YOU DON'T HAVE TO BE GOOD

Sabrina Broadbent's debut novel, *Descent*, won
the WHSmith Raw Talent Award. Author of a
second novel, *A Boy's Guide to Track and Field*,
she used to teach English at a comprehensive
school in north London, and now works for
FILMCLUB, which works with teachers to set up
and support free after-school film clubs in schools
throughout the UK. She lives in London.

ALSO BY SABRINA BROADBENT

Descent
A Boy's Guide to Track and Field

SABRINA BROADBENT

You Don't Have to be Good

VINTAGE BOOKS

London

Thanks to the Arts Council England, to Tom Badger
and Dal Chahal of the Metropolitan Police, to my
father, John Broadbent, for his tireless editing,
to mi amiga Olivia Lichtenstein, for Spain.

Published by Vintage 2010

2 4 6 8 10 9 7 5 3 1

Lines from 'Ithaka' from CP Cavafy: *Collected Poems*; translated by
Edmund Keeley and Philip Sherrard, published by Chatto & Windus.
Reprinted by permission of The Random House Group Ltd.

First published in Great Britain in 2009 by
Chatto & Windus

Vintage
Random House, 20 Vauxhall Bridge Road,
London SW1V 2SA

www.vintage-books.co.uk

Addresses for companies within The Random House Group Limited
can be found at: www.randomhouse.co.uk/offices.htm

The Random House Group Limited Reg. No. 954009

A CIP catalogue record for this book
is available from the British Library

ISBN 9780099535553

The Random House Group Limited supports The Forest
Stewardship Council (FSC), the leading international forest
certification organisation. All our titles that are printed on
Greenpeace approved FSC certified paper carry the FSC logo.
Our paper procurement policy can be found at:
www.rbooks.co.uk/environment

Mixed Sources
Product group from well-managed
forests and other controlled sources
www.fsc.org Cert no. TT-COC-2139
FSC   © 1996 Forest Stewardship Council

Printed and bound in Great Britain by
CPI Bookmarque, Croydon, CR0 4TD

For Mum and Dad

And if you find her poor, Ithaka won't have fooled you.
Wise as you will have become, so full of experience,
you'll have understood by then what these Ithakas mean.

C.P. Cavafy, 'Ithaka'

Gone

FRANK FIRST noticed his wife was gone a month before she disappeared.

It was night-time, in the dead hour. It was long before dawn, before the milk float and the blackbird, when he woke and saw a face inches from his own staring at him. The room smelt peaty.

'There's someone in the house.' Her voice was afraid, dry like a quill scratching parchment.

'Bea?' he said, peering through the grainy dark.

He raised himself on one elbow and listened to the house. Light from the landing leaked into the room and he felt a shift in pressure, as if a door somewhere closed. Dry-mouthed, he looked down at her and saw that she had gone. It wasn't Bea lying there beside him on the rumpled, sweat-soaked sheet. Not Bea, but a grim-mouthed stranger with clammy skin and a sour tang on her breath.

She brought one finger to her lips and said, 'Shhh.'

Frank held his breath.

And then they heard it. A small, quiet sound like the click of the latch being eased gently home. Her eyes held his for one last time and then, heart racing and with the cloyed slowness of the dream, Frank struggled from the bed. Naked and slack-bellied, he took two steps to the window and parted the curtains a crack. Outside, Oyster Row was deserted and still. Narrow terraced houses stared back at him, blind and dumb. He watched the space between the crumbling gateposts, but no figure slipped through to hurry down the street.

'Frank?'

He rubbed the rough skin of one buttock and caressed the bald dome of his head.

'Frank?'

A shudder ran through him. He was afraid to turn round and look at her.

'Nothing,' he said, eyes still on the street. 'There's nothing there.'

DOWNSTAIRS IN their frayed dressing gowns, the draughty floor chilled their feet. The fridge hummed, the boiler ticked and the sweet smell of decay drifted up from the bin. Nothing appeared to be missing and there was no sign of an intruder. Relief made Bea smile as she switched the kettle on to boil.

Frank came in from the front room and checked the back door again.

'You were brave,' she said, feeling shy and strange.

He moved away from her and looked out into the hall.

She heard him open the front door, close it again and turn the key in the lock. She waited.

When he appeared in the doorway, his face was like putty. A laugh escaped her.

'You look like you've seen a ghost.'

She sat down at the table and pushed a chair out for him with her foot. She wouldn't sleep now. It could be nice, a dawn cup of tea, just the two of them.

'Your tea,' she said, holding a mug out and sipping her own.

She was thirsty, always thirsty. What she lost in the night in sweat, she replaced in the day with tea. She was becoming a tea lady, a teapot, a tea bag . . .

She laughed down her nose. 'Oh dear,' she said.

Frank saw nothing amusing in the situation. He sighed. 'I might as well get some work done now I'm up.'

Bea watched his old-man slouch and the sheen of his head. Crestfallen, she thought. That's what I'm seeing. Your crest is fallen, Frank, and let's face it, so is mine. She felt wrung out, hung out to dry. Perhaps they should see someone, a counsellor, a doctor, or a priest. There were books they could read, *Mating in Captivity* or *Hanging on to the Bitter End*. She should smile more, she knew that for a fact. The plumber said so, and so did Frank. She pulled her mouth wide, and looked at the crowded years of the walls and shelves around them. Apart from the floor, the kitchen felt warm and safe; their home, their hutch.

'I'll sleep on the couch,' said Frank and left the room.

Bea said, 'Ouch.' Then, 'What work?' to the space where he had been.

We've reached the couch stage, she told her window reflection. She could hardly blame him. She had sweated litres of herself during the night, cocooned in her larval bed, metamorphosing in their marriage swamp. She wished there *had* been an intruder in the house; some drama or event, Frank doing battle on the stairs, defending his homestead, his wife and his chattels . . .

'Don't be so ridiculous,' she said aloud.

Her reflection looked back at her from the garden, where a solitary bird had begun to sing. She drank her tea and saw herself there, on the outside, looking in.

What

JUST THEN, a wolf did come out of the forest.

Frank raised his fingers from the keyboard and looked at the sentence he had written. He shuffled forward in his chair, stared at the crack in the wall two feet from his face and nodded. The writing had gone slowly today. Ten words since lunchtime, and now it was half past five. But, he peered at the screen, this was something.

He cleared his throat, got to his feet and read out loud, stepping around the piles of clutter on the floor of his work-room. 'Scene 24. Ext. Marsha's flat with the woods behind. Night. We watch Marsha hurry from the bus stop, look up at the moon and enter the building. Peter steps from the shadows. Dr Anton (Voiceover): Just then, a wolf did come out of the forest.'

Yes, he had found a way to bring the predatory Peter into Marsha's world. And he had managed to create the requisite sense of threat, inevitability, animalism and— He sat down abruptly and felt his lower lumbar seize. He was tempted to email his agent right away and let him know that great progress was being made with *Lupa*, but his agent had yet to reply to the last email, in which he had told him that *Lupa* was proving problematic. Frank frowned. How long was it since then? Two months? Three? The floorboards behind him creaked.

'Would you rather be stupider than you look, or look stupider than you are?'

Frank sighed and looked up at the crack in the wall again. Adrian, his nephew, had crept into the room.

'What?' said Frank without turning round. He had a shocking headache advancing up behind his eyes. He could do with a drink.

'Would you rather be stupider than you look, or look stupider than you are?'

Frank closed his laptop and swivelled slowly round in his chair.

Adrian had a way of standing in whatever space he found himself in that reminded Frank of the way tall seaweed swayed upward from a rock. At thirteen, he didn't pose and he didn't slouch. He just was. In his school uniform, a dismal array of greys in acrylic and polyester, the most striking thing about him was his head of frantic flaming hair. Like a Caravaggio, Bea always said; like a young Bob Dylan, his mother, Katharine, always said. Like a young Frank, in fact, thought Frank, stroking the smooth dome of his own head and wincing at the worrisome fact that all the really great writers possessed a head of magnificent hair. The evidence was there for everyone to see. Hair and genius go together. Look at Chekhov, Balzac, Beckett. Frank's eyes scanned the shelves to his left. Look at Hemingway, Ibsen, Strindberg. Every single last man of them crowned with a glorious mane of hair. And when it wasn't what could be called a crowning glory exactly – for example, Dickens, Trollope, Tolstoy – then there was a beard the size of a beehive. Damn. Was this the real, the awful, the actual, the inescapable reason that he had not had a script or play accepted for . . . what was it? Five years? Had all his creative energy fallen away on his forty-fifth birthday, the year he wrote an episode of *Casualty* and he and his hair parted company for ever?

'Would you rather be—'

'Yes, yes, I heard what you said.'

Adrian rubbed his bottom this way and that across the ribs of the radiator in a way that Frank found faintly offensive. The boy didn't swear, had a brain the size of a planet and liked girls. He was an anomaly, and exceedingly irritating. He was at an age when the unconscious child in him had yet to be put to death by the scimitar of sex and surliness. That wasn't a bad phrase. He ought to write it down, but Adrian was still sweeping up and down the radiator and was now doing a boggle-eyed, slow, head-rolling-back-on-his neck movement that suggested he was entering the nethermost reaches of boredom.

Frank tried to apply himself to the question. As it happened, he felt far from brilliant and looked appalling. Perhaps it was the strangeness of the night before. Now he came to think about it, he felt shredded and unaccountably close to tears.

He raised himself from the chair, paused until his lower back spasm eased, and made his way carefully to the fireplace, managing to become more or less upright by the time he got there. A bust of Chekhov frowned back at him from the mantelpiece. A string of red beads dangled from its neck. Wanda's no doubt. She was pushing it, leaving things like that around the place. He sighed, lifted them off and dropped them in the waste-paper bin. *Wanda*. Even the thought of her failed him these days. There had been a time in the last year when the knowledge of what he had with Wanda made all the difference, when just the image of her name in his head, the feel of her name in his mouth, *Van-da*, would be enough to set his blood racing. But lately, the 'what' had been bothering him. What was it that they had exactly? The answer, knocking quietly and persistently at a small door down some long corridor in his mind, was becoming difficult to ignore.

Adrian started up an urgent fingernail tapping on the radiator. 'Fra-a-nk.'

'I'm thinking!' Frank said.

A gold bullet of lipstick and a tube of mascara lay in the ashtray beside Chekhov. He really must speak to her about her encroachments. He had, after all, made it completely clear that the relationship could never edge towards the domestic, although as Wanda was in fact their cleaner, boundaries were possibly not as clear as they should be.

Adrian came and hovered alongside him, opened the lipstick and sniffed it, then repeated the question in a loud whisper. 'It's not a riddle,' he added and began rocking from one leg to the other, knocking Frank's arm in an arrhythmic beat. He drew a crimson smear across his lower lip and pouted at his uncle.

'For God's sake, Adrian.' Frank gave the boy a shove so that the lipstick dropped from his fingers and fell to the floor.

Frank leaned forward to study himself in the mirror. There was something tired and diminished about him today, he thought as he scanned his face, taking care not to look himself in the eye. He turned his head a little and examined his profile. His nose was good, sculpted and rather fine, and he had what some had called a sensual mouth. Wanda told him that the crest of greying copper curls above his ears made him look distinguished as long as she kept it trimmed and neat. He leaned closer to the mirror. His eyebrows could do with a trim, and the tops of his ears too. It was strange what was happening to his hair. Having retreated from his head, it seemed to sprout and flourish in places it had never done before. Thank God for Wanda's nail scissors and tweezers.

Adrian was back by his side and making kissing noises in the mirror.

'You see, if you look stupider than you are—'

Frank held out a finger to shush the boy. He needed to collect his wits for this one. He laid his hand on Chekhov's head and thought about it. Chekhov had an impressive mane of hair and a sublime, extraordinary face. No doubt about it, Chekhov looked like a genius, and when last winter Frank had studied the late manuscripts, seen the beauty and the power scratched on the page, seen with his own eyes the man's conflict about which direction the piece should take, he had felt he was in the presence of divinity. He ran his thumb across Chekhov's lips. The fact was that Chekhov's face, though magnificently clever-looking, probably appeared stupider than he was. He nodded and turned round.

'I would rather be stupider than I look.'

In the pause that followed, Frank had the sense that he had fallen short of the mark and was a disappointment. Adrian wandered over to the window and drew a face in the dirt. When the phone rang, they both leapt for the table but Adrian reached it first. Frank glared at him.

'Bea!' said Adrian, hugging the handset to his ear. He placed one hand over the mouthpiece and said, 'It's your wife.'

Frank snapped his fingers for the phone but Adrian flapped him away. He listened carefully to his aunt and said, 'Oh,' 'Er,' and 'What?'

'What does she want, Adrian?' said Frank, getting slowly down on his hands and knees and looking under the couch for Wanda's lipstick.

Adrian said, 'She's in the river at Grantchester and can't get out.'

A vision from the night before surfaced in Frank's mind. He sat back on his heels and sneezed. 'Grantchester? What on earth is she doing all the way down there?' There was plenty of river at the bottom of their road. Grantchester was two miles away.

'She says she was attacked by cows.' Adrian listened carefully to Bea, then added, 'Well, not attacked exactly. Menaced.'

'Menaced?' Frank stood up painfully. 'Give me the phone, please.' Adrian slipped easily out of reach so that Frank had to follow him round the room with his hand out like a child trying to get his toy back. 'Stop messing about.'

'A whole herd?' said Adrian. 'They can be quite dangerous

if they have calves with them. Did they have calves with them, Bea?'

Frank cornered him by the coffee table but Adrian jumped over it, then trampled along the duvet on the couch. At the bookcase in the alcove Frank nearly had him but Adrian put his hand up to warn him to stop. This was no time for silly games.

'Bullocks,' said Adrian. 'Bullocks *and* cows maybe. They turned nasty so she had to escape into the river. Which is where she is now. They won't let her get out.'

'And what does she want me to do about it?'

'Frank says, "And what do you want me to do about it?"' Adrian listened some more and said nothing.

'Well?' said Frank.

Adrian walked calmly to Frank's desk and sat down. He set himself off on slow revolutions on Frank's chair, using the table leg to maintain momentum.

Frank saw that he had the phone in his lap. 'Adrian, what in God's name is going on?'

Adrian stuck his foot out and brought his orbits to an end. 'I'm just waiting for her to reach the shallow bit.'

Frank closed his eyes and tried to gather his thoughts. Something he didn't understand was happening to his wife.

Faintly, Bea's voice called Adrian's name.

Frank shook his head, put his fingertips into his trouser pockets and adopted what he assumed was an expression of piercing insight but which reminded Adrian of the bewildered and worn-out old bull in a *toreo* he'd once seen on the television in Spain.

'Bea, Frank wants to know what on earth you're doing all the way over in Grantchester and also, what's for supper?'

His eyes roved the room as he followed the originality of her logic. He relayed the information back to Frank. 'It was beautiful . . . it was warm . . . soon summer will be gone . . . spaghetti.'

'And kindly ask whether I am to bring you, your sister and her friends to Grantchester too,' said Frank, hands on hips, vexation, indignation, consternation and many other kinds of 'ation' making him feel suddenly alive and upright for the first time that day.

'We're all coming to get you,' Adrian told Bea. 'Oh, and Bea?' he added. 'Would you rather be stupider than you look, or look stupider than you are?'

Adrian listened, then handed Frank the phone. He headed for the door.

'Bea would rather look stupider than she is,' he said. 'And her battery's going.'

Cow

WAIST-DEEP IN river water and fully clothed, Bea held her phone clear with one hand and clutched at reeds with the other. Her left foot succumbed further to the river bed's muddy embrace while the current coiled around her other leg like rope. She lurched towards a thicker clump of bulrushes near the bank and felt her long skirt float out behind her. She thought she could hear a weir somewhere, roaring out of sight, round the bend.

All at once the situation seemed serious and sad, as if she were hearing the story from someone else: Woman Found in River. Things could change and slip out of control so fast. She shouldn't have sounded calm and cheery on the phone to Adrian. 'You're so calm,' people always said to her. But she didn't feel calm very much of the time. A bit stunned perhaps, but not calm. She managed to take another step forward and the river's drag on her legs lessened.

Those bastard cows were still looking at her. A gang of five or six crowded at the bank by the wooden footbridge, their heavy-skulled heads blowing and puffing. One or two had got as far as placing hooves into the steep, broken sides of the water's edge. Cows Drown Woman. What bovine slight or trespass could she possibly be guilty of? She looked at the swirling brown eddies of water and realised she might have to swim upstream in order to get out. Perhaps if she headed for the middle, the current would be weaker. She had seen people swimming here, she was sure of it. To her right, a mass of bright reeds flowed past like green snakes.

'Are you all right?'

On the bank behind the press of cows, a young woman ran slowly on the spot. Tiny black pumas leapt up the tongues of her shoes.

'I'm fine,' said Bea with her hapless, sexy smile. She was thinking she needed a new word. 'Fine' didn't quite do it these days.

The woman on the bank had the artless, honest face of the very physically fit. *Nike* was emblazoned on her chest. Her body seemed impatient to get on with the running but her head remained turned towards the odd sight of this handsome blonde woman, fully clothed and up to her breasts in the river. 'You sure?'

No. She wasn't quite herself; had the sense that she had become tiny and remote, vanishing down the wrong end of a telescope, and that the last few years had been a long dry spell, a lonely crawl through desert and scrub, and that she was tired and desperately thirsty and in truth she did not know how she had ended up in the river except that she felt something bad was about to happen and tried to create her own ending rather than have one happen to her. A new and powerful current tugged at her lower legs. She hoped Nike saw the scene for what it was: a woman getting out of her depth.

'I'm afraid of the cows.'

'They won't hurt you. They're just curious.'

'Well actually,' Bea pushed the mobile phone down into her cleavage and braced herself against the current, 'actually they kill five people a year. Women mainly. Women walking dogs.' Sludge oozed up between her toes and something nibbled her knee. The main cow chewed at her insolently.

This cow was definitely giving her evils, as Laura would say. A long tongue, like a tentacle, swiped drool from its aqueous nose. Nike flapped her arms at them.

'Shoo!' she shouted, then delivered a volley of curses.

'Watch out for that big buttery-looking one,' warned Bea. 'It encouraged the others.'

'Get out of it!'

The cows looked sheepish. They blew down their noses and shuffled off, bumping their bony angles and heavy sides against each other, cleft hooves trip-trapping across the bridge. They fell into single file and ambled along the path that led towards the far meadow.

Bea pushed forward towards the bank, where the water was warm, and here, at the shallow margins, the sludge between her toes was rather pleasant in a forbidden, 'Don't do that, Bea, it's not nice' kind of way. She beamed up at Nike, who offered her hand and helped her up through the hoof-pocked mud. Tussocky grass spiked at her ankles and feet.

'Wave your arms around and swear your head off. My dad told me that.'

Bea glanced down at the swags and pleats of her mud-slicked skirt. She looked odd, she knew, alien and primordial. *Then the fish clambered out of the swamps and the world was changed for ever.* Her father's voice, as they searched for fossils among the rocks and chalk of Hastings beach, her hand in his. She flicked a creature off her calf, remembered Patrick's hot, angry grip on her wrist on this very bank two months ago, his voice clear in her ear: *I've never forgotten you and I never will.*

'I'll walk back with you if you like,' offered Nike, beginning to jog on the spot again. 'Which way are you going?'

'Really, I'm fine. Thank you for your help.'

Bea wished her gone now, unsure how to handle the kindness. She looked towards the line of willows at the turn of the river. The cows grazed peacefully. Seed heads and butterflies spun and danced in the soft light.

'Sure?'

'Yes, honestly,' she said, thinking how rare it was to have an adult to help. She had Wanda of course, although she couldn't really afford her and didn't truly need her, the house was so small. But without Wanda, cheerful curator of objects and clutter, converter of creases to flawless expanse, she sometimes thought it would be hard to come home after work. Wanda was all Flash and muscle, she was Pledge and sparkle, and if it weren't for Wanda, Bea suspected that the jumble and chaos of life in Oyster Row would rise up and close over her head. Her phone fell from her cleavage as she wiped at the mud on her shins. 'I phoned my husband just before you came.'

Nike nodded. She looked up the path and shook her arms and wrists.

Yes, thought Bea, as she flicked away some dark, wriggling things that were inching across her chest. Husband. Oh, yes. She tried the word on for size. Hus-band. For better, for worse. My husband. 'My husband is on his way.' She froofed her curls into shape and thought of the other husband, the one that wasn't hers but someone else's, the one she had given the best ten years of her life to, the husband called Patrick not Frank. They'd said goodbye, goodbye again, finally, one last time, two months ago in buttercups and clover, not far from this very spot.

'Well, that's all right then.' Nike was waving goodbye and moving down the path at a slow jog.

'Yes, goodbye!' called Bea, waving. 'And thank you for . . .'

But she was gone, head bobbing, narrow, upright body swaying into the light, covering the length of a child with each easy stride, putting distance between herself and the middle-aged river woman who had climbed out of the water and on to the bank.

Fetch

FRANK MARCHED into the kitchen and put the phone on its charger. Coffee spluttered on the stove and the boiler whumped into life. A blast had killed sixty-four in Baghdad and Frank despaired at Bea's flagrant waste where the hot-water timer was concerned. It was half past five. Who was going to be having a bath at this hour? *The fighting in Afghanistan is extraordinarily intense. The battles are close and personal and hand-to-hand. Unless more troops—* Frank said, 'Bloody hell,' and silenced the radio with a stab of his finger. Close and personal. He knew what that meant. That meant bayonets. What in God's name were they doing bayoneting the enemy in the desert in the twenty-first century?

He went to the foot of the stairs and shouted up at Laura and her friends. He knew they were in because he could hear the thudding of their moronic music through the ceiling. Earlier he had heard their shrieks and thumps.

Here he was, he thought, staring up at the landing, herding teenagers at the age of fifty, and not a play or a script sold in five long years. The stairs did their mean and narrow rodent yawn back down at him, silent witness to the night before. It wasn't supposed to be like this. It was supposed to be a wide and sweeping staircase in marble and mahogany.

It was supposed to be a glorious gleaming glide from one pinnacle of literary achievement to the next.

'Laura, I'm going to fetch your aunt!' he bellowed, climbing halfway up, where he was startled to find his niece's head hanging upside down in the gloom over the landing banister. Her hair dangled, and her mouth split into a lunatic grin. Her tongue, bright purple from some toxic confection she had been drinking, protruded from between stained and haphazard teeth.

'Cool.'

Frank sighed. 'Laura, you should probably come with me.' He hesitated, and saw the others lurking and listening. 'Don't your friends have to go home now?'

'Huh?' Laura braced herself on the bottom of the banisters and raised her lower body up in the air until she was perpendicular. Her yellow top fell over her head. Her hair fanned. Frank looked away.

'Laura, get down. You'll have an accident like your aunt.'

'Can my friends come, Frank? Please? They're allowed.'

Laura's friends called, 'Hello, Noddy!' and collapsed on to the carpet in hysterics. Laura rolled on top of Rachel and Chanel thumped Rachel's backside hard with a cushion. Laura said, 'We're doing homework.'

'Come on, Bea's stuck in the river.' Frank turned resolutely around and went downstairs shouting for Adrian and thinking it was absolutely preposterous that he should be left in charge of all these damned children. Here he was, trying to do the hardest thing, to write, to create a work of genius, and yet more often than not he spent half his day hanging about looking after other people's offspring. Frank took in a deep breath of righteous indignation. Adrian and Laura weren't even his flesh and blood, they belonged to Bea's sister, Katharine. The others upstairs, whatever their names were, well heaven knows who they belonged to. Frank let out a heartfelt sigh. Where the hell were the mothers, for God's sake?

'Wait for us!' called Laura.

The girls came downstairs in every possible way but normally. He wondered whether their school, Colgate Community College, might ever consider it sensible to teach them some Trollope or Rachmaninov every once in a while, something they *didn't* know about, instead of all this Media Studies and Sex and Relationships nonsense. Probably not. Education was rendering the younger generation quite incapable of serious thought. Of course, if grammar schools existed such as the one that rescued him from a lower-middle-class background of cultural and intellectual poverty, things might be different. He despaired sometimes, he really did.

Adrian nudged him and said, 'Er,' looking pointedly at Frank's head.

'Yes, Adrian? Any chance of some language, child? You know, *words*, a phrase? Push the boat out perhaps and try a whole sentence? Hmm?'

'The nodding,' murmured Adrian. 'You're doing it again.'

The girls pushed each other into the coat pegs and ran back upstairs to the bathroom. Then there were several minutes of footwear confusion, followed by a tedious conversation in which Frank said, 'You're not going out like that, are you?' and they said, 'Like what?' before they finally all spilled out into the front garden.

A hooded boy appeared from nowhere on a bicycle and accompanied them down the street, keeping his front wheel rampant the whole way and hawking up phlegm whenever the conversation, such as it was, dried up. Rachel and Chanel swooped and swerved round him while Laura trotted on the pavement saying, 'Oh shame, man' and 'Oh my days, I, like, don't believe it.'

Adrian said to Frank, 'Do you like my sweatshirt?' for the tenth time.

It took a while to find Bea's car, which was parked round the corner near the flyover. By the time Frank had bundled the teenagers into it, negotiated his way through the Cambridge rush hour and endured their bawdy clamour, he was very nearly beside himself with fury. Here was another day frittered away and precious little achieved.

When they reached Grantchester Meadows, the children ran from the car before he had time to ease himself from the driving seat. He shouted after them to wait and was about to bellow dire warnings of what would follow if they didn't do as he said, but instead he rested for a moment against the warm bonnet of the car. The sun was gentle on his face, the scent of apples and beer filled the air and from the garden of the pub came the buzz of early-evening drinkers. He had forgotten. He should get out more. How pleasant to be in the Meadows on a late-September afternoon. As he began to walk, he felt the weight on his shoulders lift, the pain in his back ease a little. The trouble was, since his last birthday, a leaden dread had settled inside him. It made him snap at the children and droop at the shoulders when he walked. The dread weighed heavier each time he read the words 'bright young talent', 'extraordinary promise' or 'playwright of the year'. It kept his eyes to the ground when he walked, like now, and it beat out a refrain to the rhythm of his feet on the path. 'Your best is past. There's no more to come . . .' Enter Wanda.

Frank paused and looked about him. No sign of the children or of Bea. How typical of them all to disappear. He turned and began walking back to the car. He would call Bea's phone from the pub and wait for them all there, and anyway, he really could murder a drink. Now Wanda was a woman who could hold her drink. Bea used to be able to hold her drink, but all of a sudden, quite recently, she couldn't. Wanda, though, my God, she could knock back the vodka like it was water. And Wanda was very calming where the writing was concerned. She told him that her father was still writing when he died at the age of eighty-three (which, as Bea pointed out, meant that

Wanda's father was in his sixties when Wanda was born). Frank flicked away that thought with a shake of his head. What about a screenplay set in communist Poland? A woman in the secret police falls in love with a much older dissident writer. Frank quickened his step and tugged at his cuffs. *Close and Personal*, he could call it. Thank God for Wanda. The ideas were coming thick and fast now. He should walk more often. He would phone his agent tomorrow and tell him all about it. He felt suddenly better. Last night had been a wake-up call, a kind of ghastly sleepwalk or waking dream. It was a warning not to neglect his creative impulse, a sign that he must take his work more seriously. This nonsense of Bea's and the children's had to stop. He would make himself unavailable for as long as it took to complete the script.

He heard shouting and looked back. The girls sprang through the grass like puppies, shedding shoes as they went. Adrian ran large circles round them, chasing first one and then another. The willows and chestnuts burned gold and red and the sun was low. Overhead, the sky stretched away, a rippled sea of pink and blue. His throat ached and the view blurred. He would have loved a son.

Adrian swerved inches from him, panting and bounding over waist-high grass.

'Stop larking about,' snapped Frank. 'And just remember that we're looking for your aunt.'

Love

FRANK DIDN'T have to walk very far before he heard the children calling and laughing and he saw Bea walking slowly towards him. Back-lit by the sun, the shape of her skull was silhouetted so precisely in its halo of hair that he could feel the shape of it in the palm of his hand.

'I'm a bit wet,' she said when they reached each other.

He looked at the space around her.

'Where are the cows?' he asked. 'The stampede?'

'Oh, I was rescued.'

He smelt of stale whisky and he had his shirt tucked in. What an unspeakable disaster, she thought, waving the children over. I married completely the wrong man.

Rescued? He looked at her then, at the broad swell of her belly, at the place on her breasts where the wet fabric clung. Of course. He nodded. Always this. Always the knight in shining armour standing in the wings. Who had she been here with? Bloody Patrick Cumberbatch? Surely he wasn't still sniffing about the place, was he? No, Mr Cumberbatch had been booted out of Shire Hall (ha!). He had been told to take his bonhomie, his management skills and his skinny-arsed wife and take a running jump to Corfu or Costa Early Retirement or wherever.

'Frank? Is your back bad?'

He wanted to crush her with a cold comment but her nipples had an insolent, brazen look to them. His eyes travelled up her throat as she swallowed, up to her neck where the skin was creased and crêpey. He looked at her uncertain mouth and offered a pained smile in the direction of the river.

'Where are your shoes?' She smelt weedy. It was important with Bea not to make too much of anything. Keep things on an even keel. She longed for melodrama and, like all women – not Wanda perhaps, but most women – she seemed to need a crisis once in a while.

Screams and shouts curtailed by a series of splashes informed them that the children had managed to fall in. Adrian ran towards them, arms flailing, legs leaping, laughing and shouting that all three girls were in the water, that Rachel's phone had sunk, Chanel couldn't swim and Laura's foot was stuck. Frank tore towards the river in his lopsided run. Bea gathered up her skirt and followed him, heavy-thighed and slow. She watched him sprint ahead of her, arms pumping, zigzagging round the tussocks, racing with surprising speed towards the emergency, and she remembered vaguely what it was like to love him.

When she reached the bank, she found the dripping forms of the girls draped like leopards along a low willow branch. They were panting and smiling and swinging their hands and feet in the shallow water. Frank was supporting himself with one arm up against the trunk, catching his breath and trying to speak. Laura waved over at Bea and called, 'We fell in too! Brutal!' Adrian whacked the tree with a stick and said, 'Are you all right, Frank?' Laura pulled off her shorts and said, 'I'm only going to have to walk back in me keks!' Rachel said, 'Minging,' and Chanel said, 'This branch is doing me an injury, innit though?' Frank said, 'Right, that's it,' and strode away towards the car park. They watched him go, stretching his arms down and splaying out his fingers, a gesture that had become a habit since Bea once commented that all his shirtsleeves were a little on the long side. He stopped and called back furiously to them.

'Come on! I have a deadline to meet.' Yes, he nodded to himself. There's *Lupa*, there's *Close and Personal* . . . The others stared at him like cattle. 'And I do not want my evening to seep into your evening of non-sequiturs, pantomime hysteria, pizza crusts and . . .' He took a few steps towards them and the girls scuttled, giggling, behind Bea. He pointed at them. Bea took a long, slow final breath in. Was he really pointing at them? Yes, I'm pointing, thought Frank, because things are about to change around here. Then he shook his finger at them and Adrian looked up at the sky. 'I don't suppose your mother has deigned to inform us of her expected time of arrival, but if you don't mind, I would like to get back before it gets dark!' Then he turned on his heel and set off for the car park.

Halfway to the end of the path, he wondered if they were following and hoped that Adrian and Laura understood that it wasn't that he didn't love them. Of course he did. Well, he loved Adrian. Perhaps not Laura. Fond, yes. Love, no. There was something hard about her, and all that *blingish* she talked. What was that all about? An affectation. He was fairly sure that Laura wouldn't know a US gang member if one came and bit her on the backside. The girl had too much of her mother in her. Katharine Kemp was a fierce, cold woman – ruthless, calculating, clever – the complete opposite of Bea. How Katharine and Bea had emerged from the same parents was a mystery. How Adrian had emerged from Katharine was a bloody miracle.

At the end of the meadow was the kissing gate, where Frank had to stop while a young couple went through. The girl and then the boy became trapped and then were freed with a kiss. Frank waited and coughed, aware of the ache in his lower back beginning to climb. He could smell charcoaled meat from the beer garden, and laughter rose up from the hum of voices. He looked back the way he had come, saw the swallows dive and swoop in the evening air but saw no sign of the others. When the gate was free, he let himself through, going through the paces of the silly foxtrot of love on his own, went to the car and got in. He waited, eyes closed, door open, listening to Bob Dylan on Radio 2. Funny, he thought, how they had reached the stage in life where they listened to Radio 2. They would have laughed at that ten years ago when they first met.

The first time he saw Bea was on the *Oriana* en route to Madeira. In the lounge a pianist played Abba medleys on the white baby grand to an empty dance floor. When heavy rain forced passengers down from the top deck, the dance floor filled with pensioners and a red spotlight swept the crowd in time to the music. Bea walked up to him then with wet hair and a lost expression on her face. He loved her mouth straightaway. It had a vulnerable look to it that made him want to open doors for her. She was holding a Dubonnet and lemonade and a Bloody Mary and said, 'Have you seen an elderly lady in red?' They both laughed. The dance floor was a swarm of old women, swaying together to the strains of 'Lady in Red' at half past three in the afternoon—

'Frank!'

It was Laura, calling and waving from the entrance to the car park. Bea and the other girls were behind her, wet and muddy and cheerful. Bea had her jacket tied round her waist and no skirt on. Rachel wore Bea's skirt like a sarong. Laura wore just a bra and what appeared to be Adrian's school trousers. Chanel had a long furry-hooded winter coat zipped up to her nose and shoes that squelched when she walked.

Frank got out of the car. 'Where's Adrian?' At the sight of the empty path, he felt suddenly sick.

Bea put the front seat forward so the girls could get in.

'He's being slow because he's so gay,' said Laura.

Bea sat in the passenger seat. Frank got in beside her and waited. Then he got out of the car and went to the gate just as Adrian appeared. Adrian wore only the sweatshirt, which barely reached his thighs.

'The cows started following me,' he said. 'I think it's their path. I had to stay near the hedge.'

'Someone told me they only threaten females,' said Bea.

'That's what I said. He's so gay,' said Laura.

'Come on, get in,' said Frank.

Adrian dipped his head inside the car, then stood up and looked mildly at it. 'Problem,' he said.

Frank looked at Adrian and then at the car. It was full.

'Ah,' said Bea.

'I'll walk,' said Frank, tossing the keys on to the driving seat. 'It'll be a pleasure.'

'I'll come with you,' said Adrian, following Frank up the lane. He waved to Bea and the girls as they drove past.

Frank turned to look at his nephew and said, 'For God's sake, Adrian, take that bloody sweatshirt off.'

'But then I'll be nearly naked.'

'Turn it inside out then. You look like a bloody fool.'

'The girls made me wear it,' said Adrian, beginning to lift it over his head. 'For their homework.'

'You're talking gibberish now, Adrian.' Frank began to stride up the lane, towards the main road. 'I have rather a lot of work to do, so if you want to come with me you'll have to keep up.'

Adrian stumbled along beside Frank but his head became stuck in the neck of the sweatshirt. Frank stopped and gave it a tug. Adrian yelled. What Frank needed now was a large drink and a good blast of Beethoven at his most tortured. He gave it another yank. What he needed now was Wanda, naked, face down on the couch, swearing in Polish.

Frank stopped pulling and gave the headless torso a push.

It staggered and fell into the blackberry bushes. 'I very much doubt that Laura's homework was to make her brother wear a sweatshirt saying "Nobody Knows I'm a Lesbian".'

Adrian put the sweatshirt back on inside out. His ears were red. 'It's ironic,' he said. He held Frank's hand as they waited to cross the main road. 'They had to find an example of irony. And I'm it.'

Hot

KATHARINE STEPPED through Bea's front door backwards, throwing the central locking on her 4x4, which was parked in the middle of the road, hazard lights flashing. She said, 'Damn this sodding car,' and 'Sorry, sorry about the time,' and 'Two trains cancelled then unbelievable traffic all the way from the station,' and 'What's wrong with your phone? I've been trying to ring all evening.'

Bea said, 'Mum rang.'

'What?' said Katharine, turning and looking behind her. 'Where?'

'She phoned me.'

'Oh.' Katharine stopped. 'What did she want at this time?'

Katharine looked at her watch, at the flyers by her feet for pizza, tandoori and minicabs, down the hall for signs of the children, back at the car and then at Bea. Why didn't she do something about her hair? 'Adrian! Laura!' she called. 'Sorry, yes, go on about Mum. Where's Frank?'

Bea shrugged. 'She didn't want anything. Just to talk.'

Katharine shut the door and put her briefcase down, then picked it up again. Some people they knew had been robbed like that because kids look through the letter box, see the briefcase, handbag, whatever, break the glass, release the door latch and take the bag. All over in ten seconds. Good heavens, was it really half past eight?

'How is she?'

'Quite,' said Bea so that Katharine looked at her properly, which was when she noticed that her sister looked suddenly older. Bea walked away from her, slow and heavy, towards the kitchen. All she needed to do was to lose a few pounds and get her hair done. It wasn't beyond her, surely.

'What do you mean, "Quite"?'

Bea stumbled over the children's school bags and shoved them against the wall with her foot. 'I mean, she *is*, as in she's still alive, existing. But the *how*, well, I don't know.'

Katharine scanned the notes and letters on the kitchen counter. Nothing of interest there. Bea was being obtuse. Best not to provoke her.

'Well, if only she would agree to move closer to us. Of course she's lonely, stuck out there in the sticks.'

She noted her sister's ridiculous collection of souvenir donkeys trooping across the windowsill, noticed the wilting flowers and the half-finished glass of wine and thought, this is what happens if you don't have children or a challenging job. She sat down at the table and stopped herself saying, 'I hope they aren't watching crap TV on your bed,' and 'You haven't let Adrian buy any more of those fireworks, have you?'

Bea began clearing the table. 'Let's give Mum a surprise birthday party.'

Katharine felt weak at the thought of it all. The move to London, her new job, Laura's school problems. 'But it's so soon.' Was it soon? October sometime, wasn't it? 'There's no time, is there?'

'It needn't be a big deal. Just the family. We'll have it here.'

Katharine looked round the cramped kitchen. Bea's collection of ceramica from Spain and Greece adorned every space of wall while jugs and bowls filled every shelf. Dusting those must be a full-time job. They gave the room a warm vibrancy, Katharine couldn't deny that, but it was absolutely too cramped here for a birthday lunch. And as the front room was where Frank did whatever it was that Frank did in there, well, you couldn't really have a party in a two-up two-down, could you? She watched Bea make a neat pile of the children's school clothes and suddenly wondered whether her sister was all right for money.

'Oh, but our house, surely,' she said, except it couldn't be their house, they were moving any day now. Katharine wondered whether Bea would be offended by a cheque.

'Here will be fine.' The party would be swamped at Katharine's in her chilly dining room that seated sixteen. What Bea envisaged was a cosy, informal gathering round her own kitchen table. They could open the back door and put Adrian in charge of a firebasket on the patio.

There was no point reasoning with Bea. Katharine could tell she had already decided. 'Well, the next few weeks are impossible so I would have to leave the arrangements to you. Get Wanda to help maybe.' She looked again at her sister and wondered whether something had happened to her. She hoped to God she wasn't ill. 'Have you been swimming, Bea? Your hair looks . . .' No, knowing Bea, she probably just needed to ease up on the alcohol.

Bea touched her head and mumbled something about the river. She felt foolish now. Frank had said not a word to her about it and she decided to let the children tell Katharine. She barely knew how to describe what had happened herself. It frightened her a little, how she had ended up near the fast-flowing centre of the river. Her skirt was soaking upstairs and it had turned the water green. Adrian had found a gleaming black leech jerking determinedly up the side of the bath, and now she was bone-achingly tired and what she really wanted was for everyone to go so that she could watch television in bed and pass out.

What Bea really needs, thought Katharine, is a complete restyle with a proper hairdresser, not that little place round the corner that she's been going to for years. The woman needs a total overhaul and a new job while she's at it, because languishing in Shire Hall all these years is probably doing no good at all for her self-esteem, let alone her bank balance.

Katharine said, 'How's work?' and then she said, 'You know, if I do get the consultant paediatric job in London, there's no way I can commute.'

Bea tried to arrange too many glasses on the top shelf of the dishwasher. 'We've been restructured. Efficiency measures. And we're about to be inspected so everyone is—' There was a crack. She pulled out a broken glass and dropped the pieces in the bin.

A small explosion on the front doorstep was followed by screams, thundering footsteps upstairs and the smell of gunpowder.

Adrian's voice called down from above. 'Sorry!'

Katharine went to the foot of the stairs and shouted up. 'Come on, Adrian, we have to go. Where's Laura? Laura!' She took a few wary steps upwards. 'Come on. Time to leave!'

Bea stood in the hall and heard Laura's voice wheedling from the landing.

'Do we have to go now? We haven't had our ice cream.'

'Well, we'll have that when we get home,' said Katharine.

'There isn't any. You know there isn't.'

'We'll get some on the way. Sainsbury's. Who's up there with you?'

'No one. I'm doing my homework.'

'That's a lie,' said Adrian.

'Shut up!'

'I think you're tired, darling,' said Katharine.

'I'm not. I need a shower.'

'That's true,' said Adrian.

'Shut up!'

'You can have a shower at home, Laura.'

'I fell in the river.'

'You fell in the river?' Katharine looked to where Bea had been standing but Bea had disappeared. Really, things had got completely out of hand with this arrangement. 'What happened? For heaven's sake, Bea? Bea!'

'Bea fell in too.'

'But it's nearly October.' (Was it nearly October? It could be nearly March – time just flew.) 'And there's Weil's disease, darling, you don't want that. You might . . .' She took a step up towards Laura, who shrank from her. Katharine stopped where she was. What was the matter with the child? All Laura's boundaries were becoming blurred. God knows what was going on at that school. 'Are your glands up? Do you feel achey at all? Where's your uniform?'

Laura coughed and looked ill. 'Can I stay here tonight?'

'What's that noise?'

'My French tape.'

'Are you watching television up there?'

'No.'

'I can hear it.'

'Well I'm not.'

'That's a lie,' said Adrian.

'Shut up, ugly!'

'Yes, be quiet, Adrian. Don't provoke. Go and wait outside.'

'Mum, school said they're sending you a letter. But it's not true, what Stella said I did. I didn't write those things . . .' Laura began to cry.

Adrian leapt from the house, saying, 'Abort. Abort.' He landed just past Bea, who was sitting on the doorstep.

She tried not to smile. She had put his filthy trainers by the wall so he wouldn't forget them. She could smell autumn in the air and saw it in the curled dry tips of the wisteria leaves. She waved at Nesrine over the road. Nesrine was watering her front garden, where she coaxed a little bit of

Cyprus in vine and fig from the fenland soil. Adrian crouched on the path and lit a twisted wrap of paper that puttered and plumed blue and red and green and smelt of cordite and sulphur. They could hear voices raised from inside. Chanel and Rachel skittered past them into the September dusk trailing 'Bye's in their wake.

Adrian stuffed his feet into his trainers, treading the backs down, and climbed on top of the garden wall. For the hundredth time that day, heat roared up inside Bea, coursing from her solar plexus through veins and nerves to the top of her head. Whatever aberrant process was going on, it had the force and struggle of that hot air balloon she watched once from her mother's lap as it struggled to ascend, gasping and breathing fire, scudding low, too low over the trees on the clifftop at Hastings. Three Die in Hot Air Balloon Tragedy.

Bea cooled her head against the wall. The Jeep crouched in the road, its orange hazard lights throbbing like a pulse.

Adrian sat on the wobbly slab on top of the gate pillar and said, 'Would you rather be cremated or buried?'

'It depends what happened to me,' said Bea.

A door slammed from upstairs.

Adrian said, 'I think I'd rather be cremated.'

'But then you wouldn't really *be* anywhere. You know, for people to visit.'

Frank appeared at the end of the road. He loitered just out of sight, waiting for Katharine to be gone.

'And then I'd like to be sent up in a firework,' said Adrian.
'Really?'

'Some of them reach five hundred feet.'

'What happens when you start to come down again?'

He jumped down off the wall. 'I'd be all over the place.'

She wanted to hold his body tight to hers. 'Sounds like a good way to go.'

Katharine marched past them. Laura followed, pouting, a

slow swagger of disdain. Adrian said, 'Bye, Bea. Don't forget to release the leech back into the river. I've put it in one of your egg cups,' and climbed into the car.

Katharine started the engine, switched on the lights and wound down her window. The Jeep lurched and rocked, eager to be off.

'Thanks so much, Bea. We must catch up properly soon. Before we move. Come to dinner. I'll call you.'

Bea nodded and waved them away, watching the car until it vanished from sight. Nesrine was sweeping the crazy paving in furious movements, turning this way and that as though plagued by ants. Bea thought of the chores that waited for her indoors. She could feel them behind her back – dishes to clean, rubbish to sort, plants to water, Wanda to pay, her marriage to mend. She sat with her knees up to her chin and examined the river grime between her toes.

Frank appeared at the gate and shook open the paper.

'Labour Admits: We Made Mistakes on Afghanistan.' He nodded at the paper and tapped the page. 'I mean, I could have told them that,' he said, disappearing into the house.

Work

JOSIE AND Darren from Births, Marriages and Deaths were huddled over cigarettes in the shade by the wall. Bea waved hello as she hurried up the steps, then punched the entry code into the security panel, pulled her staff ID tag over her head, greeted Archie on reception ('Oh, someone had a late night last night'), said, 'Morning,' to Nertili, who was swabbing the floor, saw just in time that it was Louise from Leisure and Culture waiting for the lift ('I've got to go for more tests . . . this time they think it's my—'), cut through Housing and let herself into the stairwell, where she began the long climb up to the sixth floor and her office in Land Registry, Covenants and Deeds.

On the third landing, she passed Angela from Transport and Streets. Angela was a firm believer in the stairs' ability to keep cellulite at bay and used to be fleet of foot, but today, in the sixth month of her pregnancy, she held tight to the rail and waited with one hand on her stomach. Bea asked if she was all right and Angela nodded, pointing wordlessly at Bea's chin. 'Toothpaste,' she mouthed and waved her on. Bea dabbed at her chin with one finger, dabbed and licked and plodded onwards, hoping she'd remember to check her makeup in the mirror before the day swept her up and carried her off to lunchtime. At the next turn in the stairs, her legs felt so heavy and slow, her thighs were so chafed and sausaged up in the too-small tights that twisted and squeezed that she had to stop and rest too. Perhaps I'm pregnant, not menopausal, she thought wildly, looking down the stairwell, where she could see the top of Angela's head, the grey beginning to show. Bea's woman's brain, which could perform complicated calculus in units of twenty-eight, reeled backwards to the last time, the one last time with Patrick by the river three days before he left Shire Hall, Cambridge and, finally, her. Backwards through the weeks and months, taking into account those with days of thirty not thirty-one, back, back through September, August and July to 30 June. Yes, yes, she told Precious whose desk was next to hers, of course it was finished, years and years ago, but then something that never officially existed could never really be over either.

The doors to the fifth floor on the landing above her burst open and Jonathan from Policing and Public Safety flew past, taking the stairs two at a time, the scent of lime and something spiky in the air around him. He called, 'Morning, Bev, how are you?' but by this time Bea was breathing too heavily to say either 'Morning' or 'I'm not Bev, I'm Bea.' Her chest rose and fell, there was an ache at the back of her lungs and she wondered when the breathlessness had begun. Was it before the summer? Before Patrick left and vanished into an Ionian sunset? She ran her tongue over her top teeth and thought, God, yes, he'd done it. By the skin of his teeth, Patrick had actually done it — escaped with a pension, a marriage and two family homes all safe and intact. She didn't know whether to hate him or admire him.

Bea pulled at her skirt, which had migrated up and back as she climbed, had bunched mid-thigh the whole time she had walked to work and was yet another item of clothing that would be sent to the charity shop after only one wearing. Nothing she wore these days looked right. She tried to slow her breathing and stand up tall. She pulled her stomach in and tightened her *bundas*, as Precious was always telling her to do. She had never understood just exactly where her *bundas* were, was unsure if she actually had any, but she tried her best to pull everything between her navel and the tops of her thighs up and in. Of course, the affair with Patrick had been over for years by the time he left. And *breathe*, Precious would remind her. Well, 'over' in as much as they didn't spend Thursday afternoons in the Novotel any longer, no, not since she married Frank. Relax your face, Precious would say. Not easy when you're trying to hold your *bundas* in as well as keeping a listing marriage afloat and seeing the man you love but lost every day of your working life, thought Bea, pressing fingertips to the skin on her jaw and her cheeks and her forehead. Christ, how long till her mother's birthday? Two weeks? She would ask Frank's father, Lance. They got on rather well at the wedding. Her mother was losing her mind and Lance was losing his legs. They were almost made for each other. She would buy her mother a CD player and get Frank to tell Lance to buy her a CD. Margaret and Lance. Perfect.

At the double doors to her floor, she applied a smile, adjusted her bra and prepared herself for the day. It was a week since her river baptism, and Frank was still sleeping downstairs. They should probably have a talk.

She took a deep breath and made her entrance. The air was heavy with ozone and static. Photocopiers churned, faxes spooled, phones chirruped and flashed. Across the entire top floor, every seat at every desk was occupied except for her corner where she sat with Precious and Karen. At the far end of the room, the new boss – Barry, was it? Charles? – was being ushered around by Human Resources. Bea sank on to her swivel chair and tried to calm her breathing. She watched him, noted his youth and his gelled hair, the new suit and stiff demeanour, then swung round and saw that Precious had materialised from nowhere and was switching everything on while sweeping magazines, coffee cups, Tampax and soup sachets into a drawer. Their corner was normally calm and ordered, but in the last weeks they had become overwhelmed by paper, laminated notices and stapled documents the weight of a Christmas turkey, which had been dispatched by every department from Fostering and Adoption to Recycling and Environment. In the summer weeks between Patrick Cumberbatch's departure and Barry Charles's arrival, the council had become a febrile hothouse of accountability anxiety, frantic manic machinations devoted to 'the covering of the arse', as Precious liked to put it. Preliminary Scrutiny and Assessment exercises were carried out, and Bea's Accounting and Record-Keeping Skills were found wanting. A mock inspection occurred in early September, where Land Registry, Covenants and Deeds was deemed to have slipped from Satisfactory to Poor. Precious, Bea and Karen were sent on professional development courses to bring them up to speed, but despite being PowerPointed half to death with compressing, zipping, archiving and merging, Bea had found it hard to leave go of the old way of doing things.

She switched on her computer and Adrian and Laura leapt into life, mid-jump above the river, white limbs wide, hair spiking the air, mouths open and eyes tight shut. Bea pressed at a tear with her fingertip and tried to reel herself in. Her days with the children were numbered; summer was gone and soon Adrian and Laura would be gone too, to London, new schools and a new life. The computer whirred and chugged and a chaos of files and documents scattered themselves across her screen. She looked up. The group with Barry Charles began to step their way, heads nodding and small twitchy smiles. Where the hell was Karen?

Bea swivelled round in her chair. 'Precious,' she said, pointing at her computer screen.

In a second Precious was leaning over her shoulder, fingers dancing across the keyboard and mouse, and her screen was suddenly a clear corporate blue, no icons or children in sight. Bea put on her headset and wondered whether Frank was going to sleep downstairs for the rest of their marriage.

She bent down and eased two boxes of deeds dated 1926 to 1940 out of sight beneath her desk and smelt the fear and anxiety rising from her armpits. She opened her desk drawer and rifled through the pens, spare reading glasses, staples and Nurofen, and just for that moment couldn't for the life of her remember why she had married Frank in the first place. She found a packet of Wet Ones, gave each armpit a quick wipe while bending down behind her desk, and remembered that meeting Frank and living with Frank and eventually marrying Frank was her way of being good, of ending the affair with Patrick, of bringing an end to the not knowing, to the waiting to be wanted. She had thought that if she was good, really good, like Katharine, then who knows what might happen, children weren't out of the question at forty, were they? And it didn't break her heart, because in the ten years since then, she had seen Patrick most days at work and – she dropped the Wet Ones in the bin – it was enough. Yes, it was enough. It had to be. But now—

'Bea,' hissed Precious and passed her the Audit of Accounts folder. 'Karen's on a course. She's being fast-tracked.' She passed over the Accounts and Governance Review and the Review of Financial Systems Report. Bea fumbled in her drawer for one of many pairs of cheap reading glasses, stuck on a pair that did not sit entirely true on her nose, and then Barry Charles was standing in their corner.

Bea tried to stand up but found she was tethered by her headset. She smiled and put her hand out neverthe-less. He took it briefly and she heard someone saying, 'As Head of Finance, Barry Charles will be responsible for implementing the council's Reshaping for Excellence Strategy.' Bea nodded and kept the corners of her mouth turned up because she had read an article in a magazine recently that said that women who smile have better job prospects than women who don't. The burner fired up in her and she wondered what Barry Charles would do if the pretty, faded woman with the headset and the poor database skills in front of him spontaneously combusted and became a column of fire. Precious asked him about his last job, although everyone knew everything already. He had been parachuted into post following Mr Cumberbatch's early retirement and his brief was to ensure the council improved its financial reporting, for which it had got 2 out of 4 the last time they were formally inspected. This, Barry Charles had made clear in his introductory letter to staff, would not happen again.

The visitors were discussing tactics over Bea's head with Sunita, assistant to the Regional Director.

Barry Charles said, '. . . robust management of budgets . . .'

Sunita said, '. . . challenges facing the council for the future . . .'

'. . . performance indicators . . . ?'

'. . . implementation and outcomes.'

'. . . risk assessment project management of Private Finance Initiative . . .'

'. . . action plans have been developed and strategies are in place . . .'

'. . . strategise the way forward and take it from there . . .'

'Waste Management Private Funding Initiative?'

'Oh, certainly.'

The light on Bea's phone came on. She replaced her headset and took the first call. The first call of the day always made her tremble. After that it was usually downhill unless someone rang who was either very rude or very nice to her. The rest of the calls meant nothing, they were just voices that she cut as short as possible, listening to their request or enquiry and putting them through.

Sunita was leading Barry Charles away from their desks.

Bea looked up as he was swept on through to Social Care and Housing.

Precious slid a tub of rice pudding from her drawer and peeled off the top.

'That went well,' she said.

'How old do you think he is?'

'Eleven?' Precious put a spoonful of pudding into her mouth. 'Twelve maybe?'

Bea's phone rang again. When she picked up, she heard Frank's silence on the other end. She waited a moment, filling the cells of the spreadsheet on the screen in front of her with figures from what she hoped was the correct version. Her mouth was dry and she wished she had had time to collect a cup of tea from the canteen on her way up.

'Frank?' she said.

'Do we have life insurance?'

'I'm covered by work. You don't have life insurance because you decided—'

'So what does that mean?'

'It means if I die in service you get a lump sum.'

'So we are protected?'

'You are protected. Why do you ask?'

'Just doing a mortgage thing, you know. Seeing whether it'd be cheaper to switch.'

'Right.'

There was a silence. Bea glanced at Precious, who was being very busy with a new printer cartridge.

Bea spoke quietly. 'We should talk, Frank.' A call came in on her phone. She watched the red light blinking at her and waited for Frank to speak.

He said, 'It's probably not worth switching.'

'Probably not, no.'

'Right then.'

'Okay.'

She replaced the receiver and did not meet Precious's gaze.

Endgame

'IS IT because you snore?'

Frank's pencil point was poised above the page, ready to make corrections. Really, this was impossible. He was never going to finish *Lupa*, let alone make a start on *Close and Personal*, unless the childcare situation was sorted. This was the third day in a week that Katharine had dumped her children at their house. Could they not afford a nanny? What was the problem? The problem was that Bea wanted them here. The problem was he quite liked them here too. He closed his eyes and gave his head an irritable little shake. Then he tipped his head back so that when he opened them again, his eyes met Chekhov's. Chekhov said nothing. Frank said, 'I beg your pardon, Adrian?'

'The separate rooms thingy.' Adrian was lying on the couch, legs cycling the air, hands on hips. Beside him on the coffee table a game of chess was laid out.

'You've fixed your pawn on the colour of your bishop.'

Frank turned round on the piano stool and glared at the chess board. 'What are you talking about?'

'Nothing.' Adrian continued cycling, but in reverse.

Frank got up and gazed down at the chess board. He nodded sagely at the framed poster of his college production of *The Seagull in the Cherry Orchard*, which the local paper

40

had hailed as 'uneven and overlong'. It had probably been a mistake to roll the two plays into one. He stood up straight and raised himself on his toes, then snatched a look at Adrian, who was gazing mildly round the room while he waited for Frank. 'Hmm,' said Frank, looking at the small glass trophy he had won for his first radio play, *Three Brothers,* based loosely on *Three Sisters* but set in Burnley. No, it was not nothing to be BBC Lancashire's Promising Newcomer of the Year at the age of twenty-three. He turned and nodded fiercely at the chess board. It was not nothing to have always remained true to his art and to have laboured day and night getting the words down on the page. He blew the dust from his trophy and wiped it with his cuff. No. Not nothing.

'What?' said Adrian.

Frank looked at him. 'What do you mean, *what?*'

'You said something.'

'Oh, I did, did I?'

'You said, "Not nothing."'

'You're not making any sense, Adrian.'

Frank let out a short, exasperated laugh. He bent down and put his thumb and forefinger on the head of his bishop, nodding and humming cunningly to himself. Adrian stopped cycling and watched. Frank pursed his lips and pushed the bishop along three squares. Adrian carried on cycling again. Frank rubbed his hands together and nearly said *Ha!* but stopped himself. The boy was just a child, after all. Beating him at chess was hardly a victory to crow about.

Frank returned to his desk, picked up the pencil and read the words 'A duck flies into the tree . . .' A duck? In a housing estate? Well, yes, it was possible, there were parks and ponds and lakes up there, but even so, a duck was possibly taking the *Peter and the Wolf* connection a little far. He crossed out 'duck' and wrote 'magpie', then read it through again. Yes, 'magpie' had the requisite sense of the ordinary and the omen, the vulnerable yet avaricious, it was both a sign and a—

41

'Your turn.' Adrian was sitting up, chin in hands, looking down at the chess board.

Frank looked over. His bishop was imprisoned behind Adrian's back row. It was staring at him with that mournful expression that bishops have. He stuck his pencil behind his ear and marched over to the chess table.

'Hang on a minute. Just show me what you did there, please.'

Adrian showed him. Frank puffed out his cheeks and shook his head. His back didn't hurt today. Wanda had worked miracles on it the day before. She certainly knew the meaning of the word massage. He sat down and studied the board. Inexplicably, things did not look good. Things did not look good at all. His king was backed up in a corner, his pawns were doubled up and his knights were doing bugger all.

Adrian said, 'Knights belong in the middle of the board . . .'

'Er . . . yes!' snapped Frank sarcastically. 'I am aware of that, I believe. If I wasn't trying to work right now as well as babysitting, I might be able to keep my eye on your cheap tricks.'

Frank clasped his hands in front of his mouth. Nothing happened for quite a long time. Adrian counted his blinks. He had got up to one hundred and twenty-eight when Frank scratched the top of his head and grimaced before pushing a pawn forward two squares.

Adrian took his move and said, '*Is* it the snoring, though?'

'I don't snore in point of fact, Adrian.'

Frank sacrificed his white knight to tempt Adrian's queen.

'How do you know?'

'I think I would know if I snored!' snorted Frank. 'I would wake myself up.'

'But it's unconscious. People don't snore when they're awake.'

'Your aunt has been known to snore whilst gardening.'

'That's not snoring.'

'What is it then?'

'Panting. Grunting maybe.' Adrian looked at his watch. He stood abruptly, flung both arms above his head, groaned loudly and sat down again. 'Hurry up.'

'It's your turn.'

'No. I've been. Look.'

Frank looked. Somehow Adrian had sneaked his queen across the board and was now menacing Frank's king. The phone rang. Frank snatched it triumphantly and listened.

He looked up at the ceiling and opened and closed his fingers into fists. After a while he said, 'Hello, Margaret.' He rolled his eyes at Adrian. 'No, Bea's out. Yes . . . yes . . . hmm . . . Oh dear. I'll get her to call you, shall I?' He put the phone down.

'Was that Granny?'

'That was Granny. Something about a variegated shrub and a funny noise coming from the oven.' Frank waved his hands in the air, shaking all that tedious detail off him. 'Now let's get this over with, shall we?' He lifted his bishop and took Adrian's queen, then got to his feet humming to himself.

Adrian took Frank's queen with his rook.

'Check,' he said.

Frank stopped halfway across the room. 'I beg your pardon?'

'Checkmate, actually.' Adrian unfolded his long legs and got to his feet.

Frank looked across at the board and nodded knowingly. 'I taught you well. Not bad, not bad. Now if you don't mind, I have work to do.' He walked to the door and held it open for Adrian.

'I mean, Mum and Dad share a bed.'

'And your point is?' Frank craned his head forward, mouth turned down. Adrian looked faintly surprised, so Frank brought his head back up again and looked at the ceiling. What in God's name had possessed them to paint it mushroom gloss all those years ago?

'You should share a bed too. Marriage is like a game of chess.'

'Marriage is like a game of chess, is it?' Frank was doing the nodding again but he couldn't stop himself. The boy was absurd. 'Had a lot of experience yourself, have you?'

'Identify the weakness. Fix the weakness.'

'Well when you've been married for as long as your aunt and me, Adrian, I shall seek your advice again. In the meantime, just stick to chess, hmm?' Frank waved him out.

'Not sharing a bed is not nothing.'

Wanda passed the open doorway carrying the vacuum cleaner. 'Hello, boys!' she called.

'And maybe just check the snoring,' said Adrian, going out.

Urn

AT ELYSIAN Fields Garden Centre Bea had, over the years, spent a good proportion of her salary from Shire Hall. It was a place she often took the children, even when they were tiny. Nappy-wadded, Adrian and Laura tottered along winding paths between shrubs and perennials while she indulged her fantasy of a verdant garden filled with scented blooms. They preferred the garden centre to playgrounds for it had a raised pond with newts in it, a café and places a child could safely get lost in. Two weeks after she walked into the river, Bea took Adrian and Laura to the garden centre for the last time.

She stood before the display of spring bulbs and considered its promise of snowdrops and crocuses. She moved away. No bulbs survived the squirrels in her garden, but here, in Autumn Colour, she could see some possibilities in fuchsia and chrys-anthemum. No. They reminded her too much of her mother's home in Hastings. She turned the corner and found herself in Conifers, Heathers and Alpines. Absolutely not. She didn't want the north or the cold even though her garden was north-facing and overlooked by large trees; it was only a matter of time before she would have to surrender to the darkness and grow nothing but hostas. But what was the point? Hostas were immediately sacrificed to the slugs. Her own garden had become enemy territory. There used to be a sunny patch over by the fence where flowers could grow but shade encroached a little more each year, stealing more light and sky. And to make matters worse, she couldn't read anything these days without a pair of glasses, and as she intended to resist, until the final moment, the wearing of glasses round her neck on a string, she had begun to find that the world of words was retreating unless she *peered*. Not a good look, sweetheart, Precious reminded her. Peering now at the labels on a display of *Hedera helix*, she stood upright and grimaced. Who in their right mind would buy ivy? It had invaded her garden; *Hedera helix* grew up the fences, along the ground and throttled everything in its path. It spread and clung with the tenacity of a malignant disease, however often she was out there with secateurs and gloves.

In the last aisle she found herself in Water Features. This was more like it. She could abandon the lawn and dig a lake. There would be frogs and newts, lilies and kingcups. It was the answer to her gardening problem. Look, here there was even a fountain and a low trickling waterfall.

'Bad idea,' said a voice. 'All those leaves.'

It startled her, she hadn't heard him approach. She turned to see a tanned, shaven-headed man. He wore yellow work gloves and an open-mouthed smile.

'Oh,' she said, smiling too because she recognised him. 'Haven't we . . .'

'Urban,' he said, with a faint trace of an accent that she could not place. He pulled off his gloves and dug his hands into his pockets. 'Urban Feake.'

'Of course!' Bea laughed with relief and thought, what sort of a name is that? 'You're Wanda's friend, aren't you? You did my patio last year . . . I'm just looking for a . .' She was jabbering. He was very attractive . . . *earthy*. It had been joyous having him and Wanda work in her garden. Precious had come round one day after work and helped her cook for everyone.

They'd stood at the sink, she and Precious, nudging each other like girls as they watched Urban wield the sledgehammer. And now here he was again, looking at her like an old friend. She stopped herself and glanced around her. 'Now . . .' She turned away so she could adjust her bra and straighten her blouse. 'I think I've lost my children.'

She blushed. Urban must know the set-up. But even so, sometimes it was easier to pretend Adrian and Laura were her own children. It could be so complicated explaining they were her sister's, and anyway, they looked like Bea. Well, Laura did. She glanced at Urban, who hadn't moved. Stocky and muscled, he gave the impression of being wound tight like a spring. His English was good, she remembered that, but 'nephew' and 'niece' might be tricky.

Scattered gravel made them turn round. Chanel raced towards them, giggling as though she were having an asthma attack. She whisked past and took a running jump at a collection of faux-terracotta urns, four feet tall and enough to take a good-sized tree or teenager.

'That's not one of mine,' said Bea, pointing. 'She's a friend.'

Laura skidded round the corner and looked wildly about her. 'Where'd she go?'

Bea gestured at the urn. Laura ran up to it and looked inside. Snorts, shushes and guffaws ensued as she swung one leg up over the lip of it and hopped on the other foot.

Chanel started to giggle.

Laura said, 'It's not funny, man, I'm gonna wet meself, innit though?' She carried on hopping.

Chanel stood up in the urn and gave Laura's leg a yank.

Laura let out a shriek. 'Mind me mufti!'

Chanel started to hoot.

Bea said, 'Stop it, both of you,' and looked shamefacedly at Urban, who had rolled a cigarette. 'You're going to damage the pot, now get out.' She took a step forward and grabbed Laura's foot.

Miraculously, Laura slid easily into the pot and the two girls fell silent, faces looking up at her from the inside, pleading with her not to tell.

Adrian wandered over. Bea leant back against the pot and smiled, running a hand through her hair. I am flirting with the gardener, she thought. So what? There was something about the outdoors, something about the non-Englishness of Urban that made her feel like her old self. Women of her age didn't thrive in England. It was the damp and the dark and the tabloids. Urban lit his cigarette and watched her coolly.

She said, 'Adrian, do you remember Wanda's friend Urban?'

Adrian said hello and Urban nodded, looking away at the stacks of larch lap fencing.

'Like the pope?' said Adrian, studying Urban.

Urban smoked silently.

'Are they a band?' Bea said, remembering that she hadn't bought the meat yet. And the milk was running low when she left that morning. They would have to go to the supermarket on the way home.

'The pope was a pope,' explained Adrian. 'During the Crusades. Pope Urban. There were lots of them.'

Urban looked none the wiser. Can't be a Catholic thought Bea. She seemed to remember Wanda telling her he was Czech or Chechen, neither of which sounded like they'd have much truck with popes, but then Wanda was Catholic and she was from Poland. Bea shook her head. Personally, she welcomed the falling of borders on the continent. It widened everyone's horizons and it gave her hope, but Katharine said the NHS was buckling beneath the strain. The urn behind them squealed and rocked on its base. Adrian looked at Bea. Bea looked at Urban.

'Do you work here?' she said, noticing a small tree motif on the pocket of his sweatshirt.

'Parks and Gardens,' said Urban. 'I've come to pick up

some masonry.' He gestured at her empty trolley. 'Find what you were looking for?'

'Oh.' Bea looked around them vaguely. 'I wanted a water butt . . .'

A shadow of a smile crossed Urban's face. 'Ah yes. Wanda told me. Over here.' He started to walk away, back towards the building. Bea followed him, pushing the ungainly trolley along the gravel paths like a mother who has lost her overgrown baby.

Adrian paused by the urn and looked about him. The girls' whispers began to echo inside it. Soundlessly he crept behind the urn and lowered himself to the ground. The whispers got louder.

'I'm gonna wet myself.'

'You better not.'

'I am. I so badly need a piss.'

'You think he's gone?'

'Honest to God, it's coming out.

'Shush. I can hear him breathing.'

There was a silence, then a plaintive cry.

'You are gross, man! I don't believe it!'

'I told you!'

Spiralling laughter looped up out of the urn and Laura's head shot out of the top of it like a fast-growing tropical shrub. She tried to hoist herself free of the neck, her face a pantomime of horror and hysteria. Adrian put one hand experimentally against the curved side of the rocking urn and held it there a moment before giving it a little push and scrabbling away behind the garden pots. He heard the rumble, the screams and the laughter but didn't hang around to see the damage.

At the checkout, Urban was lifting a water butt and a humane squirrel trap on to Bea's trolley while she paid the assistant.

'There you are,' said Bea to Adrian. 'Where are the others?

Thank you so much, Urban.' She was keen to be rid of him now. He was loitering and she sensed that Adrian was judging her. She shouldn't really flirt in front of the children. 'Adrian can help me get it in the car.' Be bright and light, she told herself. Just be bright and light, Precious had told her. Patrick's not going to want a weeping wreck on his hands, is he? And it was good advice. It had worked for years and years.

They wheeled their trolley out of the shop towards the car park, where they found Laura and Chanel, who had stopped by a stand of cyclamens with their pale pink and lilac flowers. Laura pushed Chanel towards the plants. Chanel squealed. Laura's laughter made her whole body jerk and stagger. She tried to run but Chanel held her school bag so that she boomeranged backwards. Both girls half fell and found their faces inches away from the flowers' purple-stained mouths. There was a silence.

'They're freakin' me out. I'm serious, man, they're pervy!'

Laura stared, then pranced back from the flowers. 'Ik! Uggers! They look like them old singers my granny likes.'

Chanel got to her feet, stuck her hands deep into her pockets and backed into a table of pansies. She shook her head and said, 'They ain't natural, man, I swear. No way.'

Bea looked at the cyclamens and started to laugh. 'Come on,' she called. If they didn't get back soon there would be no time for food. And she still hadn't done anything about her mother's birthday party. But she would definitely come back for a few trays of cyclamens. They'd look lovely on the patio.

When they reached the car, Adrian said, 'What do you do with them?'

'What?' said Bea. 'They're just being girls. They'll be women soon and they won't find that so funny,' and she added a laugh to let Adrian know she was only joking. Sort of.

'The squirrels.' Adrian wasn't laughing.

Bea opened the boot and put the squirrel trap inside.

'We release them,' she lied. Actually she was going to lower them inside their traps into the water butt. The squirrels had decimated her garden. They were going to have to go. But humanely. Drowning was reputedly one of the easy ways – some struggle and panic but then a sleepy dreaminess.

'Help me in with this butt.'

They heaved it into the boot and tried to shut the door.

'It's too big.' She started to laugh again. Laughing was the other side of crying, she thought. You could go weeks without doing either, becoming more and more wound up and burdened, and then, snap, out it would come. They took out the water butt, put the squirrel trap on the roof of the car and tried the butt the other way. The boot door only half closed. Bea took a step back and looked at the car.

'Damn,' she said, laughing. She looked at Adrian. 'Don't say it.'

'Don't say what?'

'What you're about to say.'

'What?'

Laura and Chanel danced up to them, their school ties pulled almost out, their skirts rolled over at the top so that they only just covered their bottoms and their shirts knotted just below their push-up bras. Urban watched from the Sand, Pebbles and Gravel section.

'That geezer thinks he's so sprung and he's so not sprung,' said Chanel.

'He's *un*sprung,' said Laura.

'Yeah, zero sprung.' Chanel glowered in Urban's direction and sucked her teeth.

'Come on,' said Bea. 'Get in.' She gave the butt a final shove. They would just have to drive home with the boot half open. She got in the driver's seat and slammed the door. The children bundled in through the passenger door and Bea started the engine. She put the car in reverse and backed into the fence.

Adrian said, 'Mind the fence.'

'Whoops,' said Bea. 'I can't see a thing.'

The car leapt forward and then stalled.

'Laura's boob just popped out!' shouted Chanel.

'Don't look, Adrian, you *paedo*,' said Laura.

'*Paedo*?' said Bea.

Adrian turned to Bea. 'Your butt's too big,' he said.

Pray

THE NEXT Tuesday, Bea half walked and half ran up the hill to school, two bags of documents tugging her arms and a laptop banging at her hip. She prayed she hadn't missed the children. She had promised to take them to the cinema, a promise she made before she realised it was the council inspection the following day, but she never cancelled a Tuesday or a treat with the children. Tuesday was their day together come what may, and so, breathless and sweating, here she was when she should have been in the office and getting the paperwork done. She heard Laura's voice from twenty paces. She was arguing with Chanel on the other side of the hawthorn hedge. Bea waited out of sight. She loved their noise and their chutzpah. It enraged and dismayed Katharine and Frank, but she found that it made her glad. No one was going to grind these girls down. Well, not for a while anyhow.

'No. Listen, right? It's. Thing is. Everyone's different. You get. You got your. Take me, right? Other. Other people. Other people, right? Other people might. Like other people might pray for. Pray for their daily bread. Right? But. But I. But I pray for. I pray. I pray for—'.

'Praying, Chanel. Praying. Praying's gonna get you like. Nowhere. No. Where, Chanel. It's a waste of time. Who prays these days?'

'What you saying? That's bad, man. What you saying?'

'I'm saying. I'm saying, right? I mean, if there was a God? If there was a God then how come we're not all millionaires?'

'You saying there int a God? I'm movin' from next to you, man. 'Cos something bad's gonna happen. You say stuff like that. Something bad's gonna happen.'

''S right though, innit? If there is a God then how come there's bad stuff happening in . . . A God wouldn't. A God wouldn't do that.'

'If there ain't a God, then how come there's prayers? Answer that. Answer that then. Answer that then 'cos you can't, see! Can you? Can't answer that one, can you?'

'No, shut up, yeah? I dint say that. I dint say there weren't. Didn't say there weren't a God. I said, right? I said how come, right? If you was listening. I said—'

'You're gonna get a thunderbolt, you are. I'm movin' to here, man! I ain't standin' here to be struck down!'

'Why int everyone millionaires, yeah? 'Cos. Think about it. Think about it. If there was a God and you pray to him—'

'You're a. You're a. What they call it? You're a. You're gonna burn at the stake!'

'Shut up! Listen. Shut up! Listen. We could all be rich, yeah? Have whatever we want. You know, a Nokia thingy. Live on nothing but Twixes.'

'Twixes? Creme Eggs. Creme Eggs and KitKats. And M&Ms. And a. A Motorola—'

'They're ming. Samsung more like.'

'Like that one you jacked?'

'I never jacked that, man!'

'You said you jacked it.'

'I never. I was given it.'

'Yeah. You so jacked it, man. You told me. You so jacked that phone.'

'That was a Sony whatsit. They're hot. Buff, man. I mean it, man! Them phones are buff. That's what I'd get.'

'And Twixes.'

'And Creme Eggs!'

'And Bounties. Innit though?'

Chanel popped her face round the corner of the hedge. 'It's your auntie.'

Bea stepped through the school gates and waved hello. It had always been her day since they started nursery, although lately they had been at her house most days. Katharine's work was getting more pressured and Richard's work had always been impossible. 'Impossible,' Katharine said, when Bea asked how things were. 'Absolutely impossible. We're going to have to move.' Meanwhile, on Tuesdays, and sometimes Fridays, and last week Monday too, Bea left work early and made up the hours getting in early and working late on the other days. She always felt guilty, though, creeping out at two forty-five while Precious and Karen stayed at their desks.

'You don't have to be good,' Precious told her. 'You do more than enough hours for this place. And you've never had maternity leave. Go on. Take your Tuesdays and enjoy them.'

But Tuesdays had become awkward since Barry Charles's arrival. Nothing had been said, but Bea sensed the disapproval. So today she had left work late and then she had missed the bus.

Laura put her face right up in front of Bea's.

'Can I go to the shop?'

'Well . . .'

'Please, Bea, please.'

'Well, I suppose so, but Laura, where's Adrian?'

'In homework club!' Laura ran down the pavement after Chanel. 'I won't be long!'

Bea looked back up the road and her heart jumped. There

was Katharine getting out of her Jeep and talking to a waiting mother. What was Katharine doing here on a Tuesday?

Bea collected up her bags again and wandered over to her sister and waited for her to finish her conversation. Passing mothers and children nodded and smiled when they saw Bea standing there. She smiled back and leaned against Katharine's car, feeling like a child herself. When people asked her whether she had children, as they inevitably did, there was always the pause after she said no. Sometimes during school holidays, like the one that had just finished, it felt to Bea like the answer to that question should be yes. After all, Laura and Adrian spent almost as much time with her and Frank as they did with their own parents. But really the answer was no, and the pause that followed would rise up sometimes only as far as her thighs while the questioner changed the subject; sometimes it would rise right up to her chest, and on a bad day it would lap at her throat so that Bea had to stretch out her chin and draw a long breath in. And in the pause, she would see the questioner realise what a trespass the question was, as if they had asked about her bowels or her sex life.

Katharine's voice was getting shrill and strained.

'Well I'll have a word with Laura, but I absolutely know that she would never do anything to jeopardise her relationship with Stella . . .'

The woman talking to Katharine shifted her feet unhappily, turning her head away as Katharine tried to plough on.

'As I say, I'll have a word, but—'

'But I'm not sure that discussing it is going to help. I just want you to tell Laura to stop the negative comments.'

'Absolutely. I think we may very well find that this is something that has been blown right out of proportion. Obviously, I will sit down with Laura and ask her if she has friendship issues she'd like to look at . . .'

'I don't think Stella's blowing anything out of proportion.

She doesn't want to go to school. There are things written on the toilet walls about her that—'

'I absolutely and totally understand how upsetting it must be. Honestly. You see, the thing is, *because* of Laura's dyslexia . . . she is in actual fact very very bright and she's really interested in boundaries and where she can take them. We're not happy with the way the school has been failing to support her, and as you may know we are moving very very soon . . . Bea! What are you doing here?'

Bea smiled at the two women. Someone's phone bleated.

'Is that your phone?' said Bea.

'It's you, isn't it?'

'Not me,' said Bea. 'My phone's been nicked.'

'God! It hasn't, has it? Then it must be me. God. I pray that doesn't happen to me. It is. It's me again. Hello? Damn, missed it.' She waved off the aggrieved mother.

'Katharine. I think one of us has the days wrong.' Bea looked away, up towards the school gates. 'I thought Tuesday was my day.'

'God, that woman is a pain in the arse. She's paranoid about her bloody daughter. Convinced that Laura is getting at her. I mean, can you imagine Laura being a bully? The real problem is with the mother, of course. The poor child is in dire need of a parentectomy—'

'Today's Tuesday. Tuesday's my day.'

'Well it is. Normally. But didn't you get my text?' Katharine grasped the shoulder strap of her handbag, lifted her sunglasses up on to her head and took a few steps towards the school fence. Trip-trap, trip-trap.

Bea looked at Katharine's shoes, patent black leather slingbacks. They pointed north, north-east, east and then north again. Leaves scuttled along the gutter. I am paying too much attention to everything, Bea told herself, and concentrated on slowing her breathing. Adrian appeared by her side. Laura slunk up behind him.

'There you are,' said Katharine. 'Come on now, we need to get back.' She looked at Bea and added, 'I'll take you home, Bea.'

'We're leaving,' said Adrian.

Bea felt something let go inside her. 'What?'

Katharine shooed everyone into the car. 'Bea, come home with us for a short while. Then I can tell you what's happened.'

Go

INSIDE KATHARINE'S car, Bea sat in the passenger seat and watched as Cambridge peeled past her, silenced and removed. This is what money buys, she thought. This is the reward that success brings: a hermetically sealed corridor through the world.

The traffic was stop-start and the meadows by Fen Causeway shimmered in a pollution haze. Katharine fixed her mind on slipping through the spaces caused by the hesitations of less *driven* drivers. The man in front of her was dithering, not driving, and the lights up ahead were on green for precisely seven seconds. Seven seconds was enough to let two cars through, one if drivers were barely conscious, as the one in front appeared to be. This, if she was honest, was why it was easier for the children to be at Bea's house after school. She did not want them negotiating the traffic and then returning to an empty house, and while she could have got an au pair for the autumn, there didn't seem much point given that they knew they were moving to London just as soon as her job was sorted out. Now, in fact. Almost immediately.

She glanced at Bea then revved the engine and flashed her lights at the car in front. Yes, it would have been simpler to have done what Richard suggested in the first place and sent the children to one of the private schools in the city, but at the time, it was Richard's infuriating assumption that that was what they *would* do that enraged her. Richard and his family, with their benign wealth and bemused detachment from the rest of humanity, behaved as if education was an inoculation against unpleasantness. Katharine pressed her palm to the horn and wondered whether a gentle shunt with her cow bars on the bumper of the car in front was, strictly speaking, illegal. Yes, it was Richard's fault they were at the community college in the first place. If he had not been so smug, so blinkered— What in God's name was the man in front doing now? Not a three-point turn surely? She blew her horn again. If Richard had not blithely assumed that Laura and Adrian would go private, she might not have kicked up such a fuss, because, after all, *she* hadn't gone to a private school. No, she had gained a place at the local grammar school, unlike poor old Bea who had gone to the secondary modern. Katharine shook her head and took a quick look at Bea. She was just sitting there, saying nothing, face closed. School had not done Bea any favours, that was for sure. Perhaps, in some ridiculous way – Katharine softened at the thought – *perhaps* sending the children to the school near Bea had been an act of contrition, an acknowledgement, an attempt— A heavy clunk brought her up short. Her wing mirror had been knocked askew as a stream of students on bicycles weaved their way in and out of the stationary cars. 'Hey!' Katharine shouted through the closed window.

The traffic began to move, was moving quite fast now, and the bloody clutch was sticking so that when she finally did get the car into gear, a long space had opened up ahead of her. She accelerated into second, punishing the engine. With any luck they would make the lights. Yes, she had hammered her point home to Richard, given him a lecture about equality of opportunity and social division (really, sometimes she suspected he didn't have a clue what she was talking about) and all of a sudden he'd bloody well gone and given in. She'd won. 'Damn it!' Katharine braked hard and squealed to a halt inches from the car in front.

She swept the hair from her face and found the whole of her upper body was as rigid as an iron pike, the sort that kept the tourists out of the college wine cellars – her back, her neck, her shoulders, her jaw were painfully fused and unmoving. 'What the hell do you think you're doing?' she yelled at the driver in front. Bea looked bewildered and alarmed, damn her. She would have to tell Bea that this was their last week in Cambridge. It wouldn't go down well; now was not a good time. Bea was doing her whipped-puppy look, her poor-me look, her it's-all-right-for-you look. There was no putting it off. Katharine put the hand brake on and took a deep breath.

'Oh, by the way, we've got some news.'

Bea looked straight ahead of her as she listened, heard the words flow past her in an unstoppable stream. After months of thinking about it, talking about it, delay and second thoughts, places had been found for both children at schools in London that would challenge Adrian and push Laura. Amazingly, they could start next week even though term had already begun, and so, what with places being like gold dust, and what with one thing and another, especially the nonsense going on with Laura, they'd decided that this would be best. A bit of a rush, but really, what with Richard's job already being in London and her consultant job at the London hospital being more or less a foregone conclusion, (hopefully, fingers crossed), there was nothing keeping them in Cambridge any longer. She would manage the London–Cambridge commute somehow until the London job came through, and so the sooner they moved the better for everyone, otherwise Christmas would be upon them and they'd probably all have nervous breakdowns if they left it till then, and believe it or not, crazily enough, that meant this weekend. Well, Friday actually. Mad, isn't it?

Bea looked at her hands and said nothing. She thought of them, numb and raw with cold, holding Katharine's smaller one in sodden wool mittens as she pulled her whining sister up the hill home from school; the happy-sad pain of them against the red bars of the electric fire. She thought of her hands against Katharine's, fingers clenched tight so she could feel the bones; Katharine's knee on her belly; the sick ache and helpless struggle for breath; Katharine's face inches from her own and the hissed threats not to tell. She thought of the giggling, soaring release when one well-aimed kick or bite sent Katharine reeling, screaming and coiling back. Their mother at the door, face like an anvil, words an icy stream from her mouth. And she thought of the shock and shame of it, the burning, stinging pain of it when her mother's hurtling hand landed on her face. Hate and rage. Slap-bang. Branded.

Katharine looked at Bea. Looked and drove, looked and talked, adding details, making it ordinary, trying to soften the blow. She asked whether Bea thought Mum would like a day up in London on her birthday. Tea at the Savoy maybe. What was she talking about? thought Bea. They had agreed it was going to be a meal at Oyster Row. Wanda was going to help. Lance was coming. Mum could sleep in the spare room and Lance could sleep on the couch in Frank's room. Frank would have to sleep upstairs again with her. Bea looked at the satnav on the dashboard and at Katharine's wedding ring as she held the steering wheel. She tried to think of some words to say, something to calm Katharine's deluge about mortgages and travel times and careers and schools and how they had tried their best to do the right thing but that when push came to shove they were spending a fortune on tutors and Claudia at Richard's office had a brother who was admissions tutor at Durham and he said they never even looked at candidates who didn't get at least ten A*s at GCSE and when all was said and done, they couldn't rely on the school to make sure that happened, well, Adrian would probably be all right other than being bored to death, but Laura . . . they'd never forgive themselves if Laura ended up pushing paperclips in an office for the rest of her life.

Katharine turned the car into the shade-dappled road, where children played on bicycles and glossy dogs trotted smiling on leads. The gravel crunched as she swung into the driveway of a caramel-bricked, double-fronted house and brought the car to a halt. Bea thought, Why would anyone want to leave all this? Then she thought, What's she brought me home with her for? She looked at Katharine. Katharine looked at Bea.

'Damn,' said Katharine. 'Damn and damn it.'

'Don't worry.' Bea undid her seatbelt and tried to open the door. It didn't matter, and anyway, she was pleased to put some space between herself and Frank. Perhaps she would go to the cinema after all.

'I wasn't thinking,' said Katharine.

'Let me out, I can walk.'

'No, you can't possibly.'

'I'd like to, really,' said Bea and started to laugh.

She bent down to untangle the strap of her laptop case, which had twined itself round one foot. She opened it, stuffed the papers from one of the two carrier bags in and forced the zip shut. Heat consumed her head and she thought that if she had to continue laughing one moment longer her skull would split.

Katharine saw her sister beside her, the house in front of them, thought of the champagne chilling in the fridge, the lists to be made and phone calls to be planned. It was going to be such a busy evening and the traffic had seemed heavier then ever, really, Cambridge was worse than London when it came to rush hour. Her throat felt tight and a band of tension had begun to grip her forehead. If she got a migraine now, it would be a disaster. It would take an age to drive Bea home but Richard would disapprove if she let her walk. Too bad. She undid her seatbelt. Here she was, just like work, trapped as usual in an interminable loop where doing the right thing proved nigh on impossible. And here was Bea laughing and rummaging around with her coat and things like some old bag lady. Well, they were here now. The children were tired and there were things to do. She pressed at her forehead with her hand to keep the pain at bay, then rolled her head and closed her eyes with a sigh. It was just too bad, she thought with a guilty sense of release as she swallowed and allowed selfishness to throttle decency.

Bea had stopped laughing and was looking at her.

'What, *walk*?' said Katharine.

'Honestly, it's fine.' Bea struggled with the door handle. They were locked in. Safety feature. Automatic.

'What, all the way?' Katharine stared at the wiring on the front of the house. She must remember to notify the utilities of their move date.

'Well, yes.'

'Round the ring road?' Claudia could do all the phone calls though. Thank God for Richard's PA. It was invaluable having one of those. Like a wife.

'No, along the river.'

Katharine looked at her watch. Her mobile began to ring. The ringing increased in volume. Bea longed for her own phone, which she had lost. It had Adrian's voice as the ringtone, Adrian's voice saying, 'Ans-wer the phone. Ans-wer *the phone!*' in a rising tone of barely controlled hysteria. That hadn't gone down terribly well at work during her one-to-one Targets and Objectives meeting with the head of Human Resources a few weeks ago. Katharine's phone continued to ring.

'I feel so bad about messing up your last afternoon with the children, Bea . . .' She gestured at Laura on the back seat who had earphones in and her eyes closed. 'But everything is such a bloody rush suddenly.' She released the central locking and Bea opened her door.

'Really, it's all right.' Bea climbed down on to the gravel. Christ, she hadn't even got them a present. Tomorrow. She would nip into town at lunchtime and send it round in a cab.

'Oh God, it's the estate agent. I'd better take this!' shouted Katharine. She waved the door keys over her shoulder. 'Adrian! Keys! Bea, I'll ring you later. Sure you're okay?'

Bea hesitated between the house and the car as the children trooped up to the front door. 'Hey!' she said.

They turned and looked at her and she held out her arms. Adrian loped towards her and let himself be enveloped by her embrace.

'Maybe see you at Granny's birthday,' she said into his hair.

'Do you think she'd like fireworks?'

'Definitely.'

She let him go and looked at Laura, who was feigning indifference by the sundial. Her face was pale and blotched. Spots threatened beneath the skin of her forehead and her brow was furrowed. Bea smiled and took a step towards her. Laura frowned, pulled out one earpiece and reached for Bea in a sudden clumsy movement. She dropped her head on to Bea's shoulder and leant against her, arms hanging passively down by her sides. Bea hugged her soft form and kissed the side of her head. She smelt of shampoo and chewing gum.

'Goodbye, my beautiful girl,' she said. The tears rose up in her then and she concentrated on not sobbing. Laura brought her arms up and gave her aunt a fierce squeeze. Hair slides and clips pressed painfully into Bea's cheek.

Laura pulled away and looked at the ground, her mouth tugged downwards like a clown.

Katharine's voice sailed out of the car. 'Absolutely not. Absolutely out of the question.'

'Say goodbye to your mum for me.'

Laura spluttered a laugh. Bea smiled and turned away.

Rip

FRANK SAT back on his heels and admired Wanda's bottom. She lay face down on the couch before him, naked apart from her blouse. He had the letter from Lancashire Arts in one hand and a glass of Scotch in the other. Joy flooded his body, chased by a riptide of fear. Joy that his literary career might be about to be resurrected; fear that, like his early success, this moment in the sun would be just that, a moment. He looked again at the letter. There was to be a perform-ance of his play by the Burnley Amateur Dramatic Association as part of the council's Winter Arts Retrospective. Lancashire Arts would be delighted if he would attend the first night and take part in a short question-and-answer session on stage beforehand. Wanda was impressed.

'You must be very clever,' she said, raising herself up on her elbows and flicking through the pages of *The Seagull in the Cherry Orchard*. He had written it in his final year at university, and his parents had spent their holiday money getting five hundred copies printed and bound. It was a gesture that Frank had appreciated, although the cover had always irked him. An enormous seagull, sketched by Lance, had been pasted on top of a cherry tree (found in his mother's gardening catalogue). Frank had, not very kindly, explained that the title was not literal; the play was not *about* a seagull in a cherry orchard, it was an exploration of the Chekhovian understanding of all our sorrow – that neither love nor work will rescue us. This comment was lost on his parents because love had indeed rescued them – for the time being.

Wanda said, 'What is the seagull sitting on?'

Frank raised his eyes to heaven and took a slug of Scotch. He felt the spasm in his back relax a little and asked whether she would like a signed copy. He had four hundred and seventy of them in a box under the couch. Wanda was delighted and tried to turn over but Frank told her to stay as she was because, in all honesty, he found the front of a naked woman rather – what? Offputting? Intimidating? *Demanding* was the word he was looking for. Roughly he took the copy of the play from her, rested it on her bottom, and began to write an inscription. 'For Wanda,' he wrote, then hesitated. Thank you for cleaning my house? Don't be ridiculous. My Masha? No, she'd probably never read *Three Sisters*. The pearl in my oyster? He was getting sentimental now. Hastily he signed his name, 'Frank Pamplin', and handed it back to her.

'Your father drew the seagull!' she cried. 'Oh, your parents must love you very much.'

He nodded and watched with satisfaction as she turned the pages of his play. Oh yes, he was loved. As a child, he was stuffed with love, loved half to death by his mother, who smothered and cosseted and fussed and pressed him. Like his clothes that she ironed every evening in front of the television while he got on with the time-consuming business of being clever and winning a place to Cambridge. But once the play was performed at the Cambridge Arts Club in his final year there, once he had decided that his future was to be a glittering career as a playwright, things hadn't quite panned out the way they were supposed to. Wanda giggled.

He drank more Scotch and let it roll, burning a little,

across his tongue. *Cambridge*. He was the first in his family to go to university, and that wasn't nothing either. Not like where Wanda grew up. In Poland everyone went to university and everyone was clever. But in England it was different. People said he would go far and he had. People expected him to get a First and he hadn't.

Frank put the bottle down. He wouldn't drink any more because, on top of the painkillers he took for his back, it wasn't helping with the potency issues he had been experiencing lately. Sad to say, where Bea was concerned, this was largely a case of a loss of desire. Hence, Wanda. The life cycle of a man was complicated, something that Bea failed to understand. Wanda was what he needed at this stage in his life. There was nothing wrong with it; all great artists required a younger woman at some point. Look at Picasso, Dickens, Tolstoy . . . He glanced over at Chekhov. Well, he shrugged, not *all* perhaps.

Wanda was impressed that he had been a Cambridge student. She was turning the pages while swinging one leg up and down at the knee so that her bottom shuddered. Frank looked away. He felt perplexed. Why had his viva for a First gone so terribly wrong? He had nursed the scene of this missed opportunity for decades. He saw it now as the crucial moment when his life took a wrong turn and he still felt the sting of it. The whole interview had been awkward, like talking to a girl. In the Senior Tutor's study he had faltered and strained after the finer points of Milton's *Paradise Lost*, he had mouthed platitudes about the Age of Reason and then dried up altogether while the clock on the wall ticked the slow minutes away. The tutor had said, 'Well, I think that is all,' and pressed a brown bell in the wall by the fireplace. Frank sat and stared stupidly for a moment until the green baize door opened and a short man dressed like a waiter said, 'Thank you, Mr Pamplin' and held the door open for him. He got clumsily to his feet and tore the silence with the cry of his chair leg on the parquet floor. His crêpe soles squeaked the long clown's walk from the window overlooking the quad, away from his future, his past and into the cramped and dimly lit anteroom that smelt of dust and leather.

'And will your parents be at the performance in December?' asked Wanda, turning on to her side.

Frank got off her legs then and sat on the edge of the couch and picked up the letter again. He shook his head.

'My mother died the year I left university. It was a shock. The last thing I was expecting.'

Wanda put her hand on his back and stroked it. That was what Bea had done when he told her all those years ago, stroked his back tenderly.

Wanda asked how she died but Frank didn't answer because he didn't really know. His mother had hidden her illness and he had never asked for the details. He knew it concerned the dark female interior of her, the unspoken secrets lodged inside her woman's body. Lance told him she ignored the signs for a long time, carrying on with her secretarial job and running the home until the pains became agonies that made her lie down in the day and sit up all night.

'What else you write, Frank?'

He cleared his throat. He told her about the radio plays and the brief stint on the television soap *Brookside*. He told her that in those first years after his mother died he had written a lot; there had been a flurry of interest, enquiries from agents, the occasional invitation from theatre groups. He pulled down a file of cuttings and read some out to her. 'Frank Pamplin has an original voice'; 'Could this be the Chekhov of Burnley?'

'And women, Frank? I bet the girls go crazy for you.'

It was true that every time a play of his saw the light of day, a woman appeared with it. He told her about Sandra from the BBC and Valerie from Northern Arts, both relationships that managed to make it to three months, but his heart was never in it and after a while they would take the hint and that would be that. The most difficult part was telling his father. It mortified Lance to think that his son might never marry and have children of his own. He couldn't understand it, and in truth nor could Frank.

'And Bea?'

'Be what?'

'Then you met Bea! I like Bea very much.'

Frank hardly felt it was appropriate to be discussing his wife. It was even less appropriate for her to *like* Bea. But of course she did. Everyone liked Bea.

'Bea is a good woman,' said Wanda.

'She wasn't very good when I met her.' Carrying on with a married man was hardly exemplary behaviour in Frank's book, after all. 'I made her good,' he heard himself say.

'Like God?' Wanda had a smirk on her face that he didn't appreciate. She erased it. 'Where did you find her?'

'On a boat. En route to Tobago or somewhere.'

'How romantic.' Wanda held her hand out for the Scotch bottle. 'What were you doing on a boat?'

Frank told her. He had learnt to explain his cruise ships story as a rite of passage. He avoided the details of those ten soul-sapping years on board the *Oriana* and *Island Star*. Once he moved out of his father's house, and after a few years in London – flatshares, bedsits, the YMCA – he found himself, despite three more plays, staring thirty in the face and without enough to pay the rent on a decent place to live. He was too proud to go on the dole or into teaching, so when he saw an ad for cruise liner work it seemed like the answer to his problems. An income and a place to live, a chance to see the world and time to write. As 'photographer' on the *Oriana*, all he had to do was snap the passengers on Polaroids, then take their money.

'How romantic,' said Wanda again.

'Oh yes, plenty of that. Now lie down.'

Wanda did as she was told and Frank wondered about taking off his trousers. Sex was the very last thing he felt capable of right now, but perhaps if he just sat on Wanda's legs again and took photographs . . . God, he had taken some depressing photos in his time on board those ships, and that was just off duty. Nameless encounters with numberless passengers and staff in his tiny cabin below the water line where it smelt of oil and sewage and was unbearably hot.

'Lucky Bea,' giggled Wanda.

He didn't tell her that when Bea stood before him as the pianist blanded it out on the baby grand, he was at such a low point that it was enough that she looked him in the eye and smiled. She was a good listener too, and at that time she appeared interested in his work. What was more, he soon discovered she had a house and a job and she wasn't bad looking for a woman of forty. He had begun to feel doomed to a life on the ocean wave, ploughing pointlessly from port to port and unable to get off. Every ridiculous voyage seemed to take him further away from the distant promise of his youth. He was getting old. He needed to feel the ground beneath his feet and a roof over his head. He needed someone, to have and to hold, just one. He needed a wife.

Frank sank his thumbs into the dimples either side of Wanda's lower spine. Wanda turned and reached for his thigh. Frank hesitated. He didn't want this to go anywhere. His back was bad today and one shoulder was stiff. He resolved to keep his clothes on and just take photographs. He took the front of her blouse in his hand and gave it a tug. She pulled away in mock alarm and he heard the fabric give a tiny tear and rip.

'Oops,' she said and tipped her head on one side.

He watched her through the viewfinder as she lay down on the couch again and looked up at the ceiling, a distant smile on her face. Her body looked damn good in a photograph, but in real life it was almost too masculine. She was so lean and long that if it were not for her breasts, she could almost be a boy. Wanda stretched and yawned and closed her eyes. Frank raised the camera to his eye and took a shot. The great thing about this digital camera was that it didn't really matter what you pointed it at, it always looked tremendous. Clear as a bell. Too clear if you happened to point it at anything over the age of twenty-eight, of course. Wanda squirmed and made a mewing noise. She claimed to find the sound of the shutter arousing. Wanda claimed to find just about everything arousing, especially when she'd been at his Scotch.

A sad, small voice nudged the corner of his mind. It told him he was beginning to tire of her no-nonsense Polish promiscuity. He ignored it and rubbed at the pain in his shoulder. He didn't want to stop just yet. He was using her to sort out this difficult period with Bea. And, he burped discreetly, he had no qualms about using Wanda, seeing as Wanda was using him. She was building up a portfolio of very professional-looking photographs—

A noise from the hallway made him stop and listen. Bea had said she was taking the children somewhere and wouldn't be back till later. He turned to look at the door and felt a draught of cool air on his feet.

Wanda raised her head and met his eyes, pouting. His heart was beating fast. He looked at the letter again and thought that perhaps, after all, he might be capable of some mild erotic moment. Just concentrate, he told himself, concentrate on those astounding half-moons joined by a narrow waist, the long ridge of the spine, the shoulders and neck . . . He put his hands either side of her legs and moved his groin up towards her bottom, then sighed and rubbed the top of his head. It was no good; these days he barely felt anything at all. Even lust was deserting him now, and this too he felt was not unconnected to Bea. Something had happened to the woman. He had seen it that ghastly night four weeks ago.

Some retreat in her, some duplicity. He had seen it before, or rather he had sensed it creeping up on him, laughing behind its hand. It had always been there. And it had a name. Oh yes, it had a name all right. He reached for the bottle and swallowed a good long mouthful. Patrick Cumberbatch.

Wanda twisted round, sat up and kissed him on the lips. Frank wondered what on earth had possessed him to put on Beethoven's String Quartet in B Flat Major. It didn't begin well, with its grinding dissonances and unresolved themes. It was a piece that was best described as 'unusual'. What torture must the old man have endured to compose something like this? A jarring, jangling dance of discrepancy blended with an impossible yearning sweetness. Wanda giggled. He was tickling her foot. He tickled it some more and she prodded his groin with her other foot. Actually, that hurt. He grabbed her instep and gave it a little twist. She squeaked and lay still. The thing about Wanda was that she showed respect and she never laughed at him, not the way that Bea did. Bea had a way of looking at him and just laughing. He took Wanda's other leg in his hand, heard her sigh and parted her legs a little. How uncomplicated Wanda's body was compared to Bea's. God alone knew what was going on with Bea's body right now. She was leaking, spreading, boiling, melting – really, it was the stuff of nightmares.

He slapped Wanda on the bottom, hard this time so that she shouted something in Polish into the pillow. He wanted to extinguish Bea, flatten her and turn her to stone. And so, bit by bit – when was it now? two years ago? three? – he had begun.

Van-da.

He took a long drink and grimaced. What had surprised him was how hard it was to stop. The thing was, having turned away from Bea, he wasn't entirely sure he could find his way back any more.

Suddenly Beethoven was silent and they heard the kitchen

door slam. Frank leapt to his feet and set the Scotch bottle spinning across the floor. Wanda raised her head. She had a rather stupid expression on her face, a wide-eyed silent movie calamity face.

She said, 'Oh no!'

He recognised Bea's footsteps in the hall. What the hell was she doing back so early?

'I forgot,' said Wanda.

'What?' he said, recoiling now at the sight of her pale sprawl. The female body was so indiscreet, with its mounds and gapes and sudden eruptions of hair. 'Forgot what?'

He stood up and threw Wanda's bra at her so that it hit her in the face. Good. She looked at him dangerously and wrapped herself in the tartan rug, his mother's rug.

'Get dressed,' he said.

'I meant to say.' She shook with silent laughter. 'Your wife rang!'

'But she was taking the kids to the cinema.' He pulled the rug from round her and pushed a pile of her clothes into her arms.

'She rang to say she was coming back early.'

Frank stared at her and realised she was drunk. He shook his head in disbelief. If he wasn't very careful, this was all going to explode in his face. Wanda held her blouse up to the light and frowned at it as if she couldn't remember which way to wear it. What was she playing at? He felt the familiar ground of their betrayal lurch and shift.

He needed to take control of the situation. The important thing was for him not to act like the guilty philanderer. What he did in his workroom was entirely his business. Anyway, Bea was in a world of her own, and that, he told himself, looking in vain for one sock, was half the trouble.

Wanda gathered her hair back in an elastic band. 'Okay, I'm going now.'

'Wait,' said Frank.

He listened by the door and watched Wanda apply lipstick in the mirror. He could hear Bea in the kitchen, then heard her come into the hall, heard the chink of a tray and a small, timid knock on the door. Wanda spotted her lacy red knickers draped on the lampshade and dropped them into her bag with a giggle and a shrug.

Frank put his finger to his lips then listened some more. He heard Bea's heavy tread on the stairs and the bathroom door shutting.

He nodded at Wanda and unlocked his door. 'Come on, hurry,' he said, putting Beethoven back on.

Wanda slipped out of the house, said a quiet 'See you,' and was gone into the darkness.

When

B EA CAME downstairs in her dressing gown and found
Frank standing in the hall. He had the sort of surprised
expression on his face that looked as though it had been
applied a little before any actual surprise.

'You're back early,' he said. He put his hands in his pockets,
pulled them out again and peered at a patch of wall. 'Been
in long?'

He was standing in the way. From the open door of his
room Beethoven could be heard shaking his fist at the world.

'What?' she said.

Frank gave the door of his room a push to open it further,
as if he wanted to show it was empty. She rarely looked in
there and she avoided looking in there now.

'Where are the children?'

She stared at him. There were specks of dandruff on his shoulders. He shouldn't wear dark shirts. 'Wrong day apparently,'
she said.

Something had happened to her face.

'I got some good news today,' he said and fetched the letter
from the floor by the couch. He handed it to her. 'It appears
that I have been invited . . .'

She looked past him towards the kitchen and shook her
head again. 'I can't find my glasses.'

'What?'

'My glasses. They must have fallen out in Katharine's car.'

She walked past him. The skin on her forehead was moving all by itself and her fingertips tingled. He followed her into the kitchen and Beethoven died away without conclusion.

'They're leaving for London this weekend.'

Frank held the letter limply in one hand. 'Who?'

'Katharine and the children. She just told me.' Bea filled the kettle because she had better be good and have a cup of tea although what she really wanted was a double vodka and tonic. She sniffed the air and turned round to look at him. 'Have you been drinking?'

'They're leaving?'

'Yes.'

'But that's very sudden.'

'We knew it was on the cards.'

She leant against the worktop and looked at her discarded shoes. Grass cuttings and mud smeared the soles and now all Tuesdays would be like this. Just the two of them in the kitchen, waiting for the kettle to boil and batting questions to each other. Any minute now Frank would put on his but-that's-*ridiculous*-face and say, 'You mean they're *moving*?'

'You mean they're *moving*?'

'The children have places in schools starting Monday.'

She poured water into the pot and looked out into the garden. A squirrel bounced and hopped on the grass beneath the squirrel-proof bird table. She would plant no more bulbs this autumn or any other. Last year the bloody squirrels dug up every single one of them. A dozen daffodils, six lilies and ten hyacinths. She could murder the little bastards.

'Monday? But they haven't even sold their house.'

Bea decided not to offer him a cup of tea. She was always making him tea and finding it hours later, cold and untouched. He could pour his own. She put the pot on the kitchen table and unzipped her laptop.

'Their house will sell in a day.'

She ought to make a start on some work. There was so much to do before the inspection tomorrow that she had no idea how she was going to get it all done.

'But I haven't said goodbye to Adrian and Laura.'

'You'll see them at Mum's party.'

'What?'

'You did tell Lance, didn't you?'

'When?'

It would probably take hours. When she printed out the budget summaries before leaving the office, she noticed to her horror that the figures still didn't tally. She had brought everything home, all the figures and reports going back three years.

'In a couple of weeks.'

'What, here? How many?'

'Well we can't use the front room because you're in there, Frank.'

'How many are we expecting?'

'About ten.'

Frank looked at the kitchen table that sat four, then squinted at Bea, who had gone to the window again and was pre-occupied by something in the garden. It was impossible to tell if she suspected anything. Not that anything had happened. Photography was just a way of earning a bit of money, but all the same . . .

Bea banged hard on the window with her hand. 'Wanda's helping,' she said.

There was a silence as they watched the squirrel climb the squirrel-proof pole of the bird feeder and swing itself up to the seed on the platform like a trapeze artist.

'You bastard,' muttered Bea.

Late

THE NEXT morning, Precious, armed with an extra layer of purple lid shimmer and a thorough slicking of lipstick, got to work early. It was 7.15 and she knew she would find Bea already at her desk, looking terrible and preparing the final papers for the Spectres. There were no errant smokers by the wall, no Nertili mopping the floor, and on reception, Archie had been replaced by a woman in what appeared to be a prison officer's uniform. Louise and Angela were in the lift looking pale and ragged and Jonathan had less of a leap in his stride when he made a run for it as the doors closed. 'Good luck,' they whispered to each other, avoiding eye contact, whenever someone got out. Up in Land Registry, Covenants and Deeds, Precious found Karen, bound from head to toe in black and perched on Bea's chair. She peered at the computer screen and gave Precious a guilty look.

'What you up to?' said Precious.

'I'm looking for the work Bea did yesterday.'

'Leave that to Bea. You'll bring up the wrong file. She took them home to check.'

'But she's not here.'

'It's half past seven in the morning, girl. Give the woman a chance.'

'The thing is, Barry Charles wants everything on his desk by eight.'

'Yes, we know. Bea will do that.'

'He asked me to do it.'

'You what?' Precious delivered a withering look. She took a pair of glasses from her drawer, checked the arms and lenses, and laid them on Bea's desk.

Karen swallowed. 'He asked me to. Yesterday. He told me to bring the papers up to him and . . .'

'And what?'

'Make sure everything was in order.' Karen looked wretched. 'Sorry.'

'Get off.' Precious flicked her away from Bea's chair. 'Bea will be here any minute.'

At 8.15, Barry Charles's PA rang and asked where the papers were. Precious said they would be with her shortly. She asked to speak to Bea. Precious told her Bea was away from her desk. She asked to speak to Karen. Precious told her Karen was also away from her desk at the moment. When Precious put the phone down, Karen's lips had gone white.

'Was that a good idea?'

Precious went to Bea's computer, opened a file and began printing a document. 'I tell you what would be a good idea.'

'What?'

'It would be a good idea if you fast-tracked your sorry arse down to the photocopier and ran off a copy of this.'

'But you said it wasn't the latest version.'

'It's an inspection. Nobody actually reads any of this stuff. Now go. Double-sided and stapled at the spine.'

At 9.17, Precious picked up the phone and dialled Bea's home number. It rang for a long time and then switched to the answer machine. She put the phone down and dialled again. Karen's face appeared over the dividing screen. She communicated silently with eyes, lips and hands. *They're coming.*

Precious had the phone to her ear and stared back at Karen, one finger up in the air.

'Hello, it's Precious Mtandwa here. Mtandwa. From Bea's office. Hello? Is that Frank?'

Karen took a swift look behind her. Barry Charles was down the other end talking to Sunita and the Spectres. The whole office was subdued, everyone at their desks, no chat, no phones. She gripped the metal edge of the screen. Sparks flew and static crackled.

'Ahh!'

'Shh!' said Precious. 'Frank? What time did she leave?'

Karen needed the toilet urgently. She held her palm to her shrunken belly and watched as Precious listened to Frank. Precious's body was wrapped in bottle green with a slice of black-spotted magenta silk that dived down to her capacious bosom. Karen thought that Precious was watermelon while she herself was celery. She half wondered what it might be like to eat for pleasure. Precious put her hand over the mouthpiece and said to Karen, 'He doesn't know when she left. He was asleep.'

'Well we are a bit worried, yes. It's so unlike Bea to be late and not call . . .'

Karen held her fingers to her lips and smelt the cigarette she'd smoked on the way in. She whispered, 'What about her mobile?'

Precious shook her head. 'Stolen,' she mouthed.

'Did she leave her laptop at home, Frank? Bags and things?' She closed her eyes and tilted back her head while she waited for him to look.

'He's still in bed,' she said.

Karen looked at her watch.

'He's a writer,' Precious explained.

'They're going,' said Karen, giving a little clap. 'They're going into Barry's office!'

Barry's face appeared over the screen. His forehead gleamed in the strip lighting.

'Well?'

'We can't find Bea,' Karen told him, sliding on to her chair and beginning to type.

He clenched his jaw and strained his neck up, away from the punishing grip of his collar. This was the problem. This was precisely the problem. Hang on to substandard staff who have been in the job too long and they always let you down. Beatrice Kemp should have been put out to grass years ago. His eyes wandered absent-mindedly over Karen's body. He glanced over to his office, where the inspectors had retired and shut the door.

'Has she phoned in sick?'

'No, just nothing. There's been no word from her at all.'

Precious put her hand up to quieten them. Frank was back on the line.

She listened and then said, 'Of course it's strange. She's left for work with her laptop and folders and she hasn't arrived in the office.' She looked pointedly at Barry Charles. 'Bea is never absent and she's never late . . . Yes, why don't you do that. And then call us back.'

Precious put the phone down and said, 'Something's not right.' She told them what Frank had told her. That Bea was stressed about work last night, said she had a lot to do, and he thought he ought to give her some space.

Barry looked at his watch. Karen looked like she might cry.

'And he didn't take her a cup of tea this morning even though he knew it was the inspection.'

'So what's the plan?' asked Barry.

'He's going to retrace her route to work and ring her mother and her sister. I think we should call the police.'

Barry nodded. The woman might well have fallen under a bus or jumped in the river or something. What with the Investors in People review coming up next month, it was best to do everything by the book.

'The police?' said Karen and hurried to the toilets.

FRANK PUT the phone down and scratched his head. He hummed a few bars of Beethoven's Fugue in B Flat Major but found it was near impossible to imitate the demented flight of the violins at the start of that piece. From the kitchen window he scanned Bea's small garden, its curve of patchy lawn, its unhappy shrubs and border plants. He saw that she had raked the first fall of leaves into a pile near the patio and that some potted flowers were lined up ready for planting. They had argued about that patio. He thought there was no sense in having one, seeing as the garden faced north-east, but she insisted and got some friend of Wanda's to lay it for next to nothing. A spade stood up out of the soil where she'd been digging at the weekend.

He wandered out into the hall and looked up the staircase. The house felt unpleasantly still. Had she seemed herself when he last saw her? Well that did rather presume a notion of *character* that he didn't subscribe to, especially where women were concerned and most particularly where Bea was concerned, for Bea was nothing if not inconsistent. How had she seemed last night? He could hardly tell Precious about the evening before. They had barely spoken until much later, when he was ready for bed. He went into the kitchen to find her packing away her laptop and he said something like 'All right?' He was trying to be nice, trying to offer an apology of sorts. He didn't see her face and she didn't answer at first, but then she gave a funny little laugh and said, 'Not dead yet.'

He thought of the bedroom door shut at the top of the stairs. Fear coiled up inside him. He dug his fingers hard into the ache in his back and climbed the stairs, a sick excitement in his brain. He opened the bedroom door and looked in. The bed was neatly made, as always, the old patchwork quilt sewn by Bea as a teenager a jangle of tiny colours and angles like something broken and glued back together. There in the alcove was her egg cup collection, over fifty of them arranged on three shelves – china, metal, Bakelite, plastic, porcelain, glass. They stood huddled together: curvaceous, expectant, empty. Frank felt the bedroom was no place for egg cups. Along the floor and on two chairs were bags of clothes, shoe boxes, her hairdryer, the television, a basket of ironing, a tower of videos and DVDs, books and more bags of God knows what.

By her bed lay the books she'd been reading. 'Has Bea read the script you're writing?' Adrian asked him the other day. Frank shook his head. 'Bea is not a reader,' he said, by which he meant that Bea was a woman reader. She read women. He bent to examine the titles, turning them towards him as he did so. P.D James, Stephen King, Marion Keyes, a biography of Holbein, and on the top, her spare reading glasses folded on its cover, Dickens's *Bleak House*. The book was distended and swollen as if it had been in the bath. He picked it up and opened it where a card was tucked inside the pages towards the end. It was a photograph of a man with thick curling hair and a tanned face. The face was out of focus as if he were moving his head forward when the camera caught him. In the foreground, the back of a woman's bronzed shoulders, short, pale curls shining in the light of the flash. The man's eyes were laughing and his mouth was pursed, kissing the air.

A pulse started up at the corner of Frank's eye and the pain in his lower back made him lower himself carefully on to the edge of the bed. The photograph was of them, taken with the Polaroid by the pianist on the *Oriana*. He looked down at the open page of *Bleak House*, surprised that Bea had apparently persevered with such a novel. It was years since he had read any Dickens and he remembered it as dense and deadly dull. He read the lines at the top of the page, a letter from Lady Dedlock: 'I have done all I could do to be lost . . .' That was the thing about Dickens – always resorting to letters, which was rather a lazy narrative device in Frank's opinion. 'I have nothing about me by which I can be recognised . . .' And here again, very typically, was plot, plot, plot, as if lives really were lived with such–

He peered at the page. The words wobbled and seemed terribly small. He reached for Bea's glasses and put them on. Something was exploding quietly inside his chest, small detonations occurred in his throat and shoulders and it was hard to see. He could not remember the last time he had wept.

Missing

FRANK OPENED the front door on to a heavy grey day and smelt the river. Oyster Row led down to the edge of Stourbridge Common, a stretch of rough pasture that ran with the river, north-east, away from the city and towards the fens: Fen Ditton, Fleem Dyke, Devil's Ditch. There were no tourists or colleges in this direction; no pinnacles or minarets, no King's, Christ's, Trinity or Jesus; instead there were the remnants of an industrial age – the towering chimney of the old pumping station and the ironwork bridge that carried the railway line over the river.

He stopped at the end of the road and looked the other way, westwards, the way that Bea's walk to work would have taken her, beneath the flyover, over Midsummer Common and on up into the city. A boy rode at him on a bike, cycling in lazy swerving loops, both hands in his pockets. Frank dithered in the middle of the road, stepped first one way, then the other so that they nearly collided. The boy swore and shouted, 'What you think you doing, you wanker?' and Frank thought, I am retracing her steps, a thought so preposterous that he nearly shouted it out loud after the boy. Really, wasn't this a job for the police? He hadn't had the courage to say that to Bea's work colleague. There was something in her voice that gave him no option. She didn't sound like the kind of woman you could say no to. So, while he didn't really have the time himself to go wandering about Cambridge, he would have to go through the motions for appearance's sake. After all, it wasn't beyond the bounds of possibility that the police were watching him. The end of *Lupa* would have to wait for the time being, despite the fact that he had planned on getting a good morning's writing done and then sending off a few emails. There was his agent, Lancashire Arts . . . Frank stopped. He had reached the under-pass beneath the flyover and he suddenly thought he should look for Bea's car. Sometimes she drove to work if she was late and had a lot to carry. He looked around him at the parked cars, then behind him the way he had come. Damn it. If he was going to follow the car lead he would have to go back to the house and start again. He set off in the direction he had come, feeling really rather irritated with Bea, the police and the woman from her office. Quite how he had got himself into this situation he didn't know. He had spent a lot of his time recently going backwards and forwards looking for her. Now that was an idea, he thought as his feet hit the path. It could be the solution he was looking for with *Lupa*. He would start the narrative again in the middle, after the wolf came out of the forest. We see Marsha's face in the window, we see Peter's shadow by the tree, we see . . . not the attack but cut to black then close-up of Marsha's laughing face when she's three years old and playing near the wood! Brilliant. Frank quickened his pace and found himself outside the house. Damn it, it was so hard to keep the creative mind focused on the here and now, and here was Bea's car so that theory was out the window and now he had better get going again.

Back he went, hands dug deep into his coat pockets, down towards the river and off towards Midsummer Common. He kept his eyes on the ground for clues and occasionally he stopped and surveyed the common, the benches and the river, the trees and rough patches of bramble and weed. He noted the names of shuttered and silent houseboats: *Chubasco*, *Awol*, *Kestrel*. A couple of ducks and a swan hung about for bread and a solitary rower glided downstream, her oar strokes a whisper like the rhythm of a sleeper's breath.

'Robbers Beware. Police Operate in this Area.' Frank paused at the sign on the tree. He tried to imagine the scenario: Bea walking this path, early this morning, laptop and bags weighing her down. He thought of her inert body on the gravel of Katharine's drive last Christmas. He'd tried to get her to her feet but she was a dead weight so he left her there to sleep it off. He winced and looked around him. Unfortunate that Richard and Katharine had arrived home from the Seychelles very early the next morning and found her prostrate by the sundial. 'I couldn't lift her off the ground,' he'd told them when they gave him the third degree. 'You mean to say you left her outside? All *night*?' Katharine was tossing that long face of hers, all chestnut and tanned, whinnying and baring those higgledy-piggledy teeth, while Richard in his crumpled linen suit stood watching as though hanging in the air, a heavy sadness around him. It didn't look good, Frank understood that, and he was sorry that Adrian and Laura had seen their auntie in a heap in the dark. 'What the hell kind of a husband are you, Frank?' Katharine had jabbed her finger at him. Jab, jab. And then she'd given him a push on the chest with the flat of her hand, which she shouldn't have done. No, she shouldn't have done that. Violence bulleted up through him then, obliterating fear, hangover and shame. Richard had led her away; had told the children to go upstairs and check whether Bea needed anything.

He walked on carefully towards the bridge, placing the whole length of each foot upon the ground, not just the balls of his feet but putting his heel down too with every step, for the last thing that Katharine had spat at him the night of the senseless-Bea-in-a-heap-by-the-sundial was, '*Autistic.*

You're *autistic*, Frank. You *bounce* on the *balls* of your *feet*. It's a *known* indicator of *autism!*'

He headed north, toe, instep, heel, *toe* . . . No, that's wrong. He skipped a step and then continued. *Heel*, instep, toe, heel, instep, toe, over Magdalene Bridge, up the street and towards the council offices on Castle Hill.

'I'm looking for Beatrice Pamplin,' he told the receptionist at Shire Hall. 'She works here.'

The woman looked down her list and shook her head. 'I don't have a Pamplin here. Do you know the department?'

Frank thought for a moment. 'Admin?'

She paused and looked down at her list. 'Well it's all admin really.'

'Accounts?' His mind tried to retrieve the details of Bea's work. Something to do with deeds and figures. 'Finance?'

The receptionist waited. He could see she wasn't going to let him through without a name, and a department.

'I had a call from her colleague to say she hadn't turned up for work.'

'I need a name, I'm afraid.'

'Don't worry,' said Frank, turning away. He'd had enough of this. First Bea doesn't turn up for work. Then it turns out Bea doesn't actually go to work at all. What in God's name was going on? 'I'll go to a phone box and dial directory enquiries. It'll probably be easier.'

'Just a moment, sir.' The receptionist called him back. 'I have a Beatrice Kemp in Land Registry, Covenants and Deeds,' she said. 'Would that be her?'

'That's her,' he said, tugging at his cuffs and struggling with the splinter that was Patrick that he could not remove, had never managed to be rid of. Yesterday's Scotch was beginning to take its toll. It hurt that Bea used her maiden name at work, but of course she did. It was where *he* worked.

'Out the door and round the corner.' The woman pointed with her pen. 'Park House.'

Behind the handsome, carefully restored building Frank found a warren of walkways running between featureless blocks thrown up too close for light or views. Kemp? Pamplin? Who on earth did Bea think she was? She was Pamplin for the mortgage and the insurance. Mr and Mrs Frank Pamplin. He nodded angrily to himself then looked up at the grey concrete in front of him that looked a bloody mess, like it had been slapped together by a bored child. He had only a dim image of Bea at work; it was a rear view, in a pencil skirt and heels, carrying sheaves of documents down the polished parquet of the building he had just left. But now he suspected this might have been an error. He looked about him and had the queasy sensation of being on the edge of some vast area of her life he knew nothing about. What on earth did she do here all day? A noise behind him made him jump. The door to Park House opened violently and ejected a thin woman in her twenties. She had stockinged feet and carried a pair of stilettos. She was blowing her nose noisily into a man-sized tissue.

'Oh!' she said when she saw Frank.

'Excuse me,' said Frank. 'I'm looking for Bea.'

The woman took a step backwards. The unlit cigarette she was holding broke in her fingers and fell to the ground. She fumbled for another one, then shook her head and her face crumpled. 'Jesus Christ,' she said. 'I'm Karen. Are you . . . ?' She searched her bag for a lighter. 'Are you . . . ?' She stopped herself, fearful of making a mistake.

Frank said, 'I'm her husband,' and felt, for the first time that day, in control. The girl looked as though she was from another time. She had the serious, ailing face of a nineteenth-century novelist.

She grasped his arm. 'Thank God.' She scrabbled some more in her bag and pulled out the lighter. She took a quick look back at the building and pursed the cigarette between her lips, cupping her hand round it and bending her face as if to kiss it. 'We can't find her.' She took a deep inhalation and exhaled, blowing the smoke away from Frank and flapping guiltily with her hand. 'Sorry, sorry,' she said.

'I've retraced her steps.'

Karen's eyes widened. She looked at the burning end of her cigarette. 'Oh my God.'

'I told the person in her office I would.'

Karen nodded feverishly. 'Yes. Precious. Yes.' She tapped excitedly at her chest and nodded. 'I was there. I work with Bea.' She opened the cigarette packet and took another one out before remembering the one in her fingers was still lit.

Frank looked around him. He thought perhaps he should go in and try and see this Precious woman. He moved towards the door. Karen put a hand out to stop him.

'I wouldn't if I were you. It's hell in there.'

Bad

'Y ou let her walk?' Richard took a look at his wife. Her face was turned away from his as she bent over papers and lists.

'Yes. She wanted to. Now where did I put that rentals list?'

The children had left for school and they should both be at work but Katharine had a plan to execute and he knew better than to get in the way of that.

'Even so, darling. It's quite a long way and some nasty things have happened on that path. Remember the girl who was dragged into the—'

'Richard, please! My sister is a grown woman. I cannot continue to spend my life watching over her. Here.' She passed him a brochure. 'I think this place looks fabulous. Beautiful garden.'

Richard had been quite pleased at the suggestion they meet back at the house for coffee after the school run. He had envisaged a leisurely breakfast, some calls to work and a jolly time choosing a place to rent in London. If he were absolutely honest, work was a little quiet these days and on occasions he found himself standing in the vast atrium of his office and feeling like the captain on the bridge of a ghost ship. He missed the buzz and hustle of the coalface of finance, but his current post did at least leave him more time for family.

Katharine poured more coffee and took another slice of toast. The woman had quite extraordinary drive, a bit like his mother. And he was very proud of her work. At least she did something useful, he always told her. Saving babies all day long, now that was a real contribution, whereas he, well, some days he was hard pressed to say what he did all day.

'I think we call this one today, now, put the deposit down and drive up and camp there this weekend. Adrian will just adore that.' Katharine put half a slice of toast and marmalade inside her mouth and gulped down her coffee. Richard looked at the brochure and nodded.

'It looks marvellous.' He glanced at the front. 'Good lord, is that really the price? Per month?'

Katharine took it away from him. 'It's the going rate. But it'll only be for three months or so. Oh God.' She reached for her list again. 'Uniforms! By Monday.'

He had been careful not to crow over the schools issue but he was glad she had come round to his way of thinking at last. It was reassuring that Adrian would have the same sort of education as he had, without the boarding of course; Katharine would never agree to that. *In pectore robur* had been his school motto, 'With a heart of oak', and oddly enough, it was the way he had led his life. His mind ambled off to a forthcoming meeting with shareholders. Claudia, the bottles of Perrier, air-conditioning, and the soothing upward gradient of profit and sales. It was strange that he'd had no calls.

'And anyway,' continued Katharine, 'she'd got the day wrong.' She pushed her chair back. 'I'm going to get Wanda in for the day tomorrow. If Bea doesn't mind.' She glanced at her husband. A quiver of irritability ran through her. 'I thought I might set her to work on the cellar. And the children's rooms. She knows what she's doing and she's incredibly cheap.'

'Well, ask Bea first.'

'I called her but her phone is off.'

There was a pause. Richard returned to the here and now. 'Are you sure she wasn't upset yesterday?'

Katharine peered at the details on the brochure. 'Oh, you know Bea . . .'

'I imagine it's a shock for her. The children will miss her.'

'She didn't say much.' She got up and put more bread in the toaster, then turned on him. 'Richard, don't look at me like that. I've done what I can for Bea, I really have.' She marched over to the fridge and put her head inside. 'I rescued her from that ghastly betting shop in Hastings, I found her the job at Shire Hall, helped her buy the house, did what I could to stop her wasting her time on that man Patrick, and practically *gave* her my children in the absence of any of her own.' She brought two jars of jam to the table. 'I mean, just what else am I expected to do?'

The toast popped up and Katharine sat down. Richard noticed the vein in her temple start up a warning throb. He put his hand on her arm and rubbed it.

'I was simply suggesting—'

'Well don't,' she snapped. 'It's not simple.'

Richard surrendered to her unreasonableness. This was marriage, he told himself with a long breath in. There were ups and there were downs and once there were children, well that was an end to it. He opened the paper, lifted himself from the scene and sent his mind off to the office again. Claudia would be running the show as usual, answering his emails, organising his diary and fielding calls. They would take a trip to the Seychelles again at Christmas and stay at the house on the beach. Katharine would relax there, the children would grow happy and brown and they would return to start their new life in London. He considered a lengthy visit to the lavatory with the newspaper.

Katharine felt better for her outburst and leant across to kiss Richard's hand. He was extraordinary. She could throw anything at him and he just went on being there. That was what was so frightening. She was completely in control. Everything she decided on happened. Even Richard happened because she made him. He was Plan B. Plan A was escape from Hastings and become a success, and at twenty-nine when she found she had achieved that, she looked about her and noticed she had failed to achieve a husband. Time was short and she needed to act fast. When she came across Richard in the hospital, numb with grief and looking for the chaplain's room, she showed him the way. Her friend Jane urged her on. 'Snaffle him fast,' she advised. 'Widowers are *perfect*. But they only last a few weeks.'

It wasn't very difficult. She looked after him and amused him with her breathless grip on life. She knew that her work impressed him and that her body comforted him. Within a year they were married and Laura was on the way and she knew she had a good man. But there was a part of her, a narrow, bad part that crouched below her ribs, that wanted to push him to his limits, wanted to see what would happen if she made herself so hateful that one day he broke her, walked out and never came back. Part of her wondered at the terrible fear and destruction that this would bring, longed to feel that pain, the Tuesday pain when Daddy never came home, never came and never came, the slow, empty terror of it that was more real than anything she had felt before or since.

She screwed the lid tightly back on the jam jar. A terrifying part of her needed a sacrifice to make her whole again.

Sign

THE VAN driver was shouting. He was strutting and jabbing, effing and blinding at Nesrine, who stood in the middle of Oyster Row, a fistful of bindweed drooping from one hand. The courier held the parcel up and shook it at her like a birthday gift.

'All I'm asking you is to just sign for it and keep it for them!'

Nesrine wiped her hands on her apron and looked unhappy. Her front door was open and the hosepipe lay on the crazy paving, water running down the path and into the gutter. Frank quickened his pace and reached the gate, hopeful suddenly.

'Is it for me?' Lancashire Arts had promised to send him some books.

The van driver swung round. 'Number seventeen. That you?'

Thank God, thought Frank. He could do with a parcel. He badly needed an arrival, an entrance, a prop. He said, 'That's me. I'll sign for it.'

'She don't understand a word I'm saying,' said the courier, jerking his head in Nesrine's direction. 'Sign here.' Frank squiggled blindly on the tiny screen. He held his hand out for the parcel. 'Print as well.' He did as he was told. 'That'll be two pounds fifty.'

'I beg your pardon?'

'Excess postage.'

Frank looked at the package. It was wrapped in battered brown paper that looked like it had been used many times before. Evidently it had been backwards and forwards for some time. Several different-coloured stamps were stuck unevenly across the top and someone had written, 'Not known at this address.' Bea's name was scrawled in blue pencil. The postcode was wrong. Frank stuffed the packet irritably into his coat pocket and paid the courier.

The van roared off and Nesrine shook her head apologetically.

Frank tried to smile. He had never acknowledged the woman before, much less spoken to her.

'Have you seen my wife? Bea?'

Nesrine shook her head and said, 'Yes. Oh yes. Your wife is very kind lady.' She dropped the weeds and stepped towards Frank, patting her cheeks with her palms, mouth wobbling. 'When my husband die, I didn't know what to do.'

Frank took a step away. He didn't want to get involved in any kind of rerun of the grieving process.

'Every day she speak to me and one day she give me the roses.' Nesrine turned to look at the bush by her front door. 'Wait there,' she told Frank. Nesrine went into her front garden and bent down behind the dustbin. She re-emerged holding a potted lily and came back across the road.

'This is for her. I've grown it myself.' She held it out to him and turned back to wave a hand in the direction of her garden. 'She give me the roses, see? They're beautiful.'

Frank took the lily and let himself into the house. He dialled Katharine's number. A woman answered immediately, efficient and brusque.

'Dr Cooper's phone.' Frank hesitated. Cooper? So Katharine took Richard's name. He asked if Katharine was there, pointlessly, he realised, because presumably if she were, she would have answered herself. Or perhaps not, Frank thought, realising he had little idea how things worked in Katharine's world of work. He was told, rather rudely in his opinion, that Katharine was in a meeting. The woman sounded rushed and keen to get back to whatever it was he had interrupted – Frank imagined parents sitting before her, being given bad news about their premature baby.

She said, 'Who's calling?'

'This is her brother-in-law. Frank Pamplin.'

'What's it concerning?'

Frank had had enough of this. 'It's all right. I'll try her mobile.'

He put the phone down and sat at the kitchen table. The phone rang at once and hope soared inside him then fell and died as he heard Margaret's voice on the other end. Bea's mother.

'Is she there?'

Before Frank could answer, a shadow from the kitchen window moved across the table and he swung round to see a short, heavyset man crossing the patio. He wore yellow gloves and carried a rope in one hand. Some sort of metal cage swung from the other.

'Who the hell is that?'

'It's me,' said Margaret.

'There's a strange man in my garden.'

'Is that Frank?'

'Bea's not here . . .'

'It's not her I want to speak to.'

'Now listen, Margaret—'

'No, you listen to me. I don't want a party.'

Frank watched the man lift the cage. Claws, teeth and grey fur sent it jerking through the air with what Frank felt to be an obscene energy. He grimaced.

'It's the patio man.'

'No, Uncle Derek told me, so I know she's planning one.'

'Hey!' Frank banged on the window.

'Pardon?' said Margaret.

Frank watched as Urban tied the rope to the top of the cage. He removed the lid from the water butt, raised the trap close to his face and said something to the squirrel.

'Hey!'

'Oh, she won't listen to me. That's why I'm calling you.'

'Margaret, something's happened.'

'And I'd want to get my hair done, but Leslie is in Lanzarote until the Monday, so that's no good.'

Urban lowered the cage into the water, paying out the rope. Then he replaced the lid.

'I think I've lost Bea.'

Urban lit a cigarette, then winked at Frank.

'Frank?' said Margaret.

Frank watched him smoke and stare wistfully up at the sky.

'Well what do you mean, lost Bea?'

A protracted ring on the doorbell made Frank jump. 'Margaret, I have to go. Could you call Katharine on her mobile and tell her we don't know where Bea is? And keep an eye out for her yourself. She may have taken the train down to see you. She may have . . .' Frank's voice trailed off.

MARGARET PUT the phone down and looked out over the great expanse of sea. Bea coming here? To Hastings? Whatever was she coming to Hastings for? On a Wednesday, of all days?

Because

MARGARET WATCHED the deserted beach through the window. The sky was stacked with clouds riding west and the surface of the sea danced and spangled in the October sun. Seagulls floated in the air and a tanker made its way steadily across the horizon. Margaret had watched from this window for fifty years. It pleased her that nothing very much was happening today. Events had a nasty habit of changing everything; she always lowered the blind if there was a storm.

From the cupboard over the sink she took two bottles and poured herself a Dubonnet and lemonade. She added an ice cube, carefully refilled the ice tray and took her drink into the lounge. Beneath the window, Eamon's stereo stood in its smart teak casing. Its meshed speakers were where Bea used to press her face and see white horses cantering in a ring. Stockinged feet deep in the carpet, Margaret looked steadily at the round mouths of the laquered mesh and tutted. It annoyed her that she could never see these speakers without thinking of Bea's nonsense. She knelt in front of the stereo and ran her fingers across Eamon's record collection. All their favourites were there: Frank Sinatra, Elvis Presley, Perry Como.

She slid the Perry Como album out and let the vinyl slip from its sleeve. Opening the lid of the record player, she set the turntable going with a click and held the record between spanned hands as she lowered it on to the spindle. She loved these preliminaries, the small sounds and sensations, like the roll of coins from Eamon's trouser pockets on to the lino of the bedroom floor.

She took a mouthful of Dubonnet, held the bitter plum taste in her mouth and watched the soothing undulation of the turntable. She closed her eyes at the scratch and hiss of the needle in the liquorice groove, the quiet rip of fabric, the heat of Eamon's mouth in her hair as they danced. The label at the centre lost its letters in a dissolve of magenta like the giddy spin of her in satin and net, Eamon's hand at the base of her spine. For the good times.

His fossil collection was on the windowsill next to a photograph of him below the cliffs. She hadn't walked there in years. That was where he searched for the remains of *Lepidotes* and *Iguanodon*, among those boulders and stones. He taught her all the names, showed her the drawings of three-toed footprints as big as bicycle wheels in a rock found along the eastern beach. Eamon loved a storm. After the winter storms, he and the girls would be there with hammers and chisels searching for their very own dinosaur footprint. To be truthful, Margaret doubted that Hastings had been a delta swamp inhabited by giant lizards 140 million years ago. It just didn't seem very likely. She preferred it as it was, the town laid out below their front door just as a town should be, with its mossed slates, its pretty blue and pink masonry. She was never that keen on the beach, always preferred the clifftop walks where they did their courting – Ecclesbourne Glen, Covehurst Wood, Fairlight, Firehills. Such romantic names.

She would worry sometimes that there would be a cliff fall or that he would be cut off by the tide because that happened to people every year. There were stories of children being swept out to sea, fully grown men dropping to their deaths from the unfenced path near Warren Glen, dogs chasing seagulls off the cliffs and tumbling to the boulders below. But Eamon never came to any harm on the beach, and he never got the chance to find anything more than those few muddled remains of teeth and shell because the bread van took the corner too fast when he was coming the other way on his bicycle that Tuesday afternoon.

Perry Como had stopped singing and the record player had returned the arm to its cradle in a way that Margaret found gentle and considerate. She picked the arm up again, set the turntable going and dropped the needle down heavily so that it popped and crackled. 'I'm afraid I have some bad news,' the policeman said with his helmet under one arm. The girls were already in bed and for a moment she thought it strange that he should choose her door to knock on to tell his bad news to. 'It's your husband,' he said. But Eamon had only popped out to collect the balsawood he'd left at work. He was going to finish making a piece of furniture for Bea's doll's house. It was a sideboard with tiny drawers you could open and close. The policeman was only young and he had a red rash climbing up his neck. 'I'm afraid I need you to come and identify the body,' he said.

She put on her mackintosh, pulled her headscarf from the pocket, tied it over her hair, put the key under the mat, just in case he came back while she was gone, and closed the door behind her. She followed the policeman down Tamarisk Steps and over to the High Street where his Panda was parked outside the Washeteria.

When they got there, she was led downstairs and along a custard-coloured corridor, and she thought Eamon wouldn't have liked it here. He hated hospitals, doctors, dentists, anything like that. It was the smell as much as anything, he said. The room they had put him in had no windows. It was chilly and smelt of his butterfly collection. The policeman said something she didn't catch and left her alone in there.

In front of her, a high metal bed was covered with a white sheet. She felt very nervous, like a bride.

She only knew what was expected of her because of what she had seen at the pictures on Saturday evenings at the De Luxe where they had first kissed. The sheet at the top of the bed was crumpled and peaked in a strange way that frightened her. There were rusty yellow smears on it. The silence was terrible.

She remembered she had left the pie in the oven and she knew it would begin to burn if she wasn't back soon, so she looked down the other end where one foot was uncovered and pointing upwards at the ceiling. A brown label was tied to his big toe, she couldn't think why.

She felt shy lifting the sheet so she could see both feet properly, but when she did, she knew that they were his because, well, she would know those feet anywhere.

The policeman knocked and put his head round the door. He gave her a sad, questioning look and she nodded because her jaw and tongue and lips were slow and heavy as if she were trying to talk in a dream.

'This way,' he said, very polite, very kind.

He took her back upstairs where they gave her a paper bag marked Personal Effects. When they asked her to sign for it, the pen was stone in her hand and her signature looked like someone else's. Inside the bag his clothes were neatly folded. His bicycle clips were there too and his keys, wallet and a small bundle of balsawood tied with string.

It was October, a week before her birthday, and so it was still light in the early evening. She couldn't understand it. She couldn't understand why the van hadn't seen him at five in the evening when it was practically broad daylight.

For ever such a long time after that she hadn't been able to play his records, but these days she didn't seem to be able to stop, especially 'For the Good Times' because Perry Como sang as if he were in the room, singing just to her.

Six and seven the girls were, and that's what they all were after that, at sixes and sevens, because even telling them had been impossible.

Well, they wouldn't believe it and she didn't believe it herself, because who knows, perhaps somehow or other she had made a mistake with his feet and one day he would walk right back in through that door carrying an ammonite from Kimmeridge and laughing at her for worrying. *Always at sixes and sevens, you are, Margaret*, and then they'd all sit down to his favourite, a chicken pie, Fray Bentos, because she kept one in the cupboard. Even now, always.

Night

I T WAS much later that night when Margaret rang Katharine to tell her that Frank had lost Bea. After the phone call, Katharine walked into the bedroom, where Richard was propped up against one pillow, chin on chest, glasses on the end of his nose. He looked at her over the pages of the report he was reading.

'Something wrong?' he said.

She sat on the bed and eased off her shoes.

'I'm not sure.'

'Mmm?' Richard patted the bed beside him and held out an arm without looking up. Katharine saw their reflection in the open door of the wardrobe. Two successful forty-somethings in a high-ceilinged bedroom with antique furniture and heavy curtains. The bed gave a groan as she stood up and stepped out of her sensible brown skirt.

'Bea's gone off somewhere.'

'Hmm?' said Richard.

She crossed to the wardrobe, took off her cream blouse, folded it over the chair and closed the wardrobe door so that the mirror could not be seen. She did not go so far as taking the running jump of girlhood from the door to the bed to prevent herself being snatched by witches under the bed, but mirrors she knew were not a good idea if one woke in the night.

And besides – she padded back to the en suite and ran her toothbrush under the tap – she was old enough now to know that under the bed was not where the witches were.

Katharine came back into the bedroom brushing her teeth fiercely. She paced the room picking up clothes and straightening things. Richard watched her angular body in the no-nonsense underwear. Sometimes he wondered what it would be like to see Katharine in the kind of clothes Claudia wore, where the cut and the colour spoke of the female form moving beneath. She padded off into the bathroom and he heard her spitting and rinsing into the sink. She stood in the doorway and undid her bra.

'Bea's disappeared,' she said.

It sounded so improbable, spoken out loud like that. She shrugged and turned back to the bathroom, where she finished undressing and stepped into the shower.

The phone call from her mother had been more than usually confusing, she thought as the water streamed down her narrow body. She squeezed her eyes tight and rubbed soap rapidly all over herself. Her mother's words were slurred and slow and asked whether they had found Bea yet. It took a while to get the story straight, for everything had to be repeated, asked again, checked, rewound and waited for. Even now, Katharine couldn't be sure what had actually happened.

She turned the water off and reached for a towel. Katharine never spent long in the shower and she spent even less time getting dried. A childhood habit from the days when their bathroom in Hastings was so cold that she and Bea would pull on rough vests and jumpers, shaking and shivering, before their skin was properly dry. When she emerged from the bathroom she was in blue checked pyjamas and rubbing night cream into her face with speed and vigour. Richard didn't much like the old-lady smell of it but hadn't the heart to tell her.

She straightened the curtains, set the alarm and threw back the duvet. He held his arm out for her again and she allowed herself to be gathered briefly up against his side. She waited for the throat-clearing that always followed and felt his heart against her temple. Richard slept naked except at weekends when the children sometimes came into their room in the mornings.

'Disappeared? Really? Good for her.' He turned a page and marked a paragraph with a highlighter. He had a stack of market reports on the table beside him. They weren't essential reading but he liked to feel he was ahead of the game, and most nights he worked his way down a pile, marking sections in fluorescent pen.

Katharine disengaged his arm from around her and sat up. 'Something doesn't feel right,' she said and got out of bed again. She took her mobile out of her bag and checked it. 'I mean, why didn't Frank ring me himself?'

Richard turned to look at her and took his glasses off. He was calibrating the seriousness of this conversation. Perhaps he needed to give it his full attention.

'Frank's terrified of you, darling. He's probably feeling a bit of a fool. I mean, what exactly happened? Did they have a row?'

'I'm going to ring him now.'

Richard watched as she spoke into the phone. 'Why the hell didn't you call me?' was her opening line. 'I've only just heard,' was the next. 'The police?' made him put his pen down. When she finished the call she shook her head in disbelief.

'Christ knows what she's doing married to that man,' she said. 'Apparently he rang Mum in Hastings this morning and asked her to ring me, which of course she forgot to do until just now.'

'And the police?'

'That was her friend's idea.'

Richard looked at his watch. 'So Bea didn't go to work today and hasn't been seen for about sixteen hours.

Hardly an emergency yet, I'd say. It isn't illegal to take yourself off, after all.'

'No. But all the same, it's not like her. I mean, if she was planning a trip . . . She didn't say anything to me yesterday.' She turned and plumped up her pillows, lay down and then sat up again. 'I told him that if there's no news tomorrow morning I'm going to her office first thing. No point relying on Frank. "Neither use nor ornament," as my mother would say.'

She lay and blinked up at the room. The wardrobe door had swung open again as it always did and Richard's family wealth was reflected back at her in mahogany and oak. She sat up and wrote a note to herself to get it all valued – the wardrobe, the tallboy, the bureau, everything. In their new house they would have different furniture. She'd talk to Richard about it in the morning. He said himself there was too much of it. She put her earplugs in, adjusted the eye mask round her head and lay back down. Then she sat up and kissed him blindly on the cheek. 'Night night.'

Richard put his glasses back on. 'Sleep well, darling.'

IN THE silent stillness of night, Katharine sat bolt upright in bed. She pushed with frantic movements at the darkness. Her eye mask had dropped down to her neck and she fixed her stare on the cornice above the bathroom.

'*Oh, no . . . Oh, look!*' Her movements were slow and deliberate, like a mime of terror, her voice small and pitiful like a child's.

She twisted her head back and forth at the blackness high above their bed. She cowered against the wall, raised one arm in a sweeping arc before her face and ducked her head away. '*No . . . Oh, no . . .*'

Richard stirred, reached one arm to the space where she had been, found nothing and tried to speak before sinking back down into deep and thoughtless sleep.

So

THE NEXT morning Katharine woke early, thought instantly of Bea and got out of bed. She heard Richard in the shower and wondered how long he had been awake. Downstairs, when she checked her emails and phone, she found no messages or missed calls. She hurried upstairs to find Richard standing naked in the room with his socks on and rubbing his hair with a towel.

'Good morning.'

'I'm phoning Frank,' she said, dialling his number.

'What, now? It's six thirty in the morning.' He yawned. 'I hardly slept a wink. Dreadful night's sleep.'

Frank answered immediately, his voice hesitant and careful. Katharine told him she was going to contact the police and file a missing person report. Someone had to get a grip on the situation, and as usual, it was going to be her. Frank explained that all that had been done. He added that the police had come to see him yesterday.

'You didn't tell me that.'

'Nothing to tell. All very routine. Name, address, age, et cetera. It would seem this happens quite a lot. They didn't seem unduly concerned. But the Missing Persons Unit is coming round later today.'

'Well I will go and see them this morning.'

Frank said nothing. He was infuriating. He was Bea's husband, for God's sake. He must know what was going on.

'Are you still there?' she asked.

There was a pause and then he said, 'Yes.'

'Look, are you sure there's nothing you can think of that might have made her go off like this?'

Frank sighed. 'Last time I saw her she was fed up about work. She said it didn't matter how much she prepared for the inspection, it wouldn't be enough.'

'But apart from work? Did you have an argument or something?'

'Well, she was a bit upset about your move being brought forward . . .'

Katharine turned to see that Adrian and Laura had slid silently into the room. She told Frank she would ring him back and hurried them downstairs. It was a school day today and she needed them out of the way if she was going to have a hope in hell of getting everything done.

Downstairs she made toast and coffee and began writing lists.

'What's happened?' said Adrian.

'We can't find Bea.' She kept her voice level and brought cereal boxes to the table.

Adrian opened his eyes wide so that his hair moved. He sat down and poured sugar puffs into a bowl. Katharine wanted to press her face into his hair but she didn't. She didn't touch either of her children now. Laura appeared in her school blouse and tights. She dipped a breadstick into the Nutella jar and held it between her fingers like a cigar, sucking the end.

'Laura, where's your skirt?'

'I left it at Bea's.'

Adrian said, 'Bea's disappeared.'

Laura stopped eating and sat completely still.

Katharine moved backwards and forwards between the dining-room table and the kitchen. Keep moving, she told herself. Keep things on an even keel.

'I expect she's got the dates wrong and gone on a course, lost her mobile or something. You know what Bea's like.' Katharine searched through the pile of letters by the phone. She checked the answering machine again for messages.

Richard came in doing up his tie. He poured coffee and touched Katharine's shoulder as he handed her a cup. Adrian chewed and watched them as they began talking in whispers at the other end of the kitchen. That was the trouble with grown-ups. They thought that children knew nothing when the reality was entirely the opposite. Children saw everything and knew far more than parents could ever imagine. Parents, on the other hand, knew less the older they got. They had no idea what went on in their children's world, or anyone else's as far as he could tell.

Katharine began talking, as if reading a part in a play.

'You take the children to school, darling, if you don't mind. I want to talk to Bea's colleague . . . Paula, Priscilla . . .'

'Precious,' said Laura.

'Come on then, you two,' said Richard. 'I'll have to drop you early, I need to get a move on.'

Katharine was gulping the last of her coffee and studying the calendar.

'Laura!' she cried suddenly. Laura cringed and flipped the top of her school bag shut, moving it closer to her chair with her foot.

'What?' Her mouth was smeared with chocolate and a fleeting vision of her as a toddler in her high chair passed before Katharine's eyes.

'You've got an orthodontist's appointment at ten. Oh for heaven's sake!'

Laura ran her tongue over her teeth and thought of Chanel's mouth, which was filled with metal tracks and screws. Chanel was always at the orthodontist's. She hadn't been to Double Science for months. Laura couldn't wait to get tracks herself.

'We'll reschedule it,' said Richard.

'No. It's taken forever to get to this point. Umpteen visits for measurements, for impressions, for fittings, for God knows what. We can't start all over again in London. He's going to wire her up today.'

Adrian inserted a quarter of orange peel in front of his teeth and gave Laura a smile. Laura had been practising cutting people with her eyes and she dropped a lidded flicker at her brother now. The orange peel popped out, leaving his lips baggy and pale. Laura gave him the finger from behind the milk carton.

'Well I've cancelled everything anyway. I'll just have to take her with me. Come on, Laura, we're going.'

'You've already cancelled everything?'

Funny how parents had to say everything twice. Adrian drank the remains of his breakfast from the bowl.

'Yes. Outpatients, training, supervision and a meeting with the Chief Executive. Everything. I know I've taken on too much but it's so difficult to say no, and we're *so* overstretched in Paediatrics . . .'

Richard left the room to get ready. Adrian followed him.

'Greedy,' said Laura quietly, swinging one foot.

Katharine glanced in the mirror. She combed her short brown hair with sharp, impatient strokes.

'Mmm?'

'You're greedy,' Laura said to her.

'Who?' she said, looking at Laura's reflection in the mirror. Why oh why did the child insist on doing that to her hair? Where on earth was the logic in going to the hairdresser and asking for black highlights when she had perfectly nice fair hair?

'You,' said Laura.

The comb caught the corner of her eye. She blinked and pressed the tear duct with a tissue. What did this girl know? She opened her eyes again. Everything, the look assured her. Everything.

'And in what way am I greedy?' Voice hard and bright, Katharine turned, one hand holding the comb.

'All those jobs you've got. Why not leave a few for some-body else?'

Something, some feeling she could not name, fluttered at the base of Katharine's throat. 'It's not a matter of greed—'

'How many jobs you got, then?'

Where was the love? That was what she wanted to know. Where was the love and the gratitude and the respect? Really, she had taken her eye off the ball as far as Laura was concerned. They both had. Sending her to that school had been the very worst thing they could have done. Thankfully they had seen the error of their ways before it was too late. There had been one hell of a row when they broke it to them the other night, but children were children, they adjusted very quickly.

Katharine banged her cup down harder than she intended. She sighed. No doubt Laura was struggling with all sorts of feelings about Bea. Lord knows, they all were. She tried another tack.

'Look, don't worry about Bea . . .' She allowed a pause for Laura to fill. Laura stared at her and put an entire half slice of toast and Nutella into her mouth. Katharine wanted to say that perhaps Laura had had enough breakfast now but she stopped herself. It was such a tightrope, girls and food.

'I have a feeling that she's taken herself off for a little holiday.'

Laura drank milk and watched her mother.

Katharine took her cup to the sink. 'I can't remember the last time Bea and Frank went on holiday. They went to Spain, was it, for their honeymoon years ago and she and Granny flew to Mallorca for a weekend last year for Granny's birthday, which didn't sound like much of a holiday . . .'

There was that feeling in her throat again. 'We'll just pop into her office and chat to her colleagues before your appoint-ment, and then . . .'

She turned round. Laura had left the room.

Memo

'PRECIOUS MTANDWA is expecting you. Top floor.'

The receptionist handed Katharine a visitor's badge and pointed to the lift, where Laura was trying to be invisible. On the way up Katharine concentrated on trying to pin the badge to her lapel but her hands were trembling. Laura took the badge and did it for her.

'Show-off,' she said.

'What?'

Laura nodded at the badge. '*Dr* Katharine Cooper.'

When the doors opened, Precious was waiting for them.

'Look at you,' she said, taking Laura's face in both her hands. She turned to Katharine and held out a hand. 'I'm Precious. And you're Katharine. Oh, yes, I see the resemblance,' and she laughed so that Katharine put one hand up and checked her hair.

They followed her into the main office, a windowless maze of desks and partitions where men and women sat transfixed at their screens. At a small area in the corner of the room Precious stopped and patted a desk.

'Here we are,' she said. 'I was just going through her emails.'

Katharine stared at Bea's empty corner. There was nothing personal on the desk and the bare pinboard facing her chair had dark empty shapes on it where photos had recently been removed. It was unsettling to be seeing a part of Bea's life that she knew nothing about. Her eyes were drawn to the clutter under the desk. Ledgers, boxes, files, carrier bags and a pair of shoes were pushed together in a pile. By contrast, Precious's desk was calm and ordered.

'Where's all her photos of us?' said Laura, pointing at the board.

'Oh, we had strict instructions to remove all personal items for yesterday's visit from on high.' Laura made a face and Precious smiled and said, 'That's what I thought. Oh, I nearly forgot.'

She pulled something out of her bag and put them in Laura's hands. Laura opened the tissue paper and found two egg cups in cobalt blue with *Adrian* and *Laura* written in white across their sides. 'I found these on holiday and kept forgetting to bring them in. Why don't you take them home and keep them safe for her.'

Laura cradled the cups in her hands. She looked at Precious and didn't speak.

Katharine noticed that Bea had 278 unread emails in her inbox. 'My God,' she said. 'Is this normal?'

She thought of her own inbox, sifted and checked by her secretary, of her office, clean and bright, guarded by two ante-rooms and three staff. She thought of her consulting room and the wards. She didn't come across mess, she realised, not even in theatre. In theatre there were all those pairs of hands ready with the swabs, the suction and the sutures.

Precious said, 'Well . . . Let's just have a little look . . .'

They watched as she scrolled down the list.

'Memo, memo, memo . . .' said Katharine.

'What's a memo?' said Laura.

'Usually they're nothing,' Precious said.

'They're a quick way of communicating with a lot of people,' said Katharine. 'I find them invaluable, I must say.'

'I think Bea's attitude is that if you ignore them for long enough they'll go away or at least become irrelevant.'

'Like homework,' said Laura.

'Probably,' laughed Precious. 'Trouble is . . .' She opened an email titled 'Urgent. Immediate Action Required' and looked at Katharine. 'Trouble is, they can catch you out sometimes.'

Katharine looked at Laura and wished she would go somewhere out of earshot.

Precious said, 'Do you remember where the photocopier is, Laura?'

Laura nodded.

'Would you mind doing twenty-five copies of this for me?'

She handed her a sheet of A4. On it was an enlarged image of Bea taken from her staff pass. 'Beatrice Kemp' was printed underneath and 'Have You Seen Her?' across the top.

Katharine peered at the fifteen-year-old photograph of Bea, the dated hairstyle and embarrassed smile. 'That's not Bea,' she said, shaking her head.

'Oh, I know. She doesn't look her best in that one. But I thought it would do for now, until we get a recent one from you or Frank.'

'And isn't she Beatrice Pamplin at work?'

'Pamplin?' Precious shook her head. 'She's always been Bea Kemp here.'

Laura went to the far end of the office with the poster and Katharine sat down on Bea's chair and blew her nose. This was all horribly, prosaically real and awful and she wished Precious would stop being so cheerful and practical about everything. As soon as Laura was out of earshot, Precious's face became sombre. She sat down too and drew her chair over to Katharine.

'I have to say, I am worried about Bea,' she said.

'So am I,' Katharine said, more sharply than she meant to. 'I've been so busy these last few weeks I've hardly seen her. Has she been . . . ?' The words failed her and she shook her head helplessly.

'I'd say she's been up and down for a few months.' Precious's voice was low and kind. Katharine nodded, afraid of what she might hear. 'But the last few days she seemed pretty good. Busy but –. She's been making all these plans for your mother's birthday.'

'And Frank? How were things in that department?'

Precious wondered if Bea talked to Katharine the way she had talked to her. Wondered whether Katharine had heard Bea say that in the first years their lovemaking was earnest rather than passionate, dedicated to the making of a child, and that there was something monk-like about Frank that she couldn't quite work out, so that pretty soon, when the child didn't come, she went back to Patrick, in her mind for the most part, and it was Patrick's face she saw whenever Frank made love to her, although, Bea said once, the words 'made' and 'love' were inaccurate really. Come to think of it, she added, so was the word 'her'.

'Things weren't easy,' was all Precious had time to say as she watched Laura return.

'But did she say anything to you, anything that made you think she might . . .' Might what? Disappear? Do a runner? Die?

'Nothing out of the ordinary, but you never really know what's going on, do you? Mostly I think people cope all right at work even if they are depressed. I know there were some money worries and she was certainly fed up with work. We all are. She hated the way it was going – targets, appraisals, reports to write that no one reads. And then there was the pressure on us to raise our grade from the last inspection. She had done a lot of extra work on some of the figures. But in truth the figures are impossible, they're imaginary almost. You must know that from working in a hospital.'

Katharine found figures extremely useful. You just needed to know how to make them work for you. Katharine found figures turned easily into money for her department, her research, her bank account. She thought of her recent pay rise and blushed.

Laura put the photocopies on Bea's desk. Katharine checked her watch.

Laura said, 'I'm getting braces today.'

'Are you? My two have braces now. You know why all you girls are getting braces? Your brains are getting bigger and crowding out your teeth.' Precious held Laura's chin and laughed. 'It's true! It's intelligence evolving in front of our very eyes.'

Katharine bent to pick up her bag. 'Oh, I don't know about that.'

Laura opened her mouth enormously wide like a hippopotamus and shut it again when Katharine straightened up.

But

'WHAT?'

'Mispers. Missing persons. There are thousands of them out there. Gone without trace. Six hundred a day.'

'Six hundred?' Katharine didn't think this could be right, but the Missing Persons officer nodded. He had told her his name — Pete, was it? Jim? She couldn't remember. There were two of them sitting opposite each other across a pair of desks. 'Michelle' followed by a phone number and 'Sudden Death' were written in green on a white-board across the wall facing her. On a poster next to it was a list: Missing Persons Risk Assessment — High, Medium, Low.

'They get up one day, leave home and disappear.'

He wasn't making Katharine feel any better, this short, sallow-faced cop speaking in riddles like he was on a television show. She straightened her back and prepared herself to say something that would let him know the kind of woman he was talking to.

'Listen, my sister . . .'

The skin contracted against the front of her skull and across her cheeks as if she had stepped into a cold wind. The muscles of her throat ached and the throbbing was beginning at the front across her forehead.

'Most reappear eventually,' said the taller man. He cleared his throat. 'But there are a few, a very small number who—'

'Oh God.'

He pushed the box of tissues across the table towards her, the sound of a hand stroking satin; Bea's palm on Katharine's wedding dress, their laughing mouths tickled by champagne bubbles while the guests gathered in the room below.

Jim cleared his throat. She looked up at him, grateful for his kindness. His eyes were brown and the skin below them looked loose and bruised.

'There was nothing, there was no reason . . .' She stopped and blew her nose with surprising force and noise.

'So your sister was last seen when she left the house at around seven on Wednesday morning. That's about thirty hours ago,' said the smaller man. 'Let's just begin with some facts about her appearance.'

Katharine told them Bea's approximate height and weight. She gave Bea's eye colour, hair colour and age, all of it meaningless, she thought, just numbers and adjectives that gave no sense at all of who Bea was. She wasn't even completely sure of the facts herself. Bea's eyes were always described as blue, but in certain lights and in certain moods, it seemed to her, they were more of a slate grey. When Bea stood up straight she was taller than Katharine, but lately she seemed to have shrunk. When he asked her whether Bea had any distinguishing marks, any scars or tattoos, Katharine recoiled. She felt tricked. These questions were not to help find a living person; they were to help identify a corpse.

'No. My sister has no distinguishing characteristics,' she said coldly and the two men exchanged the briefest of looks. But how could she be sure about Bea's body? she thought. She hadn't seen her naked since she was fourteen.

'And what name did she go by?'

'What?' They had Bea's name. What were they talking about?

'There can be some confusion over identity where married women are concerned,' said Jim. 'Sometimes they use more than one name. We have Beatrice Pamplin down here. Is that her married or her maiden name?'

Maiden? Katharine suppressed an image of Bea in a wimple and gown, traipsing the meadows and glens of Hastings. 'Kemp,' she said, 'Bea Kemp. I have a feeling she used her married name, Pamplin, for some things but not for work. She's been there so long, perhaps it felt odd to change it.'

She put her hand to her mouth and looked at the white-board. How were they going to find her if they didn't even know her name?

'I know this is difficult for you,' said Jim. 'But can you think of any reason why your sister may have decided to leave? Did she seem depressed, unduly worried about things? Were there problems at home perhaps?'

Katharine was shaking her head, impatient with this man, this room, the slow, tedious business of forms and protocol. She felt desperate to speak to Bea, saw now not Bea but a gap where she had been, the negative space of her sister. She couldn't remember the last time they had had a proper, serious conversation together that wasn't about time or objects or children.

'She seemed tired but fine. I mean, I think things with her husband hadn't been easy for a while.' She stopped and wondered whether they had met Frank.

'Things hadn't been easy for a while?' The short one was talking now. 'In what way?'

She looked at them. They were asking whether Frank was violent.

'He has a temper, I do know that, but it is mainly these dark moods. He's capable of not talking for days . . .' She shook her head. 'But Frank's not violent, I don't think, no. His main problem is he doesn't really have a proper job. I mean, a writer, for heaven's sake.' She suddenly wondered how on earth Frank and Bea managed for money.

While Jim wrote this down, she could feel the other one looking at her. His scrutiny made her blush. She had made up her mind about Frank a long time ago, dismissed him and closed her mind to him. He was a man who was disappointed with life and as a result adopted that ridiculous mantle of false pride. It would be so easy to drop Frank in it right now. Here she was, talking about violence when all they had asked was how she got on with her husband. She shrugged and tried to smile.

'All I mean is that if I woke up one day and found I was married to Frank, I would probably run screaming into the sea.' She gave a laugh. They looked at her. The phone on Jim's desk rang. He ignored it and it stopped after three rings.

Now she felt like a suspect. Shame prickled at the roots of her hair. 'Look, we're not particularly close to them as a couple, if you know what I mean, but our children are. They're very fond of Bea. They're fond of both of them. Adrian adores Frank.'

In her mind she saw Frank as the opposite of violent, as spineless and impotent. But how could she be sure? She swallowed and wondered whether she had been reckless with her children's safety, leaving them in the care of a man she did not like, much less knew in any real sense of the word.

Jim entered some information on the computer. He was bringing the interview to an end and Katharine rubbed at the tingling beginning in her hands, saw the lights in the room flare up then retreat as a migraine threatened. She didn't want to leave. How was she going to find Bea? She must be somewhere. What if she had had an accident, fallen in the river, been attacked or murdered? Why was there no word from her, why was there no trace?

'This, all this . . .' She brought her hand up to her head and looked wildly about her. 'Oh God . . .' All this was the stuff of newsprint and television, not Bea and Katharine.

Jim straightened his tie and stood up, gesturing gently at

the door. He began to speak, something about 'The investigation is already underway. We will be visiting her husband later today, making enquiries and contacting the main agencies . . .' Katharine stayed where she was; she wasn't going anywhere. She needed some inside information. She was a hospital doctor, for God's sake, she knew how the system worked. She needed to be fast-tracked, given the names of the best people to see; she wanted the truth about survival. This was twenty-first-century Britain; there could only be a limited number of possibilities. There was the bank, the doctor, passport control. We're all on CCTV, we have mobile phones— She stopped herself, remembering that Bea's phone had been stolen.

'Please,' she said.

'I know it's hard.' Jim sat down again. 'When a loved one goes missing, those left behind can often become lost themselves in a kind of—'

An animal noise rose up from inside her. She covered her face with her hand. This was appalling. She was out of control. She heard the other one switch on the kettle, the rustle of tea bags in a jar. Jim waited. His hands rested together on his laptop. His fingers were long and tanned. He wore a gold wedding ring.

'But why?' she whimpered. She hated that question. It was the question grieving parents asked of her, the question she always deflected with statistics and a cool professionalism. 'But why do people go missing?' she said, her voice small and hopeless. It was a stupid, unanswerable question. He nodded and cleared his throat, and she held her breath and tried to look him in the eye because it seemed as though he was going to say something important, something that might save her from the storm, that would bring Bea back, but fluid was running from her nose and from her mouth and eyes all over again.

'The missing tend to fall into four categories: young people in care, men in their twenties, middle-aged men, and elderly people suffering from dementia. Sexual abuse, financial worries or mental illness are often the reason. It's rare for women your sister's age to take themselves off. Women tend to be firmly bedded into their lives, to family, friends and so forth, and that is why we are treating her case as high risk.'

'You think that something's happened to her?'

'Most Mispers are found or return home of their own accord. It is only a very small number, a tiny number, to whom something untoward has happened.'

'What we find,' said the other man, 'is that it's never really a mystery. Somebody in the family always knows why they've gone. It may take a while till they realise they know. But it's just a matter of time until they tell us.'

Katharine disliked what he was implying. Horrible little man, with his cheap shirt and brand-new trainers. She shook her head and snapped two migraine tablets from their foil. 'Not Bea. This is completely out of character.' No. Not Bea's face fading on posters. Bea was solid and real. She was flesh and bone and blood, laughter and words and breath. Bea could not just vanish and melt away into nothing. Katharine fumbled about her for a tissue then reached again for one of theirs. She pressed it hard against her nose and mouth as if to block out the stench of death.

The phone rang again. Jim excused himself and answered it. *Mispers.* Katharine tried out the word silently inside her mouth. It had the papery whisper of something that could not be told; it had the shifty sibilance of secrets and of shame.

Jim hung up and told Pete that Erkan had just been found. 'Got a train to Manchester and was picked up sleeping rough round the back of the station.' He looked at Katharine. 'This lad's been missing three weeks. He stole money from his uncle to pay off a gambling debt. Then he was too afraid to go home.'

'What shall I do?' said Katharine. 'I can't just sit around waiting for her to turn up.'

'We will be working with CID and conducting house-to-house interviews. They may carry out a thorough search of the area with dogs, helicopters and divers. But it's early days yet. The chances are your sister will turn up.'

'I see.' But she wasn't sure that she did. So now they were going to be looking for a body, not a live woman.

'Often, when people take themselves off, they go back to places they knew well.'

'Hastings,' Katharine said. 'It's where we grew up.' She got up to go and checked her watch. She was impatient now to get out of the room, away from the whiteboard with its names of the lost. There was no time to lose. She would find Bea herself. She would go to Hastings as soon as she possibly could. Not today, there was so much to do. Tomorrow perhaps. Or Sunday. Monday at the latest.

Wife

FRANK SAT in the kitchen and poured milk into his cup of tea. He had showered, put on clean clothes, shaved and trimmed his ears. The knock at the door made him jump, even though he had been waiting for it since breakfast.

Without uniform but wearing pale blue shirts and dark trousers, the two men on the doorstep looked more like salesmen than police officers. The tall, handsome one with the tie flipped his warrant card open. The silver badge flashed and Frank saw his eight-year-old self, fringed Stetson, sheriff's star, *I'm the Milky Bar Kid and the Milky Bars are on me.*

'I'm Jim Woods from the Missing Persons Unit. Mr Frank Pamplin?'

An instant later the warrant card was flipped shut and back again in Jim Woods's pocket. He introduced the smaller man without a tie, who looked like he could throw a punch or two.

In the kitchen they stood round the table and the tall one looked kindly at Frank while the short one cast his eyes around the room. Frank gestured vaguely at the sinkful of dirty tea cups and the curdled milk on the table and said, 'I was just going to get some more milk.'

'Don't worry about that,' said Jim. 'Is it all right if we sit down?' He pulled his pocket book out. Frank nodded and sat across the kitchen table from him. Pete, the short one, stood with his back to the light. Frank wanted to see what he was doing, but it would have meant turning away from the tall one, who was looking him in the eye and straightening his tie.

'I had a visit from the uniformed branch yesterday,' Frank said.

'There is some concern as to the whereabouts of your wife, Mr Pamplin.'

'Can't say I'm terribly confident about their powers of deduction.' Frank chuckled, then wished he hadn't. The informality of these men confused him. Was it sympathy or a trap?

'Are you worried about your wife, Mr Pamplin?'

Well, that was a complicated question. They had to realise they were dealing with an intellectual here. Worried about Bea? Bea had always been able to look after herself. Worrying was Bea's department. Writing was his. He pressed hard at the ache in his back and said, 'Yes, of course I'm worried.'

Jim crossed his legs and began the questions, making brief notes as Frank answered. First, a description of Bea. Frank swept a glance round at Pete but couldn't see his expression. He told them she had green eyes and was about the same height as himself. He wasn't sure about her hair colour because it kept changing. He thought it was probably blondish. He had no idea how much she weighed, although she had put on a bit of weight recently. 'I couldn't lift her off the ground,' he said. Jim's pen paused.

'We can usually get an idea from her clothes.'

'Well, she buys enough of them,' said Frank, risking a smile.

'You wouldn't believe how often we hear that,' said Pete.

Frank relaxed a bit. He turned and smiled at Pete, at his boyish face and military haircut, but Pete was frowning at the floorboards.

Jim asked if they owned a car.

'We do. It's up the road. But she usually walked to work. You know, along the river.'

'Quite a long walk. Wouldn't it be quicker to take the bus?'

Frank shrugged. 'Oh, she liked to walk. She needed the exercise, so she said. To keep her weight down. I told her running was what she needed for that.'

'Can you tell us what she was wearing when she left for work yesterday morning?'

Frank swallowed. 'She generally wore something fairly smart.'

Pete waited.

'You know, dark. A skirt. Blouse. That kind of thing.'

'Coat?'

'Probably, although she did complain a lot about being too hot.'

'Colour?'

'Well that would depend which one she took.'

There was a pause. Pete flicked back through his notes. 'What time exactly did she leave the house on Wednesday morning?'

Frank blushed and said, 'Er . . .'

'It's quite important as you can appreciate,' said Pete.

'I didn't actually hear her get up.'

Jim and Pete exchanged a look. 'You mean you didn't see her at all before she left for work?'

'Not as such.' Shame crouched in Frank's chest. 'I worked late the night before and slept on the couch downstairs.'

'So the last positive sighting we have of your wife is Tuesday evening.'

Nobody spoke. It didn't sound very good, Frank had to admit. Somebody cleared their throat.

'Do you own a computer, Mr Pamplin?'

'Yes.' Frank's voice was faint. He tried again. 'Yes, I do.'

Jim looked at him and waited, but Frank had nothing more to say. His desultory late-night surfing would be there for all to see, he knew that, and some of it, especially after the second bottle of red, was not especially edifying.

'Is it a shared computer or does your wife have her own?'

'She has a laptop she brings home from work. My wife . . .'

Frank stopped. The word 'wife' hung in the air and he thought how Bea disliked the word. She said it sounded cold and sharp and that it was never a word the world used warmly. Jim was asking how long they had been married, while Pete was looking out at the garden. Frank said they had only been married a few years but had been together for ten. Pete looked in the vase on the low shelf by the door and found the door key. Frank heard himself saying that Bea's sister, Katharine, persuaded them to get married because of inheritance tax and pensions. Bea made him promise not to call her his wife. I'm still Bea, married or not, she said, and Adrian had said, To be or not to be, is that the question?

'And how was her state of mind, would you say?'

Frank said, 'Well, you know . . .' and stopped short of finishing the sentence, the rest of which had been 'women', because there was something about Jim's calm face and gentle voice, something about the gold ring on his long-fingered hand that suggested he did indeed know women and in a way that Frank quite possibly did not.

Pete stepped out on to the patio, looked at the ground and pressed gently with his toe on a loose paving stone.

'I think she said they'd got a new boss at work. You know, some young upstart. She went on about that.'

Outside, Pete was pulling something out of the water butt. Frank got to his feet and went to the door. 'Ah. That is the work of a local handyman. Drifter type. Goes by the name of Urban, believe it or not. He just appeared yesterday in my garden and I have no idea how he got in. Claimed to be sorting out the squirrel problem at the request of my wife.' Frank warmed to his theme. 'I didn't like the look of him.

Something rather threatening about him, if you want my honest opinion.'

'Urban?' Jim made a note. 'Urban what?'

'No idea. He's a friend of a friend.' Frank paused. He would prefer to keep Wanda out of all this. 'I mean, he does odd jobs about the place, you know, he's . . .' His voice died away as they watched Pete examine the squirrel trap, from which the dead squirrel dripped water. He put the trap on the ground and looked over at them.

'I think you'll be wanting to bury that,' he called. 'It's not going to be smelling too sweet.'

Jim closed his pocket book and got to his feet. 'We'd like to take a look around if that's all right with you. Oh, there was one other thing. Do you have a toothbrush of your wife's that we could take away?'

Frank was watching Pete, who had squatted down to stare at the garden spade standing in the flowerbed. Then he looked around at the lawn, turning his head slowly from left to right as if measuring up.

'I beg your pardon?' said Frank.

'Toothbrush, hairbrush, something of that sort?'

Frank blinked at him.

'For DNA,' said Jim.

'Ah.' Frank's mouth was dry.

'And we'll need a recent photo.'

Recent? It was years since he had taken a photo of Bea, in fact he couldn't remember the last time he had. He looked around him. On the mantelpiece were school photos of Adrian and Laura and an old one of himself on graduation day. Pete came in from the garden brushing dirt from his hands.

'We'd like to conduct a preliminary search of the premises in order to secure and preserve appropriate evidence,' said Jim. 'Is that all right with you?'

'Yes, of course,' said Frank, feeling that it was very much

not all right. He wasn't even sure if it was entirely legal. His wife was missing. What was the point therefore of looking in her house? 'How do you want to do this?' he said. 'One of you take the upstairs, the other downstairs?'

'We stick together mainly,' said Pete. 'Why don't you show us round?'

Frank watched while they did a cursory search of his workroom. They noted the duvet and the pillow on the couch, they gazed around at his vinyls stacked on shelves, the books and CDs and piles of reference books and papers. Scotch bottles and tumblers littered the wooden floor and a few tea mugs with mould in them stood on the coffee table. The place was really a bit of a tip. Perhaps he should relent and let Wanda clean it up. He never let her touch this with the hoover or the duster – it would be a disaster for his work. He led them upstairs into the bedroom, which smelt of Bea, some kind of flowery, sweet scent that she used. The room felt crowded with three men in it, and when they pulled the curtains open and let the light in, its shortcomings were glaringly obvious. They hesitated in front of the egg cups and Jim picked up a blue striped one from the Mull of Kintyre. Frank looked down at the floor and saw that the white carpet Bea had bought long before she met him was grubby and grimed with age. He watched Pete look up at where the faded curtains had come away from their tracks.

'She was always on at me to do the bedroom,' he said, and Jim gave the smallest of smiles. 'Peppermint rarely works in my experience,' he added, indicating the walls. 'My father swears by wallpaper. Says it gives a room substance.'

Jim opened the wardrobe and surveyed the clothes on hangers. Pete opened the chest of drawers. They looked at each other and Frank explained that his clothes were in the spare room. Pete ran his hand across the hangers and asked whether these were all the clothes Bea had. Frank looked and said that he really had no idea. It seemed like plenty to him, but he wasn't sure whether it was a lot or a little for a woman pushing fifty.

He was relieved when they went into the spare room, which Bea had decorated for the children. Apart from his clothes in the small wardrobe there, she had made it entirely theirs and spent quite a bit of money on it. There was an orange sofabed and new curtains, a little desk and lamp for homework, funky wallpaper that made him feel seasick, pink furry cushions, a television and music centre and an electric guitar and amp – old ones of Frank's that he had given to Adrian. Frank explained about the children and Jim nodded, seeming to know all about it.

Back downstairs Jim said, 'Is it all right if we take this?' He had their wedding photograph in his hand. Frank couldn't think where they'd found it. It must have been when he left them to it upstairs and came back down to the kitchen to wait. He stared at the photo. It was years since he had seen it. Bea was smiling, one hand up, holding on to the ridiculous hat she had insisted on wearing. It was a small black fez with spotted net that reached to just below her eyes. It was understood that the hat was her way of making a joke of it. He stood beside her, eyes almost closed so that he looked like a halfwit; Lance stood at the edge in his funeral suit next to Margaret while the children grinned from either side. It was an absolute pig's ear of a wedding photo, but that was what happened when you left it to an amateur. Richard had taken it. 'Smile!'

Beach

'YOU DIDN'T tell me I was gonna be the only black person here.'

Chanel had both hands pushed deep into her coat pockets, her hood was up and she had her face turned towards the Slots of Fun amusement arcade. No one in there was smiling.

'I wish we'd stayed at school now.'

'Don't be stupid, it's Friday.'

'I like Double Art.'

'Shut up, will yer?' said Laura, giving Chanel a push. 'You're prac'ly the only black person in Cambridge too so get over yourself.'

But Chanel wasn't going another step.

'I wanna go back,' she said and plugged in her earphones. 'Anyway, I can't understand a word you're saying.'

Laura looked about her and ran her tongue across the metal in her mouth. The wind hurt her teeth. Behind them was Hastings's derelict pier and up ahead was the Old Town. Chanel was right, they hadn't seen another black face since the train left Orpington, and as the journey took them further south she had become more and more subdued. The only fun they'd had so far was hiding from the conductor. It was rubbish being here with Chanel if she wasn't going to be a laugh. The inside of Laura's mouth felt alien and metallic. For some reason she wanted to cry.

Up ahead on the corner she could see the Italian Way ice cream parlour, where they had red check cloths and vases of carnations on each table. 'This is the way that ice cream should be eaten,' Bea always said each time she took them there. Laura pulled at Chanel. They pressed their faces to the window and peered inside. The tables were just as she remembered, but it was empty apart from an elderly couple eating knickerbocker glories. They blinked at Chanel and Laura, glanced at each other and looked back down at their ice creams. Each lifted a spoonful to their mouth.

'I'm starving,' said Chanel, misting up the glass with her breath.

The sun came out sudden and bright, illuminating the beach like a stage.

'Come on,' said Laura, dragging Chanel across the road. 'Last one to the sea's an A star.'

'Yeah, like Delilah.'

Delilah got A star for everything, even maths.

They climbed the barriers at the side of the dual carriageway and squealed and darted their way between honking cars and vans. As they crunched along the shingle Chanel's mood lifted. There was no one there apart from a young Chinese man sitting facing the sea, hunched over a textbook. When they staggered past he looked up and gave them a melancholy smile. Laura shoved Chanel towards him. Chanel thumped her hard and said, 'What's your problem, bitch?'

The water rolled and rippled as far as the eye could see. A racing sky and bright sun kept the light shifting from sullen to dazzling then back again. Gulls wheeled and cried around them. One hovered low, directly above their heads.

'What's it want?' whimpered Chanel, ducking and swerving towards the water's edge.

Laura waved her school bag at it and shouted. The gull drifted off and landed on stones up ahead of them.

'It's freakin' me out, all that sky,' said Chanel.

Bea always said, 'If you're feeling down, get on a train and take yourself somewhere else. You'll feel better when you get there.' That was how Laura knew Bea had gone to Hastings. She wasn't sure exactly where, but most likely they'd find her in one of their favourite places, like The Fish Hut or up on the cliffs. Of course Bea would probably pop in on her mum while she was here, but she wouldn't stay long. Granny didn't like long visits.

Chanel was holding her phone above her head and filming herself in catwalk poses against the backdrop of the sea.

'Look at this,' she screamed against the wind, holding her phone out for Laura and parading along the ridge at the water's edge.

'Chips?' shrieked Laura, starting to run.

Chanel struggled after her, both of them moving in slow motion, heavy and clumsy through the shifting shingle.

Chanel caught up with Laura and stuck one foot out so that they both fell on to the stones. They were laughing and panting and struggling to get upright. Chanel held the phone above their heads and took a picture. They were silent when they viewed it. With their heads against the brown stones, the fur of their hoods framing their faces and the sun in their eyes, they looked strange, otherworldly.

Then Laura started to laugh. 'We look like them igloo people.'

Chanel giggled, grabbing at the phone for a better look. She began to hoot. 'What, them Innits?'

'Innit though?'

'No, *Innits*. That's their proper name.'

Laura snorted. They kicked their legs in the air and screamed. An Old English Sheepdog bounded up to them, a flurry of white fur.

'Oh my God, it's a polar bear, man. I am not joking, it is . . .'

'It's a wolf thing, man, an Ark-tic fox!'

They scrabbled to their feet and crouched back to back, sobbing with laughter and holding their bags to their knees. The dog ran round them barking and jesting before dashing off up the beach.

'Ooh . . .'

'Oh . . .'

'Oh my God . . .'

'Oh my God, man . . .'

Drunkenly they helped each other up and pulled their clothes straight. They picked up their bags, spasms of laughter breaking out every time they caught each other's eye.

'Come on. The chip shop's over there.'

With linked arms they staggered up the beach.

It was some time later, as they sat outside the chippy, fingers gritty with hot salty oil, that Laura remembered why they were there. They should get a move on. They had to be back in Cambridge by five at the latest.

'You're not looking!' she said to Chanel. 'We need to keep an eye open for my auntie.' She swung round on the bench and squinted at the sea.

Chanel nodded and loaded more chips into her mouth. She looked around them. In the Dolphin pub just along the road, two big women sat drinking pints, a fighting dog on the ground between them. Behind Chanel, a few people queued at the jellied eel bar next door.

'Where's your granny live, then?'

Laura pointed with her bag of chips up the hill behind the shops. 'That way. Not far.'

'That's what I'd do,' said Chanel, nodding.

'What?'

'I'd go up me mum's.'

Laura shrugged. She blinked at the horizon, suddenly unsure of her theory. After all, most people ran away *from* home, not to it. She looked at the boatyard, where small trawlers were festooned with tattered black flags. They leaned on the stones as if injured. Rope, chains and nets lay in chaotic piles between them. 'Sweet disorder,' Bea called it. She used to say it about her bedroom and her kitchen, that chaos was much under-rated. 'Careful chaos and sweet disorder.'

Laura pulled a postcard from her jacket pocket. It pictured the beach at Hastings, a brightly painted fishing boat pulled up on the shingle. She turned it over and addressed it to Bea in Cambridge. She wrote, 'I came to find you. Miss you lots, love Laura,' then stuffed it back in her pocket again. Her granny would have a stamp.

She looked up at the black net sheds that stood tall between them and the sea. The sun went in and she shivered.

'Let's go.' Laura swung her legs off the bench seat and headed for the steps that led to her grandmother's house.

What

MARGARET WOKE with a start and looked about her. Her neck hurt and her glasses had gone awry. The record had stopped and the needle was lisping. There it was again. A rattle at the door. She sat up and patted her hair straight.

When she went out into the hall, she could see a shadow the other side of the frosted glass. A pair of eyes looked at her through the letter box.

A voice was saying, 'Hello? Hello?'

'Beatrice?' said Margaret.

'Let us in,' said the voice.

'What?'

'It's me.'

'Bea?'

Laura rapped on the glass. She watched the shape retreat and become indistinct. After a while it became visible again from the left, where the kitchen door was.

'Who is it?'

'It's me, Laura.'

Margaret thought for a moment, put her hand to her lips and looked back towards the kitchen.

'Beatrice?' she said again.

'We've come to look for her,' said the voice.

'She's not here yet.' Margaret put the chain on the door and opened it a crack.

Laura stood up and said, 'Granny. It's me, let me in.'

'Well why didn't you say so?' said Margaret and shut the door. She removed the chain and opened it again. Laura came in and Chanel hesitated outside.

'Come on,' said Laura.

Mute, Chanel followed Laura and stood beside her in the hall, tugging the hem of her skirt.

Margaret put her head out and looked up the street.

'Well, where is she?'

'Who?'

'Who brought you?'

Laura moved into the kitchen and reached for the biscuit tin on top of the fridge.

'Have you got any of those chocolatey ones, Granny?' She prised open the lid and looked inside.

Chanel thought they ought to be getting back and said, 'Laura . . .'

'Want one?' said Laura, offering her the tin.

Chanel looked inside. Pink wafer ones, dry plain ones, round ones with jam in the middle, custard creams, but no McVitie's Milk Chocolate Digestives. She took a custard cream and tried not to drop crumbs as she ate.

'Did Bea bring you?'

'We've come to get her.'

Margaret gave a little sigh and filled the kettle. She looked around for the teapot.

'Bea's not here.'

'Are you sure?'

'Well she might have come in while I was having a nap. You ought to get those teeth seen to, you know.'

Laura looked across the hall at the closed door of her mother's childhood bedroom.

'I'll just check.' She squeezed past and put her hand flat to the bedroom door. She listened. 'Bea?' she said.

She turned to look back at the kitchen, where Chanel was taking another biscuit and Margaret was opening cupboards, searching for the teapot.

'Chanel,' hissed Laura and waved her over.

Laura opened the door. Two single beds with mauve candlewick spreads stood side by side. The window above them was draped in nets. Chanel wrinkled her nose. It smelt of cats.

Laura sat on one bed and Chanel sat on the other.

'We should go,' said Chanel. She felt homesick here.

Laura looked about her. The room was bare. No sign remained that two girls had grown up here.

'She'll probably be back soon.'

'No she won't. She's not coming. Come on, my mum's gonna kill me. What time's the train?'

'Shut up a bit.'

Chanel pulled up her tights and raised her zipper to her nose. 'Is your nan a bit, you know . . . ?'

Laura pulled an exercise book from her school bag and ripped a page out of it. Kneeling on the carpet she scribbled a note.

'What's that say?'

'It's to Bea.' Laura signed it with several kisses. 'Just letting her know we've been looking for her.' She slid the note under the pillow then straightened the shade on the bedside lamp. 'She'll see it when she gets here. Come on.'

They paused in the hallway. Margaret was in the lounge, looking out of the window, watching the sea. Laura took a stamp from the drawer in the hall table.

'We're off now!' she called. 'Thanks for the biscuits.'

Margaret turned and waved. 'Oh. Mind how you go then.'

Outside, Chanel hurried to keep up with Laura. They walked back up the main road alongside the beach. The sun had disappeared behind a blanket of grey. They passed a large complicated sign warning of tides and currents. She couldn't understand how anyone would want to live in a place like this and she wished they had never come.

'So your granny's a bit . . .'

Laura kept walking. She was sniffing and her jaw was clenched. At a postbox she stopped and dropped the postcard to Bea inside.

'She's a bit, you know, what's it called?' persisted Chanel as they made a dash for a traffic island and stood stranded in a heavy rush of cars and coaches and vans.

'Yeah,' Laura said . . . 'She's—'

A continental juggernaut sped inches from them, drowning her words.

'What?' yelled Chanel.

'She's a bit gone!' shouted Laura.

Sorry

KATHARINE WASN'T sure she could endure an evening at the Elliots' but Richard had persuaded her it would do her good.

'After all,' he said, 'it's not as if you're in mourning. Bea hasn't died or anything. She's taken herself off somewhere, she's having a break . . .'

His voice trailed off as he pulled the laces tight on first one shoe, then the other. His shoes were one of the things she loved about him. He had unerring taste where shoes were concerned, rare in a man, she suspected, and the ones he had on tonight, classic black calf, with a rich sheen, had a dependable, no-nonsense air to them. Katharine abhorred nonsense. She just couldn't stand it. It was part of what made being a mother so very testing. There was so much nonsense around even the simplest of things. But with Richard, there was never any nonsense. He was like her, the epitome of sense: intelligent, reasonable, sane and smart.

He finished with his laces, lifted his jacket off the coat-stand and called goodbye to the children. They waited for a response. Katharine stared at the floor and thought how she had learnt to tie her laces at three. She had sat on the doorstep, her mother and Bea waiting, while she tied a not very tight but very good-looking knot. 'See that, Bea?' her mother said.

'Fancy being able to tie your laces at three.' They had all looked at Bea's black T-bar sandals, the white socks that dented dumpy calves, and Katharine had felt the rush of being best enthral her. Their mother had clapped her hands. 'What a clever girl.'

Katharine battled a brief disturbance in her guts. She blinked in dismay. She was never sick. Absolutely never sick. 'Sorry,' she whispered. 'So sorry.'

Wanda appeared from the kitchen. Her hair bounced and shone. So did her teeth. Richard beamed at her. He can't help it, thought Katharine. It's wired in. She thanked Wanda again for agreeing to babysit. At least Wanda knew Bea, understood the situation and would be cheerful with the children. She said she would cook something for them and seemed unperturbed that the fridge held nothing very promising in this respect. Katharine knew too that on their return the kitchen would be spotless and Wanda would find her own way home.

Earlier, the children had said they didn't need a babysitter. Laura was old enough to be left alone, after all. Katharine would not hear of it, not since the incident with the vodka. They asked to go to Frank's instead but Katharine refused.

'Why not?' asked Adrian.

'It's not appropriate.'

Richard backed her up. 'No, he's probably—'

But Katharine jumped in before he could finish, a habit of hers he had grown to ignore. 'He's probably out looking for Bea.'

'Absolutely,' added Richard, looking around for his wallet and keys. 'After all, I expect Frank is—'

'I expect Frank is exhausted.'

That seemed to settle it. Adrian had gazed into the middle distance then left the room. She hadn't seen the children since.

Richard put on his coat. Katharine said goodbye to Wanda.

'We won't be late.'

'You go out and enjoy yourselves.' She waved them away.

Katharine hesitated on the doorstep, looked down and said, 'Oh, no.'

'Are you all right, darling?' Richard put his hand beneath her arm.

'Your shoelace,' said Katharine. 'It's undone.'

As SOON as the front door closed, the children came downstairs. Laura looked Wanda straight in the eye.

'Where's Bea?' she said.

Wanda had found a tin of baked beans and was looking in the freezer for something to go with it. She made her eyes wide, as if it was all a big secret. 'I think she's having a holiday, don't you?'

Adrian stood against the radiator. Wanda had a sharp chin and the straightest nose he had ever seen. Her hair was blonde, the practically white sort, like her skin. He tried to see her eyes but couldn't put a colour to them. They should be blue but he didn't think they were. He wondered if they were orange.

'Mum says it's completely *out of character*.' Laura jerked her head up and made her arms spring out, a withering and precise impersonation of her mother's no-nonsense demeanour. 'And that's why they're worried.'

Wanda frowned. 'Out of character? What does this mean?' She turned the heat up under a frying pan, poured in a dollop of oil, and opened a packet of fish fingers.

'It means that they think Bea is very reliable,' said Adrian.

'You know, in my country it is against the law to go missing. Here in England it is allowed, I think.'

'What, like, in Poland they'd put you in prison if you went missing?' said Laura.

Wanda laughed. 'Probably.' The fish fingers sputtered in the pan. She turned them over with a fork, something that Katharine expressly forbade.

'That's so stupid.'

Wanda asked Adrian to lay the table and he checked her eyes. Yes, they were orange. Well, hazel. But similar to the tiger in Woburn safari park that had walked up to their jeep, raised itself on its hind legs and glared with malevolent intent into their car.

When they sat down to eat, Wanda gave him six fish fingers without even asking. She was nice, not like a tiger at all.

'I'm doing a YouTube Missing video for Bea,' said Laura.

Wanda thought that was an excellent idea and that Bea would love it.

'I've got to say if she had any distinguishing marks.'

Adrian had arranged his peas in a double helix down the centre of his plate. He was eating the fish fingers sandwiched between pieces of bread.

'The little finger on her right hand is bent where she shut it in the car door,' he said. 'Like this.' He showed her.

Wanda asked whether he was going to eat his peas. He shook his head.

'No, children don't eat green things.'

'And why is that?'

'It's the yuck reflex. Makes you gag.' Adrian gave a demonstration. 'It's a survival mechanism. Anything green is liable to be rotten or poisonous . . .'

'Or vomit,' added Laura. She started jiggling one leg and chewing her lip. 'Can I go finish the YouTube thing?'

'Of course,' said Wanda, scraping Laura's peas on to her own plate. 'Don't forget her tattoo.'

There was a silence. They watched her forking peas into her mouth.

'What?'

'Bea has a tiny one.' She pulled up the bottom of her jumper, and drew down the top of her jeans. 'Here. Just below the bikini line.'

'A tattoo?' said Laura. 'What of?'

'Of a bee, of course.'

Laura flicked her eyes over at Adrian. She wasn't sure this was the Bea she knew at all.

Best

IT WAS a relief to be out of the house and moving. Katharine just wished they didn't have to arrive. It reminded her of when the children were very small, babies really, and how she would drive round the ring road for an hour to avoid getting home. It was the mess and the clamour she couldn't bear. She preferred to arrive home after seven when the nanny had prepared them for bed. Bea had been invaluable with the children in those days. More often than not she would be there when Katharine got back from work. Her job was so much more flexible than Katharine's.

It wasn't Katharine's fault she was the clever one. She had worked damn hard to get where she was. Hours she used to spend on her homework, absolute hours, while all she remembered Bea doing was eating peanut butter sandwiches and watching *Blue Peter* and *Magpie*. Even at weekends Katharine would get up, cycle to her riding lesson, come back, do a few hours' homework and then go into the lounge to find Bea was watching *Champion the Wonder Horse* in her pyjamas. That was one reason Bea was always . . . not fat exactly, but heavy. 'A big girl,' was what people said of Bea. 'Stolid,' aunts would agree, followed by, 'Isn't Katharine getting tall? And *so* slim,' and the pride spread inside her then like a sugary drink. But there was no doubt she had worked hard to get where she was. She and Jane had been the only medical students in their year to get Firsts, and what people didn't understand was that while her life might seem luxurious compared to Bea's – two cars, six-bedroomed house, three foreign holidays a year – it hadn't been without a lot of hard graft. After all, Katharine had not taken a series of gap years after school as Bea had. And Katharine had actually gone to university, unlike Bea, who, despite the gap years, never quite got round to the university part of it. 'Gap from what?' Katharine thought now, remembering Bea's announcement that she was going travelling again at the age of twenty-five. She tried to recall where Bea had gone during that time. France? Spain? She had never really asked for details; she'd been too busy. She had gone straight into training after her degree, worked herself to the bone, endured that punishing housemanship for three long years, snatching a few hours' sleep a night, woken by her bleeper at three in the morning because the twenty-three-weeker had gone into cardiac arrest. Oh, the horror of those nights, trembling so much she couldn't work the buttons on her clothes, arriving at the intensive care unit blind and stupid with exhaustion to find a white-faced infant in its Perspex basin looped up with tubes and lines and the monitors flat-lining all around. The panic of those night calls. The wordless dread at the prospect of child death. Sometimes, often with heart cases, death had already occurred and she would have to snip at the stitches there and then, no time for gloves or iodine, her own heart beating so hard she couldn't keep her fingers still. Somehow she would expose the tiny heart, already showing the dull blue lustre of the lifeless organ, and would try to palpate it with her own clumsy fingers the way they had practised on a sheep's heart in medical school. Often the baby died. They were too tiny, too ill. Trying to save them was just going through the motions.

Yes, she had worked damned hard to get where she was. And as Jane was always reminding her, at least they were doing some good with their lives, giving something back. Not like Frank, pretending to be a writer and getting absolutely nowhere. What Frank needed was a job. A proper job with a salary so that Bea didn't have to—

'Katharine?'

She looked at Richard. He had stopped the car outside the Elliots' house.

'You all right?'

She rubbed her neck and stretched her head back. She just wished she could sleep. But she couldn't. She was too angry. Rage engulfed her. Rage at Bea, at Frank, at the children's school . . .

'We don't have to stay long. They'll understand.'

Katharine nodded, straightening her skirt, her blouse, the strap on her bag. 'I'm fine,' she said. 'We can't duck out. It's Jane's birthday.' She reached over to the back seat and lifted the wrapped gift towards her.

'What did you get her?'

'A fish kettle. I've had it for years but never took it out of its box. Who in their right mind ever uses a fish kettle? But it'll look good with all the rest of her stainless steel.'

'Well, Jane certainly is stainless. And made of steel.'

'Shut up, Richard.' She got out and gave the car door a good slam. 'She's my oldest friend. She's my only friend, come to think of it.'

'Oh darling, don't be silly. You've got lots of friends.'

'I hope to God they haven't asked anyone else. They did say it was just us, didn't they?'

Scream

LAURA WAS one of the outstanding screamers of her year. She had a pair of lungs on her that could rupture a tympanic membrane. She had a mouth the size of a pelican's; a gullet with the capacity of a python's. Screaming was her thing. She was best at it. At birthday parties, when the candles were blown out, she led the screaming; outside the sweet-shop near school, when the bloke with the mangy Alsatian walked past, she led the screaming; on Thursdays, when the very nervous French assistant took the lesson and a wasp or a fly or once just a dust mote floated through the window, Laura led the screaming. It was a girl thing, as far as Adrian could work out, or maybe it was a bird thing, like the way swifts and swallows had screeching parties in the summer over the meadows. Whatever the reason, Laura Cooper was the Maria Callas of screaming.

So when Adrian and Wanda first heard the screaming as they loaded the dishwasher, they were inclined to ignore it. Usually the volume and pitch were in inverse proportion to the size of the emergency. But after approximately three bars, Adrian suspected something was amiss. The screams began as the usual long screel. Adrian looked at Wanda. Wanda looked at Adrian. Then they upgraded to a kind of *staccato furioso*. Wanda dropped the fish slice and took the stairs two at a time.

Laura had stopped screaming by the time Wanda reached the third floor landing and was standing outside the bathroom door, holding it shut. Nothing was coming out of her mouth but she was shaking.

'What? What is it?' panted Wanda.

'There's a man in the bath,' said Laura.

Wanda's mouth thinned. She took a deep breath, seized Laura by the shoulders and steered her in the direction of the staircase. Adrian was plodding up round the final turn in the stairs and Wanda called to him to take his sister down again and out into the garden. The instructions were clear and calm: Take your sister all the way down to the bottom of the garden and into the summerhouse.

'But it's dark.'

'Please don't argue.'

'And it's raining.'

'I will bring you ice cream.'

'With sprinkles on?'

'Go.'

They went.

Wanda opened the bathroom door and said, 'Get out.'

Urban raised his knees and sank his head back, slipping down so that the water surged over the sides and he was submerged. Wanda waited. After a few seconds, with one powerful motion, he broke the surface, rose and stood in the tub, water streaming down the gullies and ridges of his body. His torso and legs, even his scalp, were deeply tanned from his work outdoors. She pushed a towel towards him.

'What are you doing here?'

Urban stepped from the bath and stood steaming on the mat in front of her.

'Waiting for you to finish sitting on the babies.' He flashed a smile at her and rubbed his face in the towel so that she could hear the bristles. 'Thought you might come up and join me.'

'Get out. This isn't funny.'

'What's the problem?' He pressed himself up against her. She turned away.

'Bea's disappeared. I want you to go. Now.'

'Yeah?' He opened the bathroom cabinet, took out a razor and filled the sink.

'The police are involved and I'm worried. It's been three days.'

'Three days is nothing.' He looked at her in the mirror as he spread shaving cream over his face. 'I've been gone for years.'

Wanda watched his back, the S of his spine, bound with ropes of muscle, and she thought of Frank's wan and muted flesh, his grave look and the words in his fingers. She pulled the plug out of the bath and rubbed at the sides with a cloth.

'It's different. Women of her age don't just disappear.' She squirted cleaner over the enamel.

The blade scraped on Urban's cheek. He rinsed and said, 'But it's easy. Women her age are invisible.'

He finished his face and then began on his scalp.

'Please just go. It's not safe.'

Urban examined a bottle of Richard's aftershave. He unscrewed the top and sniffed it. 'Perhaps she has a fancy man.'

'Not Bea. She's too good.'

'Perhaps she's gone and got herself some good loving.' He smiled as he patted the aftershave over his face. 'Because Frank—'

'No.' Wanda elbowed him aside and cleaned the sink, rubbing energetically at the tidemark he had left. 'She was too tired for that.'

'Ah.'

She checked the toilet, flushed it, gave it a scrub with the brush then flushed it again. She bent to tidy the floor, wiping the pools of water with a towel, hanging up the bathmat, rinsing the flannels and the sponge and arranging them over the heated towel rail. She worked fast, the way she did in people's houses. A line of sweat beaded her hairline. She needed to decide how to handle the children. She needed to get this situation under control. When she straightened up, Urban was gone.

DOWNSTAIRS, WANDA double-locked the front door and loaded ice cream into three bowls. The doors to the garden were open. She hurried through the soft evening drizzle towards the wooded area at the far end, where she could see torchlight beams playing on the summerhouse windows.

Inside, Adrian and Laura were sitting on deckchairs, swinging their legs.

'Here we are.' Wanda passed them ice cream, sat on the floor and ate some herself.

Laura ate silently. Between mouthfuls she checked Wanda's face in the half-light. Then she said, 'I'm going to tell.'

'Oh, I looked for the sprinkles but—'

'I'm telling.'

Wanda dug deep into her pocket.

'Here, I found these instead.' She handed each of them a Flake.

There was silence while Laura ate it. An owl called over from the river. Somewhere nearby, a fox barked.

'Still going to tell.'

'Well that's a pity,' said Wanda.

'Yeah, it is.' Laura screwed the Flake wrapper up tight, threw it in the air and kicked it out of the door with her foot.

'Because that means I will have to tell too.'

Adrian hesitated, then licked out his bowl.

'What?'

'I had planned on keeping it secret, but . . .'

Laura's tongue was seeking a stray blob of ice cream from

under her lower lip. She had got back from Hastings well before her parents arrived home from work. Nobody knew except Granny, and who would believe her?

Adrian licked his spoon clean and said, 'Sweetened pig's fat.'

'But,' continued Wanda, 'I'm afraid that if you tell on me, then I will have to tell on you.' She peered out into the garden.

'If it's not dairy,' said Adrian. 'The ice cream. If it's not dairy, then that's what it's made of. Sweetened pig's fat.'

'Shut up,' said Laura. 'What secret?'

Wanda held her hand out for the bowls. 'The mobile phones in your bedroom.'

Laura looked like she'd been slapped. She blinked, her mouth went slack and her face burned.

Wanda laughed. 'You have to learn to hide things better than that.'

Gin

U NDER THE glare of the security light, they arranged
their collars, their hair and their smiles and rang the
doorbell.

Paul opened the door, his arms already wide, his head and
face tilted in sympathy.

He embraced Katharine warmly but she slid away from
his clasp. She never felt comfortable with all that. He greeted
Richard. They shook hands and hugged and slapped each
other on the back. They said, How are you? And *Good*, thank
you, *Very* good, and laughed, and Katharine thought, what
had to happen for them not to do all that?

'Any news?' Paul asked as he took their coats.

'Not really,' she said. She felt uncomfortable with pity, it
made her large and clumsy, which wasn't her at all. She prided
herself on being slim and controlled. She looked down the
hall to the brightly lit kitchen, where loud laughter had been
cut short and people were waiting for their entry.

'Shall we . . . ?' said Richard.

'Yes. Oh yes, go through,' boomed Paul, ushering them
down the hall.

The kitchen smelt good and looked warm and cosy. How
did they do it? wondered Katharine. Jane kissed them and
hugged Katharine hard. Over Jane's shoulder, Katharine saw

another couple getting to their feet and looking stranded by the sofas. She wanted to go home. She couldn't do this. Not with strangers. Richard marched over, stuck out his hand and introduced himself.

'Oh, we're not staying,' said the man. 'We just dropped in to say hello.'

'Oh, but do stay,' said Paul automatically. 'There's plenty to eat.'

'We just moved in next door,' explained the woman to Richard, gathering up her bag.

'Don't rush off just because we've arrived,' Richard said. 'Have one more glass.'

'Oscar's a life coach,' said Paul. 'And Suzanne is a couples counsellor.' He beamed with pride, as if he were presenting his children. 'Here, what's everyone drinking?'

Paul unscrewed a gin bottle and looked at Katharine with a smile. She wandered over to him, watched as he poured over a tall glass of cubes. Sometimes, it was this smell, juniper and bitter almonds, that was on her mother's breath when she tucked them in, both of them in bed by seven, out of the way early so their mother could get on with what she'd been waiting to do all day. To Katharine, gin was Gene Pitney played over and over again late into the night; it was not enough furniture, paraffin heaters and tinned chicken. She shook her head.

'No?' said Paul. He made a ridiculous curtseying sweep, taking one long stride towards Suzanne, holding the gin and tonic glass aloft like a trophy. She accepted it with a little 'Oh!' and a skitter of heels on the stone floor.

Katharine found a carton of orange juice and mixed herself a fizzy drink. Richard was rocking back and forwards on his heels, hands deep in his pockets, shouting 'Ha!' every now and then as he listened to Oscar's tales of hilarious house-moving mishaps.

'Any news?' asked Jane, coming alongside her and helping herself to a drink. 'Sorry about the others. They'll go soon.'

Katharine shook her head. 'The police visited Frank today. Tomorrow they're searching the common and the river . . .' She struggled with her face as it crumpled.

A silence opened up. The guests scanned the floor and walls for something to say.

Richard said, 'Frank says the police keep asking him about whether they were into anything funny. They seem to think Bea has run off with a man from the internet or . . . come to some harm.'

'But the Missing Persons man I saw yesterday was very reassuring . . .' said Katharine.

'And it's been what, two days?'

'Three. Since Tuesday night. The last time Frank saw Bea was bloody Tuesday night.' Katharine took the wine bottle and poured herself a large glass. Richard wondered about checking who was driving but thought better of it.

'Well it's early still, isn't it? I mean, she may well have just . . .' Jane turned the gas off under the rice. 'You did say she was pissed off with everything. Come on, let's eat.'

Oscar was hungry for details. He wanted to hear them offered in words from Katharine's mouth, to pick over the possibilities, taste the fear. A forty-nine-year-old woman goes missing. Just vanishes on the edge of the common at seven in the morning one October day. Well, anything could have happened. It didn't sound good.

'We're fairly sure she's done a runner. Temporarily,' said Richard.

'What does she do, your sister?' Suzanne asked.

They were all aware of the need to stick to the present tense. It made them nervous so that they spoke carefully, like foreigners practising their English.

'She works for the council.'

'Managerial?'

'Admin.'

'Something to do with finance, isn't it?' added Richard.

Unlikely, thought Katharine, looking in vain round the table for some reminder of what it was exactly that her sister did to earn a living. Between the pepper grinder and the water jug she caught a memory of Bea at the long trestle table outside their primary school office, stacking coins – sixpences, pennies, shillings and threepenny bits, furrowing her brow over the pencilled sums to her right while Miss North watched over her, mouth a thin seam of disapproval. Dinner Money Monitor was one of the things Katharine always excelled at, whereas Bea . . .

'Well, she changes around a bit,' said Richard. 'They keep restructuring.'

'Has she worked there long?' asked Suzanne.

'Quite some time,' said Richard. 'How long would you say Bea's worked at the council, darling?'

Katharine chewed joylessly. She attempted to laser Richard into silence but he was in overdrive; his tact sump was empty, he was trying to compensate for her own numbness and also – Katharine dropped him a pitying look – also, he was flirting.

'Well paid?' Suzanne lifted her glass to her lips and sipped. She swallowed meaningfully in Richard's direction.

'I think she gets by,' he said, distracted for a moment by the wine bottle that Paul was waving at him. 'But not, you know . . .'

Katharine watched Suzanne tearing ciabatta then dabbing it in the sauce on her plate. She knew this type, knew what she was up to, on and on with the personal questions, not stopping until she had her subject pinned and spread, all intimacies surrendered. She was nourished by the disasters of others. When other people fell apart, Suzanne felt complete. Katharine looked to Jane for help, but Jane was flailing down the other end of the table, trying to fend off Oscar's interrogation about local schools and house prices. Katharine pushed back her chair and got to her feet.

Suzanne looked up at her and said, 'Jane tells me you're an absolutely brilliant paediatrician and a wonderful mother.'

Katharine sat down again. Richard confirmed that this was true.

'And does your sister have children?'

Katharine shook her head.

Richard cantered to the rescue, sweeping up the wine bottle by the neck on his way. 'But our children adore her. And she's devoted to your mother, isn't she? Keeps in touch and what have you.'

'A maiden aunt. Invaluable,' said Paul. 'I used to have one. They have so much more time and energy.'

'Not married, then?' asked Suzanne.

Richard nodded. 'Oh, yes. To Frank. A writer.'

Oscar pricked up his ears and leaned towards the conversation. 'A writer? Really? Anything I'd have heard of?'

'Some radio plays, I think. *Holby City* every now and again.'

'Ah.' Oscar studied his plate.

'Yes, I'm afraid Frank isn't what you'd call prolific. He's something of a freeloader really, old Frank. Well, we think so, don't we, darling?' said Richard.

Katharine couldn't speak. Something was catching in her throat. Cardamom? Chilli? She took a gulp of water and forced it down. Something sharp was burning. Torn lamb lay on the white plate in a smear of dark gravy. Her eyes watered. This can't be happening, she thought. I can't be about to spew out a mouthful of chewed meat or die of asphyxiation in front of all these people. She coughed, spluttered and knocked over her glass of wine. Her eyes searched out Richard's. He looked appalled.

Jane came towards her with napkins. 'Sorry. Did you get one of the chillies?'

The spasm passed. Katharine opened her eyes and drank some water.

'Sorry.' Her voice sounded small and weak.

Suzanne was shaking her head in faux befuddlement. 'Obviously I know nothing about your sister, but from what I hear . . . sometimes people reach their fifties . . . they take stock of their lives and if it's been a bit . . . *dull* . . .'

The wine worked abruptly on Richard. His face flushed, his mouth widened and he began taking up more space. 'Well,' he said, too loudly, threatening to roar with laughter. 'It would bore the pants off me, working in that office then coming home to bloody Frank every day. He's a grumpy old sod.'

Katharine stood up and said, 'We need to get back.'

Jane was by her side saying, 'I'll get your coat.'

Katharine got herself to the kitchen sink and ran the tap over her hands. They smelt of work despite the fact she hadn't been at work since the day before. No matter how often she washed them she could still smell the chemistry of illness and drugs. To her left, by the knife block, stood the gin bottle. She spun the cap off and poured a measure into a dirty wine glass, knocking it back while the others were apologising, reassuring each other and getting to their feet. She shuddered. It tasted rank and bitter, like stems left too long in a vase.

Cold

A T NINE o'clock the next morning, when CID and Forensics arrived, Frank was still asleep. He had tidied the front room, ignored the Scotch bottle and worked late the night before, hunched over a final printout of *Lupa*. He sat quietly with his back to the open door, a shy hope perched patiently on his shoulder. He had left the door open so he might hear her come in and she would see him labouring there all alone. By two in the morning his throat was sore and he was shivering. By three, he cursed women in general for their lack of concern, drank a large glass of brandy, swallowed the remains of an old bottle of Night Nurse and fell asleep on the couch.

He was woken by long, insistent rings and aggressive hammering on the door. When he finally blinked out into the Saturday morning light, he found two very tall police officers on his doorstep. One of them was holding a piece of paper and speaking the lines about a search warrant. The other one barged into the house and straight through to the kitchen. Out in the street, two more officers were climbing out of a white van.

He was told that a full and exhaustive search of the property was to be carried out as part of their ongoing investigation into the disappearance of his wife. It was suggested that he might find it more convenient to vacate the premises for the duration of the search. He was also informed that they would be removing his vehicle and computer for forensic examination. Blue and white tape was wound between the gateposts and a tow-truck pulled up outside. A small crowd gathered in the street. Nesrine watched from her upstairs window.

Frank had pulled on his coat to cover himself before opening the door. The weight of the parcel still in the coat pocket rested lightly against his thigh. It would be best to let it stay there, he thought. He indicated his naked legs beneath the coat and said he wasn't dressed yet, and the officer said, 'That's easily remedied,' and escorted him upstairs.

From the children's room, where he was dressing, Frank could hear something heavy being dragged through the hall. Out in the back garden, two men were climbing into white body suits. He heard a dog bark and van doors slamming. It's a bloody liberty treating a man this way, he thought. Anyone would think he was a suspect. The whole thing was an outrage.

The phone rang.

'Can you hear me? Frank? Frank, can you hear me?'

It was his father, Lance. Something was going on and he didn't understand. The police had just rung him, for goodness' sake. They had asked all kinds of questions, unpleasant questions, questions he wasn't too sure how to answer. At first he wondered whether it wasn't the police at all but the press; perhaps one of Frank's plays was going to be on the television. But no, it was the police and they wanted to know whether Frank had an interest in clubs and videos of an adult nature, whether Frank had, to his knowledge, ever visited a prostitute, been involved in swinging at all, got into trouble as a boy, and how relations were with his wife.

Frank looked down at his yellowing toenails that were becoming impossible to cut and tried to get a word in edge-ways. He said, 'Calm down, Dad,' and 'I'll be round to your place in half an hour and take you down the pub for lunch,' but Lance wanted to know what on earth was going on; it was a shock and he didn't know what to think. He said he sometimes wished he had never moved down to Cambridge. It wasn't as if he saw Frank very much and he might as well have stopped in Burnley for all the difference it made. Lance often said this. It was one of the few things that he and Frank agreed about.

The walk to the pub with Lance took longer than Frank expected. His fingertips caressed the packet while he walked at a snail's pace beside his father. It was a while since he had seen his father because Bea usually popped in on him most weeks; his sheltered housing accommodation was on her way back from work. But something seemed to have happened to the old man in the few weeks since Frank had seen him last. He shuffled stiffly at an angle that threatened to tip him forwards on to his face. Every few moments he stopped dead and turned to look back the way they had come. Then he would start with the infuriating questions again: The police? In your house? What, now? Searching? Searching for what? By the time they were in sight of the pub, Frank began to think that time had ceased and gone into reverse. It reminded him of walking with Adrian and Laura when they were toddlers, not a stage he had a natural affinity for and one that he'd avoided as much as he could. All those whats and whys, all that stopping and looking; it completely clogged up his narrative drive.

'So did you have a tiff or what?' Lance asked when they were seated in the pub. They were going to have a coffee and then maybe an early lunch, although Lance said the last time he'd been here he'd had a crab and egg sandwich, then been up half the night with a funny tummy.

At Lance's request they had chosen a table near the toilets, and once the coffees were brought over, and then a couple of Scotches and two pints of bitter, he let Frank get a word in. Frank explained that the police were searching for evidence. Evidence of what? Frank shrugged. Evidence of Bea, he supposed. Well do they think she's been kidnapped? asked Lance. Frank said this might be a possibility. There came a point in conversations with Lance when it was easier to answer in the affirmative because negatives merely provoked supplementary questions and requests for clarification. Lance shook his head and said he was confused. Had something untoward happened to Bea? She hadn't said anything when she brought his shopping round last week. Frank was aware of the barman listening and wished his father would lower his voice. He tried to steer the conversation towards more familiar ground by saying he hoped the police didn't damage the front garden or the patio.

'Ah, patios,' said Lance. 'They're like wallpaper. Hide a multitude of sins.' Lance had always enjoyed a bit of DIY. 'Did a patio for a chap up Skipton way once. Foxes kept digging up the family pets. He had two dogs, a cat, quite a few rabbits, a gerbil and a fish out there. Well, you can imagine. Put a patio down and problem solved. And somewhere nice to sit in the summer. It was that patio, come to think of it, where I broke my foot . . .'

I am drinking Teachers whisky and Kenco coffee with my father in an empty pub on a Saturday morning, thought Frank. He looked at their feet facing each other on the carpet and worried that *Lupa* had inner conflict and outer conflict but did it have personal conflict? He was not so sure any more. Perhaps he should leave it for a while and make a start on *Close and Personal*. He watched his father's mouth working away on the words and the whisky and sighed. People took up so much *time*.

'I said to myself, if I don't get out of this blinking hospital right away they'll have to carry me out in a box. So I goes up to the nurse and I says, "I need me clothes back, I've got work to do, where are they?" Well you know what they're like. Half of them can't speak English. I said to her, "You know my son would find this highly amusing." Then I said, "He's an acclaimed writer and one-time photographer on the *Oriana*." Well that made her listen up. "What's his name?" she said . . .'

Two plates of ham and eggs arrived at their table and Lance stopped talking.

What if this is the future? thought Frank, looking around for the sauce bottles. What if this is the final act? A stained carpet, the smell of stale beer and listening to his dad in a chilly pub? Had this moment been waiting in the wings all through these last few years that he and Bea had spent together? Had it poked him in the ribs those mornings he'd turned over and pretended to go back to sleep? Those mornings lately when Bea had stretched a clammy hand towards him in bed? He inched away from Lance, who had pierced the yolk and was wiping a chip through the dreadful gelatinous flood that bled towards the pineapple ring. He shuddered. There was a draught coming through the windowpane behind his chair and his neck was going into spasm. A cold shoulder, that was what he had been to Bea lately, he knew. He squirted brown sauce on to his plate and nodded. Lance paused in his eating and gestured at the bottle with his knife. Frank squirted Lance's plate too and wondered briefly whether the old man had been feeding himself properly. He was wolfing the food down like he hadn't eaten in a week. Frank swallowed a mouthful of chips and had a dismaying thought. What if the police came across the photos of Wanda that he kept among his vinyl collection? Lance had his head on one side and was pointing with his fork. He was saying that sometimes, in a marriage, sometimes patience and forgiveness was what was needed and it might be necessary to swallow your pride and—Frank shied away from the father-and-son chat he saw plodding towards him and caught the barman's attention. 'Yes, I know,' he said. And to the barman he called,

'Same again.' His father's eyes were shining and watery and something was tugging at the corners of Frank's mouth, so he pushed his plate away angrily and said that Bea hadn't been herself since before the summer. She had changed, and not just on the outside. Lance looked at him, and Frank added that it had been a difficult few months, that Bea had wanted a holiday somewhere hot but he couldn't possibly go because he had too much work on and she had spent all her spare cash on the bloody garden. There was the patio, endless new shrubs and climbers, herbs for this and that and the other. Her latest plan was a pond, yes, a pond if you don't mind, as if there wasn't enough water around the place already.

They were silent for a while. Frank frowned. It was becoming difficult to think clearly. Had he shut the door on her. Had he wanted her to beg? To beg him to stop? Do you surrender? *Do you surrender?*

'Pardon?' His father looked at him, glass half raised to his mouth.

'Do you want another drink?' said Frank, pushing away his half-finished food.

Lance wiped his mouth and shook his head. 'I wouldn't mind some of those chips, though.' He pulled Frank's plate towards him. 'Whatever you've done, son, go and make it up with her. A man's no good on his own. A man needs a woman around the place. Do you know, not a day goes by when I don't miss your mother.' Lance was getting teary. Frank glared at the barman. 'A man's no good on his own and that's a fact. I always thought I would find someone else because I know that's what your mother would have wanted, but when it came down to it I just didn't have the heart . . .'

Frank closed his eyes and stopped listening. A wave of nausea crept over him, which could have been the eggs and could have been the thought of Bea with her old flame, Patrick. Patrick the Prick, as Frank liked to call him. He had never been entirely sure that it was over between them; after all, they worked in the same building. He had met Patrick once at one of Bea's work do's. It was the first and the last such event that he attended. She had introduced them. Patrick was tall and gangly, with an effeminate taste in shirts. He had stooped elaborately to shake Frank's hand, pumped his arm up and down and asked how the writing was going. Needless to say, by the time Frank composed a reply to this, someone else had swooped over to request the Chief Executive's attention.

'What's the betting she'll turn up at the weekend, Frank, cheerful as you like, telling you she's been to see a friend down Hastings way or some such?'

Frank remembered Katharine had told him she was going to look in Hastings. Katharine had taken over, of course. Barging in as soon as she got the phone call. He was surprised she'd found the time, and she didn't have the kids with her, which was a rarity in itself. Got on the phone to Bea's mother. Got the poor woman all worked up and then told her not to worry. Typical. That's a bedside manner for you. Must be scary coming round from an operation and finding Katharine by your bed with a clipboard, equine face all angles and bone, blood counts and bleeds and secondary spreads, no nonsense, telling you like it is through twisted teeth . . .

Lance rose, getting unsteadily to his feet. He needed the toilet. Frank got up and helped to shuffle him in. Then he waited and shuffled him out again.

Lance said, 'Shall we take a wander then? See whether they're done yet?'

'I'll go, Dad. You stay here.'

But Lance would not sit down. He gripped Frank's arm. 'What do I want sitting in here all on me tod?'

There was no way they could walk back. Frank looked over to the barman.

'Can you call us a cab? It's my dad. He's not been himself lately.'

Tender

FRANK FELT it before he saw it. The front door had a melancholy look and the hairs rose on the back of his neck. Inside, the hallway smelt of polythene and dust. Lance hovered on the doormat saying, 'Have they gone, then?' while Frank looked tentatively in at the downstairs rooms. Every object, all Bea's plates and jugs and bowls and figurines, had been taken from its place and put back awry; shelves gaped empty or half stacked with their contents the wrong way round; cupboard doors hung open and the computer was gone. CD cases were open and strewn across the floor; furniture was moved from the walls; rugs and carpets had been dragged askew and the floorboards bore the marks of a crowbar and hammer.

Feeling old and ashamed, Frank climbed the stairs. In the bedroom, in the children's room, even in the bathroom, the same wreckage. He sank on to their double bed and tried to draw breath. Something in here was odd though, surely. He looked about him, at the carelessly repacked plastic bags, the disturbed drawers and wardrobe, at the dust balls exposed where the bed was dragged away from the wall. Then he saw them. Her egg cups lined up, precisely spaced as always, apparently untouched and watching him in silent reproach. He heard Lance calling from the kitchen.

Outside, they stood in the sand and cement where the patio had been and stared at the ruin of her garden. The lawn looked like a vandalised graveyard with its split turf, dug pits and dislodged paving stones. Clumps of ivy had been ripped up and piled up. A thrush hopped in the fresh soil, stabbing at grubs and worms. Someone had tried to replant her magnolia sapling but it leaned half in and half out of the soil, delicate twigs already drooping. Her shrubs were uprooted and the border plants, which she had begun to carefully prune and mulch to protect them from frost, lay with their roots and tubers exposed. Tender? Was that what she called them, the ones that needed covering for the winter? Those dark red ones with tips like asparagus that she wrapped in black plastic and bound with twine? He heard Lance say he needed a sit-down, he saw the drenched corpse of the squirrel still in its cage and he wondered what Adrian had been told. Abruptly he turned and marched into the kitchen.

Lance sat at the kitchen table, hands spread out before him.

'Come on, Dad,' Frank said, voice gruff as he slopped water over a tea bag in a mug. 'Don't start. It's routine police semi-boiled procedural stuff.'

'I don't know about that, son.'

'Here, drink this.'

Lance looked dubiously at the cup filled to the brim with grey liquid. He shook his head.

'I think I need a lie-down, Frank. It's the beer.'

'Come on, Dad.' Frank took the old man's arm in a clumsy gesture of tenderness. 'You can kip on the couch downstairs.'

WHEN FRANK woke up a few hours later, he went down to the kitchen to find Wanda snapping on a pair of yellow rubber gloves. She turned on the tap so that water gushed at full force, spraying the tiles and plate rack. She squeezed washing-up liquid into the bowl, spun the tap to off and said, 'We'll soon have this place back the way it was. Then when Bea gets back, it will look lovely.'

Frank wondered whether she had misunderstood. 'Bea has disappeared, Wanda.'

She tossed a laugh up at the ceiling and he wanted to hit her. 'She will be back. It's Saturday afternoon. Next Wednesday is her mother's birthday. She wouldn't miss that.'

'How the hell do you know that?' The woman had no boundaries whatsoever.

'She's having a break. And I don't blame her. At least now I will get a chance to clean that front room of yours!'

He watched her hoist the vacuum cleaner out of the broom cupboard and lift a bucket of sprays and dusters with her other hand. She looked at the mess they had made of Bea's ceramics and tutted to herself. Piles of painted china littered the floor and kitchen table. Under the rocking chair lay the family of Portuguese donkeys in white clay. One had lost its head, others their legs.

'They are bastards to do this,' announced Wanda quietly.

'You'd better go,' he told her gruffly, hoping that she wouldn't leave without clearing up. There was something improper in her being here, even he could see that. He didn't want her here if the police came sniffing round again. Did the police interview cleaners in such cases? he wondered. Somehow it seemed unlikely.

'Don't be ridiculous!' Wanda strode out into the hall, banging the bucket as she did so. 'What if she comes back and it's like this? She'll run away again.'

With Lance in the front room and Wanda roaming the house, Frank wanted very much to be alone; or rather he wanted to be here without Wanda so as to be able to think clearly about being here without Bea.

'Oh my G-o-d,' sang Wanda. 'What have they done to her garden?'

Frank ignored her and went into the front room, where

he sat on the edge of the couch next to Lance's motionless form. He winced at the sight of Chekhov with a pair of Wanda's tights tied like a bandanna round his head. Some joker from CID, no doubt. He noticed his camera on the coffee table, the memory card removed. Well, it wasn't illegal to take photographs of naked women if you were a photographer, was it? He got up and peered at the bookcase, where a stack of records still lay on the shelf. Perhaps the search had been a rushed job, a careless job, designed to intimidate more than anything else. He looked inside the sleeve of *Tubular Bells*. The photos of Wanda were still there. It wouldn't do for the police to find these. That would make everything so much more complicated.

He lifted out the photographs, a cool handful of slippery gloss. There was Wanda face down across the couch, Wanda astride the chair, Wanda bent backwards over the coffee table. One by one he held them over the metal waste-paper bin and snapped a lighter at their corner. He watched the jaundiced flame climb up each print, watched it darken, flare and curl before dropping it, a stinking, sooty mass, into the bin.

'Whatever are you doing, Frank?' asked a voice from the duvet.

'I am disabling one of Adrian's pyrotechnic devices,' said Frank, impressed, as always at his ability to dissemble.

'Adrian?' Lance poked his face out above the duvet. 'Is he here?'

Frank picked up the chess box and began laying out the pieces.

'I'll give you a game,' said Lance.

Frank nodded and wondered whether he would see Adrian again.

'Okay, Dad, yes. That'd be nice.'

Stairs

W HEN ADRIAN opened his bedroom door late that
Saturday night, he found Laura sitting on the top
step, knees drawn up to her chin, head cocked in the direction of the kitchen door. She slid him a look as he sat
silently on the step below her and pressed his forehead
against the banisters. The voices of their parents drifted up
towards them, rising and falling as they moved about the
kitchen. Laura sniffed the air. Cigarette smoke lingered
high up near the ceiling. Smoking was taboo in their house,
but on rare occasions, in that extraordinary way that only
parents are allowed, Katharine broke her own law. Distress
signals was how Adrian thought of his mother's smoking
transgressions. The sour, hopeless scent of burnt tobacco
in the house meant that things were slipping beyond the
manageable.

Adrian felt Laura's eyes on the side of his head and he
looked up at her. She had the schoolgirl's demonic ability to
stare unblinking at a foe until they withered or turned to
stone. He opened his mouth to speak, to say that it didn't
look like they were going to new schools on Monday after
all, but she intensified her stare and his words died on his
tongue. Katharine's voice, jangled with wine and worry,
reached them clearly.

'I'm not sure I want the children alone with that man right now, Richard.'

The chair creaked and they heard the cat meow once.

'Well that seems rather harsh in the circumstances, darling. He could have them tomorrow while we go to Hastings.'

'No, I'll go on Monday while they're at school. We do not need to bring Frank into this.'

They heard a cigarette packet flipped open, then the flare of a match. A chair was pushed back suddenly as she got to her feet. Both children prepared themselves for flight, but the doorway remained empty except for the cat, which came and sat and looked up at them.

'But the man must be in torment.' Their father's voice again.

'Would you *please* stop being so damned reasonable!' Something clattered on the table. 'Every time I ring Frank they've dug up his garden or they've searched his house again. What do you think they're looking for? Buried treasure?'

'But they've also searched the river and the common. They're just doing their job.'

They heard the clink of a bottle and the slide of a glass across the table. Laura put her lips to her knees and licked. Her mother would smell rank and stale in the morning and she would have a mood to match. Their father's voice burred indistinctly. They heard 'police procedure' and 'leave no stone unturned', which prompted a 'Christ, Richard!'

The cat meowed up at them.

'If they thought he was a suspect they would arrest him, Katharine. *Do* be reasonable.'

Adrian winced and looked down at his toes. They waited for the explosion.

'For *fuck's* sake!' Katharine's voice was shredded with alcohol and fear. The cat scuttled down the hall and into the front room. Something between a grimace and a smile visited

Laura's face and she clasped her hands at her chin, curling in on herself. There were no more words, but they heard their father get to his feet. He would be holding her now, pressing her head to his chest.

His voice was gentle. 'We have to keep things in perspective. For all his faults, Frank really does not have it in him to . . .'

Katharine was crying now and her words were gulped and swallowed like a child's. Laura started to stand. She punched Adrian hard between the shoulder blades with her fist. He didn't respond.

'I mean, think about it, darling, the man's lost his wife . . .'

The chair scraped again and fell with a clatter to the floor.

'Well he should have taken more care of her!'

'Katharine!'

But she was already below them in the hall, bumping against the wall, footsteps heavy and uneven.

Both children scrambled up and out of sight before she reached the bottom of the stairs, but not before Richard came to the doorway, looked up and spotted their feet darting like startled fish round the turn on the landing. He sighed and looked back at the debris on the kitchen table. *In pectore robur.* He collected up their wine glasses, the ashtray, Katharine's cigarette packet and matches. He wiped down the tabletop and rinsed the glasses out in the sink. He heard Katharine blundering into furniture and doors above his head. He hesitated by the dining-room window and heard, but could not see, the branches of the trees tossing in the strong October winds. One of these days a tree was going to come crashing down. He looked up at the sky for a moon, but there was no trace of one tonight.

Sometimes he wondered what it would have been like to stay a while longer in the pale sheath of grief that Katharine lifted him from sixteen years ago. Sometimes, with difficulty, he remembered the tenderness of Sophie, her head on his chest or her fingers at his mouth. Sometimes he wondered about another life, Hong Kong, Singapore, New York, and the wife and the children he might have had there. But mostly – he persuaded the cat out of the cat flap with his foot and switched off the kitchen light – mostly he performed the tasks expected of him; and he gave the rear end of the cat, for it had hesitated halfway through the cat flap, a firm shove with the toe of his shoe.

Fair

FRANK OPENED the front door on Sunday morning to find Adrian standing there, just dangling there in that way that he did, his face white against the flames of his hair. He could have kissed him.

Adrian did kiss him. A cheese-and-onion-flavoured peck on the cheek. He said, 'Hello, Frank. I think we know each other well enough now to do that.'

Frank stepped out into the front garden. He didn't want Adrian seeing the house right now. It was in a state. He'd had a bit of a night.

'What are you doing here?'

'Mum and Dad have gone to the Salvation Army – they find missing people as well as playing carols at Christmas – and Laura's making a YouTube Missing video.' He squinted up at the sky, a gentle pearly grey with occasional flickers of sunlight.

Frank looked up the road. 'I'm not sure that your parents want you here.'

'Yes, but that's not fair.'

Adrian was jumping, both feet together for maximum effort, up on to and down off the step. Ah yes, fairness, thought Frank. That rare and quaint concept beloved by children and eroded by adults and experience. Adrian told Frank, panting, and in rhythm to the jumps, that the move to London was postponed, that they weren't leaving school after all, and that he thought Frank should come for a walk with him because he shouldn't neglect his health given his age and circumstances.

'Did anyone find Bea's passport?' panted Adrian.

Frank shook his head and confessed he had no idea where she kept things like that.

'That's good then. It means she's gone away somewhere.' Adrian stopped jumping and nudged Frank down the path and out of the gate. 'Come on.'

'Where to?'

'A step to Stir-Bitch Fair?'

'I beg your pardon?'

He followed Adrian down the street to the common and the river. A few feet before the cattle grid where the common began, Adrian took a sudden run at it and leapt across, mooing loudly. He waited for Frank on the other side and pointed to a National Waterways sign that said 'Stourbridge Common'.

'Stir-Bitch. It's what Stourbridge used to be called. Site of the largest fair in Europe once upon a time. Isaac Newton came here. Everyone did.' Adrian patted his man-bag, something that Frank was quite certain he would never wear himself, and added, '*The Pilgrim's Progress*. It's all in there.'

Stir-Bitch, thought Frank as he fell into step beside Adrian. Stir-Bitch indeed: Katharine, Wanda, Precious, Richard too probably. Even Bea, damn her, creating all this upheaval. And very little progress, when all was said and done.

'They used to sell everything here,' said Adrian casting an expansive arm around the grass and hedgerows. He flicked through the pages of the book he pulled from his bag until he found a place he had marked. '. . . titles, kingdoms, lusts, pleasures . . .'

Frank let the boy drone on. He felt a good deal stupider than he suspected he looked today and found the dank river smell that pervaded everything faintly nauseous. It was no doubt a fitting flavouring to the unfolding nightmare of his days.

'. . . whores, bawds, blood, bodies, souls, silver, precious stones . . .' continued Adrian, reading from the book.

The last time he had slept, proper easeful sleep, it seemed to him, was in the moments before the phone call from Precious five days ago. Other than the bloody police, only Lance had been near him these last few days.

'Also, if you wanted juggling, cheats, fools, apes, knaves and rogues . . . then this was the place to come.'

Frank felt a momentary breathlessness looking at the path ahead and the sense of the past and the present and Adrian walking into the future without him and how Bea had loved this walk and all the times he had let her do it alone. He quickened his pace, afraid that Adrian would stop his recital and look at him. The boy was already taller than him, not so much a growth spurt as a fountain or geyser. It showed no signs of stopping, just as there seemed no limit to the space inside his head from where information and words and ideas seemed to gush. Physics, chemistry, history, the stars – everything, even literature now, for heaven's sake, Adrian was overtaking him, while Frank felt he himself wasn't learning anything new. Frank rubbed his head and nodded. He straightened his spine and tried to breathe. It was a daily struggle to hang on to what he had in there already.

'And not forgetting thefts, murders, adulteries, false-swearers . . . Are you all right, Frank?'

They were opposite the mustard-coloured Penny Ferry pub, which stood across the river. Ahead of them were ditches and patches of brambles and hawthorn. Scruffy piebald ponies dotted distant fields.

'We should go back.' Frank was abrupt. He suddenly felt uneasy being out here with Katharine's son. 'Where do your parents think you are?'

'Oh, I've gone to buy trainers. These ones hurt my feet.'

A train flew along the track that bordered the far meadow, clanging across the old ironwork bridge up ahead. A chill breeze cut through his jumper and the sky had a bruised and purplish look. Frank pulled at the thin beige machine knit. Today's jumpers were no good for keeping out the wind. What he needed was a home-knitted one. Bea had laughed with him at the Fair Isle tank-top Margaret knitted him that first Christmas. Both were reminded of the jumpers of childhood, the fierceness of knitted care in cable and moss stitch, the way they twisted and rucked at throats and under-arms, the purl and the plain, the drop one and knit one. God knows where that tank-top was now. It had vanished somewhere down the years. He remembered it had beautiful colours and shivered. It was nearly November and he ought to have worn his coat. Bea hated the winter. He was fairly sure that what Bea liked best was the light and the sun. He stopped and looked at Adrian, who wore no coat and no jacket, just a T-shirt.

'Bunyan,' said Adrian, tapping his book.

Frank doubted the boy had a bunion, at his age, but who knew what went on inside the footwear of the youth of today?

'John Bunyan. He wrote *A Step to Stir-Bitch Fair.*'

Adrian passed Frank the book and stared hard at a cyclist approaching from the far side of the common. He thought of the hundreds of fairs this common had seen, held his breath and looked hard to eliminate the cyclist, the newly planted trees, the women with buggies and dogs. He tried to conjure the noise and the smell and the crush of people in 1665, tried to pick out the curling grey hair and long nose of Isaac Newton, and wondered whether if he could just find the spot, the very exact spot, where Newton bought the prism he used to show that light is made up of many colours, then—

'Perhaps we should go back,' said Frank. He didn't like it here, the interminable, flat horizon. It felt hopeless.

They were at a small footbridge that crossed the ditch into Ditton Meadows. The ditch was choked with brambles where shrivelled blackberries still clung to some of the stems. Something scuttled in the dense, dying undergrowth. Adrian hopped across the bridge.

'Let's go on to Fleam Dyke. Bea liked it there,' he called back across his shoulder. 'And then we have to buy my trainers.'

Exit

KATHARINE HURRIED through the underground car park, unlocked her car from twenty paces, threw in her briefcase, coat and handbag, slammed the door and started the engine, reversing at speed into the path of an oncoming Mercedes, which braked hard, tyres squealing and horn blaring. Seatbelt warning light bonging, Katharine threw the car into drive and went forward into the parking space again. Cursing, she checked the rearview mirror, saw the coast was clear and put her foot on the accelerator. The car leapt and surged forward, hitting the car parked ahead of it with a sickening force and the crash and splinter of breaking glass. Stunned by the violence, for a moment Katharine did nothing. Then she got out and looked about her. No one was around. She went to the front of the car and was surprised to find not a scratch on her machine; the cow bars had absorbed the impact. Glass crunched underfoot and her eyes skimmed the damage to the Daimler in front of her. The headlight had gone for sure; perhaps there was damage to the bonnet too, it was hard to tell in the gloom. She wavered for a moment, wondering whether she should leave a note on the windscreen with her number, but a Daimler, for God's sake: the cost was likely to be wildly out of proportion to the damage. By the time she had told herself it was akin to leaving a blank cheque on the windscreen of a total stranger, she was back in the car and in search of the exit.

She drove in circles, up and down the narrow, low-ceilinged concrete vault, eventually coming to a ramp that pitched down sharply at a T-junction. EXIT LEFT. Terror reared up in her and she braked violently. A few feet in front of her the concrete floor vanished in an abruptly sheer drop into darkness, like the surface of an underground lake. She gripped the steering wheel and leaned forward, heart hammering at her ribcage. What she was looking at was the glassy surface of water that had flooded and filled the dip between two ramps. She glanced up. The shallow water was reflecting the angles of the concrete roof and had given the illusion of a drop. Reluctantly, she inched the car forwards, sitting high up in the seat, half expecting the lurch and fall into darkness.

Shaken, Katharine drove nervously, the world suddenly a fearful and unfamiliar place where disaster waited to ambush her at every turn. And now, in addition to the Bea-shaped void that obscured her vision, she was aware of a lumpen figure in yellow, herself in pigtails aged eleven, first in the queue to go out to play, turning her back on Bea sitting alone in the dinner hall, hands on her head before an uneaten plate of fish and beetroot. She checked the mirror and accelerated, an ugly sense of her own badness lurking at the back of her head. She pressed the central locking, checked her speed and relaxed into the leather embrace of the driving seat. Career, Children, House, John Lewis, Missing Sister, Mother, Hastings. She could handle this.

It was Monday morning. She had got up early, long before the children or Richard, and had driven to London to get things in order at the hospital before dashing into John Lewis for curtains, carpets, sofas, wardrobes for their new house. Now she was en route to Hastings, where she would find Bea before returning to Cambridge late that night. The drive to Hastings could be done in just over two hours if she pushed it and was lucky with the traffic. At least it could last time she went, which was a few years ago, because, really, all four of them traipsing down to Hastings for the day was rather impractical when it came down to it. It worked much better when her mother came up and stayed with them. And anyway, Bea visited once a month because Bea had the time.

Katharine found herself a few feet from the bumper of a Renault that didn't understand that the middle lane was not for cruising at sixty-five; it was for overtaking. She flashed her lights and pulled out, glaring at the driver dithering at the wheel of the other car. The Salvation Army woman was full of statistics. She said that the average age of persons sought was forty-eight years; that the department's success rate was eighty-five per cent, which was about ten reunions a day; and that a record reunion took place in 1999 between sisters who had not seen each other for eighty-three years. Katharine jiggled her shoulders and tried to relax her jaw. How people could be as careless as that was beyond her, frankly, but still, these numbers reassured her. It was going to be all right. The Salvation Army were on the case and prayers were being said for Bea. Yes, prayers! Bea would probably laugh at that and it had made Katharine feel a bit odd, but Richard was all for it. It always amused her to be reminded of Richard's faith. She thought of it in the same way as his school motto that he was so fond of quoting. Arcane and completely irrelevant. Still, they had quite liked Major Whatever-her-name-was. At least she had until they got up to leave, when the question of a fee for the Family Tracing Service was mentioned and then the suggestion about donations. It was absurd in her opinion, although of course Richard went overboard and wrote out a cheque, then a monthly tax-free pledge for God knows how much. And she hadn't liked the last thing the Major had said to her as they left. 'Please remember,' she said, 'that although we have an eighty-five per cent success rate, it's not always a happy ending.' Patronising, thought Katharine. That was the trouble with religion.

And Missing People, the other organisation devoted to the thousands of the lost, were on the case too. From what she could tell from their website and from Hazel, the woman she had spoken to on the phone, they seemed to have all kinds of contacts and means of obtaining information that even the police didn't have. The police, it turned out, could not even get information from a GP if the GP chose not to give it. But Hazel was very warm and reassuring. In all likelihood Bea had simply done a runner, would at some point pitch up in Hastings, and after a chat and a cup of tea and a bit of chivvying along would come back to Cambridge and they could all get on with their lives happily as before.

Katharine imagined a sisterly reunion as she drove. The door would be opened by her mother, a look of mild surprise on her face. In the kitchen, she would see the expanse of sea through the window, moiled and grey, the photos on the windowledge: her parents' wedding, her own wedding to Richard, and a faded photo of the two of them with their father on the cliffs at Fairlight, the wind snatching at their hair and skirts. And round the corner, sitting at the scratched Formica table, would be Bea, her hand in her hair, that rueful look on her face. The kitchen would smell of pie and tea and she would go over and hug her and say, 'Oh, Bea.' No need for questions or explanations.

The next road sign that hurtled past informed her that the turnoff to the A21, the Hastings road, was in a hundred metres. She checked her rearview mirror and knew she couldn't make it, and sailed on in the fast lane of the M25 headed west.

Damn! A whole new section of motorway appeared to have been built since she last drove down here.

House

'JUST IN case.'

That's why Richard was working at home for the day. He hadn't pressed Katharine with just in case *what* exactly. Presumably she had some idea that Bea might turn up or call or that the police might come by. She felt that the house should be occupied while she looked for her sister in Hastings. And so Richard had spent the day working from home, which he never normally did, and had found the experience something of a challenge. With no meetings, no lunches, no Claudia to pass on messages, calls, appointments and reminders, his day was alarmingly formless. He kept checking his phone for calls and emails but there were none. He had printed out hundreds of pages of documentation but had not been able to concentrate sufficiently to make head or tail of them. He wandered for the hundredth time into the kitchen and gazed out into the garden, which was looking a little neglected what with one thing and another. The children's climbing frame, unused for years now, looked ugly and the grass beneath the apple trees was littered with rotting fruit. The cleaner was vacuuming upstairs somewhere and half their belongings had been packed into boxes. He thought wistfully of the marble and glass of his office in Canary Wharf, the view of the Thames from his window; he thought of his desk of chrome and leather, which must look abandoned like the bridge of a ship. Several times during the day he rang Claudia, his secretary.

'Richard here.'

'Oh, good morning, Richard. Any news?'

'No, I'm just manning the phone, so to speak, at this end.'

'Of course.'

'Everything going to plan?'

'Oh absolutely. I'm at your desk now as a matter of fact. I've rescheduled Tokyo and Louise is meeting with Bonn.'

'Right. Shouldn't we cancel and set up another?'

'We did suggest but they have Mergers and Acquisitions all next week and wish to put things in place well ahead of time.'

'Accounts have done their homework, I presume?'

'Oh yes, I have it all here. They've done an excellent job as usual.'

'And will Legal be present?'

'Yes, Legal, Accounts and Marketing will be there.'

'Oh, good. Good.'

There was a pause.

'Shall I call you after the meeting, Richard?'

'Yes, yes, do. Unless you think we should set up a conference call.'

'We could do that, but . . .'

'Too late to synchronise all the others, I suppose.'

'A little late, yes, but if you would like . . .'

'No, no, no, I'm sure it'll be fine.'

'Don't worry. It will.'

There was another pause in which Richard could just hear the drone of a helicopter approaching and the ping of the lift that opened directly on to Claudia's office. He heard her clear her throat.

'Was there anything else, Richard?'

'Er, no, I don't think so.'

'Well, I'd better get off to the fourteenth floor then.'

'Oh, there was one thing.'

'Yes?'

'Who's chairing the meeting?'

He heard the bong of her computer saving a document.

'I'm chairing and Louise is doing the presentation.'

'Oh. Right. Yes. Excellent.' The cat came and sat at his feet and stared up at him. What in heaven's name could it want? 'Get back to me when you can.'

The cat followed him around and mewed continuously. Richard looked at the list of things Katharine had left for him to do. There was nothing about the cat. He trawled the various missing persons internet sites and he phoned Jim and Pete at the police station. He wandered round the house, half of which was packed up in boxes and the other half of which was on hold until the business with Bea was sorted out. He checked with their solicitors that the vendors in Chiswick hadn't taken fright at the delay. He looked out at the garden and tried to remember why they were uprooting themselves. He liked coming home to this place. He liked the commute, the Docklands Light Railway to King's Cross, the train to Cambridge, the taxi home. It barely took an hour and it was like a series of debriefings or airlocks that allowed him to reacclimatise on re-entry to domestic life.

He had got in a muddle in the morning about school uniform as it was the first time he had been in the house on a school day when the children left. Usually he was out by six thirty and the house was still sleeping. He had some memory that Laura was supposed to wear a tie, but this she denied. He was also not convinced that the odd way she had rolled the waistband of her skirt over and over so that it sat on her hip bones and ended barely below her bottom, nor the way she had tied her shirt in a knot above her navel was adhering strictly to school rules, but Laura told him it was fine, and anyway his daughter was a mystery to him; that he was prepared to admit to anyone who cared to ask. It's just a stage, Katharine kept saying, but there were no stages in his own childhood for himself or his siblings that involved rudeness and the vast consumption of chocolate and American television shows. He thanked the Lord that Adrian was a gentle giant, a gentle genius by all accounts. There had been times, when the boy was little and slept with that rare stillness peculiar to children, when he entertained the extraordinary notion that in Adrian resided the spirit of Sophie.

Richard tripped on something in the darkened hallway and looked down to see Laura's coat. She must have left it behind in the rush to leave the house. He picked it up and hung it neatly on a peg by the front door. When she had finally left for school that morning it was half an hour after Adrian because she was waiting for Chanel to knock. Even then he had to call her back because she had forgotten her school bag and her lunch, which Katharine had made for her the night before. He had stuffed the lunchbox in the bag and dashed down the road after them, calling Laura's name and waving the bag above his head like a rugby ball. Laura had screamed back at him from the other side of the road: 'I don't need it, Dad! I don't need it on a Monday!'

When he went back inside and looked properly in her school bag he found it was completely empty. Katharine was right. Laura probably did need to attend a school where the Protestant work ethic was not a cause for embarrassment. Adrian, bless him, probably needed to attend a university. Yes, Richard's and Katharine's genes had merged to form a powerful conglomerate in Adrian's DNA but something had gone awry where Laura was concerned. He unwrapped Laura's lunch and began to eat the evidence. Hummus and cucumber. Not bad. Laura perhaps had received a little too much of whatever Bea had in her chromosomes, a lack of application and cerebral fission, which, when combined with Katharine's fierce determination, made for a volatile mix. He started on the rice cakes with honey, which were dry but not unpleasant. Still, he thought, giving the cat a series of encouraging small kicks away from his clean trousers, no doubt she would turn out all right in the end. He swallowed hard. Although endings, as he knew well enough, were not necessarily something to be hoped for, much less the ever or the after that came with them.

Flat

TAMARISK STEPS in Hastings was steeper and narrower than Katharine remembered, and she had to get her breath back at the top before she knocked on her mother's door. When there was no answer, she let herself in with her key. She found Margaret standing in the hallway dressed in a fluffy lemon dressing gown and a pair of gold slippers. She looked smaller than the last time Katharine had seen her. The flat smelled of bleach.

'Hello, Mum.'

'Katharine?'

Katharine gave her a kiss and looked in the sitting room. The flat was tiny. How could a person survive in such a confined space?

Margaret felt annoyed. She so wished the children would phone before they turned up. Now here she was, looking a fright, no doubt, and they'd be fussing and telling her she had to decide about things. She knew perfectly well what they thought. They thought she was losing her marbles. Well the fact was, she was merely giving them away. She had far too many in the first place. It was a blessed relief to be rid of some of them.

'This is a surprise.'

Katharine ignored the *froideur* and went into the kitchen to make tea.

'I tried to ring you,' she said. 'Is there something wrong with the phone?'

Margaret shuffled back down the hall and closed her bedroom door. She didn't want anyone prying in there. So what did this one want now? Something about the birthday, probably.

'Is it today?' Margaret said, standing at the kitchen table.

'Is what today?'

Oh here we go, round and round. Why couldn't people just be straight with her? She was so terribly tired of all this nonsense.

'My birthday.'

She had written it down somewhere because Bea had told her to. Where exactly she had written it escaped her right now. Katharine was washing two cups under the tap. She kept rubbing round and round them with the spongy thing, peering inside and then back under the blessed tap again. If her birthday party was today then that was just too bad. She would have to give it a miss. She wasn't going to any party without a visit to the hairdresser.

'But we cancelled your birthday, Mum. You asked us to. Just till we find Bea. I've come down in case she's popped in to see you.'

'Well of course she did. She was here yesterday . . . was it yesterday? No, it was last week sometime. She was with her coloured friend.'

Katharine put down the cups.

'Thank God. Oh, thank God.' She cursed herself for not coming earlier.

It was all going to be all right. They would celebrate with a wonderful party, all of them, down here. Why not? Wanda could help. Perhaps Wanda and her friend could even come and decorate the flat. They'd make it a party to remember. And they would sort out some sort of arrangement to look after Mum. Perhaps Wanda might like a different sort of job, here in Hastings.

Her mother sat folding and unfolding a paper napkin. 'Oh, she went again.'

Margaret watched her daughter opening and shutting cupboards. Always a fusspot, this one. Never satisfied. To be honest, it was easier when Bea came to visit, not Katharine. And today, well, it wasn't the most convenient of times. There was so much to do. Sorting and clearing. And always the dust.

Katharine gave up making the tea and smiled. Through the window, beyond the wooden roofs of the net sheds, the sea shone and glittered and she felt happiness soar inside her. She couldn't remember the last time she had felt this way. Bea was here somewhere and Richard was right – she had found herself someone else or she was making a fresh start. A gull dropped from nowhere inches from the window, dangling a chip in its beak.

Margaret said, 'Are you staying long?'

Katharine spoke carefully; she kept her voice slow and level, kept a pleasant smile on her face. 'Mum, Bea's missing, you know that, don't you? She's left home as far as we can tell. I just need to know she's all right and perhaps leave a message for her.'

She would make her mother something to eat and then go out and . . . She looked in the cupboard next to the cooker. Nothing but tinned pies and cans of peas. It didn't smell too good in there. And were those mouse droppings? Bea was right. They couldn't leave their mother living alone any longer. Something would have to be done.

'She's shot up, hasn't she?'

'What?'

'She's taller than me now.' This was the trouble with visitors. They always said they'd be no trouble, but as soon as they stepped through the door they wanted feeding and watering morning, noon and night, whereas left to her own devices she could go weeks without going to the shop. Well she wasn't going out in this wind.

'Mum, Bea's been taller than you since she was fourteen.'

'Not Bea, the other one. It's her daughter I'm talking about.'

Katharine's scalp prickled. 'Laura?' she said.

'Laura, that's the one.'

'Laura's *my* daughter, Mum.'

Margaret swept this detail to one side with a vague wave of her hand. She shrugged. She would like a lie-down now.

'Are you telling me Laura was here yesterday?' Katharine's mind slalomed through yesterday's events. She couldn't recall Laura in any of them. 'With Bea?'

'You see, there aren't any coloureds in Hastings.' What was she going on about Bea for?

'Mum!' Katharine reached Margaret in one stride and held her arms roughly. 'Listen to me!' She stopped herself. Don't murder your mother, for God's sake. At least, not like this. She pulled up a chair and sat opposite her.

'Is Bea here?'

'Who?'

'My sister? Your daughter? Frank's wife?'

Oh, she'd had enough of this. 'I haven't seen anyone.' Margaret pushed her chair back and got to her feet. Katharine held on to her sleeve and looked up at her, imploring.

'Mum, please. Bea has vanished. We think she's run away. We hope she has.'

Margaret looked at Katharine's hand on her sleeve.

'Don't,' she said, her voice like stone.

KATHARINE CLOSED the door quietly behind her and stood in the abandoned bedroom of their childhood. Their twin beds were narrow and flat, the candlewick bedspreads a faded mauve memory of girlhood, sisterhood, the past. This one, the one she sat down on now, was her own and slightly better than Bea's because it had a headboard of padded velour. Here – she pressed her hand on to the thin mattress – was where she had slept six thousand nights, sat cross-legged with her homework beneath the frosted ceiling light and planned her escape. She looked at Bea's bed and battled briefly with despair. What would bring Bea back to this? Was this what it was like for Bea left behind when Katharine left for university at eighteen?

A row of empty wire hangers hung in the wall cupboard. Katharine was shocked at the emptiness. Their mother must have had a clear-out. It smelled of school and cheap perfume in there. On the floor of the cupboard was a cardboard box. She knelt on the cord carpet and opened it. Inside were school exercise books, reports, a fountain pen and bottle of Quink. Her own exercise books were neatly filled with turquoise ink, titles underlined, dates given, every page affirmed by a tick in red – the codes and signs of the clever student. She stroked their cool surfaces and bent her face, hungry suddenly to smell again the secret language of success, the logarithms, declensions and past perfect of it all. That was second nature to her, but to Bea . . . Bea had not applied herself at school and no one was surprised when she left with nothing but O levels in art and cookery. Katharine sorted through the remaining books, searching for one of Bea's. At the bottom of the box she found a green geography book with *Beatrice Kemp* written on the cover, smudged, careless and covered in doodles. She flicked through the pages, noting that the book felt thin and that many pages had been torn out. Bea's handwriting sloped first one way, then another; at times her e's were looped; at others they were like backward 3's. A similar experimentation occurred with a's and m's. Katharine shook her head. The pages were a mess and the teacher's impatience was plain to see. 'Always underline the title', 'See me', 'Where is your homework?' then tailing off eventually into no response at all, just a series of unfinished, scrappy work. She pulled out another book from the bottom of the box. It was a school copy of *As I Walked Out*

One Midsummer Morning, with Bea's name written inside and the date, 1972. On the inside cover was a map of Spain that showed Laurie Lee's route from west to south. She put the book into her bag. The children might enjoy reading it. In another box she found their singles record collection – 'Son of a Preacher Man' by Dusty Springfield (Bea's), 'Dedicated Follower of Fashion' by the Kinks (shared) and 'Hey Hey We're The Monkees' (hers) – and loose at the bottom a tube of Miner's frosted lipstick (Bea's) and a Biba cream blusher (also Bea's) that still smelt of sugar and promise. Next to these, in two pieces, was a green pottery dinosaur (Bea's) and a glazed brown thumb pot (hers).

Katharine's foot had gone numb. This couldn't be all. What had become of those years? She looked about her, trying to remember what it was. Was it before or after? She could barely remember the before. His long legs in tan trousers. His shoes. A strong warm hand round hers. It wasn't him, though. It was Bea. Before and after. Bea drawing, drawing, filling pads, scrap paper and cheap floppy-backed books.

She eased herself up off the floor and looked at her watch. How it had got to ten past three she had no idea. She sat on Bea's bed and rubbed the life back into her foot with one hand while she dialled Laura's school with the other. The school secretary confirmed that Laura had been absent the previous Friday. She rang Richard and told him the news.

'I can't believe we've let things get like this,' she said. 'I mean, our own daughter.'

'Laura's fine, darling. She's a teenager.'

Katharine allowed a pause. 'What does that mean?'

'Well, I'm sure that when you were fifteen—'

'I went to school every day and I always did my home-work. It was damn hard, as a matter of fact, living here. All I thought of was how to escape.'

'Well there you go. There was a rebellious streak in you.'

'It wasn't a matter of rebellion, Richard, it was a matter of survival. We didn't all grow up like you.'

'Katharine, you know I have nothing but admiration for the way that—'

'But it hasn't worked,' she cried. 'Don't you see? Nothing is certain any more. My mother can't live here alone, Bea's gone, and now Laura . . .'

'Darling, would you like me to come down on the train and then I'll drive you home?'

'No! Don't be ridiculous.' She blew her nose so that Richard had to hold the phone away from his ear. She sniffed and sighed and gathered in all the pieces of herself, wiped them with the tissue then tucked it up her sleeve. There had been a time at school when the place to tuck your hankie had been up one leg of your knickers. My God, she thought, she might as well have come from another planet for all the connection her life had to Laura's. Richard was saying something about the apple trees, about leaves, about the cat, for God's sake. 'I need to stay a bit longer.' Katharine told him. 'Bea could still turn up. She may be wandering around the town without her memory or up on the cliffs . . .'

'Right-o.'

Katharine didn't speak. Sometimes, just sometimes, she felt like taking off herself. Typical of Bea to up sticks and scarper. She'd scarpered one time before, when Katharine was doing O levels. Turned out she had hitched to Brighton and was gone three whole days. Apparently she had some idea in her head about applying for art school there. Katharine straightened the bedspread and noticed something beneath the pillow.

'Did Laura get off to school today?' she asked, lifting the pillow. She pulled out a tightly folded note.

'Yes, she did. No need to worry. And I rang the school and checked she had arrived.'

'Did you tell them we're not moving for a while?'

'Yes, I did.'

'Was she on time? You know what she's like. Sometimes I think that girl needs nothing more than a damn good slap.' She got the note open and saw Laura's handwriting. 'Oh, Laura,' she said, so quietly that Richard missed it.

'Well there's no more news at this end. Perhaps now you're down there, darling, you should stay the night.'

There was silence from the other end.

'Katharine?'

Temp

I T WAS nice, just the three of them in the kitchen after school. No one did any homework or practised the violin and they ate beans out of a tin. Laura showed Richard and Adrian how to dance with just your bottom, and when it grew dark, no one turned on the lights. When Adrian suggested an indoor firework display, Richard said he didn't think that was allowed but agreed to hold a sparkler anyway. Laura told him she had been good at school that day, not bad like she usually was, and when he asked whether she had enjoyed being good she said it had been so boring she couldn't remember anything about it. Richard told them that at boarding school, if they were good, they got turned into prefects, which wasn't good at all: it meant you had to spend your breaks standing in the cold trying to catch people smoking. Laura shuffled up closer to him and thought she would rather live with one parent instead of two. It was more equal like this. She felt promoted. She told him they had gone to Bea's office after school because Precious said they could drop by any time they liked. On Mondays Bea did yoga at work with Precious. They thought she might have sneaked back in.

'Sneaked back in?' said Richard.

'To her life,' said Adrian.

'To her work,' said Laura. 'To the bit of work that didn't have work in it — Precious and yoga and drinks in the pub round the corner.'

'Ah,' said Richard. He could certainly see the logic of that. After all, one lived more than one kind of life. There was the office, there was home, there was the conference, the work dinners, the squash court . . . He tried to think of the constituent parts of Bea's life, but he was finding it difficult to keep Bea in his head, even now, when they were supposed to be looking for her. It was as though she'd been gone for years.

'Someone was sitting in Bea's chair,' said Laura.

'Really?' Richard thought uneasily of his own office chair with Claudia in it.

'Someone was using her computer and drinking tea from her cup.'

Richard stretched his feet out and lay down on his back. The room looked rather peaceful from this position. The cat came and sniffed his face. He sighed and felt unaccountably content. He couldn't remember the last time he'd had a conversation with the children that wasn't about PE kits or lunchboxes. Come to think of it, he didn't have even those conversations with them; he listened while Katharine had them.

'Who was sitting in her chair?'

'A temp,' said Adrian.

'A temporary Bea,' said Laura.

'To tackle the backlog,' said Adrian.

'She had a fat head,' said Laura.

The doorbell rang and the cat scuttled out of the cat flap. Nobody moved.

Laura closed her eyes and prayed it was Bea. She promised that she would be good for ever and ever and to give back all those trespasses that she had trespassed against. Adrian lit a small green cone called Vesuvius that spewed a long coil of curly ash. Richard thought it would probably be children collecting for Guy Fawkes, and as he only had twenties on him there was little point in going to the door. He was reluctant to break the spell.

The bell rang again and a woman's voice called through the letter box. 'Hello, anyone home?'

Richard recognised that voice from somewhere. He got to his feet and switched on the lights. On the doorstep he found Jane and Paul. Jane was halfway through the door before Richard had said hello. Paul stood on the gravel near the shadows. He looked smaller than he had done before the weekend.

'Katharine rang from Hastings,' said Jane, handing Richard a bottle of wine. 'We thought you could do with some adult company.'

'Oh,' said Richard. 'Well, come in and say hello to Laura and Adrian. They're just through here.'

But the kitchen was empty. Richard looked around. Jane tapped him on the shoulder and said, 'Looking for these?' and handed him three wine glasses.

'Well, the children *were* here.'

'I expect they're watching *Friends*,' said Jane. 'Ours are.' She gestured to Paul to find the bottle opener. Richard smelt wine on her breath.

'Yes, ours watch it nonstop,' said Paul. 'They're addicted.'

'It's because it's about friends and there's no sex or violence in it,' Jane said, watching Paul open the wine. 'It's a safe world of friendship and laughter.' She laughed and turned her back on Paul. 'An utter fantasy, of course.'

Jane looked at Richard, who was dressed in jeans and a sweatshirt. She rarely saw him in casual clothes. Usually he wore a tie and rather 'old man' trousers pulled high up his waist. There was something so proper and public-schoolboyish about him that she didn't really notice him in a sexual way. And anyway, she only ever saw him with

Katharine, and Katharine, after all, was the one who commanded the attention. But now . . . she noticed that he really was deliciously tall and boyish. He had sleepy-looking hazel eyes and large hands and lots of dark hair on his head. He was really most unusual for a man pushing fifty. She looked around for somewhere to sit, then put her hand on his arm and took him with her to the sofa by the French windows. No doubt about it, she thought, battling an un-sisterly impulse, Katharine had certainly fallen on her feet where Richard was concerned. And Katharine had never been what you could call *beautiful*. She sat down and patted the cushion next to her. Husbands, she thought, noticing her own lowering himself with difficulty on to an old pouffe on the floor; it was so difficult to know what it was exactly that you were getting.

Richard raised his glass encouragingly to Paul and hoped he wasn't going to wander off anywhere or be completely silent. Jane could be so intense.

'I just can't stop thinking about Bea,' said Jane. 'Did you see the piece in the paper about her? My heart goes out to Katharine, having to read something like that about her sister. "Fears Grow For Missing Wife".'

Richard said, 'Oh, Katharine thinks it's important to keep the public interest alive.'

Paul was having difficulty with his drink. Each time he raised his face to his glass, he slipped further on to his back. Jane watched and extended one leg towards him so that Richard could get the full benefit of its length. She had a strange body, Richard saw now. Truncated above the hips and elongated below, as if she were somehow the wrong way up. There was something odd about them both tonight. He wished Katharine were here.

'I was surprised to hear about the affair,' Jane said suddenly.

Paul coughed and struggled over on to his side. Richard hesitated. Hadn't Katharine said that Paul was a little prone to the extramaritals? Surely they hadn't come round to discuss that with him?

'That long affair she had with a married man,' said Jane. 'Katharine always worried that Bea was sacrificing her thirties and her chance of a child to a man who would never leave his wife.'

Richard wasn't sure it was right to be discussing Bea's love life in this way. He wondered whether he should get up and close the door. He didn't want the children hearing anything they shouldn't.

'Yes, well that is more or less what happened, I suppose,' he said, remembering Katharine, incandescent every time she heard that her sister was still seeing 'that man'.

'You see, I always feel sorry for the other woman,' continued Jane. 'Imagine living your life as someone else's understudy. Soul-destroying.'

Paul was on all fours now and trying to climb off the pouffe. This was what he called sailing a little close to the wind, something Jane had a penchant for when she'd had too much Sauvignon. Jane's reaction to her discovery of his most recent indiscretion, with the woman who ran the juice bar in the gym, was to not react at all. No row, no screaming, no threats or ultimatums. It was baffling. She just appeared to carry on as normal, except that things were not normal. He had the uncomfortable feeling that he was walking the plank, and that if he put a foot wrong he'd be done for. He sat back on his heels and tried to get comfortable on the floor. His belt cut into his paunch, a paunch that was proving impossible to shift no matter how often his trainer took him round the park.

'What women don't realise,' said Jane to Richard, 'is that marriage is a fortress. There may be the odd incursion or skirmish at the ramparts every now and then, but essentially it is impenetrable. No man would willingly leave the comfort and security of a marriage; he'd have to be thrown out.

They know they wouldn't survive a moment out there on their own.'

Richard wished Paul would steer the conversation to some more neutral ground. Infidelity was not something he felt much of an expert on.

He said, 'Bea was always very discreet, I believe,' and tried to summon an image of Bea when she was younger. He could remember her dancing round this very room with Adrian in her arms, and he could see her out on their lawn being a pony with Laura on her back. But he could not imagine her as a mistress. 'She would never have asked this man to leave his wife and children for her. I'm sure she would have thought that was . . . wrong.'

'So you don't think she's gone to be with him then?'

Richard shook his head. 'Why would she? She's got Frank.'

'Oh, *Frank*. Do you know, I had forgotten all about him,' said Jane.

'I gather the police haven't,' said Paul. 'I'd be bloody worried if I was Frank.'

There was a silence. True, Katharine had told him they had searched the house twice, and dug up the garden. And Frank had given a statement, or was it two? But all the same, Richard thought, murdering your wife. That was just too Inspector Morse. He was Frank, for God's sake, not—

'. . . biggest cause of death in women aged sixteen to forty-four.'

The two men looked at Jane.

'What?'

'Domestic violence.'

'What, bigger than . . .' Richard tried to rally some statistics for all the kinds of cancer that women died of – breast, cervix, womb . . .

Paul chuckled. 'You've got to be joking.'

'Why would I joke about that?'

'I am quite sure it's nothing melodramatic,' said Richard.

'My feeling is that she had a tiff with Frank and she's taken herself off to calm down a bit. It's a temporary blip.'

'Either that or she's topped herself,' boomed Paul, getting to his feet. Now the conversation had turned to murder, he seemed to be feeling more his old self.

The cat meowed and the three of them looked over to the door, where Laura and Adrian stood silhouetted in the light of the hallway.

Over

BY THE time the sun set in Hastings, Katharine had put posters up all round the town. To her surprise, it had been good to be back in the old place. She couldn't understand how so many years had passed since her last visit. The shopkeepers and restaurant owners, the publicans and waitresses, the fishermen and the man who ran Swan Pedalos, everyone had been interested, sympathetic and attentive. In the eel shop they gave her free eel and chips, and in the Dolphin pub they told her about the missing nurse from Berkhamsted found sleeping rough in the net sheds. It gave her hope and had all taken much longer than she thought, so by the time she climbed the steps of East Hill to begin the cliff walk, the sun was going down and a sharp wind had sprung up from the east.

She had forgotten about the sea, the sheer expanse of it, the sigh and hiss of it and the clamour of the gulls. She had forgotten how it never stayed still and how it changed with the light, how it was magic when the night drew in and bright spots of light like sequins on net pricked out the sky and the coast and the trawlers that stitched the land to the shore.

She walked up the path where the turf was cut away into steps, where the wooden seat faced the sea, and wondered how a place could be so familiar without being trodden or thought of for thirty years. A safety fence had been put up along the edge, but when they were children it was possible to get right to the point where the grass ended and the drop began. She remembered how they lay down on their tummies and wriggled forwards, Bea in front and herself behind, how she gasped with the fear and excitement of it and how Bea would inch her fingertips to the edge and then her face and look down to the beach below. Bea used to laugh and scream into the wind, and once Katharine looked over too, but the terror of the height threatened to tip her, made the land lurch and the horizon rear up. But Bea was always brave; she was frightening and fearless in her dares and her need for fever and elation. There was the day one summer up here on the cliffs when Bea had raced away from her, running fast up the path so that Katharine had to shout out at her to wait, her voice a reedy cry gobbled up by the distance. 'W-a-i-t! Bea-e-e-e!' It had been murder running up the hill, scratching past the gorse, trying to keep Bea in sight. She had started to cry, but not real crying, just a dry lament that hurt her throat like the time in assembly when she under-stood that Daddy was dead and she had screwed up her face to try to force out the tears but none came, just the pain in her throat. As she ran, she knew that if she didn't catch Bea she would be left on the clifftop alone, all alone near the edge and far, far from home. When she did finally reach her, stumbling and spent, she found Bea suddenly, just there, so near she almost stepped on her, lying in a dip on her back in the grass, socks down, dress fluttering so you could see her knickers. She had her arms stretched out like the picture of Jesus above the school stage, and she lifted her head up when she saw Katharine. Then she sat up. There was a deadly look on her face and Katharine knew what that look meant. It was her Storm Game face, her End of the Pier face; it was the Caves Game face, and now, from today, it was the Over the Cliff face. 'We're going to go and see Daddy!' Bea shouted from her back on the grass. The wind buffeted her words and her hair and Katharine felt the cold cut through her knitted cardigan. She wished more people were about and that the sky was not so blank. She shook her head. They didn't talk about Daddy except at night in the dark when they talked about everything.

'Come on.' Bea sat up. Katharine shook her head and tried to warm her hands under her armpits. Bea got to her feet and brushed the grass from her clothes. Then she stood up straight on her toes, like a dancer, and looked towards the nothing above their heads. 'You want to see him, don't you?' she said.

Time slowed as Katharine understood what Bea was going to do. She hoped it was some dreadful trick, but up here alone with the wind and the racing sky she felt help-less. 'Don't,' she pleaded. 'Don't and just shut up!' Their father was dead, they knew that. A teacher at school had told them and they had seen the letter from his work. Eamon Kemp Deceased. Katharine turned round and headed back down the path but Bea grabbed her hand. 'We run to the edge and then we jump. That's how you get over to the other side. I've done it before. It's the best feeling,' and then Bea's hand slipped out of hers and she was running to the place where the grass met the sea. Her dress billowed and snapped, her sandals kicked high out behind her, higher and higher, her hair flailed and at the very edge she burst up into space, stretched out her arms and leapt.

In that moment, Katharine felt every element of her burn, freeze and shatter. When eventually, somehow, she got herself to the place where Bea had jumped, she put her hands over her eyes before she looked down. What she saw through cold, shaking fingers was not a vertiginous drop to beach and boul-ders but a series of tussocky dips like grassy bowls, and in one of them, on her back in a star shape, lay Bea, laughing triumphantly up at the sky.

Falling, thought Katharine as she made her way carefully back down the path. Falling had always been a horror to her. At university everyone was doing it. All around her, bright, beautiful, highly educated women were falling in love. Their skirts, their papers, their hair flew up and out, fluttered away in the wind, while their faces became dreamy and far away. Jane had teased Katharine about her lack of a love life. 'It's easy,' Jane told her. 'Like falling off a log.'

At the bottom of the hill she crossed the road carefully and looked up towards Tamarisk Steps and their mother's flat. 'What's got into you?' their mother screamed down into Bea's seven-year-old face when they got home and Katharine had told. 'What the devil's got into you, girl?' she screamed again, and yanked Bea's arm so hard that Bea was lifted from the ground. Katharine let herself back into the flat and felt her energy and optimism falter. A thin sliver of light shone from beneath Margaret's bedroom door. Katharine knocked softly and waited but there was no reply. She had thought they might go out for supper, talk about the old days and work out together what had got into Bea, but of course this was impossible. She stood in the kitchen and poured herself a Dubonnet. She swallowed quickly, hating the taste but needing to remember it, remember the taste for Bea, who sometimes brought a glass of it into their bedroom at night. The flat had a faded, sorry air to it. She looked at the Formica and at the starburst clock on the wall and wondered if it felt like this for Bea when she visited their mother. She poured more Dubonnet as the dread settled over her like a cloak. The taste of it made her teeth chatter, and when the kitchen clock nudged nine and the light went out under her mother's door, she knew she couldn't stay. She wanted to be in her own home with Richard; she wanted more than anything to be safe and still, next to him in their bed.

She tore a page from her notebook, scribbled a message to her mother, then let herself out of the front door. She hesitated, then wrote a second note, to Bea this time. She put it under the pot of dead chrysanthemums where they always kept a spare key. Just in case.

Sorry

A<small>T THREE</small> o'clock on Wednesday afternoon, Margaret rang from the station and told Frank she was waiting to be collected for her surprise birthday party. She said enough people had been on at her about it and now here it was, it was Wednesday, and so she had done what she was told, been to the hairdresser's, another hairdresser, not Leslie, put on her best dress, but where was he? Bea had said Frank would be there to fetch her and she'd been waiting since gone dinner time, but not a sausage; speaking of which, she was starving. She said she hoped no one had baked a cake as she couldn't abide cake, it disagreed with her. Biscuits she could just about manage as long as they didn't have ginger or coffee in them, but personally she couldn't see what was wrong with a nice sherry trifle. Frank told her to wait where she was and he'd be down to fetch her right away.

He surveyed the state of the house and thought that it probably looked about right given that his life was collapsing with every passing hour. One thing was certain, they couldn't have the party here. He rang Katharine and got Wanda. Wanda said that a party at Katharine's would be difficult because everything was packed into boxes and the electricity had been disconnected. She told Frank not to worry, that he should go and collect Margaret and they would see him back at his house at five o'clock.

'Five o'clock?'

'Yes, give us time to get everything ready. It's what Bea wanted. She told me all about it but I thought that—'

'And what am I supposed to do with Margaret till then?'

'I don't know, Frank. Take her for a drive. Take her to the river.'

'I haven't got a car. The police took it away.'

'Take a cab.'

Frank said nothing. Where did everyone think the money was coming from? He hadn't got a cent on him.

'I must go. See you soon and don't forget to shave.'

Well he couldn't walk, his back was in a bad way today. There was nothing for it but to get the bus to the station and bring Margaret back on that. Frank couldn't bear public transport and avoided using it at all costs, but – he looked at his watch – at least it would kill some time. Just as he put on his jacket, the phone rang again. He thought about ignoring it, but he could never ignore the phone now, thanks to Bea. Thanks to Bea, he would always have to answer the phone and the doorbell whatever the hour or the inconvenience. Just in case.

It was Katharine. She was talking loud and very fast. She sounded out of breath. The birthday had completely slipped her mind and the party obviously had because she thought that . . . well, it didn't matter now what she thought because this was wonderful news. If Bea had arranged a surprise birthday party for their mother then Bea would be there. It was the best news she'd had for a week. She'd always known in her heart that Bea wouldn't let their mother down and it was such a good sign that their mother had remembered. A really good sign. Wanda's friend was on his way to Oyster Row now and Wanda was off to sort the food . . .

Frank said he was a bit strapped for cash and he needed

some for the taxi to collect Margaret. Katharine gave him Richard's taxi account number and password. Frank wrote it down carefully.

'Don't worry about anything, Frank,' she said. 'I've got a really good feeling about this afternoon.'

Frank rang Lance and told him they were having a party, that a cab would be calling for him in an hour and to make sure he wore something clean.

The car arrived precisely when it said it would and waited patiently outside, having politely phoned him to let him know it was there.

Frank sat in the back and felt like he did the afternoon he was driven to his wedding. Richard had sat in the back with him then and said exactly what Katharine had said. 'Don't worry about anything. I've got a really good feeling about this afternoon.' The wedding had been brief but an embarrassment all the same; neither he nor Bea looked each other in the eye and they'd had to wait out in the rain because the wedding before theirs overran. That wedding was all Katharine's idea as well. He'd overheard her telling Richard that she hoped the wedding might bring Bea to her senses and cheer her up a bit because nobody could quite work out what had got into her. She hadn't been herself since she'd been transferred to a new department at work. She'd got it into her head that her work was pointless, that she wanted to do something worthwhile with a career path, and some-body, Precious no doubt, had suggested she retrain as a social worker. A social worker! He hadn't seen the sense in that. It'd take her four years to get the degree, which it was dubious she would manage, and how were they supposed to pay the mortgage let alone the tuition fees if a regular salary wasn't coming in? They hadn't talked about it much and after a while Bea stopped mentioning it, but Katharine seemed to think she needed something to look forward to and Margaret had a fall about the same time, so Bea had taken a month's leave from work and gone down to Hastings to look after her. For a while it was touch and go whether Margaret would pull through; Bea said it was as if it wasn't just the hip she had broken but her self, her hold on life. The wedding was something for Margaret to hang on for, but once Margaret recovered, she was never very interested in anything again.

Frank had nothing against getting the piece of paper, but the actual wedding – he looked down at his hands and realised he'd forgotten to clean his nails – the actual wedding was awkward in that way that weddings always are, especially as Bea insisted on that hat and six-inch heels and he refused to wear the ring she bought him.

When Frank got to the station it was nearly half past four and Margaret was nowhere to be found. He asked the driver to wait while he went to look for her. Before long he found her sitting on a bench on the London-bound platform, dressed from top to toe in powder blue. Even her hair was blue. She told him she'd got fed up waiting and she hadn't wanted a party anyway, all this was Bea's silliness, and anyhow, she needed to get back because she had a nasty feeling she'd left something on in the oven.

THEY PULLED up outside the house and Adrian and Laura bounded out. Adrian wore a sweatshirt that said *Nobody Knows I'm a Leviathan* and Laura wore a pink dress and carried her violin. They danced round Margaret singing 'Happy Birthday' with Laura scraping out the occasional strangled note while Frank looked shyly around for signs of Bea. He tugged at his sleeves and followed the children indoors.

Inside he was astounded by the transformation. The floorboards had been hammered down, Bea's plates, bowls and figurines shone from the walls and shelves, the table was laden with coloured bottles and candles, and in the garden Urban was putting the finishing touches to the patio. Richard was out there too, building a large bonfire, and Adrian had planted fireworks everywhere. Lance looked handsome in his suit and got shakily to his feet for Margaret, leading her to the chair next to him, where they had a good view of the garden and the drinks were in easy reach. Katharine flurried in and out, looking thin and yellow. Apart from some heavy blinking, which Frank noticed afflicted her from time to time, she appeared to be either drunk or very happy. Chairs were pulled out on to the patio and arranged round the fire basket, which glowed red hot. Lance kept saying, 'I can't believe the heat from that brassiere,' and Margaret said she'd have an advocaat to start with because it settled her stomach and gave her a lift, which was what she needed, she'd been sitting that long on a bench at the blessed railway station.

At six o'clock, Frank put on an old Sinatra record and Adrian lit the garden candles. Laura looked out at the remains of Bea's garden. She heard the man singing, 'Fly me to the moon, let me play among the stars' and wanted to cry. She heard Lance say, 'I lost mine, oh, years ago now.' Margaret said, 'I lost mine when they were still only girls.' She noticed that the tips of their fingers were approximately three centimetres from touching.

When the doorbell rang, everyone froze and pretended not to. Then Laura put down her violin and pushed past Katharine to the hall.

Wanda stood on the doorstep with two plastic bags in her hands. She put her head on one side and said, 'Hello.'

Laura said, 'Oh, it's you.' She wanted to be sick from disappointment.

Wanda said, 'Can I come in?'

Laura shrugged.

'I forgot my key,' said Wanda, holding the carrier bags up high. 'I've brought the food and the birthday cake.'

Laura said, 'In there,' nodding in the direction of the kitchen and pressing herself against the coats so they wouldn't touch, then she thundered up the stairs to the bathroom and locked the door.

If Bea was coming back, she'd be here by now. She knelt with her head over the toilet bowl and tried to vomit, put salty fingers down her throat and felt the animal heave in her. She moaned and retched. Nothing, just some spit.

She gave up trying to be sick and settled herself on the tufted mocha bath mat. The room still smelt of lavender and honey from the soap Bea used. It was small and cosy and cluttered with the shells and driftwood Bea brought back from holidays. They hung on strings from the ceiling and lay piled up around the edges of the bath. The walls were painted plum and fuchsia because she'd once seen a house like that in a magazine, and there were thick towels to match. Katharine thought the colour scheme hideous but Laura thought this was what a bathroom should look like, not hard and white like theirs. This bathroom was fruity and warm and a place to be held. Like Bea.

The floor was always warm by the cupboard. Laura opened it and looked inside. It smelt of camphor and eucalyptus. Cross-legged, and beginning at the top shelf, she began lifting out tubes and packets, opening, sniffing and putting them down again. She popped a Nurofen from its bubble and put it in her mouth. It was sweet and smooth like a Smartie. She snipped the top off a Karvol capsule and shook the drops on to her dress. She peeled the foil from an aspirin and let it fizz on her tongue. The Piriton was bitter and got stuck in her throat so that she had to wash it down with a glug of gorgeous sticky-sweet Calpol, and then she just had to lick the treacly cap as well. Being ill at Bea's house had been the best thing. She smeared E45 cream on her cheeks and dabbed Preparation H behind each ear. From the garden she heard the bang and crackle of rockets. She struggled, anger rising, with the paracetamol bottle, heard the hiss and sputter of Roman candles, and still no Bea.

On the second shelf there were shampoos and face creams, aftershave, razors, body oils and toners. She dabbed Elizabeth

Arden Age Defying Night Cream on her forehead and tested the serum for limp, lifeless hair, rubbing it into a few strands of her fringe. On the bottom shelf was Bea's make-up bag, black and sequinned with a broken zip. 'Cashmere' was written in gold on the base of a lipstick, which she opened just to hear the slide and pop of it when Bea said, 'Hang on, just a bit of damage limitation,' and did that thing with her mouth in the mirror. Laura made a moue of her own mouth and drew the worn, gleaming tip of the lipstick over her lips, then rolled them together like Precious did whether she had lipstick on or not. When she opened the gold compact it released the sugary scent that smelt of Bea's neck. She lifted the sponge disc and pressed its damp felt to her face. Before they went anywhere, Bea always checked her pockets, said, 'Keys, Looks, Personality. Let's go.' Laura unscrewed the mascara wand and touched it to her lashes, brushed and stroked with her mouth agape, the way Bea did. 'Your aunt is sexy,' Chanel always said. 'You can tell from the way she walks.' Laura thought of Bea's walk through the grass by the river that day. She moved slowly; her bottom *rolled*.

What if it was Laura's fault Bea couldn't come to the party? Perhaps she had tried to phone but couldn't. Perhaps she had been kidnapped and thought she'd call the police but then found her phone was gone.

Someone was knocking on the door. Someone was rattling the door handle and calling her name. Laura reached up and turned on the taps, stretched across and flushed the toilet so that she couldn't hear. She held her mouth sideways beneath the tap and let the water gush into her. The cold hurt her teeth and she wished she didn't have tracks at all because she still couldn't speak properly, she sounded like she was stupid, it felt like she had a scourer in her mouth and her lips were always dry. She tested each toothbrush against her cheek, rejecting damp ones because it would be gross to get Frank's. She sucked the peppermint memory from the lime-green one then put it in her pocket. The knocking on the door was getting on her nerves, and downstairs the man was singing, 'The lady is a tramp.' She sat down at the cupboard again and opened a Boots bag on the bottom shelf. Sanitary towels – Ultra Plus, Ultra Normal, with wings, without, and Super Plus Tampax. In another bag there were tubes and strips for dealing with unwanted hair – bikini, facial, leg and armpit. God, it looked exhausting being a woman; she was surprised Bea ever got out of the house. Finally there was a small hand-woven basket of bottles and potions. She pulled out each one and read the label. Dong Quai, Black Cohosh, Red Clover, St John's Wort, Zinc, Calcium, B Complex and Magnesium. She opened each, shook out a tablet and put it on the back of her tongue, washing it down with water from the tap.

The door burst open and the little bolt dropped on to the carpet. Adrian looked down at her. Laura looked up disparagingly, then burped.

'We've been calling you. Mum says you've got to come downstairs.'

'What for?'

'We're going to have the cake.'

'What's the point? Bea's not coming.'

'She says it will help Granny.'

Laura dispatched a pitying look in his direction and got to her feet. 'What's Frank doing? Why can't he help with the cake?'

'He can't.'

'Why not? He never does anything.'

'He's busy.'

'Oh yeah? Out looking for Bea, is he?'

'He's in charge of the balloon firework. He has to stay near it till I get back. He's in the lilac tree.'

Laura pushed past him sucking her teeth.

Adrian said, 'Wigga.' Leapt into the bathroom and shut the door, pressing the entire weight of his body against it.

Laura kicked the air where his backside had been and slapped the door hard so the flat of her hand burned. Tears stung her eyes. She took a quick look down the stairs and tiptoed into Bea's bedroom. Quietly she opened Bea's top drawer and slipped a mobile phone right in there at the back among the scarves and bras and knickers.

'Sorry,' she whispered. 'It wasn't me.'

Venus

AFTER THE fireworks had finished, Adrian went upstairs and climbed into Bea's wardrobe. He pulled the door shut behind him and smelt the gunpowder and woodsmoke on his sleeve. He sat down among her shoes and put his face in her clothes. The floorboards creaked and he peered through the crack in the door panel. Katharine came in and stood by the egg cups, where she ran her fingers over their rims. He heard her sniff and sit down on the bed, her feet facing the wardrobe. He waited and listened to his breath for a long time, blinking in the semi-dark. When she bent to the floor, he just saw the top of her head as she reached for something under the bed. She pulled out a pale blue slipper, bent down again and pulled out the other one. Then she sat up and held them out of sight. The bed creaked as she kicked off her own shoes and bent forward to put Bea's slippers on the floor. Adrian saw the grubby blue fluff of them, the sole coming away at the toe on one. Slowly and with great care, Katharine slid her feet into first one, then the other. She rested her feet on the floor for a long time. Laura's voice shouted up from the kitchen but Katharine didn't move.

Katharine took the slippers off and put them neatly beside the bed. She went to the door and returned with Bea's dressing gown, which she laid carefully across the quilt.

Laura came up the stairs, still shouting her mother's name. Adrian watched Katharine as she went to the bed and turned down a corner of duvet. She smoothed the bottom sheet and plumped up the pillows.

'Mum?' Laura was at the door.

'Just coming down,' she said and switched off the light as she left.

Adrian eased his hip off the hard edge of a pair of boots and relaxed. Above his head hung what must be a hundred garments. Buy less crap, he had told Bea once. It's a website. You should look at it. Bea laughed at him and nodded. I know, she said, then shook her head and looked hopelessly at the clutter around them in the kitchen. It's true, I should buy less crap. But I can't seem to stop right now. And she rubbed her stomach and made a face. It's like a hunger, she said. An addiction. I want to fill my life up with stuff. He closed his eyes and took deep breaths, conjuring up Bea's shape and form in his mind's eye. He knew it was not possible for her to disappear unless she had been heated to a temperature of over one thousand degrees and vaporised, which was what happened to the people in the cellars and houses and streets of Dresden and Nagasaki. Then there was nothing left of them at all. No clothes, no bones, no *thing*. All the water in their bodies turned to steam: bones, teeth, flesh, organs made ash and dust in an instant. So unless Bea had walked into a firestorm, she would *be* somewhere. Whether she was alive or dead was another matter. She might be on the river bed with stones in her pockets, she might be asleep in the back of a container lorry in the Channel Tunnel, she might have gone to Hastings and be sitting in a rented room overlooking the sea. 'I could stare at the sea for ever,' she'd said.

'*Never?*' he had said. It was one of those times she had brought both children with her. They were on the shingle in the shelter of an upturned fishing boat.

'No, *ever*.' She didn't look at him but she was smiling.

A figure battled against the wind down near the water's edge, a black dog loping by its side.

'There's no difference,' he said.

She didn't answer him. Perhaps she was thinking about it. Probably she was somewhere else. He threw stones, waiting for her response.

'Between ever and never?'

She wasn't even trying. That was probably the problem with two X chromosomes. Frank would put up a fight but Bea just gave in most of the time, although his mother never did and she had two Xs, so perhaps it was just habit or laziness.

'Yes. They're both expressions of time. Ever is the same as never. It's why people say "never ever". They're just repeating themselves. For emphasis.' He threw a stone, watched it fly in a low arc, enter the water and disappear.

'Actually, they're contradicting themselves,' said Bea.

Adrian thought about this. 'Are they?'

'One is all the time in the world, for ever and ever, Amen. The other is the absence of time.'

She was right. He tried the word out loud. 'Neverness. You probably get that in space.'

'Probably.' She got up. The pebbles clattered and rolled. 'Come on, we're late.'

Adrian ran his hand through her skirts, dresses and trousers, making the hangers click and knock. He was surprised by how cool the fabric felt, not low down near the wardrobe floor but high up towards the shoulders and lapels of them. Her clothes were mostly dark, although one or two patches of white shone through in the gloom. He rubbed jersey and rayon, wool and cotton between his fingertips, and took deep long breaths of Bea.

There would be millions of her atoms and molecules in here; he was inhaling them right now. Where was she? There had to be a trail, a trail of molecular particles. The police had used a heat-seeking helicopter yesterday when they searched the meadows and the common. They had used sniffer dogs too, but none of that was any use, it seemed to Adrian, because the world was too full of heat and too full of smells. If there was some way of identifying her molecules here in the wardrobe, magnetising them in a centrifuge and then putting them in a canister . . . He bit his knee and thought about this. It should be possible then to call the other molecules back to the canister of collected ones like iron filings or like the way that starlings or bees will swarm and flock together. If he inhaled enough of her here, in this wardrobe, he could become the canister himself and just start walking, see where she led him, because the trail could not be entirely cold yet. It wasn't that she had disappeared; that was obviously irrational, because everyone knew that matter could be neither created nor destroyed. It was just that they couldn't see her. It was just that other things were obscuring her, like water over a stone or clouds across the sun.

She always said she loved the sun. He told her about Venus, how Venus was known as Earth's evil twin because it was born the same time as Earth, composed of the same stuff as Earth and had a similar diameter but had evolved differently. The problem with Venus, he told her, was that it had no magnetism to protect it from the solar winds. Venus lost hydrogen and oxygen through the wake. 'The wake?' said Bea, who seemed to listen but didn't always look like she did. 'The wake the orbit leaves – like the wake on a boat.' She was interested in the planets, she said. He told her that on Venus the runaway greenhouse effect meant it was 450 degrees, which would melt lead, and you wouldn't like the sun if you lived there, he told her. On Venus the clouds were made of sulphuric acid and it had a slow rotation the *wrong way*, which was very unusual. 'Is it?' said Bea. Yes, he explained. It was retrograde and no one knew why, but *Venus Express*, the European Space Mission, would be launched in 2012.

It was going to try and find out if Venus was Earth's future in 2.6 billion years, and *Mars Odyssey* would find out if Mars was Earth's past 3.8 billion years ago, and if only he was a bit older he could help.

His nose tickled and his foot had gone numb. Perhaps she didn't want to be found. Perhaps she was hiding. He had lost all feeling in his bottom. Laura was squawking his name. He should be full of Bea particles by now. He opened the wardrobe door and climbed out.

DOWNSTAIRS, THE party mood had evaporated and the bonfire had gone out. Wanda and Richard were clearing up and Katharine was arguing with Frank. Laura had done something strange to her face and looked a little like a prostitute, but Adrian knew better than to comment because he understood that fourteen was a fragile time for girls, what with negotiating their sexual identity and everything. In the front room, Frank Sinatra was silent and Lance and Margaret were sitting side by side on the couch.

It was late. Katharine wanted to leave, but before she did, she wanted to punish Frank. Laura and Adrian hovered. Laura just slumped in a space in the room and waited, while Adrian slid slowly back and forth along the wall, his eyes fixed on the floor between his mother's feet and Frank's.

'But you're always taking snaps,' said Katharine, her face blotchy from wine.

'I'm not that kind of photographer,' said Frank.

Inexplicably, she had no photographs of Bea since the wedding and had assumed that Frank would have plenty. She needed a couple for the Mispers people, for the Salvation Army Family Tracing Service, for Missing People and for more posters. Frank of course had been worse than useless, pulling out stacks of old papers and files from the ruin of his workroom, complaining that the police had left everything in a mess and failing to find anything resembling a recent photo of his wife. The posters that Precious had made used the photo from Bea's staff pass that resembled the mug shot of that woman who drove her children into a lake in New Jersey. That was who people were currently looking out for along the Cam and around the marketplace. No wonder there was no news of her.

Katharine jangled the car keys and called to Richard that they were leaving. The party had been a mistake, of course. What they had all been thinking of, she had no idea. Now that Bea had failed to turn up to her own mother's surprise birthday party, the situation seemed much more serious than before. Richard asked whether she was all right to drive and Katharine said she would just have to be seeing as he had been drinking all evening as far as she could see. Outside, torn strands of police tape dangled from the gatepost. Richard put his hand on Frank's back and said goodbye. The children waved ineffectually. Katharine revved the engine and switched on the headlights. She looked at Frank. He was wanting sympathy, she could tell, but she had none to give him. Not only did he have no recent photographs of his wife but he was also clueless as to the whereabouts of her passport, which meant she might have left the country. No financial activity might mean one thing and no passport might mean another. It didn't make sense. And Frank, it turned out, had not even slept in the same bed as Bea the night before she went, which meant that Bea might have been missing since Tuesday night, not Wednesday morning. He looked a pathetic figure to her, in the dying front garden, fiddling ineffectually with the plants on the windowsill. She felt enraged by him.

She leant across Richard and said, 'Frank, I'm putting up posters, setting up a website, arranging a television appeal. What are you going to do?'

Frank took a step back and scratched his head. 'Well, I'm going to wait here in case she comes back.'

Katharine said, 'Oh for God's sake,' and released the handbrake.

He came over to the car. He looked diminished in the sodium glow of the streetlight, grown old suddenly, and Katharine wondered if this was how Bea had seen him.

He put one hand on Richard's open window and said, 'When are you moving?'

Richard said, 'Well . . .' and looked at Katharine.

'Oh, all that's on hold now,' Katharine snapped as she put the car into gear. She looked at him and regretted her tone.

'Be in touch,' she said.

Frank watched the Jeep glide away and saw its brake lights glow at the bottom of the street. As he was turning back to the house, the car reversed angrily towards him.

Richard smiled sheepishly as he climbed out.

'Forgot to say goodbye to Margaret,' he said.

Frank realised he had forgotten Margaret too. And Lance. He felt a little better suddenly. Lance could have his room tonight and Margaret could sleep in the children's room. He followed Richard and Katharine back into the house. Tonight he was going to sleep in their bed, his and Bea's.

Daddy

NOVEMBER BROUGHT storms that felled three trees along the river, a poplar on Stourbridge Common and two willows at Grantchester. In December it started to rain and didn't stop. The days shuffled by, numbered and noted on the calendar by Katharine. Bea's fiftieth birthday came and went. Headaches and back pain nagged and worried at Katharine and she couldn't for the life of her remember what it was exactly that she had been good at in her job. Saving tiny babies, tubed and patched and wired up, seemed absurd to her now. More than once she had found herself standing in the neonatal unit, gazing over at the incubators bathed in their gentle uterine glow and wondering what on earth the point of it all was. Why all this effort to hold life together when to let it go at this stage could not really be so very terrible, could it? The fragile bird-like creatures in their tanks had barely weight nor substance enough to make a mark on the lives of others, not the way they could when they were grown, when years had spread their roots wide and deep, not the way she'd imagined the full six-footedness of her father had filled a whole side room and needed six men to carry it into the chapel. Not like the way the Bea-shaped vacuum threatened to pull in everyone standing at its edges.

The hospital where she worked had been very understanding

and allowed her to keep an office even though her replace-
ment had arrived. She went in most mornings and tried to
finish a paper she had started in the summer, but mostly she
trawled the internet for news of Bea and checked with the
various agencies that there were no developments. What
little media interest there had been in Bea's disappearance
was dwindling and dying away. Katharine knew and dreaded
this and typed Bea's name into Google several times a day.
She had a file of news about her that she hated to look at
but did look at in case it held some clue she had missed.
'Middle-Aged Woman Vanishes', 'Mystery of Missing Council
Worker', 'River Search Draws a Blank' and the one that she
hated most of all: 'Missing Woman Probably Dead Say Police',
although Jim told her they had said nothing of the sort; that
was local papers for you. Pete said it was harder to remain
hidden when you were dead than it was when you were alive.
Bodies had a habit of making themselves known eventually.
Jim apologised for Pete's lack of tact but Katharine was glad
for this information. It gave her hope.

The hospital in London where she had been due to take
up her job was being less understanding. She had spoken to
them of the circumstances and her start date had been delayed
twice. They had explained their staffing difficulties, their
teaching commitments and had written to her again. Richard
had tried to persuade her it might be better for all of them
if the family moved to London, but Katharine could not
agree to this. She couldn't leave Cambridge until something
had been resolved, discovered, understood. It would feel like
a betrayal, an abandonment of Bea. Richard muttered something that sounded like, 'I think that's already happened,' and
left to play squash with Paul. The house, which had been
packed and ready to leave, now became partially unpacked
and felt like a waiting room. More and more the children
kept to their rooms or stayed over with friends. Katharine's
eczema had flared up, something that hadn't happened since

she was a girl. She lay in salt baths and smeared cortisone on her skin. When the vendors of the house in Chiswick found other buyers, Richard kicked the cat.

They looked out into the blackness of the garden where the cat had fled and listened to the rain. The children had gone to bed.

Katharine said, 'For God's sake, Richard. That cat may very well not come back again, you know.'

Richard said, 'I know how it feels.'

Katharine looked around at the packing cases and stacked furniture and felt a migraine coming on.

'I found this in Frank's pocket.' They looked up to see Laura standing in the doorway holding a crumpled parcel. Adrian stood behind her and gave her a shove into the room.

'Why aren't you asleep?' Katharine asked.

'It's for Bea. I'm afraid to open it.' Laura put the parcel on the table and Katharine recognised her mother's writing. She sighed with irritation.

'Mum's been having one of her clear-outs. I got one of those recently and do you know what was in it?'

They looked at her. Adrian said, 'Money?'

'Yes! How did you guess? She sent the piggy bank I'd had since I was five. It was full of pennies!'

Richard laughed.

'I mean, what a useless thing to send through the post. And now of course the money's worthless. Ten years of savings. Must have been at least—'

'Open it.' Laura thrust the parcel at her mother.

Adrian helped, using a penknife to slice the layers of tightly taped paper. He tugged and tore until a plastic bag and three small red notebooks fell on to his mother's lap. She stared down at them and drew her hands away.

Laura darted forward and emptied the bag on to the floor. A bunch of keys, rusted and heavy with age, a pair of bicycle clips and some balsawood tied with string. Adrian flicked through the notebooks. They were densely filled with carefully inked drawings, speech bubbles and captions. They were graphic novels drawn in meticulous detail. Laura snatched one and opened it greedily. She saw a tall man wearing trousers tucked into cycle clips and a young girl in wellingtons on a beach. Another scene was of a museum with the girl next to a dinosaur skeleton. Further down the page, a mammoth with wild swooping tusks sank into the mud. She read the caption: 'Hastings One Million Years Ago'.

'That's Bea.' Laura pointed at the girl in the pictures. The skill and effort of the artwork bewildered her. 'I never knew.' She searched through the pages and looked up angrily at her mother. 'When did she do all this?'

Richard got down on his knees and took one of the books in his hand. 'These are really very good. I had no idea she had such talent, did you?'

Katharine shook her head. She leant down and picked the cycle clips up off the floor.

'*The Fossil Hunters* by Beatrice Kemp,' read Adrian from the title page. 'For Daddy.'

Went

'HOW MUCH do you know about Bea and Patrick?' asked Precious.

Katharine was sitting at Bea's desk. She had come to collect her personal belongings. No one had asked her to but it was nearly Christmas and she was running out of places to look and things to do.

'I know that it went on for a long time.' In the beginning, she had warned Bea countless times about getting involved with a married man. Then she had stopped talking to her about it at all. She pulled open the desk drawers. 'And I know they went abroad once. What was he like, anyway?'

'Patrick Cumberbatch is a lovely man, as a matter of fact,' said Precious. 'Very popular here when he was running the place. A good "people person".'

'Evidently. Did his wife know?'

Precious gave a gentle shrug. 'It's hard to believe that a wife *doesn't* know, don't you think? I mean, if she ever looks at her husband, or listens to him, or smells him. But who knows what goes on?'

Katharine rifled through the papers of Bea's in tray, then opened and shut the drawers of her desk.

'How many pairs of glasses does one woman need?' she asked, pulling several cheap and battered pairs from the top drawer.

'Oh, she couldn't bear it. Her eyes were going . . .'

'What?'

'Just getting long-sighted. It's an age thing, you know.'

Katharine didn't know. She had excellent vision. If Bea couldn't afford proper eye treatment, why in God's name didn't she ask for help?

'Oh!' Katharine pulled her hand away from the bottom drawer and sat up. Precious looked over at the packet of cigarettes and the pair of lacy knickers. 'I didn't know.' Katharine blushed. 'I didn't know that Bea smoked.'

Precious shrugged. 'Just occasionally. She said it made her feel more grown up.'

The familiar twist of anger coiled in Katharine's gut for a moment. Despite being the older sister, Bea had always refused to behave like one. Katharine had had to do the growing up for both of them. She checked herself and buried the feeling. For all she knew, she didn't have a sister any longer.

'So this Patrick,' she said, closing the drawer. 'It's not possible Bea might have gone to him, is it?'

Precious observed the pale, knotted length of Katharine, the no-nonsense skirt and blouse on her girl-like body. There was a prying hunger about her that she was reluctant to feed. She understood that Katharine was a woman for whom everything was a mission – work, family, marriage, and now rescuing her sister. She and Bea had laughed about it and Precious had developed a dislike for the woman sitting here now in Bea's chair. Neglect, in Precious's book, came in many forms: neglect of mothers, of children, of marriages, of sisters.

She wanted to say, 'I hope that Bea's on her way to Patrick. I hope that she's working something out. I pray nothing bad has happened to her.' Yet during her one tentative phone call to Patrick's number in Ithaca, she had got his wife. After a guarded conversation she was handed over to Patrick, who was adamant that he had no information on the matter whatsoever.

And so perhaps Katharine, with this arrow-like determination of hers, was Bea's best bet.

'I found this at home.' She slid a picture postcard over to Katharine. It was of Kioni, Ithaca. A circle was drawn round a white house nestled in the trees above the harbour. The card was from Bea and addressed to Precious's home. 'I could stay here for ever,' she had written, signing it just B.

Katharine noted the date, ten years earlier. Before Frank. Just.

'That's his place. And these are his contact details.' Precious passed Katharine a business card.

'Patrick Cumberbatch, Consultant. Oh, so quite high up then?'

'Sorry?'

'Professionally,' said Katharine. 'I hadn't realised.'

When Bea told her Patrick worked at the council, she had always imagined a cross between a street cleaner and a housing officer. She'd never been able to picture him clearly – that was the point about a secret lover, she supposed, a kind of invisible friend. But clearly he was something rather better paid than a rent collector. She peered at the postcard and felt hope flutter up inside her. She straightened the little piles of Post-Its on Bea's desk. What if some promise had been made to Bea and she was making her way there? It made her rather cross, for a moment, the thought of Bea gazing down on that translucent sea, idling away her days.

Katharine sank slowly back on to Bea's chair. Because if she was going there, she would have let someone know, she told herself, not least Patrick. She opened the bottom drawer again and lifted out the cigarettes and knickers. She held them on her lap and looked helplessly over at Precious.

'I need to talk to this Patrick. Apart from anything else, I have a thing or two I want to tell him about the way he's treated Bea.'

Precious wondered whether she was referring to the ten-year affair or the other thing.

'I told the police about the abortion,' she said, frowning. 'It didn't feel good telling them but they asked me outright. "Has she had any operations that you knew of?" They would have found out from her doctor anyway, I suppose.'

Katharine absorbed the blow.

'Sorry,' said Precious, seeing all at once that Katharine knew nothing. 'I thought you knew.'

A void opened up, a sickening drop. 'When?'

'Years ago, just before she met Frank. It was the end, really.'

Katharine did the sum. Ten years ago. Bea was forty, Adrian was two, and Laura was four. Precious pressed on. 'Bea was horrified when she found out. She was so afraid of jeopardising Patrick's marriage – he has four children. She was always very good like that. Wanted to protect him and his family.'

'Rather hypocritical really,' snapped Katharine. 'If she had really wanted to protect his family, then why see the man at all?' The harshness of her voice surprised them both and Precious regretted saying anything. Katharine blew her nose fiercely. 'Sorry.'

She waved away a fly, or was it a dust mote, something, something there just in front of her face. The skin on her forehead contracted and she lost control of the muscles round her mouth. Karen appeared round the corner of the room divider, hesitated and disappeared again. Precious leant forward and patted Katharine's bony shoulder.

'She was very matter-of-fact about it. But I sometimes wondered, as the years went by, what it cost her to do that.'

Katharine shook her head and swallowed fiercely. A high-pitched whine escaped her. She dug the fear and the sadness into the palms of her hands with her nails. All around her were notices and overflowing waste-paper bins, screens flickering as far as the eye could see, stifling static, the hum of printers, Xeroxes and phone calls. She would die if she worked here. What would she do in Bea's shoes? If she was in Bea's shoes, she would take pleasure where she could find it. If she were Bea, she would go to Ithaca. She hadn't realised how little Bea had left to lose.

She put the postcard and Patrick's details in her bag and got up to go.

Precious smiled and stood up. 'Bea talked about you all the time, you know.'

Katharine was taken aback. 'Yes. Well, we're very important to each other. We're the only sisters we've got.'

DRIVING HOME from the council, Katharine wailed at the top of her voice so that the tears blurred her vision. She cried all the way round the ring road and down along the traffic jam by Midsummer Common. She tried to recall whether Bea had ever talked about children. She could remember both occasions she had announced her own pregnancies to Bea and she could remember Bea visiting her after the births, laden with gifts and tenderness and love. Then, for quite a few years, Adrian and Laura had filled all the space of their lives, and anyway, there comes a point when it is tactless to raise the subject of children with a single woman in her thirties. It couldn't be helped. Bea had made the decision to keep seeing Patrick and she must have known what that would cost, although perhaps she could be forgiven for not knowing it would cost her a child. Katharine wiped her face dry with one hand and shook the hair from her eyes irritably. Foolish woman! To all intents and purposes Bea was single for the ten years of her life that she secretly saw Patrick, which was why they were all so relieved when she met Frank at the age of forty. Bea's met a writer! Quite a catch for Bea. No, not a writer that anyone had heard of, but still, a writer all the same. They had all got excited when they had a moment to think about it. Children weren't out of the question, but then, as the years passed and no children arrived, they all assumed that it just wasn't to be. Katharine hadn't given the matter much thought after a while – life had been such a mad rush what with her career and her own children.

The crying had stopped. She felt washed out and thought how she should have given Bea more thought. Bea had given a great deal of thought to Adrian and Laura, had always been on hand, never complained, always been ready to step into the—

From out of nowhere a woman walked out into the road. Katharine slammed on the brakes and a split second later slammed her palm down on to the horn. For Christ's sake, she could have got herself killed! The woman, wrapped in layers of feculent clothing and pulling a makeshift shopping trolley, looked neither left nor right but continued her way to the other side of the road. Katharine watched an oncoming van in horrified fascination as it bore down on the shabby figure. It slewed to a halt with inches to spare. The driver leaned out of his window and vented a torrent of abuse. The woman paused just before the opposite pavement, looked at him and hauled her trolley up on to the kerb.

Slower now and shaking, Katharine drove on. She tried to put the spectre of the bag lady from her mind. She focused on Bea. Bea and Frank. The woman in the road must once have been missed. Once, a long time ago. And then wasn't. This was not the same as the situation with Bea at all. No. Let's think about Bea and Frank. Bea and her husband. Katharine and Richard had been impressed at first and they had been well suited in many ways, having washed up on the shore of middle age together, both a little the worse for wear inevitably. After all, thought Katharine, the person you are at forty is an awfully long way from the person you were at twenty. Another country really.

She slowed at the roundabout near her turning. She was

driving carefully, gently now, looking out for the unexpected. She waited patiently for an opening in the traffic. It was one thing to think that Frank was a disappointment to Bea, but nudging at the edge of her mind was a new thought. For the first time Katharine wondered what it had been like for Frank to live with a woman who was in love with another man. Perhaps he had hoped for children as well. Perhaps he too had hoped for more than he had found.

Ithaca

PATRICK HAD taken to swimming to the village shop most
afternoons. Apart from keeping him fit, it gave his day
some purpose and appealed to his sense of the absurd. 'I'm
just swimming to the shop!' he liked to call to his wife as
he left the terrace and took the path down to the water. It
was a few hundred metres from the small pebble beach near
their house, out across the bay and over to the harbour. He
always thought it was a shame that he couldn't swim back,
although he had done so once, with Bea, years ago, swimming on his back holding the bread out of the water while
she towed the tomatoes and cheese in a bag beside her.

The afternoon sea was choppy and felt chilly when he
waded in so that he hesitated before throwing himself under
and striking out across the bay. He swam in a measured,
steady crawl, aware of his blood gradually warming his
muscles, of his breath becoming calmer and catching the
rhythm of his limbs. Each time he broke the surface for air,
he saw a freeze-frame of the rocky coast beside him. Today
the tourist season was well and truly over and the village had
a sombre, still-life look to it. The yachts and hire boats were
gone, the tavernas had closed except for Penelope's and the
waterfront guesthouse was shuttered up for the winter. His
previous visits here had always been temporary, a holiday, but

now this was his real life. Well, they were going to give it a go. At the jetty, he hauled himself out of the sea. He flicked the water off his limbs and turned to look back at their house, seeking out the white wall of the terrace in among the trees halfway up the hill. He usually gave a wave to his wife once he was standing on the quayside, but today there was no figure waving back.

The sun warmed his skin and he stood a moment looking up at the sky and letting its rays bathe his face. It rained a bit at this time of year but the sun always came out afterwards and the rain gave the air a crisp, clean edge to it. The light here was wonderful, especially off season. The light was the whole point, wasn't it? All those years in England in the bloody dark. It was one of the things he always told people. Why live in the Dark Ages when you could come and visit us in the light? Very few visitors yet, though, other than their daughter of course. He took a deep breath and ran his hands through his hair and down over his torso. He knew he was in good shape for a man of sixty; he still had his hair, his muscle tone and his height, and that mattered to him, although – he licked the salt from his lips and raised a hand in greeting to Yannis sorting nets in his boat – he wasn't sure how much it mattered to his wife.

Patrick looked over towards the shop. The great thing was, he didn't even need money. They had a tab set up there. All very civilised. A cockerel crowed and a donkey's complaint sawed the air. Yes, at this time of year it could get fairly quiet out here, but one bar stayed open and the ferry from Kefalonia still brought the occasional visitor in search of solitude and blue skies. He looked up at the house again, set among cypress and oak and eucalyptus trees. He thought of his wife, setting the coffee to boil in the kitchen and preparing the guest room for the arrival of their daughter Annabel and her children. He tried a smile and shook his head. No, no one in their right mind would give up all this.

He took a deep breath. Theirs was a quiet, careful marriage. No sudden movements or loud noises. Susan had put up with a lot and he had much to thank her for. But then he had always been careful about his marriage; there had never been any question of jeopardising his family or his home. And he would have been a fool to turn down the severance package from Cambridgeshire County Council, although some days – Yannis had untangled an octopus from the net, gathered its legs up into his fist and was striking its head against the quayside – although some days, when the hours seemed slow and the view somewhat static, he did rather wonder about that word *severance*. Yannis grinned at him and threw the lifeless octopus into a bucket.

Patrick waited. He was waiting for Yannis to finish in his boat and come ashore, he was waiting for a boat to enter the harbour or for the farmer to arrive with his mule. Once or twice he and Yannis had drunk coffee together in the bar next to the shop. He enjoyed that. It gave him a chance to practise his Greek and made him feel more a part of things. He loitered now in his wet shorts, reluctant to go into the shop and back up the hill with the groceries. The move to Ithaca had been a lifesaver really, as far as their marriage was concerned. Not that it was ever on the rocks. Not really. After all, it wasn't as if he had behaved like some media star and detonated the marriage with a lethal mix of hubris and cocaine. No, he had protected Susan and the children throughout. It wasn't until the very end that she somehow found out about some of it, and of course things had been difficult for a while. And then the restructuring at work happened over his head, which meant he would have to apply for his own job, and what with the poor inspection perform-ance of his department, the gossip at work, well, it didn't take a genius to realise it was time to jump ship. And so here he was.

Yannis stood up in his boat and put the bucket down on

the quayside. He called to Patrick and offered him a plump, gleaming fish. How marvellous, thought Patrick, taking the fish with a smile and trying to explain to Yannis that he would pay him next time he was in the village with trousers on. Yannis waved him away, started his engine and chugged slowly out of the harbour. Patrick looked at the fish. Susan would be impressed with this, he thought, making his way to the shop. She could grill it with thyme and garlic and they would eat it with bread and roast tomatoes. He put his hand on the shop door handle and hesitated. That phone call from Precious had been awkward. And an email from the police, for heaven's sake. He shook his head. No, he did not find it out of character! Not from what he knew of Bea. And no, he did not know of her whereabouts. Really, he had left all that behind him. Although sometimes, when he woke early to the sound of the cockerel, long before the cicadas started up, he couldn't deny that Bea occasionally crept into his mind.

And then he saw her.

It was Bea, a photograph of her on a poster with *Have You Seen Her?* printed across the top.

Have you seen her? whispered his wife when he climbed into bed in the dark, hoping that she was asleep. *It's all over*, he told her then, and mainly it was true. *It's over*, he told Bea and there were no scenes. She just nodded her head against his chest and said, *I know*. She was always very good like that.

Precious's phone call had alerted him, of course, but he had almost put it out of his mind. It was so hard to think of the office existing, of the people and routines, out here in this great sweep of sea and sky. A mild guilt nudged him, guilt laced with desire. He had assumed, during the conversation with Precious, that Bea had rowed with Frank, had enough of work and buggered off for few days. Leave of absence without pay. She'd done it before – played hooky with him on the occasional Friday when he'd had a local government conference in Birmingham. But this poster disarmed him. It was like an accusation. It meant they were on to him. Not Precious, here, surely? Patrick looked about him. A catamaran rounded the entrance to the bay and approached the harbour. The meat van blew its horn. He studied the poster again. A full-colour photograph of Bea looking pretty and tanned, caught in the middle of a laugh. He had seen that look on her face here, in Ithaca, the last time, the one last time before she gave up waiting and found herself a husband of her own. She had never been a beautiful woman, but she was a handsome woman and so full of life, up for just about anything, and God knows he missed that. A sickening thought occurred to him. What if this was Bea's idea of a joke? He wheeled round and scanned the empty harbour. Yannis's threadbare dog sat splay-legged in the road scratching its ear, an expression of rapture on its face. The road winding up from the village was deserted. Yannis's mother came out of the shop with her broom and swept away some nutshells. No, this wasn't the kind of prank that Bea would pull. She was nothing if not discreet. My God, he sometimes thought she cared more about the feelings of his wife and kids than he did. She was forever reminding him to delete the texts; they'd pay for the hotel rooms with her card not his. Even that last time when they'd made love by the river, she'd woken him up to tell him he should go, so that his wife didn't worry. That had been such a delicious afternoon – all the more so for being so unexpected. After all, it had been years since they'd done that. He'd thought of Frank as he moved between her raised thighs. Thought of how he was erasing that pompous old fart, imagined Frank stumbling upon them when they were too far gone to be able to stop. He hadn't realised how much he'd missed all that. There was nothing apologetic or careful about sex with Bea. Just a glorious animal fission. He looked at her face again. No, this was someone else's work, not Bea's. He reeled back through his mind for the names of the people who knew about him and Bea, but the list was a long and confused one, what with Cambridge being such a small and gossipy place. He cast a furtive glance up at his own house but the sun was in his eyes. He readjusted his grip on the fish. He jumped when the bread van careered round the bend and stopped outside the shop. With a bolting heart, he understood. It meant that Bea was dead. That was what these posters were, wasn't it? They were memorials to the departed; despair disguised as hope; the prayers of those left behind that they themselves might not be lost in grief. The catamaran dropped its anchor, the rattling chain echoing round the hillside. Who had been here then? There was a mobile phone number with an English code at the bottom. Frank? Her sister? Something leaked from the mouth of the fish and he wiped his hand clean on his shorts.

Patrick gave the poster a sharp pull and ripped it from the wooden panel. He sometimes wished Bea had been more demanding. He strode up to the other two posters and snatched them down. How could he dare to detonate his marriage if Bea never stated that was what she wanted? And what if Susan saw the pictures now? All the pain and hard work would be wasted. He might even be stranded in old age on his own. Anger filled his chest. One of the posters floated away on the breeze and settled on the surface of the water by the harbour wall. He watched her face darken and sink. It really wasn't any of his business now, he told himself as he stuffed the remaining posters into his pocket. Whoever had put these here should know better. Bea would never come here, although he sometimes wished to God she would. He began to walk, through the village, along the road that skirted the coast and up the steep path of the hill. He walked fast and without stopping to shop. He needed to get back home to Susan before whoever had made the connection between himself and Bea got there first.

WHEN KATHARINE stepped off the ferry from the neigh-
bouring island of Kefalonia earlier that afternoon, she was
exhausted. The closer she got to Ithaca, the less of an idyll
it appeared to be. The flight to Kefalonia was much longer
than expected and then there were delays in getting to the
ferry. She could see that the crossing to Ithaca might lift the
spirits, but once on the island, her very first impressions were
of starved cats, concrete and plastic bags. Tuscany was always
a safer bet. The Mediterranean could be so shabby. At the
port, there was a long wait for the bus to Kioni, the village
featured on Bea's postcard to Precious, and the journey itself
was a diesel-ridden lurch from one rain-slicked hairpin bend
to another. She wished she had hired a car, but the whole
point, impressed on her by Adrian and Laura, was that she should
follow the route that Bea might take. Bea would be saving
money. Bea was always careful with money. They were certain
she would not drive. Katharine left a trail of posters wherever she went, and when she finally reached Kioni in the
late afternoon she had no trouble finding out where Patrick
lived. The woman in the village shop took her outside and
pointed out his house, perched high above the rest, with
views across the Ionian Sea.

Katharine climbed the steep road that led out of the village
and looked down at the harbour. She had to admit that it
was beautiful in a simple, rugged sort of way. As she climbed
higher, the headland appeared and she saw three stone towers,
ruined windmills looking out to sea. She rested on a low
wall and got her breath back. Now this was a view; a silent
drama that must have seemed a million miles from Bea's job,
from the flat greys of Cambridge, from the quiet massacre
of their childhood.

When she reached the house, she climbed halfway up the
steep steps to the terrace and called out.

'Hello? Anybody home?'

A woman's face appeared over the terrace wall. Small and

pale, she didn't look like she spent time in the sun. She had a reluctant air to her, as if she didn't anticipate any visitors.

'Can I help you?' she said.

Katharine came to the top of the steps and wondered what she was going to say. Obviously this was the wife. She cleared her throat and raised her head. She took a breath and put on her work face. Businesslike and brisk was always the best approach.

'Sorry to bother you,' she said, climbing the remaining steps, panting and pulling one of the posters from her bag. 'But does Patrick live here?'

Bitter

PATRICK WORRIED that his heart might burst. His run had slowed to a jog by the time he reached the final bend and then become a tortured, drunken stagger as he made it up the steps to the terrace. He clung to the rough stone of the wall at the top and groaned for breath. His wife sat drinking coffee with a strange woman, a poster of Bea on the table between them.

Patrick said, 'Oh God,' and bent at the waist, supporting his weight with one hand on the wall.

Susan said, 'I'll get more coffee,' and went into the house.

Katharine looked at the fish in his hand and said, 'I'm here about Bea.'

She put her hand to her hair in that gesture that was Bea's, and he nodded and said, 'You're her sister.' He sat down opposite her with his back to the view and poured water for himself from a glass jug full of ice and lemon. 'Katharine, is it?'

Katharine was disappointed. She had been imagining Patrick as a balding Irish bureaucrat in an ill-fitting suit and pale skin. She hadn't expected him to be so tall or so hairy. Richard's body was hairless, even his legs for some reason, but Patrick – his chest, stomach, thighs, calves, everywhere was thatched in startling black hair. She looked away.

Red and white geraniums stood clustered in pots and she imagined Bea in his arms. She thought of Richard, with what friends described as his classic English good looks. Jane said Richard looked like Cary Grant in *North by Northwest*, and Paul remarked that he did sometimes have that being-pursued-by-a-crop-duster look about him, a comment that Katharine had not found amusing. She straightened her back and eased the fabric of her trousers at her groin. They were too tight and hot for this weather. Patrick pushed a bowl of shrivelled black olives towards her and waved a fly away from the fish.

'I ought to get this out of the sun,' he said.

She looked at his eyes, which were brown and not meeting hers. He was watching the house as though wondering whether to make a dash for the fridge. He looks French or Greek, she thought. Lethal, no doubt, in Deeds, Convents and Registrars or whatever it was that Bea's department was called.

'Bea's disappeared,' said Katharine.

Patrick nodded and she wanted to kick him. 'I saw the posters. But she wouldn't come here. We—'

'You had an affair.'

His eyes flicked to the door of the house again. She saw him calculating speed, distance, velocity, working out if he had time to deflect the missile before it hit his marriage.

'We were very good friends for a long time. An affair is not the word I would have used.'

'What would you call it then?'

Patrick poured water for them both. 'Why don't you tell me what's happened? Of course I will do what I can to help.'

She told him, while he nodded and listened, hands clasped before him on the table. He was in work mode, she thought. He was managing her like a problem from Lifts, Toilets and Parking.

When she had finished he looked down at a neat row of children's buckets and spades and said, 'What happened between Bea and myself was a long time ago. And it was a mistake . . .'

Katharine stopped him. 'I'm not here to judge.' She had done that already, she thought. Men get away with bloody murder. 'I'm here to find out more about her. I know she came here with you once.'

The olives were mean and salty. She spat the stones into her hand and recognised the painted bowl from Bea's kitchen collection.

'I've been told that when people go missing they often find their way to places or people from their pasts. Apparently, they can't help it . . .' Her voice tailed away. She put Bea's postcard to Precious on the table and pushed it towards him. Patrick looked at it fearfully.

The vast sea stretching out there to the horizon looked suddenly dreadful, and Katharine wished she'd never come. Finding Bea, so far from home seemed impossible. Neither of them spoke. The olive grove below seemed to shiver and shake like a shoal of fish, becoming silver then grey then blue.

'You think she's come here?' Patrick's tan took on a yellowish tinge. 'How long did you say again?' He looked her in the eyes briefly but his gaze kept fidgeting between the view and the postcard and the door to his house. In the end, thought Katharine, it was the house and the view he feared losing, more than her sister.

'She was last seen six weeks ago.' It sounded as if Bea was dead, she knew that. He thought there was a fair chance she was dead, she could see that on his face. 'Has she contacted you at all?'

He looked up as Susan came out with more coffee. She was small and bird-like with a precise, clever air to her. Katharine wanted to push her down the steps. Susan poured coffee with a steady hand and sat down next to her husband. The postcard had vanished.

She said, 'That looks like it might be past its best,' and waved the flies away from the fish.

'Yannis gave it to me,' said Patrick. 'It's fresh.'

'I think it needs to go in the fridge,' said Susan.

Katharine got up and asked if she could use their bathroom.

She ran water into the sink and lowered her face into it. When she raised her head and pulled back her hair, she looked in the mirror and saw Bea for an instant. Smile! She left the bathroom and hesitated in the darkened corridor. Framed family photographs lined the walls leading to the bedroom. Katharine peered at them. They looked like all family photographs – everyone smiling, smiling, smiling!

'I was just telling Susan about Bea,' said Patrick, when Katharine came back outside. He had put on a loose red shirt. 'You work with someone for years and years and then this.' He picked up the missing poster. 'It's such a shock.'

They're neutralising me, thought Katharine, hesitating and unsure about where to stand. Susan was still seated at the table, sipping her coffee. The fish was nowhere to be seen. Katharine went over to the wall and looked out at the sea.

When she spoke, she kept her back to them. 'When you last saw her, Patrick, did she seem herself?'

Patrick thought of Bea laughing on her back in the grass, saw her opening the wine and dipping strawberries into icing sugar. 'We had farewell drinks with the staff and she was her usual cheerful self as far as I could tell.' He thought of her silence as he held her familiar but strange, changed body against his. 'That was the thing about Bea. Always so full of life. Always happy.' That had been the point. Bea was the antidote to the ball-breaking business of marriage. He smiled over at Susan. My God, if it hadn't been for Bea, he doubted his marriage would have survived. She made it bearable.

The phone rang and Susan went inside to answer it.

'Bea told me that she loved you,' Katharine said.

He put an olive into his mouth. And then another.

She waited for him to say it. Up here, in this place where he and Bea had spent hidden days, she needed him to tell her that he had loved her sister.

Patrick offered the olives to Katharine and wondered whether she would be interested to know that they cured them themselves, from their own olive grove. It was one of the things they told visitors. Our own olives! Takes four to six weeks. You have to remember to remove the scum from the vat once a week. And change the brine regularly. Endless rinsing. They hadn't got it quite right yet. This batch were a little on the bitter side.

'She must have loved you rather a lot for it to last as long as it did.'

He shook his head. 'I can't believe she's just vanished.'

'Well she has,' snapped Katharine. And it's your fault, she wanted to say, except she didn't know whether it was or not. No more Patrick's fault than Frank's, than the job, than hers, their mother's, their father's for damn well going and getting himself killed before they were barely out of fairy tales and knee socks.

She explained to him all they had done to try to find her. How the police could find no trace despite a thorough search of hospitals, bank accounts, houses, commons and rivers. She told him that their one hope was that, as they couldn't find her passport, it seemed probable she had gone abroad. So far, though, there was no record of her from airports or the Eurostar or any of the places where they scanned passports, and anyway they didn't scan her own passport when she flew out here, they barely looked at it. She didn't tell him that Precious doubted Bea would have got a plane anywhere. Boats and trains, yes, but not a plane, not these days, with all that being herded into pens and all the queuing clutching your plastic bag of lotions, your documents, your keys and wallet and phone. All that being shouted at to take your boots and belts off. 'Was she afraid of flying?' Katharine asked. 'Oh no,' Precious said, looking her straight in the eye. 'Bea just didn't like being treated like shit.'

The air had grown cooler. Katharine fetched her jacket from the table and looked down the steep hill to the sea. 'I know she's alive,' she found herself saying, although being here with Patrick and his wife in their stone paradise, she was fighting a creeping notion that Bea was dead. 'But I need to ask you whether she ever said anything that made you think she would do herself . . . harm.'

She was saying the words not because she believed them but because these were the words the Mispers men had used. The word suicide stuck in her throat. It was the *sui* of it, the verb *to be* of it, the *cidere*, the cut and the kill of it. She had trawled the internet all the long nights lately looking for the many ways that the desperate found to commit themselves to the act of death. Downstairs alone in the cold blue computer light, she had learned the preferred means used by women, by men, by the young, the aged and the infirm. She had forced herself to try and see Bea with tablets, with ropes, long drops and railway lines, but she couldn't, she wouldn't . . .

Patrick was saying, 'God, no,' shaking his head. 'I don't think Bea was capable of such a thing. I mean . . .' Katharine did up the buttons of her jacket. A chill wind was blowing in from the east, the sea had turned a deep dark blue and she didn't like it here up on this terrace in their wary, beached marriage. The sight of grandchildren's flippers and masks stored in a box by the wall made her very angry. She had one more thing to say before she went.

'Not even when she lost the baby?'

Then he looked at her. That did it all right. His face slackened, discoloured and retracted as though she had punched him. He hadn't known either. Katharine felt sick. Her stomach heaved. She wanted to shit.

Susan appeared beside them, car keys in her hand and smelling of fly spray. Bea was right about perfume, Katharine realised now. It all smelt of insecticide or cat piss and people should stop using it. Susan was telling them that she was driving to Frikes to meet Annabel and the children off the boat. If they left now, Katharine would make it in time for the last flight back to London.

ZIGZAG LINES, flickering lights and nausea assailed Katharine as Susan drove her to the port. By the time they reached the waterside, the wind had picked up and waves crested with white rode the inky sea. Katharine stared fixedly at the horizon and ordered her guts to be still.

At Kefalonia she managed to get herself into a taxi. Black dots replaced the zigzags in her vision and her right cerebrum felt primed to explode. In the queue for the plane she forced down a double dose of migraine pills and threw the perfume she had bought on the way out into the bin. Once on board, she collapsed into her seat and balanced the sick bag on her chest ready for takeoff. Somebody asked if she was unwell.

'You did know your sister had been unwell for some time,' Susan had told her as they reached Frikes after a silent drive north with both windows open. Katharine asked what she meant but Susan was getting out of the car and waving at a young woman and two children waiting on the quayside with bags and suitcases.

'Unstable,' she added, walking towards her family. 'Patrick had to give her a lot of support.' The ferry blew its horn. 'Quick. You'd better hurry.'

'Unwell' was a euphemism on the missing websites Katharine had searched. Unwell meant mentally ill. 'Jason's family is very concerned about him as he has recently been unwell.' She covered herself in a blanket and put her eye mask on. She had scrolled through the hundreds of the missing on websites and podcasts, scanning their details to try and find a case like Bea's but there were very few. Most were either teenagers or middle-aged men. No mystery there,

Katharine had thought. And then a few were not from these groups and they were the ones who had been 'unwell'. No mystery there either, she thought. She knew what that meant. But Bea's disappearance *was* a mystery. She twitched away Pete's voice, or was it Jim's? One of them saying, 'It's never really a mystery. It's just that people only start looking once they've already gone.' Useless, the police had been in her opinion. Absolutely useless.

She accepted a beaker of water from the passing trolley, swallowed a temazepam and waited for oblivion.

Seen

THERE WERE a dozen people in the audience at the Burnley library's matinee performance of *The Seagull in the Cherry Orchard*, and there were slightly fewer at the question-and-answer session afterwards, three of whom were Lance, Margaret and Wanda. Katharine now employed Wanda as a part-time carer for Margaret down in Hastings. When Wanda phoned, Katharine was in Greece but Richard thought a trip to the theatre would do Margaret the world of good.

It was lucky they were there because they were the only ones who asked any questions. Lance asked what Frank was currently working on, which allowed Frank to free-associate about *Close and Personal*, which at that very moment he decided was going to be a novel, and to talk up the 'soon to be produced' *Lupa*, which he suspected was still in its envelope under his agent's assistant's chair. Wanda asked, 'Was the sex real?' which threw Frank completely until the chair of the Q & A repeated the question as, 'Is the set a reference to Chekhov's pioneering work in stage realism?' A woman in a green coat and with hair like a cauliflower asked him where he got his ideas from, then Margaret asked where the toilets were. And then it was over.

They got back to Cambridge late that night. Wanda put the parents to bed and then left for Katharine's house, saying she would be back in the morning to take them down to Hastings. Margaret slept in the children's room and Lance slept on the couch downstairs. When Frank climbed into the double bed he lay awake for a time, enjoying the new sheets and duvet. He turned on his side and watched Bea's egg cups lined up along their newly painted shelves and walls. Katharine had thrown money at Wanda and Urban and instructed a thorough upgrade of the house and garden. She hadn't bothered to ask Frank; she had just informed him it was happening and told him she wanted Bea to have a proper home to come back to. She hadn't asked if she could use Wanda as a carer for Margaret, down in Hastings either. She had just done it, or rather given Wanda an offer she couldn't refuse. True, she was paying for Lance to be cared for down there with Margaret, but even so.

Frank turned over the other way and looked at the curtains. Bea's bags and boxes and clutter had gone. Wanda had sorted through and packed everything away into suitcases. Something had happened to the carpet so that its colour warmed the room. In fact, the room felt surprisingly spacious. He had a suspicion that Katharine might be paying the mortgage, because he had waited for letters from the building society but none had arrived. He was rather hazy about the mortgage anyway, as Bea had always dealt with that. But even so – he scratched his groin – he was very short of cash. Bea's salary, still coming in for the first few months, had barely covered the bills and living expenses. Then, all of a sudden, her salary had been suspended 'pending an enquiry into unauthorised absence'. He turned over on to his back and looked up at the ceiling. Urban had painted the whole room brilliant white so that it glowed through the darkness. There was no doubt about it. He needed to earn some money. The question was, how? He thought of the garden, which Katharine had spent a fortune on in the last few weeks. Urban was digging a pond out there, a terrace of York stone had been built, which Frank was not allowed to call a patio, and there were new trees and shrubs all planted and with their labels still on.

Frank turned back on to his side and looked at the egg cups again. He needed to get on with *Close and Personal*. He should have written a novel years ago instead of fiddling about with plays. His agent was supposed to ring him back with a date for a meeting. Frank had in mind a substantial lunch somewhere like Lawyers where they did excellent traditional food and a collection of rather good wine. He heard someone in the bathroom, heard the catch of the door and the sound of the toilet flushing. He lay on his back again and straightened his pyjamas. He gathered the duvet close around him and thought about Wanda. They didn't any more, not since Bea went. And anyway they never had at night. It was understood. It had been a couch thing. An afternoon thing. Not really a sex thing at all, more a muse thing. They had never spoken about it and he supposed that Wanda felt guilty about Bea, about that afternoon when she hadn't given him the message, about abusing Bea's trust in her that way. He listened to the house. All was quiet again. He liked the feeling of others sleeping in the house around him. It made him feel a part of things, like a small creature in a colony of other creatures. Tomorrow they would be gone again to Hastings. He hardly saw Wanda now. Katharine sent a Hungarian boy round once a week to do the cleaning – Viktor. Frank turned on to his stomach and spreadeagled himself across the bed. He looked sideways out towards the thick velvet curtains that had appeared one day. Purple seemed to him an absurd colour for a bedroom. He was getting an idea. The children's room was unused now. He might get a good price for that room. He turned on to his back again. Yes. He would do it tomorrow. The answer to all his problems. He would get a lodger. Four hundred pounds a month. A nice lady lodger.

The next day, as soon as the others left, Frank sat at his computer to check on rental prices. When the phone rang he froze. He looked at it. 'Withheld' showed in the caller's number display. He considered not answering it. Phone calls usually signalled an unwelcome about-turn in his life. Any minute now it would stop ringing and leave a message. He stared at it. Withhelds never left a message. He lifted the phone and held it to his ear.

'Frank? Frank Pamplin?' A man's voice. 'Good morning, Jim here.'

Frank racked his brains. Jim? Jim who?

'Jim Woods, Cambridge Missing Persons Unit. Frank, we thought you should be the first to know. Frank? You there?'

Frank nodded and mumbled something. Here we go again, he thought. Event, incident, enter, speech, exit.

'There's been a development.'

Frank breathed into the phone. There was white winter blossom on one of the trees Katharine had bought for the garden. Tiny birds with yellow and black markings hopped and pecked in the branches.

'We have a sighting.'

He saw Bea standing at the end of a long tunnel. The house felt empty and he wished he had asked Wanda and the others to stay for breakfast. Jim was talking on the other end of the line.

'While we wouldn't want to raise hopes—'

'Where? Who's seen her? When?' Frank rubbed his hand over his face as panic tried to clamber up through the fog.

'Southampton station. We have CCTV footage which we'd like to bring over, if that's all right with you.'

There was a silence. Jim said he was sorry if this was a bolt out of the blue and Frank took that as permission to turn grief and fear to rage. These bastards had left him to rot for weeks and now they wanted to talk.

'Don't you normally just come and kick the door down?'

There was another silence. They were probably recording this call, he thought.

'We're not CID, Frank.'

'Yeah, well . . .'

'I'm sorry if—'

'Does her sister know?'

'She's away at the moment.'

'What are you saying? Have you found my wife? When was this?'

'No, we haven't found her, Frank. But we would like you to have a look at some film from a security camera. It's a few weeks old unfortunately, but . . . Would it be convenient if we dropped by in the next hour or so?'

IT WAS raining when Jim and Pete arrived. Both men were gazing round at the newly planted front garden. Jim smiled at Frank as he came in while the small one, Pete, said, 'Lovely day for it,' and gave him a half wave, half salute as he hopped into the house after Pete.

The three men hesitated in the hall and noted the transformation in the house. Frank told them to go through to the kitchen.

Jim was businesslike and brisk. He sat at the table and opened his laptop.

'We've made a DVD for you,' he said as the screen lit up. 'The quality is not what we would wish, but as you know, we follow up every lead, and other than this one there have been none at all.'

Frank peered at the screen while Pete did his weird wallflower number.

A snowstorm fizzed and then a series of frames of the station platform appeared. It wasn't even black and white, which would give some definition, it was just grey and white. Jim paused the disc.

'There,' he said.

Frank bent closer. It didn't help that he had lost his glasses and really he could make out precious little on the small screen. Jim was pointing at a woman standing at the far end of the platform. She was looking away from the camera, up the track, towards the approaching train. The next frame had skipped several moments and when it showed the platform again, the train was standing there but the woman had vanished.

'Is that it?' asked Frank.

'As I say,' said Jim. 'Hollywood it ain't. Let's look at it again.'

'Well, did she get on it?'

'That's our problem. We don't know. That is the London train, heading for Waterloo. We've checked Waterloo cameras for when that train arrived but come up with nothing. We also checked Southampton station's ticket office to see whether we could catch this individual either buying a ticket or leaving the station. The camera in the ticket office wasn't working.'

'Can I borrow your specs?'

Jim handed them to him and Frank sat ready, head forward, shoulders hunched. 'OK,' he said.

It was recorded in the early afternoon of the day she had gone. But he knew straight away it wasn't her. She didn't know anyone in Southampton. The woman was holding her head strangely, as if it was too heavy and something about her clothes was wrong. Frank had the feeling that whoever the woman was who had taken herself to the far end of the platform, he was watching a stranger. For a start she wasn't behaving like a normal person. When the train appeared in the frame and she didn't step back from the edge, he wondered whether she was deaf or blind or something, because she didn't respond like the rest of the crowd. She just stood her ground, too close to the edge. The coat looked similar to one he thought he'd seen Bea wearing, he'd give them that. And maybe the bag, although Bea had so many bags he couldn't be definite.

'Anything?' asked Jim.

Frank took the glasses off and handed them back. For the first time he felt that he had the upper hand with these two men. He could feel the tension in the air, the hope that they might have hit on something. They probably got commission for every Misper that they found. They weren't very good at this and he had been treated like shit. The whole police investigation had an amateurish air to it. He shook his head.

'It's not her,' he said. 'I'm pretty sure it's not her.'

Her

LAURA KNEW immediately it was Bea when she saw the footage. They knelt in the dusk in the empty sitting room, crouched around Jim's laptop. Katharine's suitcase stood unpacked in the hall.

'It's her.' Laura got up and walked away, knowing she would not be believed.

'I think it might be her,' said Adrian, nodding. 'That way of standing. When she's tired. She used to say her head got too heavy.'

Katharine peered at the screen and asked to see it again.

'It's terrible quality. I've seen ultrasounds clearer than this. I don't see how we can make a positive identification . . .' She stopped and studied the time-lapsed frames, the snowy blur of a woman with her back to the camera like a slowed-down silent movie. She creased her brow in an effort to make the strange jerky movements familiar. We have reached this point, she told herself. We are searching closed circuit television footage for my sister. She knew what this meant. They all did. Always, with CCTV, the gritty, grim association of death.

They watched the meagre few seconds again and again, leaning closer into the screen until they could hear one another's breathing.

'I don't know . . .' said Katharine. Her joints cracked as she straightened up.

'It's impossible with this quality,' said Richard. 'She could be anyone.'

'We can just enlarge the image a bit . . .' Adrian pressed some keys on the laptop and the screen went blank. 'Oh.'

'Classic,' chuckled Pete.

'It's her,' said Laura again. 'It's her Happy Coat.' She picked up the cat and forced it into an embrace it did not want. 'She bought it to cheer herself up. It's got a pink lining and everything.'

Katharine looked at Jim in exasperation. 'Laura is supposed to wear glasses.' He surely wasn't going to take the word of a child?

'What could she possibly be doing in Southampton, though?' asked Richard.

Pete started to pack away the laptop while Jim led Richard down the other end of the room. 'Nine times out of ten in a case like this,' he murmured in a man-to-man kind of a way, 'someone else is involved. We had a married man the other day, respectable type, lawyer in the city, et cetera. Goes to work one morning, never comes back. Family at their wits' end. Turns out he's met a barmaid called Betty in a pub in the Cotswolds. Packed up and gone to live with her. More often than not, with these older types, there's bound to be a Betty the Barmaid there somewhere. Betty or Bernie . . . someone she met on the internet perhaps—'

'It's her,' said Laura, glaring up at them and leaving the room.

THEIR BEDROOM was empty now. Katharine had put an ad in the paper and a man with a van came round and bought the lot. She preferred the house empty because it was like the way she felt. Stripped down and featureless. She lay on the mattress on the floor and looked up at the curtainless windows. Richard turned the light off and got undressed. She thought of Patrick doing the same in Ithaca, peeling off the lies of his life while his wife lay on the bed and watched him. Richard climbed under the duvet with her and she waited for his embrace, for his words of gentle enquiry and reassurance. They didn't come. He lay silently beside her for a while and then asked how long they were going to live in limbo. They had done what they could to find Bea, but what if she didn't want to be found? He asked her whether, in some dim recess of her mind, it had ever occurred to her that Bea might just have had enough – of Frank, of work, of her. He wondered whether Katharine might possibly consider that the lives of her own family – him, the children – were perhaps in need of some attention. That, in case she hadn't noticed, they weren't much of a family at all any longer, if indeed they ever really had been. He said that Adrian stood a good chance of flunking his exams because the school had no science teachers and Laura seemed to have a permanent period pain or an upset stomach or sore throat and barely attended school at all. He told her that Claudia had suggested that they hire a private detective because she had heard of a woman in Scotland who had seven children and went to empty the bin one night but never came back until three years later, when she was discovered living half a mile away with the woman who ran the hospice. A private detective had found her. Then he accused Katharine of hypocrisy. He told her she had exploited Bea for years and never given a second thought to the woman until she suddenly wasn't there any longer. He said it was a bit bloody late to be throwing money at Bea's house and garden, that perhaps she might have thought of that before, but that this was typical of Katharine, she never gave anyone a second thought; just look at Margaret.

Katharine lay in the dark and didn't speak. She waited as the words removed the layers of her self and her marriage.

She waited patiently for the flaying to stop. She listened to everything he said, ears straining to catch each word, which she took and folded carefully away in glass tissue inside her. Then she got up from the bed, picked up her eye mask and earplugs and left the room.

Out on the landing she waited for Richard to come and get her. He didn't. She couldn't go to the spare room, the bed had been dismantled. She would rather not go downstairs and sleep on the sofa. For one thing there was no duvet there, and for another, it was too much of a Frankish thing to do. She climbed the stairs to the top floor and stood outside the children's rooms. The floorboards creaked. She looked at Laura's door. Laura's door was always shut. Laura's door had been firmly shut for the last two years. It was a very long time since Katharine had been in there. She put her hand on the doorknob and turned it slowly.

A night light was glowing from a plug in the wall and she saw that Laura had unpacked some of her things. Fluffy toys sat lined up on the shelf beneath the window, a pile of children's books from long ago stacked on the floor below. Laura lay on her back, sleep-sprawled in the position that hadn't changed in her since she was an infant. A small toy monkey nestled beside her, its hand up tenderly at her chin. Soundlessly, Katharine put down her eye mask and earplugs and lifted the edge of the duvet. Limb by limb she slid herself in to the narrow space at the edge of the bed. Laura shifted in her sleep and turned on to her side away from her. Katharine hesitated, then slid one arm slowly into the gap beneath Laura's neck and rested her other arm gently around her daughter's body. She pressed her face into the nape of her neck and filled her lungs with the sweet, warm scent of her. Laura stirred again. Katharine, afraid she would wake, tried to lift her arm away. With a tight, fierce grip, Laura held it firmly where it was.

Lost

JANUARY WAS unseasonably mild. Daffodils and blossom budded early; blackbirds and thrushes, still thin from the winter, searched for places to nest. Wanda was in a hurry, her blonde hair bouncing and jerking, her mouth a thin line. She found Urban working in the cemetery. He had stripped off to a vest and he bent at his work, spade slicing the earth with powerful downward strokes. She let the gate clang shut behind her, walked over to him with quick, angry strides and gave him a push. He turned his head to her and half smiled without stopping the digging.

'Give me the passport.' She pushed him again, and this time he straightened up and grasped her wrist tight so that it hurt. 'You said you hadn't got it. I think you have.'

He let her go and stabbed the spade into the earth. 'So, how's Hastings?'

'It's not right, Urban. They need to know. They need to know she's not using her passport.'

Urban took off his gloves and raised his eyebrows at her. 'She doesn't need her passport to get abroad.'

'Don't, Urban. Have you got it?'

'I don't know. The police search that place so many times I think maybe they have it. I haven't checked.'

'Come on.' She pulled at his sleeve. 'It's important.'

Urban stayed where he was. 'What's it worth?'

'Shut up.'

THEY ROUNDED the corner of Oyster Row.

Wanda rang the bell and then unlocked the door, calling Frank's name. The house was empty and it smelt of paint. Urban pulled on his gloves and went out into the garden, disappearing behind the shed. Wanda followed. She heard him pulling up the roofing felt before emerging with a plastic bag folded flat. He handed it to her. 'Take your pick,' he said.

Wanda looked through the brown, the turquoise, the maroon and the black, each worth £500. It reminded her of the monopoly game she had played in her first au pair job here in Cambridge. She checked the photos of two British passports and handed one back to Urban.

'Perhaps I'll keep Frank's,' he said, putting it back with the others and going round to the far side of the shed again. 'Terrible photo anyway.'

Wanda didn't argue. She studied Bea's photograph. An unremarkable middle-aged woman looked back at her. Beatrice Pamplin. Next of kin: Frank Pamplin. She shook her head. 'That's not Bea,' she said, putting it in her pocket. 'I'll post it. Come on, let's go.'

'Hang on,' said Urban, winding a strand of Wanda's hair round his fingers. 'I want a bath.'

WHEN BEA'S passport dropped through Frank's letter box he held it in his hand and wondered whether this was a good sign or a bad one. He rang Katharine. Katharine told him not to touch it, to stay where he was and do nothing. Frank was still standing in the hallway when CID turned up to search the house again. He gave them the passport, walked out of the open front door and turned right, up the road and away from the river. These days he avoided the river walks. There was something oppressive to him now about its familiarity and dank odour, something crushing in its sluggish leaden flow. These days he wandered through the hushed terraced streets, avoiding the main roads, the town centre and the common. He walked to try and find a way out, a way out of the hollow, sour sense of remorse that shackled him here in this flat, squat town.

Bea had made the best of the place, he realised, its absence of cliffs and of sea, its petty Town–Gown divide. She had walked out into it every day and that was more than he had done until recently. When he first stopped working she had suggested they move away. 'Why live in one damp corner of the planet, Frank, when there's a whole world out there?' He had been disdainful. He had dissed her, as Laura would say. Disdain and opposition were his default positions. 'It doesn't matter where you are,' he told her. 'It's what's in here that matters,' and he tapped his forehead as if to say, I have worlds in here that you can barely imagine. Bollocks to that, he thought now. She hadn't given up, though. 'You could work anywhere, Frank. We could live somewhere hot, somewhere beautiful.' But he knew she was thinking of Ithaca. The Ithaca stories had been offered by her in the early days in exchange for his own sorry stories of life on the *Oriana*. It had sounded idyllic and he had sewn them inside himself with tight jealous stitches. He knew Bea was thinking of her days there with Patrick, and what she had lost. He had looked at her, seen the loosening of skin at her jaw, the slackening around her eyes, and he had swallowed a mouthful of whisky, felt it sluice the fear and the sadness in his groin. 'Don't let's die in this grey, flat town,' she had said, threatening tears and putting a hand on his arm. 'Let's make a new start.' He knew too that when Bea met him on the *Oriana* she had mistaken him for an adventurer who would take her out of the ordinary. The very last thing he wanted was adventure, and when, as the years passed, he saw the disappointment in her eyes when she looked at him, he shrank from her and grew to hate her.

To do this, he shut out the determined brightness of her voice, the plump curve of her mouth. 'What in God's name would we do perched on a hillside in the middle of nowhere in the baking sun?' She didn't answer at first. 'It would be an adventure,' she said, at last. 'It would be a disaster,' he said, because it always felt better to end a scene with his voice not with hers. Exit Bea.

He turned a corner of a street and looked around to discover that he was lost. He appeared to have come to a dead end and was about to turn back when he noticed a gate in the wall at the end of the road. It was standing half open and framed by a low arch of yew. He walked the rest of the way down the street, opened the gate and went through. Raindrops brushed his hair and shoulders and he found himself in what at first he took to be a large, wild garden. Towering copper beeches, oak and yew told him the place was old, and neatly trimmed gravel paths told him it was cared for. A few steps further in and he realised he was in a cemetery. Wild rose, heavy with hips, holly and trees and shrubs that Frank didn't know the names of but which Bea would know. There was no sound of traffic here, just birdsong.

'I'm lonely,' Frank said out loud. It was no good shutting himself away to write without the knowledge of Bea or Wanda or the children on the other side of the door. Oyster Row was his world now. He winced at the joke. A couple of years back, he and Bea had taken the ferry to Calais. It had been a cold day in February. She had spent most of the crossing up on the deck watching the horizon and being battered by the wind. They had eaten *moules* in a deserted restaurant on the seafront and got drunk on cheap red wine. It had been a mad thing to do, Bea's idea, and he was sure it wouldn't work but it had been fun. The sea had been rough, the wind had been wild and the very fact of crossing the sea, leaving England behind, had been surprisingly exhilarating.

Jim had told Katharine, 'Passport or no passport, they can

be very lax with security on ferries – especially out of season. And a middle-aged woman, well . . . who's interested?'

'I doubt she's in Calais,' said Frank.

Jim laughed. 'Ferries go all over the place. Once you're over the channel – Spain, France, Holland, you're away. It's possible to go a long way without being seen once you leave this island.'

'What about money?'

Pete looked at him and rubbed his chin so that Frank heard the stubble scrape on his palm. 'Wanda does all right, doesn't she?'

Frank blushed. So they knew about Wanda. What had she told them? Had they talked to that awful Urban too? Surely not. Wanda said that Urban had been missing for years. Crows fussed and squawked in the ash tree above his head. He hated those birds, their malevolent heads and unnatural way of walking instead of hopping.

'You can always change a name,' Wanda had told him. 'If you really don't want to be found.'

Frank read the headstones nearest him. They leaned towards one another – Nelly Read, Jess Darnell, Blanche Cooper, Ellen Leader . . . He thought of Wanda, that body of hers, close beside him. He tried to summon an image of her naked in one of those poses. At the back of his mind, a faint one flickered, then failed. He shivered. It looked like rain again.

'I want my life back,' he said.

Frank stood in the drizzle and looked at the gravel. Did he really want Bea back? It was more the parts around her that he missed: Adrian, the smell of cooking, the central heating, his escape to the writing that never had to be finished. He remembered Pete's voice, gentle and kind. 'Sometimes, when you go missing, you go further than you thought you ever could. One day you wake up and realise there is no way back.'

The rain began to fall with an intensity he couldn't ignore.

He nodded as drops hit his forehead and wondered just how long and how often Wanda and Urban had been lovers.

It took Frank a while to find the way out. The graveyard was bigger than he had thought and the paths wound this way and that so that he found himself in parts he hadn't seen before. Adrian would find this highly amusing. It was the kind of thing that would spook Laura. Perhaps he would ring them when he got home and suggest an outing. Richard would probably be all right about it.

This spot felt familiar, he thought; he must be near the exit. There were the Victorian headstones he remembered, and one that stood alone, leaning at an angle, just off the path. The name caught his eye. He looked again and stopped. Urban Feake.

Us

B Y ST Valentine's Day, Katharine had begun to lose things.
She lost her wallet, her keys, her phone. Then she lost
the job in London. When she phoned Richard at work, he
took control immediately. He asked Claudia to come into
his office. It was something he should have done a long time
ago, he told himself as he looked down over the silver ribbon
of the Thames. He waited patiently while Claudia noted
down his instructions. He wanted her to contact the
Cambridge estate agent and drop the price by £50,000 for
a quick sale, then she needed to phone round the Chiswick
agents and alert them to an urgent purchase – five bedrooms
minimum, quiet road, large garden, must be south-facing.
Will go up to £1.5 million. And if she could pop down
there in a taxi and scout around one day this week, that
would be brilliant. He asked her to call his brother,
Christopher, a consultant at Bart's hospital and arrange a
lunch date as soon as possible. Christopher, *Sir* Christopher
as he was now, would sort out Katharine's job. Finally he asked
her to phone the school they had earmarked for the children.
The places had unfortunately gone, but he was sure that
once they heard his generous promise of £25,000 to the
swimming pool appeal, the Bursar would get back to him
forthwith.

Laura and Adrian found Katharine sitting on a bench by the river, smoking a damp cigarette. Katharine was mortified and told them she was just holding it for a passer-by who had gone to find her dog. The children sat either side of her and stuffed their hands deep into their pockets. There was an awkward silence. Adrian took a hollow twig out of his pocket, took the lighter from Katharine's open bag and lit the end of his twig. He leaned back.

'Mmm, now that's what I call a mellow smoke.' Then he said, 'Does Dad know you smoke?'

'Of course. But I don't. Only every now and then. Not any more.' She dropped the cigarette into a puddle.

'. . . give us this day . . .' muttered Laura.

Adrian said, 'Bet he does know.'

Katharine shook her head.

'. . . and forgive us our trespasses . . .'

Adrian tapped non-existent ash from the end of his twig. 'Secrets aren't really secrets. People know each other's secrets.'

Laura was still mumbling. '. . . those who trespass against us . . .'

'I don't think that's true.'

'People know but they don't necessarily know they know.' There was a pause. Then he said, 'If you know what I mean.'

'. . . and deliver us from evil . . .' Laura sighed loudly.

'Are you all right?' asked Katharine.

She turned and nodded at her mother. 'I was praying.'

'Good heavens.' Katharine pushed the hair out of her eyes. 'Where did you learn that?'

'At school.'

'Does it work?'

'I don't know. Chanel says it does.'

Adrian said, 'The secrets become physical things because they don't like being invisible.'

Katharine leant her head back and looked up into the branches of the tree. The light was going and a sodium lamp had come on, shining through the tree so that the raindrops looked like shimmering jewels hanging from the black twigs. She began to cry soundlessly.

'They become a little madness,' she heard Adrian say. 'Migraines, twitches, stammers, funny walks.'

'Funny walks?' she said, gasping into a tissue.

'You know, like everyone has a way of walking. Some people walk with a suspicious limp.'

'I think you mean surreptitious, darling.'

'Suspicious. The limp is suspicious because it has noticed the secret that won't be named.'

Katharine thought of Frank's walk. Laura thought of her mother's migraines. Adrian stood up and stretched. 'My twig's gone out,' he said.

Katharine rested her head against Laura's and stared at the river. She had seen the pages of the unidentified on the Missing People website. Bodies found in woodland, on wasteland and most often, again and again, washed up on beaches. Bent over at her laptop, frozen and horrified, she studied the little photographs of the hundreds of found but not missed. Some were not photos but sketched drawings and sculpted heads taken from death. No smiles in these, only exhaustion and a vacant sadness. At the bottom of each photo was a link you could click: 'I think I know this person.' Sometimes the photo was not even of a face, just a shoe, a buckle, a tattoo. It was the other side of lost and the loneliest thing she had ever seen.

'I have an awful feeling,' she said, putting her arm through Laura's. 'I have the feeling that Bea isn't coming back.' She looked down at their shoes and struggled to stop the tears again.

'It's going to be all right, Mum,' said Laura.

'Is it?' Katharine dabbed at her face. 'I don't see how really.'

'You've got us.'

Found

I T WAS Urban who found the body. The end of February had brought freezing fog, which had blanketed the city. Its presence felt oppressive; it obscured and muffled everything beneath it like a collapsed creature too ill or tired to move. Workers and schoolchildren hurried in silence, eager to be out of it and inside. It had none of the beauty or magic of snow, it dissolved definition and deadened sound. Traffic slowed to a fearful crawl. No planes flew.

The day after the fog lifted, Urban was clearing the ditch below the railway embankment on Stourbridge Common. Torrential rains since the New Year had flooded the common and meadows. He was to clear the ditches and use the digger to create a route for the water to run back to the river.

The deserted common had an exhausted air, as if the fog had drained it of light and life. He saw her handbag first. This was not in itself a rare discovery. Muggers and burglars threw away bags and cases as they sprinted from the scene. Sometimes people just lost them or left them behind, although what she was doing this close to the railway line and so far from the path was anyone's guess.

He shuffled in closer beneath the bramble and hawthorn to pull the bag clear. When he felt the hairs rise on the back of his neck, he knew. Urban was no stranger to death, and every corpse made its presence known with that moment of suspended stillness: time and place ceased; he felt hyperalive. He froze and sniffed the air: the odour was faint but present. His eyes searched the rough brambles around the hawthorn. There, unmistakable, like a mushroom glowing from the darkness, the partially revealed globe of a human skull.

Silence.

He held his breath and bent further in beneath the hawthorn. The thorns scraped and hooked his scalp. He took off his gloves and moved away a clump of leaves. The ground was soggy beneath his knees, water trickled nearby. He exhaled and took a deep breath of leaf mould and peat. It always touched him, this, the beauty of the human skull, still, after all he had done and seen. It was the back of the skull he could see, the face turned away into a pillow of mud, the collar of a woman's coat along the jaw as if turned up against a bitter wind. Urban looked down at the toe of his boot. There, the white of bone, three fingertips curled up gracefully from the earth. He shuffled further towards her legs and uncovered a pair of feet, shod in brown leather, crossed at the ankles.

He drew himself away and sat back on his heels. A train thundered past like a jet fighter. When all was quiet again he rolled a cigarette and smoked. Compared to the corpses he had seen in the burnt hayfields and ruined towns of Chechnya, this looked to him like a good death. From what he could see, she had lain down and gone to sleep.

The handbag was stiff, mottled and blotched with mould. He lifted the flap and saw a packet of ten cigarettes, a lighter and a brown leather purse. He lifted it out: a fold of damp notes, no ID, a few coins but no cards. He held his cigarette between his lips and unpeeled a ten-pound note from the sheaf of three or four. He thought a moment, then unpeeled two more. That was a point of principle for Urban. He only took what he knew would not be missed.

KATHARINE KNEW as soon as she heard Jim clear his throat on the end of the line. She carried on walking, the tray of drinks and glasses chinking in her hands, the phone tucked between her ear and her shoulder. She made it as far as the middle of the oriental carpet; she saw Jane on the sofa next to Richard, saw Paul leaning forward to throw a log on the fire and beyond them, the thick red drapes glowing in the light of the floor lamps, the family photographs arranged in a line on the mantelpiece, a large one of Bea's wedding taking pride of place.

She heard Jane say to Richard, 'Oh, but it's lovely, it's enormous. Is that an original archway?' And then she heard Jim speak.

'We do have some news,' he said.

She waited. A half smile on her face, afraid to show what she was about to hear.

'I am sorry to break it to you this way but I knew you would want to be the first to know.'

She listened to the words then dropped the phone and raised one hand to her hair. 'Oh, no.'

Richard leapt up and reached her before she hit the floor but not before she dropped the tray. Glasses bounced and rolled on the carpet but the chilled champagne hit the side of the low table and ricocheted on to the hearth, where it exploded, sending froth and spray up the wall.

Laura looked up from her magazine and took out her earphones. Adrian shut the fridge door quickly and, appearing in the sitting-room doorway, saw his mother lying across his father's knees as if asleep. A colourless liquid leaked from the corner of her mouth. Their father cradled her head and Paul was talking into the phone. Jane sat where she was with her hand over her mouth.

Laura ran forward to Katharine and sank down beside her. She had never seen her mother this way – ashen, fallen, help- less. She crouched close but didn't dare touch Katharine's face. Something terrible had happened with her eyes. Just the whites showed between a sliver of half-closed lids.

Paul handed Richard the phone. 'It's Jim from the Missing Persons Unit,' he said. 'Shall I tell him to call back?'

Richard put Katharine's head gently into Laura's lap. 'Keep her head low,' he said. 'Stay close to her.'

He stood up and took the call. Jim told him that a woman's body had been found on Stourbridge Common near the railway line. Positive identification was not possible at this stage because the body had been there for some time, but it appeared to be a woman of similar height to Bea. A post-mortem would be carried out in the morning and they were awaiting the results of forensic tests from the site.

'They've found her,' said Laura.

'They've found someone,' Richard said, kneeling down and pulling her to him.

'They've found Bea and she's dead,' said Laura.

'Shh,' said Richard. 'We don't know that yet.'

Yet

T HE RESULTS of the post-mortem were slow in coming. CID and Forensics wanted to keep the site intact while they gathered evidence. Information leaked out, stories appeared in the papers and items on the television news – the body was badly decomposed and had been dead for some time; badgers and foxes had interfered with it; identification would be through dental records; the woman might have been a murder victim; she might have slipped and broken her leg; police were puzzled that the body had lain un-discovered so long; the woman might have killed herself; there was nothing left but bones. Three days went by and no results yet, but Katharine could not bring herself to ring Frank. On the fourth day Richard drove her up to Cambridge so that they could hear the news from the coroner in person.

She sat in the passenger seat, dark glasses on, anaes-thetised with migraine tablets. She had nothing of substance left in her body. Richard kept his hand in hers as he drove. Every now and then he would say that it was unlikely to be Bea, she had only been gone five months, the decom-position was too advanced. Katharine said that it all depended. Water could do that. Fire could do that. She said the body might have been moved, didn't the police think the body might have been moved? Who found her, that was what she wanted to know. Who were these people who came across dead bodies? What were they doing in a ditch by the King's Lynn to London line, for God's sake? In February? And in the rain? She blew her nose and winced at the rawness there. They passed a woman selling roses on a traffic island. She thought of Bea's garden. Bea's muddled and mixed-up garden, which Katharine had tried to put right but which still never got enough light and which the police had dug up again so that it looked like no one cared. Bea could have done with some help a while back; she could have done with a man on a digger to make her pond, an electric strimmer to strip the ivy, but all she had was fucking Frank. Perhaps he did it. Perhaps Frank did murder her, as the police seemed to think, hid her somewhere then threw her off the train as it crossed the common. Anything was possible. The police knew that. She could tell that Jim and Pete knew all kinds of things they couldn't talk about. She knew things too now. She'd read enough about it.

The coroner's was just round the corner from the registry office at Shire Hall. Jim and Pete were smiling and waiting for them outside. Pete had a tan that made her think of the ancient bodies they dug out of bogs, and both men had ties on and smart shoes. They shook hands and went inside, where Richard disappeared down a corridor while Katharine stayed where she was and listened to Pete tell her that the fog had delayed his flight back from his skiing holiday and he'd only got home at two in the morning but at least they'd had good snow out there in— Then Richard was walking fast back towards her; he was telling her the woman was a tourist who had gone missing in London a year before, he was saying the body wasn't Bea's, that the cause of death was unexplained, perhaps she had slipped and fallen then been unable to . . . Jim and Pete were herding her towards the door, they were speaking and shuffling to the exit, where Pete opened the door. They hesitated there, the pleasantries, the concern, the plans and next steps. Katharine longed to be away in the car, longed to be alone to cradle this newfound curdled hope. The deceased is not your sister. Bea is still out there. Still.

Snap

I N MARCH, Jane and Paul visited Katharine and Richard
in London. It was their wedding anniversary, so Jane had
booked them into the Savoy for the weekend. The Savoy!
said Richard. Well, it's where we had our wedding night,
believe it or not, said Jane. They were having a romantic
weekend for two, but first they wanted to visit their old
friends. It wasn't terribly convenient as far as Katharine was
concerned. She and the family were leaving for Spain the
next morning and they were taking Frank. She didn't want
the awkwardness of Frank and an evening with Jane and Paul.
Richard told her it would be fine, the children would be
there and it might do Frank good.

During the evening, Katharine didn't move from the sofa.
She lay with her feet tucked beneath her and looked at the
fire while Paul's words flowed over her and she watched
Jane help Richard with the drinks. She listened as Jane
spoke to him in hushed, emphatic tones. Jane wanted him
to know that she thought Katharine was going through a
process, had adjusted to the loss the way an amputee adjusts
to life without a limb. The ghost limb still pained her at
times and always she was aware of Bea's absence, but she
adjusted herself and the rest of her life to fit around it in
a way that she could manage. Jane thought the family holiday

in Spain would be just the thing, but where was Frank? Wasn't he coming too?

Katharine went to bed early. She climbed into their new, sumptuously comfortable bed and felt the relief of being alone. She longed for bed almost from the moment she got up and it was rare that she stayed up beyond nine thirty. Tonight, because of their friends, she managed to stay downstairs until eleven, but it was an effort, the smiles and the chit-chat, darting this way and that. The endless tales of winter holidays, neighbours, furnishings, schools. She couldn't bear the sound of their voices. There was only one voice she wanted to hear. She had almost stopped hoping to see Bea again but she had never stopped longing for the sound of her voice.

Richard came up the stairs to say good night. He was flushed and bright-eyed from the wine and rare conviviality. 'You seem more your old self today,' he said, setting a cup of camomile tea down on the table next to her. He smelt of brandy and garlic. He told her that he thought perhaps she was adjusting to the loss of Bea the way an amputee adjusts to life without a—

'Yes, I heard what Jane was saying, Richard. I haven't completely taken leave of my senses.'

'But still. She may have a point, don't you think?' He looked over at her. She was lying down and very still. 'And you've not had a single night terror since we moved to Chiswick,' he added, looking down at the pile of market reports that Claudia had prepared for him. She did most of the highlighting herself these days, just wrote him a little memo alerting him to key points.

Katharine was naked except for a pink satin eye mask, sequinned in black and quilted by Laura. Richard was quite keen on the eye mask. 'I'm nervous about Spain,' she said, stroking the feathery edges of it.

'Just think of it as a holiday, darling,' Richard told her.

'That's what it is. We're going to Spain for a holiday and we're going to enjoy the sun and the sights.' He ought to get back downstairs to Jane and Paul before they left.

'But we're taking Frank.'

'Yes. The children will look after Frank.'

'And really, we are looking for Bea.'

'Well that's always going to be the case.'

She sat up and pulled the eye mask up on to her forehead. 'But using Frank as *bait*. That's never going to work.'

'Frank's a changed man, Katharine, thanks to you. New clothes, new decor, decent haircut. It's a marvel what you and Wanda have done.' He looked over at her. 'Put your eye mask back on, darling, you must be tired.'

Katharine did as she was told. Then she said, 'Perhaps we shouldn't have left the route plan to Adrian.'

'It's as good an idea as any other that we've come up with. We return to the places she visited in happier times, to the places she told the children she wanted to take them to: Vigo, Andalucia, Granada.

Katharine tried to empty her mind. She drifted for a moment, imagining a tranquil ocean and Bea on deck looking out to sea.

Richard patted her leg. 'It's going to be a tour of some of the most beautiful cities in Spain. Easter is the perfect time to go – almond blossom, wild flowers, oranges and lemons . . . Try not to worry.' He glanced at the stock reports. The Asian market was definitely jittery.

'But still, attempting Laurie Lee's walk through Spain in reverse – Granada to Vigo – I can't think it's going to achieve anything. And there's no way Bea would have walked that distance even if she'd got to Vigo.'

'Of course not, but it's helped the children a lot having a project to work on. Wanda seems suddenly sure that Bea has somehow got there.'

'If Bea is anywhere, she's making her way to Greece and

to Patrick.' Katharine sighed and ran her hands down her body. She wasn't at all convinced.

DOWNSTAIRS, ADRIAN and Laura were explaining the trip to Paul and Jane, and Jane was saying quite often, 'But where is Frank?' They had it all mapped out, said Adrian. They had worked on the assumption that the future was a game of chess between the present and the past. Laura believed that the clue to the game of life was a game of snap. Frank, they suspected, didn't have an opinion one way or another, but was relieved that someone else had a plan and that he was in it. On the map of the world spread out before them, they had plotted what they knew of Bea's history so far. Laura was certain it was her at the station in Southampton and the mother of a friend of Laura's had gone to a clairvoyant and been told it definitely was. Adrian had discovered that Southampton was the port that cruise liners left from on their way to Africa and the East. Frank had verified this and remembered it was where the ship they had met on docked. 'Oh, the *Oriana*.' Adrian was astounded that Frank knew this but hadn't put two and two together, but then Frank was not that good at chess. When they looked at the routes for the *Oriana* and discovered Vigo was the first stop and had been Bea and Frank's first date, Adrian got cross and said Frank was a tosser. Frank looked shocked and said Vigo was a horrible place, no one would go back there voluntarily, so that Adrian had to explain that Bea probably would whether she liked it or not, and anyway, they had been to Granada for their honeymoon, hadn't they? She would just be drawn in that direction. 'We are slaves to our pasts,' he told Jane. 'Nothing is a mystery. Not really.' Paul felt bleary-eyed and looked at his watch. He wasn't going to have the energy for a romantic weekend in the Savoy if they didn't leave soon. 'And her school book,' continued Adrian, who was, inevitably, turning into something of a pedant, thought Jane. '*As I Walked*

Out One Midsummer Morning makes Vigo even more likely. It has a map of the route and everything. She would definitely go south.'

They were quiet for a while because each was thinking that she might well be on her way to Greece, especially when they looked at the map. She couldn't fly because she didn't have a passport but it was possible she could train and bus and ferry it. Paul said it looked a marvellous itinerary at any rate and that whatever happened they were sure to have a wonderful holiday. Jane wondered about trying to tell Adrian that you couldn't map the human heart the way you could map the stars, but the doorbell went and Frank arrived, suitcase in hand and ready for the early departure in the morning. He appeared to be unaware that he was several hours late. Richard raced around the kitchen to get him a plate of something to eat. Paul poured him a drink and Jane insisted he sit with them because really the man looked like he could do with some human contact, and anyway, she wanted to get the feel of him. Paul's theory that Frank was a murderer was plainly absurd. You needed *presence* to be a murderer, surely. Was it possible for a man to be any less present than Frank? she thought. Gently she said to the children, 'But Bea's been gone for five months. Even if she had followed this route, how can you be sure where she's got to?'

Adrian cleared his throat. He had factored in the time element. Bea probably had to make slow progress because of the need to earn money. 'Bar work, waitressing, anything casual that doesn't require ID,' he said.

Frank yawned operatically. He needed an early night.

'The sort of thing that Wanda does,' said Laura.

Frank stopped yawning.

'But anyway, Wanda says she would slip into the ex-pat crowd, no problem. No one asks questions, they're all running away from something apparently. So, let's say she gets on the *Oriana* by looking like what the local paper described her as, "an unremarkable middle-aged woman". She keeps a low profile on board and disembarks—'

'You what?' said Laura.

'Disembarks. Gets off.'

'Well why not say that, then?'

Frank was wondering whether one small Scotch would matter much. He had been extremely restrained of late. He had got up to page fifty-six of *Close and Personal* and so far he had written the whole thing entirely sober. It was an interesting experience. He sighed and thought that he ought to go to bed.

'She gets off the boat at Vigo and visits the restaurant you went to on your first date.'

'We'll put posters up in there,' said Laura.

'We'll put posters up everywhere.'

'Yeah, show people.'

'They'll remember a woman dining alone because—'

'Because it's illegal.'

'Is it?'

'Yes.'

'No it's not,' said Frank.

'In the game of life it is,' said Laura.

'Anyway, in the five months she's been gone she might even have made it to Granada, even if she spent several weeks working in four or five places on the way.' Adrian flattened out the map of Spain and traced the route with his finger. 'Somewhere on our journey between Granada and Vigo – maybe in Algeciras, Seville, Zamora – we're bound to find some trace of her.'

'Or she might see us and know we're still looking and haven't forgotten her, and she may see you, Frank, and just not be able to help herself.' Laura snorted and flung herself backwards on to the carpet.

She sat up again and looked worried. There was a pause. Leaving Frank's makeover to Katharine had not been a complete success. She'd bought him a pair of very large, brightly coloured plastic beach shoes – Crocs – the sort that were currently operating a mysterious power over the middle-aged and the middle-classed, despite the fact that they caused the wearer to resemble Bob the Builder. Laura had voiced their concerns to Richard earlier in the day.

'Never mind,' said Richard with the lack of awareness of the importance of such things that only comes with many years of marriage. 'At least she'll notice him.'

Frank was not so sure either. He hesitated on his way up to bed, turning this way and that before the full-length mirror in the hallway. He looked doubtfully at his feet, which were encased in bright turquoise plastic. Adrian thought of Daffy Duck. Laura thought of Road Runner.

'I'm having second thoughts about these Crocs,' he called.

Katharine and Richard came out of the kitchen and stood beside him. They had Crocs on too – orange and purple.

Adrian winced.

Laura said, 'What's wrong with flip-flops?'

Perhaps

THEY WERE all nervous and none of them knew what to expect.

Adrian kept his leg pressed hard against Frank's all the way over France and most of the way over Spain. Laura sat between her parents and ate her way steadily through Twixes, Bounties, KitKats and Pringles. She cast anxious glances back to where Frank sat with Adrian, and for most of the flight, she allowed Katharine to put her arm round her shoulders.

Frank tried several times to sleep. Each time he closed his eyes there would be a few moments of stillness before he sensed Adrian's face millimetres from his own. When he opened his eyes it was to find a pair of pale blue irises staring intently at him.

'Just checking you're alive.' The boy's voice was breaking these days and a crop of livid spots had appeared across his chin.

Frank sighed. 'I'm not dead, Adrian, I'm asleep.'

Frank wasn't really trying to sleep. Sleep wouldn't come, he knew that. He had his eyes closed in order to distract himself from the drinks trolley that kept being wheeled up and down the aisle, clinking invitingly. And he had his eyes closed to try to still the anxiety that had sent his back and neck into spasm so that turning his head was impossible. He closed his eyes again and counted up to seven.

'Ow! For Christ's sake!'

Alarmed, Katharine's and Laura's heads twisted round and peered through the gap in their seats. Frank rubbed his thigh ruefully, looking at Adrian in disbelief.

'Sorry,' said Adrian.

'What did you do that for?'

'Numbness is one of the first symptoms of deep-vein thrombosis. It's okay, though. You're not numb.'

The five of them were the first off the plane when it landed at Granada. They crossed the tarmac to the small terminal building. Soft, thyme-filled air was warm on their faces. Purple mountains slumbered against a pale sky; the last of the sun bled crimson in bands to the west and Katharine struggled to contain a hope that wanted to fly from her mouth in a cry. Yes, here, of course, it was possible. The hope ballooned inside her like a child and she held on to Laura's arm. Here, surely, anything was possible.

Passport control was deserted. When a member of staff did finally arrive, his cap was awry and he apologised cheerfully for not being at his post. He waved them through with barely a glance at their documents. Automatic doors swept open and they stepped hesitantly into the arrivals hall like actors surprised by the curtain. Richard cleared his throat and looked left, then right. No one was sure how this was to be managed, and now they were here they felt suddenly shy. To their right was the exit, to their left a deserted café. Katharine looked to the exit and touched Frank's arm. The doors slid open and shut. People arrived. People left.

Frank said, 'Right then,' and wandered outside.

'Come away,' said Katharine as the children tried to follow him. 'Come away over here,' and she led them to a row of plastic seats, where they sat stiffly, craning their necks to watch. 'We'll just wait here while Dad sorts out the transport.'

Pushing the hair from her face, she arranged the perhapses in her mind and stacked them carefully into a fragile tower of possibility. Perhaps Bea *had* seen Laura's Missing video, and if she had, how could she not be moved by it, by Laura's slight time-lapsed face telling Bea she loved her, by Laura begging Bea to make contact, letting Bea know of their journey to Spain? And perhaps the 'I think I know this person' response that Hazel from Missing People had reported was genuine. Hazel had warned that 'no confirmation is available at the present time', but *perhaps* (crazy thought) Adrian was right about maps and history and the routes people take through life. Perhaps her children knew her sister better than she did herself. She watched Frank, framed by the doors. But six months? Bea, here? Doing what? Living how? She shooed away the 'Unidentified' page of the website that hovered always in her mind. A page she had scoured a hundred times, 'Caution: this material may prove disturbing to some viewers', reconstructions and sketches that she knew by heart, 'found on a beach', 'found in woodland', 'found at a service station', but again and again, 'found on a beach'. Laura's leg was warm and narrow against her own. She forced herself to abandon the Unidentified and recall instead the Found, the many unbelievable stories of reunion. 'Missing brother found abroad.' Yes, she blinked hard in concentration. 'Runaway saw herself on a poster.' *Yes*, she could see how Bea might need some *space*, some *time* to find herself. She shook her head. The clichés threatened to topple the perhapses and she leant back against the wall. She took a deep breath in and began again. Perhaps. Perhaps Bea *was* here. She peered out at the glass doors where Frank hovered. Perhaps Bea would see Frank and if they just sat here a while and let them talk, perhaps if Frank remembered what to say, remembered what not to say, if . . .

And then Bea did see Frank.

From the car she sat in, fifty metres away, parked up on

one side of the car park, she saw him. She watched him hesitate on the pavement, tug at his cuffs and stare. She saw him rock on his heels, look up at the mountains and take a deep long breath of Andalusian air. Love, faint and meagre, pulled at a place low down inside her. Swifts screeled and soared. Orange blossom and aviation fuel drifted on the air.

Bea held her breath. She sat absolutely still. Vague and far off, Frank looked a stranger to her now. A plane roared and groaned and he moved out of sight. She exhaled and looked at the floor.

'See anyone?' said Kiff from the driving seat beside her.

She shook her head. She knew she must concentrate, try to pull the many loose and stray pieces of herself together. They had sat in the car park for hours. Muscle and sinew in her had turned rigid as terror prowled the edges of her mind. It was very nearly more than she could bear.

She could feel Kiff looking at her, feel him wondering whether to touch her shoulder with the hand that rested on the back of her seat. She sat forward and frowned, studying the exit. She saw Frank's head again for a moment, as he wandered to and fro behind a minibus being loaded with luggage.

'We could walk over,' said Kiff.

Walk over? She could barely sit up. The trembling she had been fighting all afternoon returned. She squeezed her eyes shut and looked into the dark. She was torn between the then and the now and the numberless nights in between, nights measured by church bell and dog's bark, prolonged and creeping nights in the shuttered dark, when panic had to be talked down like a suicide on a ledge. Sedimentary nights. She opened her eyes and shuddered at the memory of those first weeks in Spain: the slow interment of herself beneath layers of time and space until the past and the impulse to return was muffled and remote. She prayed that the children didn't appear.

Kiff wanted to check inside the building. He felt that he should. This was the last flight from London. Today was the day mentioned, repeated, emphasised by Laura in the video. He looked over at the woman in the seat beside him. She wore a peppermint shift dress cut square at the neck. One tanned knee was crossed over the other. One sandal hung loose from the toes of her foot and she called herself Katharine. You're not Katharine, he thought now. You're Beatrice. He looked at her face, which was turned away from him, her mouth moving a little to some conversation in her head. Beattie maybe? Bea? If he raised his hand, he could touch the back of her head, where the hair was darker and cropped thick and soft over bone, or there, at her temple, where it was greying and bleaching against tanned skin. She looked sometimes beaten, worn and tired round the eyes. But it was her mouth that he always looked at. She had a wonderful mouth. What was she? Mid-forties?

'Plan B, then?'

She nodded. Kiff's tired, leathery face was turned towards her. The rough beard and wraparound shades hovered near. He wasn't expecting a kiss, there was no romance in their occasional couplings; she knew he was just trying to read her. She had let him think Plan B was a journey they would take together. She had used him a little, which was bad. He was a kind man, an ex-husband, ex-builder, an ex-pat. Kiff, the estate agent, fixer and friend. He had a distracted, worn-out air that in England might look seedy, but out here in the sun and the light, busy with his building projects, his contacts and his lingo, he was rugged, hand-some almost, a cowboy riding the Sierra Nevada in his Nissan Navara.

Plan B. She had studied the road maps, the sea routes and the trains. She had them with her in her bag. She brushed a moth from her dress. It was time to move on and leave Spain behind.

'Valencia,' she said, and to herself she recited the litany: Valencia, Genova, Brindisi, Ithaca.

'Sounds good to me.'

She touched his arm. 'Wait.'

It was Adrian. He stepped from the terminal door, hair aflame above his pale face, and tall. Impossibly, incredibly tall. How did that happen? Bea smiled and bit her lip; tears pricked the corners of her eyes. Her fingers touched the door handle and pulled. His height was physical evidence of how long she'd been gone, of how far she had come. She put one foot out. He turned as he walked, looking up and around, eyes sweeping the slip road, the car park and the people gathered here and there.

He looked back to the building as Laura came out, a bundle of papers to her chest, papers that fell, then flew so that she had to chase and stamp them down to the ground. Laura hadn't grown. Her hair was longer and she wore her breasts ratcheted high up on her chest, a tight, low-cut T-shirt displaying them defiantly to the world. She looked like a small, angry woman. She stopped to stick a poster to a pillar, pressing the edges hard, then handed posters to a group near the door. Adrian swooped round her, jumped in front of the doors so that they opened to produce a trolley piled high with cases and attached to Richard, who pushed it, phone to his ear, stopping to turn and call back inside. Half in, half out, he allowed himself to be manoeuvred fully out and parked to one side by Adrian, who reached through the doors and brought out a stooped, frail figure. Mum? No. Could that be Katharine? He handed her to Laura and called his father, who had wandered away and was taking slow, deliberate strides, talking up at the sky, down at his feet, spinning on one foot and holding up a hand to his family to just wait one moment, one moment, please. Sorry, but I have to take this call, it's Tokyo. Then Adrian was running up towards the taxi rank at the front of the building, leaping into the road to avoid a gaggle of people and trolleys, hopping from the path of a bus, leaning through the window of a taxi then running back to the terminal exit to round up his family. He looked over at Kiff's car as the taxi reversed. He looked across the slip road and directly at the dust-covered Nissan parked to one side under scrubby sapling. Bea withdrew her foot and shrank down in the seat. She said, 'All at sixes and sevens, you are.'

'What?'

'Not you, me.' She dropped her head down to her knees and groaned.

She spoke into her lap. 'Have they gone?'

'Nope.'

'What are they doing?'

'They're getting in the taxi. They'll be going to the hotel. I have the name of it here.' He pulled a printout of Hazel's email from his pocket: time of arrival and departure, hotels in Granada, Seville, Vigo, phone numbers, itinerary.

Bea didn't look at it. It was too soon; too soon and too late. If they'd come during the bad time, the hollow, speechless time before Christmas, then maybe she'd have had no choice but to be rescued. But now . . .

'You should write to them,' said Kiff. 'Let them know you're all right.'

'I have.' She wiped her eyes with her hands and pulled three envelopes from her bag. Dear Katharine, Dear Mum, Dear Frank. She passed them to him. 'Can you post these for me when you get back from Valencia?' That's what she'd spent the last few days doing. Writing the letters that she could bear to send.

Kiff took them. 'I see. I'm going back to Lanjarón but you're not. Is that it?'

She knew Kiff's work was slow at the moment. She knew he fancied a short adventure with her, a trip through Italy to Greece and then who knows where. No, you don't have to take Kiff, she told herself. You don't have to be good. She sat up and looked towards the place where she had last seen Adrian. Another family stood there now. Adrian was gone.

'So, I'm coming back and you're going on from Valencia?'

Bea turned from him. Was there going to be a scene? He wasn't going to change suddenly into a husband, was he? How long had they known each other? Two months? Three? She was fairly sure she wasn't the only woman he slept with. Really, men were hopeless on their own.

'You'll be all right. There's Lesley and Jules. There's Pinkie.' She spluttered something that should have been a laugh but wasn't quite.

'Isn't that your husband?' Kiff pointed to the entrance of the car park.

Sure enough, there was Frank, quite near, helping a young woman get her bags in a car. What in God's name had he got on his feet? The woman slammed the boot closed and thanked Frank politely. He took a step towards her and pulled pen and paper from his pocket. A taxi swung into the car park and stopped. Adrian got out, sloped over to Frank and pulled him away.

'Ex-husband,' said Bea.

'What happened?'

She sat back in her seat and pressed the window closed. They both watched as the taxi drove away, four heads crowded in the rear window.

'Our marriage walked out on us. Months ago. Frank's fine.'

'And the children?'

Bea swallowed but said nothing. She fumbled in her bag and put her glasses on, spreading the map open on her legs. Kiff started the engine.

'*Vale. Vamos.*'

Falling

T HE FERRY left Valencia the next morning. Bea sat in the
stern and watched Kiff and the harbour wall recede. He
raised one hand, the hand holding the letters, and waved them
at her. As the land peeled away, taking Kiff and her time in
Spain with it, she felt her back and shoulders relax. There
were barely a dozen other passengers. A few backpackers, and
four elderly Italians freighting domestic appliances back to
their island lives. Bea had boarded the ferry, her driving licence
ready as ID, but no one was interested; it was off season, it
was the sea. The sea had its own rules, and with her shorn
hair and tanned skin, she looked, she realised now, more
Mediterranean than English.

Kiff remained where he was until he was a speck in the
distance. She knew he would post the letters, and she made
him promise not to get in touch with the family until after
the time they were due to leave Spain. She could trust him
to do that, she was almost certain. The wind picked up as they
left the shelter of the land, and Bea wrapped herself in the
cream and black Moroccan blanket Kiff had taken from his
car. It was dusty but soft and she was glad of it, for she had
no desire to leave the deck. She wanted to be transported
backwards from the land this way, with no vision of the journey
ahead. She felt steel and water rumble, shudder up through

her body. She tipped her head back and looked up at the sky. This was the way to travel. It was the art of falling, like the leaps off the cliff at Hastings.

A spasm gripped her guts abruptly. She gasped and leaned forward over the rails, panting like a dog into the churn and twist below. Yesterday at the airport had unsettled her perhaps, and for the first time in months she had drunk alcohol the night before. Two glasses of rough, raw Rioja. 'Idiot,' she told herself. Alcohol was toxic to her, the journey through Spain had taught her this at least. Precious knew that already, of course. Precious barely drank at all and never had. Once she told Bea that going through the change was just that. Change. 'You have to stop poisoning yourself the way you've been doing all your life.' In England Bea had tried cutting down on the booze but she found there was always a reason for that glass or three at the end of the day. She had one because of a bad day, because of a good day, because she was tired, because Frank was having one. Precious was right. The last year, since the menopause took hold, she felt the wine sap what little energy she had. But since she'd reached Spain – she breathed shallowly; her stomach felt tender – now it occurred to her that the repeatedly firing furnace, the hot flushes, had receded then ceased altogether. 'It's a call to arms, Precious,' she said, smiling down at the precipice of black metal below. 'Change or die! Get out of there – that toxic office, those nylon clothes, that overheated bedroom, that stalled marriage, that bloody fridge full of—' She moaned and retched violently, emptily, over the rail.

Wiping her mouth with the blanket, Bea sat down on a damp bench. She hadn't slept the night before. They had booked into a cheap hotel. Although sleeping with Kiff was the very last thing she wanted. She'd hoped for single beds, but no, it was a small double. It was the least she could do, she thought, as he laboured on top of her, and the bed creaked and groaned below. She lay awake most of the night, listening to him sleep. When she woke in the morning, it was to the end of a dream that slunk into the shadows like an intruder. Uneasy, she shook Kiff awake and made him take her to the port hours before the ferry left. She was impatient for him to be gone. She could not bear to be with him a moment longer, she thought, as he drank his coffee, ate a pastry, had another, bought a paper, chatted to the men by the water, then saw her safely on to the boat.

And now she felt bad because Kiff had been good and demanded very little in return. She had met him in late December, the night she arrived in Granada. She went into the bar by the bus stand, the bar that every Spanish town has, where the sports channel blares and a row of men watch the screen from their stools, where the floor is littered with ash and sugar wraps, and the sound of table football and pool punctuates the air. She remembered seeing him look up at her as she came in. He said he heard her schoolgirl Spanish as she ordered a drink and tapas. He watched her shy glance as she scanned the room for someone who might help her find her feet. He brought her to Lanjarón, a spa town south of Granada. It was Kiff who introduced her to others at Los Mariscos, the bar where the expats gathered. He got her a room to stay in and found work for her every now and then. She taught English conversation to the hairdresser's daughter and the garage owner's brother; she helped out in the kitchen at Los Mariscos. She got stronger. She began to sleep at night, and each day she walked. She walked for hours. From her window she could see tracks and trails traversing the hills and valleys around the town. It pleased her to find her way to one of these and walk until she could no longer see her way back. And at night, sometimes during those ten weeks, sometimes she slept with Kiff. That surprised her. She had not expected to be desired, but in Spain she began to notice that she was no longer invisible. She felt men's eyes on her, and women's too, as she walked down the street.

It was the daughter of a friend of Kiff's who found Laura's YouTube Missing video and brought Bea news of the family's arrival in Granada. It was Kiff who clicked the 'I think I know this person' button on the Missing People website, and it was Kiff who persuaded her to come to Granada airport.

Bea imagined what Precious would say if she could see her now, going the long way by sea, by train and by bus. She had been asked for her passport only once, getting off the ferry at Vigo, a lifetime ago, back in October. She had waited for a crowd and tried to slip through unnoticed but the uniformed officer had spotted her and demanded her documents. She had been rather impressed by her ability to dissemble, calling out to an imaginary friend ahead of her, 'Oh, Bea! Bea! Hang on, I think I've lost my . . .' then searching in her bag, crouching and pulling out underwear and shoes and holding up the queue. She had looked nonplussed, flustered then embarrassed, pulled out her library card, dropped her staff pass and then her driving licence and was finally waved through with an irritated shake of the head. There had been a teenage Bea, who sometimes shoplifted, took money from her mother's purse, ran away to Brighton once. Disappearing at fifty, the teenage Bea came back to her. If anything, at fifty it was easier. If you were a woman of fifty, you didn't have to be good because nobody expected you to be bad. Precious would approve of that.

Bea tasted the salt on her lips. She wondered if she were hungry and ate a handful of seeds. There were things she wanted to tell Precious that she couldn't tell Kiff. She wanted to tell her how she missed her garden; she had ideas and plans for it and hated to think of it neglected by Frank. She wanted to tell her how she could remember nothing about work, it had left no mark on her at all, and how that couldn't be right after all those years. She wondered what Precious would say if she told her the journey had taught her that mealtimes are for men and children, not women, indeed *meals* are for men and children, not women, and she would like Precious to know that she was right – she should return all the cookery books that Frank had given for all those Christmases. Not just Frank either. Patrick too. Well, he should have known better. He should. And one year he gave the same one to his wife, she happened to know that for a fact. Two for the price of one. 'You already cook for them,' said Precious. 'It's not cookbooks you need, it's a cook! I mean, look at your kitchen shelf. Nigel, Marcella, Claudia, Delia . . . *Delia*? Who are these people, Bea? And what are they doing in your kitchen?'

'Speaking of food, Precious, I've discovered something else on my travels.'

'You have?'

'The truth is that I don't much want to eat. I'm not hungry at breakfast or lunch or at dinner, and as I choose not to eat solo at a table for two opposite an empty chair, I find I get by on very little money for food. So for all those weeks, those weeks travelling from Vigo by bus through Zamora, Valladolid and Toledo, then on through Cordoba and Seville to Granada, I've eaten when I'm hungry and lived on oranges and nuts and chocolate bars.'

'That's not going to keep body and soul together, girl.'

'Body and soul manage rather better if they're apart.'

'You're too thin. And your hair . . .'

'I like my hair short.'

'You look like a stick. You look like a *match*stick.'

Bea laughed. 'And I must be fit. I walk everywhere now. I feel light and well and at home in my body for the first time since I was ten.'

'You're too thin and you look like a stick.'

'Kiff didn't think so.'

'What kind of a name is Kiff?'

'You'd be surprised how little food you need. I conserve my energy.'

'Your teeth will fall out. Come home.'

'I may go and see Patrick.'

Precious didn't say anything to that, just ate her yoghurt and scraped the corners of her mouth with a fingernail.

'What do you think I should do, Precious?'

But Precious was turned away, looking at the foamy trail of their route tapering in a lazy arc back towards the land.

'Tell me what I should do, Precious. I need your spicy bad advice.'

Bea got to her feet and stood by the rail. She bundled the blanket under one arm and looked down into the wake. She thought of the End of the Pier Game and how Katharine refused to play it. Once she got wise to it, she wouldn't come to the end of the pier at all so that Bea would rollerskate alone, past the theatre and the old people, the lovers and the fishermen right up to the furthest end where Daddy used to put her on his shoulders and pretend they were on the bow of a Viking ship returning to Denmark with plundered silver and cattle. In the days after Daddy, she would bend and lower herself upside down through the rails, turn her feet out like a clown so that she wouldn't roll in (although if she did, it thrilled her to know the skates would make her sink like a stone) and hold Teddy, Teddy who had lost his fuzz in patches here and there and who smelt of straw and sleep; hold him at the end of stretched-out arms over the roar and surge and dare herself to let him fall to the fishy deeps below. She never let Teddy drop exactly. She threw him into the air sometimes, to feel the loss and horror pitch in her belly. And once she let Katharine's doll drop. But the doll wasn't Teddy; it floated and bobbed with its eyes closed and it didn't work, she didn't get the feeling, she just felt bad and empty.

Bea retched again, leaning as far over the railings as she could. A twisted spasm rose up inside her so that she opened her mouth and waited until a thin grey stream fluttered out of her and was snatched away by the wind.

'Arggh, that was the wine, Precious, not seasickness. I don't get seasick and I don't miss the flying one bit. In fact what I like about buses and boats is how long it takes to get everywhere!' But Precious wasn't interested in transport. She said, 'Where exactly are you going, Bea? You seriously going to see Patrick? Have you thought there might be a problem with that?' Bea chewed at the seeds. She shook her head. 'There isn't a plan. There's a *map*. It's just . . . I'm just . . .' She tried to conjure an image of Patrick but his face was hazy like the horizon. She tried to summon the feeling she had once had for him but her belly was hollow and all that came to her was a damp river bank, the smell of cowshit and grass, a child somewhere who called, Mum!

She shivered and looked up. Weak winter sun warmed her face but her fingers were cold on the patched and salted railings. The blue-black flank of the sea rose and fell and her time alone in Spain, that early limbo time before Kiff and Lanjarón, flickered through her mind. She had called herself Katharine then, first for disguise, out of fear of discovery, and then for comfort. Those stunned and empty days of October, then November, she had kept moving and rarely slept in the same place twice. She was no Laurie Lee. She was too anxious and desolate to explore the town. Instead, she surveyed varnished pine, limp nets and portraits of Christ from her single bed.

She pressed the tears from her face. 'You should have stayed with Kiff in Lanjarón,' said Precious, giving her a poke with one long purple nail. Bea twitched her shoulder away and shook her head. 'No. It wasn't me.' She sat down on the metal deck, clutched her knees to her chest and cried out into the wind: 'It wasn't me!'

Ever

'H E'S NOT such a bad chap, you know, Katharine,' Richard said after their second day in Granada.

Katharine lay motionless beneath the sheet, eye mask and neck support carefully in place. They had walked miles that day, up through the Moorish quarter to the square of San Nicolas at the top. Frank insisted it offered the finest view of the Alhambra, which must be seen from afar before actually visiting it. Then they had trudged back down the hill, over the river and back up the other side to the palace and gardens themselves. It had taken hours, and as Katharine kept saying, it was most unlikely that Bea would let herself be seen in a place as public and as photographed as either of those, even if she was there, which in her opinion was unlikely. Adrian walked ahead wherever they went, consulting the map. Richard and Frank strolled together discussing the Moorish conquest and the defeat of the Visigoths. Laura lagged behind putting posters on fences and handing them out to passers-by. Katharine found herself largely alone during the day, watching her feet as she plodded upwards, past cafés and doorways that smelt of cigarettes and mint tea. Now her feet hummed and fizzed under the sheet. She hadn't realised how unfit she was, unlike Richard, who had clearly been putting in the hours at the company gym. She could hear him taking off his underpants and shirt, then wandering around the room, picking her clothes up from the floor. She wondered whether a sleeping pill might be wise. There had been a lot of barking during their first night. An awful lot of barking.

'I mean, I know he's not your favourite person, darling, but when all's said and done, he is our children's uncle and in point of fact he is remarkably—'

Katharine sighed. 'Adrian thinks he saw her.'

Richard shook his head. 'I'm afraid that he didn't. He wanted very much to see her and so he—'

'He said he saw her in a car at the airport.'

'Well why didn't he tell us to stop?'

'Because she saw us and then drove away. Or rather was driven.'

Richard looked out across at the view of the Generalife lit up against the night. There, clearly illuminated, he could see beauty and meaning and grandeur on a scale that endured. He could hardly tell Katharine that where the search for her sister was concerned, he could see nothing of the kind. Indeed, he was beginning to feel that it might be better if they never found her. After all, history was buried all around them; who was to say whether—

'Where is Adrian now?' asked Katharine, sitting up in bed and pushing up her eye mask. She looked at the clock. It was nearly midnight. 'You did hear what he told me today, didn't you? You did hear that Frank has got himself a lodger? He's got a bloody lady lodger holed up in Bea's house, keeping it warm for him till he gets back from his fucking trip! Where is Adrian now?!'

Richard cupped his balls and cleared his throat. 'He's out with Frank.'

Katharine threw back the sheet and put one leg out of the bed. Rapidly Richard pulled on his underpants and put a hand out to stop her. 'Katharine, they're looking for Bea. That's what we're here for.'

Katharine started to cry. 'They're not going to find her here and you know it.'

Perhaps Precious was right and Bea would get herself to Patrick somehow. She felt despair at having got there too early, rushed off there before she discovered that Bea had no passport. Would Patrick want her? He had contacted Precious, she knew that. Precious said he was wanting reassurance that it wasn't his fault, forgiveness of some sort, but he had not gone so far as to ask what he might do to help. And anyway, thought Katharine, what would be the point of replacing a Frank with a Patrick? Who knew what kind of a man Patrick would be without a marriage to support him? She watched Richard clipping his toenails and thought how Bea should have married someone like him – tall, dependable, solvent, normal. She felt the sleeping pill pull at her consciousness. Their father had been tall. Richard was a little like him but without the accent or the cycle clips, and Richard was hopeless with his hands – he couldn't make a balsawood model if his life depended on it.

It worried her that her memories of her father seemed only to be of his hands and his feet. She could not retrieve a complete image of him; all the complete images were in photographs and they were useless, they were lies. Once he was dead, when she was little, she feared thinking of him because of what must be happening to his body. It seemed impossible and horrific to her that he should be lying in the ground left alone to dissolve, and that had been when the sleeplessness began. There had been one night, a week or two after he died and after there came no answer to her repeated small 'Are you still awake, Bea?', when she experienced not the fall, the drop into sleep that she so dreaded and feared, but the sensation of being hurled to a place. The hurl took time, and the terrifying velocity and speed of the journey was matched by the beating of her heart and the physical sensation of terror. That place, she was sure, could only be death. Somehow she had got herself out of her own bed and into Bea's, where she clung to her sister's talcy body, shoving and poking her sides until she woke and turned and put her arm round her . . .

Katharine fought for breath like a drowning swimmer breaking the surface and sat bolt upright in bed. It came to her with a terrible clarity. That was why Bea was lost. She used men to navigate by. She set her sights on men. Fatally, Bea thought men would save her, when really, what might have saved her was . . . Katharine struggled for the answer, flailed around for the truth before it slipped from her grasp. What was it? Richard was there at her side, solid, loving, calm. She felt the warmth of his hand on her arm and tried to push it away, tried to retain the truth she had glimpsed. 'Shh. You mustn't worry.' She concentrated and closed her ears to him. It was work. That was what it was. Gratifying, demanding, worthwhile work. 'Adrian is fine with Frank,' soothed Richard, trying to make her lie down again. No. That wasn't all. There was something else. 'It's a process, darling.' What the hell was it? 'For Frank and for Adrian. A healing process.'

Katharine pushed Richard away with all her strength. She sat up. 'Nothing is *healing*,' she wailed. 'There is no healing in this.' She banged her fist to her chest, then leapt to her feet. 'Frank is *not* all right. Frank is a ruinous cunt!' She threw the alarm clock at him. 'Just fuck off out of here and fetch our son!'

Richard didn't look at her. *In pectore robur.* He pulled on his clothes. Sophie had never sworn. Never, ever.

Katharine sank back on to the bed. The travel clock lay on the carpet by his shoes. The back had come off and its face was blank. She watched the shoes as he placed a carefully socked foot in each of them, then bent to tie the laces with his large gentle hands. If he picked up the clock it would be all right. If he picked up the clock they could rewind.

Richard straightened up and turned his feet away.

She stretched out her hand to the place where he had been. 'Oh no,' she whispered. She heard him take a weary breath in and pause.

'It's the children,' she said, not daring to raise her face. She withdrew her hand and kept her eyes on the floor. 'Have we been . . . reckless?'

His shadow crossed the room and she heard a floorboard creak.

She closed her eyes and swallowed. 'Have we been careless with our children?'

When she opened them again, his feet were back near her own. She felt the dry warmth of his palm as he drew it along her jaw. He tilted her face up to him. She took his hand in both her own and held it tight against her cheek.

Steel

WHEN THE boat reached Genoa, Bea was soaked from the spray and from the drizzle that had started up in the afternoon. She waited on deck, reluctant to disembark and enter the Italian grandeur spread out before her, proud villas sweeping up from the waterfront in pink and yellow. She missed the familiar hewn ruggedness of Spain. Reaching Ithaca became suddenly urgent. She needed to get there.

At the train station, she bought a ticket to Brindisi, a port in the south-east. The journey would take, as far as she could tell, two days and involve some changes that she only partially understood. As she pushed a wad of notes under the glass, she found she had more money left than she thought. That would be Kiff's doing. It warmed her to think of that as she made her way to the platform. She should have enough to pay for a room in Ithaca for a couple of weeks at least. She folded Kiff's blanket and carried it under one arm. It was mid-March. The island would be in flower; there would be almond blossom, figs, and peppery olive oil. In Ithaca, she thought, she would buy some inks and draw.

She boarded the train, sat in a window seat and waited for the rhythm of the tracks to begin. She ought to write to Kiff and she wanted to write to Adrian. She thought he might have seen her at the airport and she didn't want him to think she didn't care. The train rolled, lurched and stopped. Iron squealed on steel as it lurched again, then reversed. Office blocks, slums, motorways, fields, hills and quarries rattled by. She smiled at the thought of Adrian. He used to say that the landscape was coded in our genes, hard-wired into our brains. He explained that was the feeling she had when she visited Hastings – saw the sea and the lie of the land, the cliffs and the shingle beach. Perhaps it was why she loved the rolling hills and farm-land of Ithaca, the rugged coast and stone beaches in deeply carved bays. It was Hastings but heated and in colour. In Hastings, with Adrian and Laura, she had showed them how to play the Storm Game, the game she used to play with her father, when they would run on to the beach holding hands, lean into the wind and shout and scream at the sea. Then their father would bundle them back up the hill, up the steps to their door, and the three of them, wet and breathless with laughter, would fall into the hall. Their mother would pretend to be cross and pull the rough jersey off over Bea's head, rubbing at her hair with a towel that smelled of pie. The radio would be on. 'Lift up your hearts,' the radio announcer said, and after dinner, it was *Listen With Mother*. 'Are you sitting comfortably?' asked the radio, and on some days, when the washing-up was done and home had a calm and lemony air to it, their mother would allow them to slide on to the slippery warmth of her full, patterned skirt. 'Then we'll begin,' and they would lie across her lap and listen, thumbs in their mouths and very still.

She had shown Adrian and Laura, from when they were quite small, the walks of her childhood – the hills above the town, the cliff path and down along the beach. Adrian said that walking was the metronome of thought, that humans needed to walk to keep sane, to keep body and soul together. The leg bone was connected to the brain bone, and if you needed to work something out, you should just take a walk until it was sorted. She thought of his slow, loose body, of how he folded his legs beneath him like a deer and told her what he thought.

Dear Adrian.

It wasn't sudden. It took me fifty years to disappear, a slow rubbing out until the final days before I went, when far from feeling absent, I felt painfully present, like a bulb filament that glows too bright before it blows, and on that last day, when I walked to work, I walked the long way and just kept walking . . .

THE TRAIN journey was a mistake. Geography had never been her strong point. She changed in Turin, Milan, Bologna and Ancona. She found the stations hectic and hostile, the information system confusing. Food and water became a problem. Often, she was too anxious about missing her connection to buy food at a station and on board the train she was afraid to leave her bag unattended. Her route was shackled by the hard, implacable iron of the tracks. She travelled north, south, north-east and south again. The train stopped frequently, at deserted stations and in the middle of nowhere. After the first twenty-four hours, at each stop she felt hope trickle from her on to the filthy track below.

On the second day, beginning the final eastern stretch, she caught glimpses of the Adriatic Sea and she prepared herself for arrival at Brindisi at any moment. Yet hours and station names rolled interminably by – Barletta, Trani, Bisceglie . . . As night fell, she woke, freezing, from a dream of needles and steel. She was alone in the carriage. The train had come to a halt and sadness lay in her lap. The aborted child of ten years ago. Had it really travelled with her all this way? She knew that it had, that now, fleeing her failed life, there was the realisation that she had destroyed the only part of her that would have made any sense.

The writing pad before her was blank.

Dear Laura.

It was nothing and everything. It was you. It was him. It was me.

Yes

A DEEP tremor ran through the body of the ferry as it docked at Ithaca two days later. Bea was asleep, wrapped in Kiff's blanket, stretched out like an effigy on the plastic banquette in the bar. She got up and was helped down the gangplank, blinking up at an Ithaca shrouded in cloud. The air, warm and damp on her face, carried on it the scent of the soil.

She took a taxi to Kioni. She was done with travelling. She had no strength or patience for the bus. The cloud lifted and they drove past fields carpeted with flowers. She asked the driver to drop her at the taverna, where she drank strong, sweet coffee, ate halva and almonds. Her body hummed with fatigue. Kioni was quiet; Penelope's, the taverna, was empty. From her table she noticed a For Rent sign not far from the waterfront. She asked about it and was directed to Elli in the village shop, who told her yes, it was available, and yes, of course she could see it. Elli called through the beaded curtain at the back of the shop —Yannis! — and talked to him in Greek. Then Yannis appeared, with a key and a cardboard box. He led Bea to the apartment, up whitewashed steps through a heavy wooden door painted blue. Inside were more steps leading up to a simple bedroom, painted white with rush matting on the floor. Next to it was a small kitchen where painted plates hung from one wall and another blue door opened on to a terrace looking away from the village over the headland and out to sea. There was a table topped with turquoise tiles and shaded by a vine. Bougainvillea and wisteria bloomed out there, and geraniums, crimson and white in terracotta pots. Yannis switched on the electricity and the water, and showed her the cupboard where linen, towels and blankets were kept. Then he left. Are you sitting comfortably? Bea peeled off her dress, dropped the Moroccan blanket in a corner, and stood on the terrace in the sun. Then we'll begin. She looked in the cardboard box. Honey, yoghurt, oil and bread. 'See?' she said to Precious. She looked around at the whitewashed terrace, the sea and the sky. 'This is why I came.'

For eight days, Bea barely stirred. From her terrace she could just make out Patrick's house, half hidden by trees in the hills across the bay. There were no signs of life. Each day she felt the sun feed her body and gladden her mind. She was happy to be mute and still. She shed her shame and shyness like a skin. The sun grew stronger and so did she, until the day came when she felt well enough to go down to the sea to swim.

She wore a white cotton dress and leather sandals, and carried a bright blue towel. She headed out of the village towards the ruined windmills standing sentinel on the headland. Where the road climbed up the hill, she picked her way down a steep trail towards a small cove, nearly a perfect O. The rock was rough underfoot and pitted with pools, pools with smoothed pink sides like flesh, where alien creatures waved up at the reflected sky. Bladderwrack sprouted at the water's edge, swaying in the swell like an animal pelt. Bea watched the sea for a long time, its slap and hiss at the rocks, the sigh in and out at the mouth of the cove. Looking down through the translucence of greens and blues, she longed to be in it. Here would be a good place, where the rock dropped away so that it wouldn't graze and cut. Tall rocks formed the opening of the cove, where the sea sometimes rose in a silent surge powered by the expanse of blue beyond. Watch the tide, her father always said. You have to know whether it's coming in or going out. She watched now and frowned. Were there tides here? She had never quite managed to work that one out.

No sooner had she taken off her shoes and put down her towel than it began to rain. Laura hated the rain but Bea would tell her that the rain doesn't matter, it's easier to get in if you're wet, and anyway, this time of year it's rain, sun, rainbow, sun, then rain again and . . . Bea looked down. Here the rock was ridged with a crop of baby mussels. She squatted to examine the glistening rows of tiny black shells, clustered on the raspberry-ripple rock. Laura would love them.

At the water's edge, Bea gathered up her dress, clung to the rock with one hand and put a foot into the sea, feeling gingerly for an urchin-free spot. The cold surprised her as the water rose up high to her knees, making her gasp, before it sank back down low in a sucking rush. Her fingers held tight as she lowered the other foot, thinking that perhaps today she would just have the coward's swim, the quick dip in, then out, without leaving go. But, she would tell Laura, it's always good to do a few strokes, however cold, because of how good it makes you feel afterwards.

The water lapped higher, wetting her dress, and she hesitated, unable for a moment to catch her breath. Yes, afterwards. That's the feeling she wanted Laura to have, when every cell of your body becomes crystal and you walk away from the sea a chandelier of light and life.

And she had seen Patrick. Yes. She saw him swimming yesterday. He did a quick dive in, then a steady, worn-out crawl towards the village, and it made her smile. He turned when he was halfway there and dragged himself back towards home. One day, when the sea was warmer, one day perhaps when Laura was with her, they would swim out to meet him. Yes, one of these days she would get in at Penelope's and swim over to his place to say hello. But not yet. For the time being she was doing nothing. She wouldn't be bad and she wouldn't be good. She would, as Adrian liked to say, just be Bea.

The rain stopped and the sun came out. She felt its heat on the nape of her neck and shoulders and knew that she should do the swim now, before she lost her nerve. She climbed out, pulled off her dress and underwear and looked down at her vanished body, thought how she was more in her body now than she had ever been before, more in herself than she had ever been, on the inside now, looking out. Yes, she thought, shivering despite the sun, and hurrying back to crouch down at the place where she could get in, that was something else Laura ought to know, and with a bold gasp and a shudder and a smile, she let go of the rock and sank backwards, down and into the sea.